The
IRISH
HOUSE

Ann O'Loughlin

The

IRISH
HOUSE

bookouture

Published by Bookouture in 2023

An imprint of Storyfire Ltd.
Carmelite House
50 Victoria Embankment
London EC4Y 0DZ

www.bookouture.com

ISBN: 978-1-80314-869-4
eBook ISBN: 978-1-80314-443-6

To John, Roshan and Zia

ONE

March, 2018

The gates of Kilteelagh House were padlocked, a rusty chain wound around the iron bars. Pushing past the orange azalea, its flowers clumped over a pile of discarded takeaway chipper bags, Marianne picked up the heavy chain draped to pull the two sides of the gate together. She had never seen the entrance to Kilteelagh look so neglected. Tugging at the padlock, she made the right side of the gate shift and creak. What had become of Kilteelagh House? Her grandmother had only been dead a few weeks.

Sodden rubbish and decayed leaves were trapped underneath the poles of the cattle grid. The avenue was littered with dandelions, the brash yellow competing with the sweep of lemony-cream daffodils which lined the edge of the driveway. Marianne shook the gate fiercely; it creaked but didn't budge. Waves of anxiety rose inside her. What was she doing here three weeks after her grandmother's passing? She should have come to say goodbye; she should have been on deathwatch for Collie Keane.

She turned away to wander down the road to the small bridge over the stream, which was part of Kilteelagh lands. Absent-mindedly, she pulled at the sage-green leaves of a butterfly bush. Plucking a leaf off, she watched it slip between her fingers and flutter through the air before landing gently on the river water. It floated away, skimming past rocks and protruding stones until it was swept by the current and flung down a small whirlpool. When it popped up the other side, she wanted to clap.

She needed to see Kilteelagh House. She needed to connect with and make peace with Grandma Collie; she needed to know Collie had forgiven her for not being there at the end. She remembered the stile cut into the stone wall on the left-hand side of the gates, but the nettles and brambles were thickly interwoven, and she could not get through. Spying a gap in the briars further down, she stamped out a path for herself until she got as far as the stone wall. Scrambling over, she was glad the brambles on the Kilteelagh side were much weaker and yielded to her urgent swipes and kicks. One briar stuck stubbornly to the sleeve of her wool coat, and she unpicked it carefully, afraid she would pull a thread in the teal-coloured weave.

Pressing on to the avenue, she briefly halted to take in the path across the field to the lake, where a fox, feeling her stare on its back, had also stopped. The fox sat still observing her until, after a few moments, it drifted away into the sea of nettles surrounding the gazebo.

She hurried up the avenue to the rhododendron bend, where she knew she could catch her first glimpse of Kilteelagh House in almost three years.

It was in worse shape than she remembered. Slates on the roof were missing and it looked like a bird was nesting in one of the chimneys. The wisteria had pulled out the plaster in places at the front of the house. Shutters were dragged across at every window except on the landing. She stood, expecting Grandma

Collie to come bustling around from the back, Benji the Labrador barking excitedly beside her.

But Kilteelagh House stood silent in the morning sunshine. Marianne shivered, tears welling up inside her. Collie must have been very ill to let Kilteelagh fall into such a state. The house looked desolate; not even the gold sunshine sparkling off the glass of the landing window signalled any joy within. A lonely uncertainty crept through her. She couldn't move forward, no matter how much she wanted to approach the house.

She had always craned to get the first peek of Kilteelagh House on their regular summer visits. Now she could barely look at her grandmother's home as it too appeared to have lost its purpose following her death. But at the same time, she didn't want to turn her back on Kilteelagh House. As she dithered, a blackbird swept low beside her to land and disappear into the shade of the rhododendron tree. Tears rolled down Marianne's face and she dipped her head.

She checked the time. She had to walk back into the small town of Balgaddy. She didn't want to be late for the reading of her grandmother's will. Swiping away the tears, she hurried down the avenue searching for a gap in the hedgerow she could squeeze through without too much trouble, to get back to the road.

TWO

Marianne stood outside the solicitor's office in Balgaddy and wondered why she had agreed to travel from New York for the reading of the will. Her head was thumping and her mouth was dry because she was nervous. She tied and untied the belt of her coat, not sure which look was best. Stepping into the building, she gave her name at reception.

'They're all waiting for you,' the receptionist said, showing her down the hall to a small office overlooking the street. Busy conversation wafted from the room as if kids were in a class-room waiting for a teacher to arrive. When she slipped in the door, Marianne felt the eyes of those inside the room turn on her.

'What the hell are *you* doing here?' a well-dressed woman who was sitting beside the solicitor's desk asked loudly.

'I was invited,' Marianne said quietly.

'Really? Is that what we should have done when Mammy was dying, invite you?' Katherine Ferguson said, standing up to emphasise her point. Her husband, Steve, put his hand out to stop her, but she slapped it away. 'You're not welcome here,

Marianne. You didn't see fit to come to Kilteelagh when I needed help, when your grandmother was ill and dying, and you didn't see fit to come when she was taking her last breaths. You sure as hell are not wanted here now.'

'I couldn't come – work wouldn't let me, because I had taken so much time off when Mom and Dad died—'

'And you expect us to believe your old excuses?' Katherine guffawed loudly.

'It's the truth, Aunt Katherine. You know I loved Grandma Collie.'

'I only know you weren't here when you were needed. You're not welcome now. I want you to leave.'

'Katherine, I didn't complain when you didn't make it to the States when Mom and Dad died. We're family, I understood. And I thought you would understand when I couldn't make it back for Collie's funeral. I'm sorry—'

'Are you indeed?' Her aunt swung around fiercely. She was wearing an extravagantly pleated dress, but the russet colour only highlighted the redness creeping up her neck and across her face. 'Sorry is a get-out-of-jail-free card for someone like you. That woman talked about you day and night.' She stopped, choking back her tears. 'I don't want your stupid "sorry", Marianne. Just go away, please.'

Feeling embarrassed, Marianne took a seat and pretended to check her phone as she tried to ignore Katherine, who moved to the seat directly in front of the solicitor's desk and insisted her husband follow.

'Maybe Marianne should be sitting up front,' Steve said sheepishly.

'She shouldn't even be here. I'm the one who looked after Mam night and day, and I'm her only surviving daughter. It's only fit and proper that I, along with my family, have centre stage,' Katherine said, her voice high-pitched.

Her words were still stinging in the air when an elderly man in a pinstripe suit bustled into the room. Katherine stood up as if it were something she should do, but quickly flopped down when nobody followed her lead. The solicitor fussed, hanging up his jacket and calling out his apologies at his tardiness, before taking his seat behind the desk.

'Let me introduce myself,' he said, but was immediately interrupted by Katherine.

'Sean, you are well known to us. How are the family?'

'Very well, thank you. But for Marianne's benefit, I would like to formally introduce myself.' He turned to Marianne. 'I am Sean Eager, the solicitor handling the affairs of Collie Keane, including the reading of her will this morning.'

'I don't want her here. She's not welcome,' Katherine said, hitting her knuckles against the top of the desk for emphasis. The solicitor looked out over his glasses.

'Marianne Johnson is here at the specific request of her grandmother, who left instructions that she be invited to attend the reading of the will.'

'And don't I have a say in this?' Katherine asked, her voice squeaking.

Sean Eager sighed and took off his glasses.

'I realise this is difficult, but the only person whose wishes I'm bound to respect in this matter is Collie Keane, and she specifically asked for her eldest granddaughter to be present. Now, let's get on with it.'

He waited for Katherine to sit down, then began to read out the last will and testament of Collette 'Collie' Keane.

Words blended together as the solicitor's voice droned on. Marianne looked out the window on to the main street of Balgaddy town to distract herself from the solemnity of the occasion. She missed her neighbourhood in Manhattan: the constant buzz of traffic, Joe in Al's Diner who always waved to her as she walked by in the morning to the bagel shop, the side streets with a little bit of edge, and the well-dressed ladies who strolled with their pooches on the same sidewalks, between the same streets, at the same time, every morning and evening, because they were too tight to pay a dog walker.

Her dad used to hop the subway every Saturday to her district, and they always had breakfast together. She felt the now familiar pull on her heart as she thought of Brad Johnson, his laugh ringing around her as her mother scolded him for one thing or another. It was several seconds before she realised Katherine had turned around and was shouting at her.

'Who the hell do you think you are, coming here for the good times and taking everything that we are entitled to? I won't let it happen!'

Marianne shrank back as the solicitor called for calm. This was not the welcome she'd expected in the only country where she still had living family. She saw Katherine lean forward to stare Sean Eager in the face.

'The girls will stay with us, and we'll sell Grandma's house. It makes sense, get rid of the old place—'

'Katherine, please listen again to the last wishes of your mother,' the solicitor said gruffly, then proceeded to read out the will again:

I leave Kilteelagh House and its land to my granddaughter, Marianne Johnson, currently resident in New York City. I also ask that Marianne becomes the guardian of my two grand-daughters, Rachel and Katie Keane, who have been living with me since the death of their mother, Aisling Keane, two years ago. I also leave to Marianne an amount of twenty thousand euros, which is to be spent for the benefit of Rachel and Katie while they live at Kilteelagh House.

It is my wish that Marianne returns to Kilteelagh House and lives there until the children reach their majority. If, after that, she wishes to sell the house, it is entirely in her hands to

*do so, but until then, she must provide a home for Rachel and
Katie at Kilteelagh House. I realise this will come as a shock,
so I propose that Marianne can, after a full year at Kilteelagh, change her mind, if she so wishes and, in the circumstances, the house would be sold for the benefit of Marianne,
Rachel, Katie, and Katherine's children, Molly and Hetty.
Rachel and Katie would then return to live with my daughter, Katherine.*

*Katherine should not feel put out. She has her home on
what was previously Kilteelagh land and I also leave the two
fields bounding the far end of the lake to Katherine to add to
and complete their farm. I also leave all of my shares set out
and attached here to my daughter Katherine, which I hope she
uses for the benefit of her family. These shares, I understand,
represent a significant nest egg, which I hope my daughter
accepts in good grace.*

Marianne didn't say anything. Her phone pinged loudly.

'It is absolute nonsense, what does she know about raising a
teenager and a six-year-old? She doesn't even have any children
herself and she's too young for all this,' Katherine bellowed,
shouting over the solicitor, who was still reading aloud.

Sean Eager raised his hand for her to stop.

'The will is very clear. Katherine, your mother has provided
for you handsomely with the land and the significant shares
portfolio. The property and land are Marianne's alone,
providing she consents to becoming the guardian for Rachel and
Katie. She must live at Kilteelagh House for one year, and if she
decides to continue after that, she must keep the house as a
home until the youngest, Katie, reaches eighteen years of age.
Marianne, it is of course your decision, but it was your grandmother's wish that you do this,' the solicitor said, looking
directly at her.

'Why did Grandma pick me? Katherine is right, I have my

life in New York and my job. I sure don't know how to look after kids. Rachel and Katie don't even know me very well.'

'See, I told you! And the children are already at our house. They are bunking down with our two and happy enough, in the circumstances,' Katherine said.

Marianne stood up. 'Do I have to decide right now?'

The solicitor closed the file on his desk. 'My advice would be to go somewhere quiet, have a long think about it, and meet back here at the same time tomorrow. If you are sure that you can't take on this responsibility, let us know and we will take it from here. But if you think you can, your grandmother has left further instructions and a letter for you.'

He reached into his desk drawer and lifted out a brown envelope.

'Can we see that letter? Surely, we have a right,' Katherine asked, her voice shaking.

The solicitor shook his head. 'If Marianne decides to honour her grandmother's wishes, then she alone will receive the letter.'

'And if she doesn't?'

'My instructions are to destroy it, unopened.'

'So like Collie Keane, always wanting the last word. What a load of nonsense,' Katherine screeched.

Sean Eager sat forward on his chair, placing his hands across the yellow jotter on his desk.

'I realise this is a very emotional time for all of you, but it is paramount that the wishes of Mrs Keane are respected. Marianne is the only one who can make the decision whether to move here or not, and we must give her the time and space to do that.'

He picked up the phone and called his secretary into the room.

'Shirley will show you all out. Why don't we meet again tomorrow at noon?'

Marianne, feeling slightly queasy, followed the others down the stairs and onto the street. She lingered beside her aunt, but Katherine turned her back on her.

'I didn't want it to be this way. Can't we talk about it?' Marianne said, gently touching her aunt's arm.

Katherine swivelled around.

'I spent every waking moment with that woman, and what did I get? Only a bunch of share certificates and two old fields! She didn't even leave me one of her rings. There was nothing personal or of sentimental value for her only living daughter. There's a lesson in that for me. It's not over until it's over. Do you really think I will let you take Kilteelagh House and its lands? Those girls need a stable home, and they are staying with me.'

'I don't want us to fall out.'

'Then go back where you came from and leave us in peace,' Katherine snarled as she got into the car, banging the door shut.

As Marianne stood embarrassed on the pavement, a woman stopped and asked was she all right. She thanked her for her concern, saying she was just tired.

'It happens to the best of us. Go home and get some rest,' the woman said kindly.

Marianne could have told her she had no home any more, not really, but instead she set off walking out of the town. When another call came in from New York, she ignored it. The road to Kilteelagh passed by a new housing estate, the red-brick houses standing pristine against the cloudy sky, their front gardens nude except for pockets of new grass peeking through the earth. The windows were polished but bare, because nobody was living there yet. A little further on, two children were swinging back and forth on a gate, chatting like old friends. When she passed, they called out hello and she smiled at them. Her phone rang again and, seeing the call was from her friend, Jay, this time she answered.

'Marianne, I've been sending you all these emails and you haven't responded. Did you even read them?'

'No, Jay, I can't right now—'

'You haven't heard the news then?'

'What? I have a few missed calls from the office, but—'

'The company went to the wall yesterday! We're gone, everything is.'

'What?'

'The Neville lawsuit – it screwed us over.'

Marianne stopped, panic tearing through her.

'What did you say?'

'I'm sorry to break the news like this, but I thought it would be better coming from me, rather than from anyone else.'

'But that lawsuit was a try-on – we know she couldn't have got the rash from the fabric.'

'The company settled, but it was leaked to the press and that Neville woman took to the spotlight like a duck to water. Within three days we were sunk. The facts only got in the way of a good story. Once the social media trolls had their say, that was it.'

Marianne slowed her pace as the road turned sharply to the right to cross the stream near Kilteelagh House. A robin flitted by and into the bushes.

'This can't be. Is there nothing we can do to stop it?'

'It was done and dusted overnight. The company folded, there was no choice. We lost our partnership with our two biggest retailers, our shareholders withdrew, and all our suppliers backed off. Just like that, boom, the company went bankrupt. We've all lost our jobs.'

'What am I going to do?'

'What are any of us going to do?'

'What about my capsule collection? I didn't think it was quite right, but Randy said it was a showstopper.'

'Darling, we all have to start over and hope we're not tarnished by this bloody fiasco.'

She watched the robin drop down to peck at the ground fiercely before launching into the air with a loud warning cry.

'Is there any way I can get my work back? There are about ten complete pieces – my drawings, everything.'

Jay sighed loudly. 'Not a hope. The offices have been shut down and staff aren't being allowed access. Everything is to be sold off by the receiver.'

'Good luck with anyone trying to make money out of my samples. I hated the stuff. I hated the damn job. I should have left it months ago. Maybe it's time to leave dress designing behind. Been there, tried that, failed...'

'Marianne, shut up. You've gone through hell and now you're going through more.'

'With a capital H, Jay. I have to go.'

He made to say something, but she cut off the call. She didn't care about the job, but the timing was terrible when she so wanted to go back to New York. What was there for her now? Her parents, Chloe and Brad, were dead; she had no job, and her work friends would probably be scattered across the States as they looked for new employment.

If she went back, she would have to move into the family home in Brooklyn. She knew she was lucky to have that option, but she couldn't face living there surrounded by past, happy, family memories. If she decided to sell, it could take months to find a buyer; best to rent it out and have some regular money coming in. Stumbling onto the stone bridge, she peered over the parapet to the water below once again. This was one of Grandma Collie's favourite places. They used to stroll down the avenue together and along the short stretch of road to the bridge. Collie told her it was there to remind everyone to take a breath, look at the water and wonder at nature. Marianne needed to take a breath.

Life had been hard these last few months, and now it was a lot tougher. Collie had never recovered after hearing of the death of her daughter, Chloe, and son-in-law Brad, when a tree came down on their car as they drove in a storm. It was one grief too many for the woman who, two years earlier, had lost her firstborn, Aisling, to cancer and had had to take over the rearing of her granddaughters. Marianne too, within a short time, had lost the most important people in her life. And now dress designing had been whipped away from her overnight. She wasn't even sure she cared about it any more.

Plucking a clump of grass, she chucked it in the river, watching as the individual blades detached from one another, each creating its own path, rolling with the surge of the water. A long blade of grass was swept away by the water rush; at sea, buffeted in every direction. Why would she stay in New York if she had no work? What was she if she wasn't a fashion designer? She had no qualifications as a mother – why would she move to Kilteelagh?

Turning her back on the river, she stopped just short of the Kilteelagh gates, pushed past the briars and climbed the stone wall. Pacing slowly up the avenue, memories were her walking companions. She had last been here three years ago, when she had surprised Collie with a flying visit while on a junket to London Fashion Week. They'd strolled through the garden together, her grandmother talking about her beloved plants. Marianne paused now to take in the rhododendron in bloom: shades of puce, cerise pink and cherry red competing with each other. Daffodils lined the avenue as if in tribute to Collie, who had single-handedly planted each bulb, when she and her husband had moved to Kilteelagh decades ago. Marianne stooped to pick some of the flowers, but she heard her grand-mother's voice in her ear, telling her to leave them for others to enjoy.

She didn't want to go as far as the house, so she turned

ahead of the bend in the avenue and went down the old path to the gazebo beside the lake. Collie loved her gazebo and often hid out there early in the morning to greet the sun rising over the lake water. Ploughing through tall grass and weeds, Marianne had to stamp on young nettles along the way. The gazebo looked dilapidated, and in places there were holes in the roof where the light dappled through, creating a pattern on the floor. She didn't try to enter but strolled to the lakeshore and sat on a tree stump. The water was dead calm and grey, reflecting the sky. Mist pressed like a cloud onto the trees, ready to roll down and blanket the water. She didn't spot Rachel at the lakeside until the girl clicked her lighter to relight her cigarette.

Not sure if she should interrupt, Marianne observed from a distance as the fifteen-year-old blew rings of smoke into the cold evening air.

When Rachel was finished, she took out an aerosol deodorant and sprayed it around herself, before hiding her cigarettes and lighter in a hole in the tree. It was only as she turned to leave that she saw Marianne.

'What are you staring at?'

'The lake.'

'How long have you been here?'

'A while.'

'Are you going to tell?'

'Tell what?'

She thought she saw Rachel relax a little, but then the young girl frowned.

'I don't care what you do,' she snapped.

'Hey, easy up, I'm not a snitch, but you know it's so bad for you.'

'I bet that never stopped you.'

Marianne smiled. 'No, it didn't.'

'Katherine is gunning for you.'

'I know. I came all the way from the States to be shouted at.'

'Have you decided if you're staying to mind me and Katie?'

Taken aback by the direct question, Marianne stammered, 'I didn't know you'd been told.'

'We weren't. Katherine wouldn't tell us a thing – there's quite a mood on her. Grandma told me, not long before she died.'

'What did she say?'

'Of all of our relatives, you were the best bet.'

'Why?'

'She asked us did we want to always stay at Kilteelagh House, and I said we didn't want to leave. It's been our only real home. We moved here with our mam after Daddy disappeared – you know, moved to Canada or whatever – until she got sick.'

The cracking of Rachel's voice made Marianne shudder. She wanted to grab her cousin in a tight hug, but instead she stuffed her hands in her pockets so Rachel wouldn't notice.

'Grandma said with New York under your belt, you must know the world. You would help us fly, not tie us to the apron strings.'

'I don't own an apron.'

'Katherine says you're going to ditch us and go back to your posh life in the States. Can we come to New York?'

'What posh life? And no,' Marianne said, too fast. Then she quickly added, 'I haven't decided what I'm going to do.'

'Whatever,' Rachel said, turning to set off in the direction of Katherine's bungalow.

'What do you think – should I stay?' Marianne called after her.

Without slowing her pace, Rachel called over her shoulder, 'It doesn't matter what I think.'

Marianne watched as she climbed the fence and sprinted across the field, dodging piles of horse dung along the way. Katherine was probably right. How could she even think of bringing up these kids? What did she know about parenting?

Her priority should be to salvage her career, which had just collapsed on the brink of a breakthrough.

Who was she kidding? *Brink of a breakthrough* sounded mighty fancy. She had lost a no-good job and she didn't even know if she wanted to work in the world of fashion any more. But still, none of this fitted with looking after two kids. She trudged back to town, not bothering to stop at the bridge on the way.

THREE

The next day Marianne woke early. Pulling on her clothes, she slipped quietly from the hotel on Main Street, Balgaddy, and turned, once again, in the direction of Kilteelagh House. She needed to go back there, to be where she felt at home as she made her decision about the future. The town was still, the curtains drawn in most of the houses. A cat on a windowsill meowed plaintively and pawed the glass to be let in. Marianne walked by the old town hall, which had been converted into a takeaway, and the stone building that had been the bank and was now a hair and beauty salon. Turning into Parnell Street, she saw Mr Butler the greengrocer setting out his produce in front of the shop.

'You're out fine and early,' he said, making her smile.

She scurried past Eager Solicitors and on to the narrow road that would bring her to Kilteelagh House. In the distance, she could hear the revving of the bread van as it made its deliveries to the shops and cafes around the town, the acceleration and deceleration like a song moving through the morning air. At the bridge, she stopped to take a breath. The water flowed, its pace not even disrupted by the latest piece of rubbish – a takeaway carton stuck between two rocks. If Collie had been here to see it, she would have slipped down the bank and used a stick to pull it from the river, then she'd have written a stiff letter to the proprietor of the town takeaway business. She had once hand-delivered a smelly, wet bag of chips to the local chipper and threatened to call in the newspapers unless the owner stopped his clients chucking their rubbish along the country lanes. A heron glided low over the water, its elegant flight filling the morning air.

Marianne continued to the entrance of Kilteelagh House, hoping to find time to think, time to confront a possible future. The two stone piers stood like soldiers either side of the iron gates. In her anorak and gloves, she was ready to take on the brambles obscuring her path. Shoving past a fuchsia bush not yet in bloom, she tucked her chin low and forced her way through, not caring what snagged her jacket. She picked individual briars out of her way and trampled on nettles until she reached the little stile in the stone wall. A streak of happiness burst through her. Nostalgia strangled at her throat for the time when she was a kid, spending summer holidays at Kilteelagh House with her mom and dad.

During those childhood visits she had accompanied Collie every morning for the long walk down the avenue to the bridge, then back to sit in the gazebo by the lake. Collie always stepped across the cattle grid while Marianne slipped through the narrow opening in the wall. Collie laughed and said it wasn't too long since she could do the same, but she had better not chance the embarrassment of becoming stuck.

Marianne felt the chill of the stone as she slid through the gap and stepped down onto the narrow path, which led around the back of the azalea. When she was young, there was always a frisson of fear that she would somehow get lost, which was immediately followed by a rush of excitement when Collie called out her name.

She could almost hear her grandmother gently urging her on past fields wet with dew, pockets of droplets glossy in the morning light. It would be so easy to believe Grandma Collie was still at home, sitting on her perch inside the landing window, watching the comings and goings of the house. A loneliness crept through Marianne and she moved along, afraid that if she stood still, she might begin to cry. On reaching the rhododendron grove, she veered onto the path to the gazebo. A thrush, surprised by her intrusion, abandoned a snail shell on the ground and hopped into the undergrowth.

Flattening the weeds and crushing the nettles, she managed to make it inside the gazebo. Dusting off the seat, she sat down on the wood, which was pocked with the carved initials of Collie's children and grandchildren. Marianne looked first for her own and then the initials of her mom and dad. It had been during one of the long hot summers; they had strolled to the gazebo and had a picnic by the lake, Brad lighting a barbecue that sent spirals of smoke across the water. Collie complained somebody might spot the smoke and take umbrage, but she tucked into her baked fish and sausages nonetheless. Afterwards, she invited them to pick a section of the seat and carve their initials.

'When I am long gone, ye will enjoy the memory of this day. Every day, try to make a good memory,' she said, and Marianne, who was about twelve at the time, had thought her grandmother was a little mad.

Eccentric was probably a better word for Collie, who clapped when she saw the letters carved within the frame of a heart. Marianne traced the markings now, her fingers turning brown as she dislodged years of ingrained dirt. Collie was right: this was a memory, a happy one. Two swans flew past, deep in their own symphony of conversation. She hoped they would come down on the lake, but they had other plans; the sunrays catching the brilliant white of their wings as they made their way to the marshy land near the sea.

It was still the middle of the night in New York. She tried to imagine the sounds: the odd siren, a solitary call from the street, a car door banging or an alarm screeching into the night air. In Brooklyn, when her father was alive, he liked to get up and read in the middle of the night, saying that was the only time he was never interrupted by anybody or anything inside the house or out. Not wanting to fall too deep into reminiscences that would stoke the hurt inside her, she got up and walked across the field to Katherine's dormer bungalow. As she drew near, she hesitated, wondering if it was too early. But then she saw Katherine's husband, Steve, giving a bucket of feed to the horse in the near paddock. He waved and she joined him, letting the horse nuzzle her hands, looking for treats.

'Come back to ours, it's time you and Katherine had a proper talk. There's no point falling out over all this. I'm sure it's not what Collie would have wanted.'

Marianne joined him and they tramped across the field to the back door. Katherine, her hair in curlers and her dressing gown wrapped tight around her, was standing at the kitchen sink. Steve said he had other work to be doing and he left Marianne to go in the back door by herself.

'I was going to ring you in a while. We need to talk,' Katherine said wearily, when Marianne tentatively opened the door.

'I was thinking the same thing,' Marianne said as she stepped into the kitchen and crossed to the table, where she sat down. Without asking what she wanted, Katherine placed a mug of black coffee in front of her niece and pushed the sugar bowl and milk jug towards her.

'New Yorkers drink coffee, right?'

Marianne smiled and nodded, scooping two sugars into the mug.

'Maybe we got off on the wrong foot. We don't know each other very well. Your mam and me, well, we had our disagreements, and she always seemed to book her holidays home here when she knew we would be away. We always got in fights when we were young. Chloe was Collie's favourite. Mother was so obvious about it. Stupid of me, but I held onto the crap from when we were young all my adult life, then one day Chloe was just gone forever. Over the years, our contact was minimal. I probably sent the wrong things for your birthdays too, because I never really knew you that well.'

Katherine stopped to pour fresh milk into the jug.

'I'm a straight talker, Marianne. Your mother could never cope with that – she was always more touchy-feely than me. She held a grudge because I thought Collie should sell Kilteelagh House and move into the town, where she could be near everything. Collie had no quality of life here, always sitting at the window looking down the avenue. She should have been in the town, where she could have joined a few clubs, had more than one friend. But that's in the past. The thing I want to talk about is the girls. I want you to leave Rachel and Katie here, and I want you to back away from Kilteelagh House.'

'That's a huge ask.'

'You can't honestly be thinking of taking over Kilteelagh?'

'I have to consider it. Collie left it to me for a reason.'

Katherine pulled a cigarette packet from the top of the dresser. Taking a lighter from her pocket, she snapped it open and lit a cigarette, closing her eyes as she blew three circles of smoke towards the ceiling.

'If your mother were here, she would say leave well alone. This is too much for you. You're only twenty-six years old, for Christ's sake! Go back to your life in New York. Bringing up kids is no walk in the park.'

'You're right, what do I know about parenting?'

'So, you will let us sell it? We won't see you short. You don't know Rachel and Katie, but I think you know what's best for them: a stable home where there's both a mother and father.'

'Thing is, I don't really know what I want. I've lost my job, I'm not sure what there is back in New York for me. And I don't want to let Grandma, Rachel or Katie down.'

Katherine shovelled three spoons of sugar into her coffee.

'Mammy is dead and gone. She had no right to try and force you to take over the house and land. As for the girls, well, they'll be fine, and—'

'What will happen to Kilteelagh House?'

'We have everything we need here, so we could sell it off. It's expensive bringing up four children.'

'But Grandma wouldn't have wanted that to happen. Isn't that why she had left the place to me?'

Katherine swung around, looking to her right and left in an exaggerated way. 'Like I said, she's dead, and thankfully she can't rule the roost from the grave. We have to do what's best for all of us. You go back to New York, and we can continue here.'

'I don't want Kilteelagh House put up for sale,' Marianne said fiercely.

Katherine took a long drag of her cigarette, so when she spoke her words emerged through a cloud of smoke.

'I've had the place valued and the estate agent is ready to put the For Sale sign up next week, once we've got over this nonsense. I'm Collie's daughter, remember – you can't go against me.'

Marianne pushed back her chair, making it screech along the tiles.

'And I am her granddaughter and the owner of Kilteelagh House. You can't bully me like this.'

Katherine laughed out loud. Moving closer, she stuck her head close to Marianne's, the reek of stale smoke strong on her breath.

'I'm trying to do this the civilised way. You know nothing

about Kilteelagh or how difficult it has been these past years to keep the old pile in one piece. We need rid of it now.'

'You mean you *want* rid.'

'Yes, I bloody well do. You haven't had to keep that shithole going all these years and listen to my mother's stupidity. It was always Kilteelagh this or Kilteelagh that with her. I was the one who stayed and looked after her. I didn't swan off to America and make a new life. I stayed behind – and look at the thanks I got for it. Collie loved those bricks and mortar more than she ever did me. However, she couldn't bring it with her, and now it's time for all of us – and especially you, Marianne – to move on.'

Marianne walked over to the back door and opened it.

'I will see you later at the solicitor's,' she said as Rachel and Katie, along with Katherine's twin girls, Molly and Hetty, came down the hallway to the kitchen. Katherine stepped closer. She stared unblinking into Marianne's eyes. 'Make the right decision, Marianne. It would be nice if we could stay friends.'

Without giving an answer, Marianne set off quickly down her aunt's gravel drive. She walked straight into the town, again too preoccupied to stop at the bridge and take a breath. Once she arrived at Eager Solicitors, she tentatively pulled back the door and approached the receptionist. She was shown to an office on the first floor, where Sean Eager was sipping his morning coffee as he prepared his files for a session of the District Court.

'Marianne, our appointment is for later,' he said as he stood up when she walked into the room.

'I wanted to ask you something.'

'Go ahead. If I can be of any help, I will.'

'Can you tell me why my grandmother chose me? I really need to know.'

'Your grandmother desperately wanted to keep Kilteelagh House in the family. The place was incredibly dear to her – she lived and breathed Kilteelagh – and she knew that Katherine, who was, and is, of course, a most dutiful daughter, had no emotional attachment to the place. I think she was looking for a custodian who would love the house and gardens. Somebody to fill her shoes. She said you were Kilteelagh's only hope.'

Feeling uneasy, the responsibility weighing heavily on her shoulders, Marianne crossed over to the window. Outside, a group of children were scuffling over a ball as they walked to the local primary school. At the hardware shop, the owner was putting out big baskets of bargain items in the hope of drawing in more customers.

'Do you think I can do it?' she asked quietly.

The solicitor did not answer immediately, but when he did, his voice was kind. 'I think challenges like this don't often come our way, and if you pass it by, you may regret it. There was a reason Collie was looking to your parents and then to you, and I trust her judgement.'

Marianne fingered the silver Tiffany necklace with the heart which Collie had gifted her many years earlier.

'It's so much to take on. It frightens me.'

'Maybe if you stop overanalysing the situation, the path you must take will show itself.'

'I don't know if I can or want to do it.'

He began to gather up his files, then abandoned them on the desk as a thought occurred to him.

'I have just the thing. Your grandmother anticipated some jitters, and she asked me to give you this letter if the need arose.'

He unlocked a drawer in his desk and took out the envelope.

'I have to get to court, but read it – it might inform your decision.'

He left her sitting in his office, the letter in her hand.

Slowly, she opened the seal.

Kilteelagh House
Balgaddy
Co. Wicklow

My dearest Marianne,

By now, I am sure you will be confused and a little mystified as to why I have made this great ask of you. I know you are still grieving. I loved your mother so much and now that she and your lovely, amiable daddy are dead, I feel a terrible loneliness.

There are many reasons I have asked you to move to Kilteelagh, and they will become apparent as time moves on. Marianne, you are such a beautiful young woman; I know you can be a wonderful parent to Rachel and little Katie. Katherine's heart is in the right place, but you understand Kilteelagh, I know, because you are your mother's daughter. Chloe loved this place, and you will too. Bring up the girls with the values your mother instilled in you, and you will be grand.

I realise I am asking you to leave your home city, suspend your career and take a step into the unknown. Take it willingly and dance with me, just for the next twelve months. Kilteelagh House needs you, and I need you to do this. Who knows, maybe you need it as well. Along the way, I hope you will not only learn much of Kilteelagh, but also of yourself. You take over at a good time, when the trees in the garden are budding, the roses are showing their green shoots, the daffodils are in glorious bloom, and the tulips are tentatively pushing through the earth.

What a time to come to Kilteelagh! I tell you, enjoy the early morning. Welcome, too, the mist coiling across the lake and around the house, the spring lambs in the front fields, the feeling of renewal as nature provides balm for the soul.

Follow nature and follow your instinct, and you won't go far wrong.

All my love,

Collie xx

She crumpled the letter into a ball. Collie had made it impossible for her to say no. She didn't know how to be a mother, but she had no job and no life any more in New York. She was stuck with Kilteelagh House. Rachel and sweet Katie were stuck with her. On reflection, Marianne thought she'd probably got the better deal. But maybe they could muddle through for the year at Kilteelagh. As for what would happen after that – who knew?

FOUR

April

Marianne pulled in at the gates of Kilteelagh House and took a heavy bolt cutter from her hire car boot. Marching over to the chain and padlock, she positioned it carefully and squeezed hard. Nothing. She moved the bolt cutter higher and tried again, but the chain didn't budge. Kicking the gate, she thought how Katherine would love to see her locked out of Kilteelagh House.

'If you want Kilteelagh House, you will have to break in and squat – I'm never going to help you steal my birthright!' The venom in Katherine's voice had been evident as she brushed off her husband's attempts to placate her and the solicitor's appeals for calm. 'Collie clearly wasn't in her right mind when she decided this. It can't be right.'

Before the solicitor could respond, Katherine had swung around to fling more words at her niece.

'Just you wait and see, you'll be begging for me to take Kilteelagh off your hands within a few months. You could walk away now and leave those two lovely girls with us, where they already have a proper home.'

Marianne made to speak, but Katherine continued to yell.

'Who do you think you are, coming over here and taking away what was my home all my life, and where I looked after my own mother? You think you can waltz in at the last minute – no, *after* the last minute, and reap the benefits. Well, missy, I have a lot of friends in this town, and they will not stand idly by,' she shouted.

Sean Eager shook his head and sternly warned Katherine that the children should not see her like this. If she impeded the orderly transfer of Rachel and Katie to Kilteelagh, he would have to take her to court.

'Katherine, none of us wants to be opposite each other in a courtroom. Accept the last will and testament of your mother and, for the sake of these young girls, try and put this behind you. Rachel and Katie should be dropped to Kilteelagh by 4 p.m. on Friday, 6 April of this year.'

'Easily known it's not *your* past that is being thrown away,' Katherine said.

She swept out of the solicitor's office, her dress swishing around her, her husband running behind, calling her name over and over.

Sean Eager waited until he heard the front door bang and Katherine and Steve scurry down the street, then handed over a small packet which included the keys of Kilteelagh House.

'I don't expect Katherine will keep this up. Let's hope she drops the girls back and you two can work something out. If there are any problems, ring me.'

Marianne took the packet and pushed it in her pocket.

When a car whooshed by on the road, Marianne hid the bolt cutter behind her back. But the car stopped and a tall man got out.

'Hi, can I help you?' he asked.

'I'm good, thanks,' she replied.

He crossed over to the gate in a few strides.

'Either you're breaking in to Kilteelagh or you are the new owner?' he said, holding out his hand.

Marianne didn't respond.

'So, which is it?'

'Homeowner, but I wish at this moment I was a burglar, because I can't get the lock and chain off the gate. I don't have a key for the lock.'

'You must be Marianne. Jack Farrelly. I believe my daughter, Sarah, and your Katie go to school together,' he said.

Hesitantly, she offered her hand and he clasped it in a strong handshake.

'May I?' he asked, pointing to the bolt cutter.

She handed it to him.

'Let's see if I can do any better,' he said. Quickly he positioned the cutter and snapped the chain so it fell away. Pulling the chain free of the gate, he let it drop under the azalea.

'Why don't I drag back the gates and you can drive up to the house.'

'Thank you so much.'

'No bother, and welcome to Balgaddy,' he said as he yanked the gates open, letting them cut their way through the gravel and mud as he manoeuvred them into place. He stood and waved her off as she steered her car over the cattle grid, the poles rattling in their settings.

Marianne was nervous, her stomach queasy. Doubt seared through her, making her want to jump from the car and say she had made a big mistake. She had already arranged for her New York apartment to be packed up and the contents of her parents' house put into storage. There was no going back now. Slowly, she drove up the avenue, stopping as she rounded the rhododendron bend.

Kilteelagh House stood three storeys tall with a sweep of stone steps up to the front door. It must at one time have looked imposing, but now it seemed tired and neglected. The wisteria was about to flower, but Marianne could see it trailed over the big bay window at the front and up to frame the higher floors. A few hens were pecking on the gravel outside; the Labrador, Benji, who had sneaked back to the house from Katherine's, was barking to warn off visitors, even though there was nobody at home to heed him.

The avenue ahead of the car was divided in two by a wide row of grass and weeds. She pulled to a stop in front of Kiltee-lagh House, which looked even more jaded from close quarters. The railings up the side of the granite steps were leaning at an awkward angle, the black paint peeling off in patches revealing the rust underneath.

The Labrador bolted towards her and began to circle wide around her. Shyly he approached, wagging his tail and craning his neck to sniff her hand. She stroked his head and he sat quietly, enjoying the attention.

Sweeping around, she scrutinised the house. Paint was flaking off the front walls; empty plant pots on the steps looked dirty and weather-beaten. She made her way to the front door as she scrabbled in her pocket for the keys. The door looked dull and was stained with dirt. Browned petals from the cherry blossom at the front were stuck in places to the paintwork and clogging up the corners, where spiders had spooled their webs.

She took out the key ring. There was only one key on the ring, which said *Kilteelagh House, for Marianne Johnson*. There wasn't a key for the front door, so she walked around to the back of the house, passing the drawing room window, which was still shuttered, and by the little path to the lake, which was unused and overgrown. The cobbled backyard was shrouded in weeds, the cobbles slippery with moss as she made her way to the back door. Pushing the key in the lock, she turned it and the door clicked open. As she slowly stepped into the kitchen, tears welled up when she saw the big Aga, now cold, and the rectangular kitchen table which once sat a family of five and where somebody had left a pile of empty cardboard boxes.

Marianne closed her eyes. Memories flooded her brain: the aroma of scones cooling on a rack on the table, a freshly washed bundle of rhubarb that needed to be chopped with a sharp knife on the worktop beside the sink, and the kettle always boiled and ready. Kilteelagh without Collie was cold and bland.

When she heard a car drive into the backyard, she was surprised to see it was Katherine arriving already. She watched as Rachel and Katie got out and Katherine opened the boot so they could get their cases. When she opened the door, Katie stepped behind her older sister.

'They're so excited about getting back home, I thought I would drop them up a bit early,' Katherine said, her voice strangely calm. Then, announcing that she had better get going as she was heading to Dublin, she got back in the car and drove off.

Marianne stepped forward to hug the two girls, but Rachel ignored her and walked by, with Katie sticking close to her. Cautiously, Rachel stepped into the kitchen.

'It feels different,' she said.

Katie ran to a box under the table and pulled it out, spilling Lego pieces across the floor.

'Grandma said only on the table,' Rachel snapped, her voice high with tension.

'I don't think Collie would mind that much today,' Marianne said, tapping Rachel lightly on the shoulder. Rachel said she was going upstairs and a few minutes later her heavy footsteps sounded on the floorboards above.

'Is Grandma ever coming back?' Katie asked.

Marianne, who was searching in the hot press beside the stove for the central heating thermostat, stopped what she was doing. For a moment, her brain fogged over as panic surged through her. When she turned around, Katie was carefully building a Lego house. Unsure of what to do, Marianne sat on the floor beside her.

'Grandma isn't coming back, sweetheart. She's dead and in heaven.'

'Grandma said heaven was a load of old nonsense,' Katie answered, her voice solemn.

'Well, that's silly. Grandma was always a silly.'

Katie smiled. 'She also said Benji loved chocolate, but dogs can't eat chocolate.'

'See, she was so silly.'

Katie laughed and Marianne wondered if it was too early to give her a hug as she sank into the big armchair beside the stove.

'What about Dolores, is she gone too?' Katie asked.

'Dolores?'

'She was my best friend, and Grandma's too.'

'I don't know, sweetheart. Let's talk about it another time. I want to give you something,' Marianne said.

Reaching for a plastic bag she had left on the table when she got in, Marianne pulled out two big chocolate Easter eggs.

'The Easter Bunny came to Aunt Katherine's house already,' Katie said.

'Well, these are my presents to you,' Marianne said as she held out the two big boxes and let Katie have her pick.

Rachel walked in. 'I opened the windows upstairs to air out the place. That was Grandma's chair – nobody else ever sat on it.'

Marianne stood up. 'Have an Easter egg while I go and get

the other windows done,' she said, as Rachel opened the fridge and asked what was for dinner. As if she hadn't heard the question, Marianne set off through the hall to the drawing room. She wanted Collie to be there, sitting in her Sunday best, a glass of whiskey, one cube of ice, in her hand.

Stepping into the room, she felt herself sink into the deep pile of the rug. She skirted past the velvet couch to the windows and reached for where she remembered the catch for the shutters to be. Pulling it up, while at the same time pushing hard on the wood, she made the shutters release. Sunlight flooded in, glaring across her face, forcing her to close her eyes. Colours danced in front of her as she twisted around to take in Collie's front drawing room. It was as she remembered: the blue velvet couch spanning the room, two comfortable armchairs in dark navy velvet either side of the ornate marble fireplace.

Over the fireplace was a painting of Collie, done when she was in her late twenties. A visiting artist had apparently painted it. It showed her in a ball gown, sitting on her favourite armchair in front of the fireplace. Behind her, through the side window, the path to the lake was visible, with the gazebo in the distance. Marianne examined her grandmother's features; the look in her eyes of not just happiness but contentment, the smile which was enigmatic as if hiding an untold story. The Collie captured on canvas was about the same age as Marianne now. How she envied the demeanour of this woman so superbly summed up by the artist. There was something about her that she hankered after: the feeling of happiness and contentment at her lot. It was a state of mind, Marianne realised, she had never felt in her life.

Shuffling over and opening the side window shutters, she stopped to look at the path to the lake. It was overgrown, as though it had not been used in years. The dog was sprawled under a horse chestnut tree. As if he sensed her watching, he stood up and ambled around to the front of the house, where he flopped down by the rose-bed. It was hard to believe she owned all this. One part of her wanted to run away, sell the lot, and her parents' house too, and buy a loft apartment in Manhattan. Another part of her wanted to slip into this simple life and hide until she felt ready to meet the world again. Maybe at Kilteelagh she could finally find some peace.

Rachel stuck her head around the door. 'There's post for you – and what's for dinner?'

'Is takeout OK?'

'We say "takeaway". Can we have fish and chips?'

'Sure.'

'Good, I can order right now.'

'Are they open this early?'

'Always on school holidays.'

'Use the card in my wallet. It should work fine.'

Marianne was relieved when Rachel headed back to the kitchen. Sitting down on the couch, she studied the painting. She'd never actually seen her grandmother wear that dress on any occasion. She remembered her mother saying Grandma Collie kept it wrapped in her wardrobe but took it out every summer and draped it on the washing line to give it a good airing. It was such a beautiful dress, made of navy-blue satin with an off-the-shoulder design that showed off Collie's slim frame. The tight bodice gave way to a full, panelled skirt, which must have swished as she walked through Kilteelagh House. A small black velvet bow was tucked under the bust and on the high waistline to Collie's right. It added a style that was more New York than Balgaddy, Marianne thought with a smile. Absent-mindedly, she took the letter Rachel had left on the bureau and tore it open. She sat up straight when she saw her grandmother's handwriting.

Kilteelagh House
Balgaddy
Co. Wicklow

My dearest Marianne,

The daffodils must be in full display. I hope you have caught the last few days before the yellow petals show tinges of brown and the loveliest of spring flowers bow as they say their final farewell. If I am right, the tulips are gaining in strength and beginning to show their colours, taking the limelight from the once proud daffodil. Every year these flowers have brought me so much joy. From the landing is the best view; let the spectacle of the daffodils lining the avenue soothe your tired brain. It always put things in perspective for me, especially in the days when even the growth of spring did not turn my heart. The daffodils stir up memories, warming me inside and giving me the strength to go on.

No matter where you are in the world, there will be days like this. Please know they will pass, and in time you will have your own memories to sustain you. Enjoy the pockets of colour as the tulips push tall and waft in the breeze, a reminder that we all need rich variety in our lives.

I know you must be anxious, taking over the parenting of Rachel and Katie, and I'm sure Katherine will have had her say about that. Katherine has a good heart – and don't be afraid to ask her for help – but you must follow your own gut. If you love those girls, they will respond to you; if you respect them, they will respect you back. But remember, teenagers also need a tough head to keep them on the right path.

Don't worry about Rachel smoking, it's her little rebellion and soon enough she will meet a young man, and if he doesn't like the taste of smoke, she will give up overnight. At least, that is what her mother before her did and, hopefully, it will turn out the same way. Sometimes, it is good to have an insight into the past! Bear in mind that a row over smoking now could set you too early on a warpath.

Before you get cross for my sticking my nose in from the grave, you must know Katie likes a bedtime story and, if you can, she would like you to stay in the room until she falls asleep. Also, don't even think about washing the disgusting rabbit she likes to cuddle. She says she will never clean it; says it smells of her mammy.

Have you noticed how the garden is budding? Get somebody in ASAP to prune the roses. It should have been done much earlier, but I think you might get away with it even now. Otherwise, let everything show its glory, slowly but surely. By the way, Katherine may offer Steve's services, but the man who is as gentle as a lamb with farm animals is like a butcher when it comes to flowers. I once made the mistake of letting him prune the wisteria at the front and I was lucky not to lose the whole lot; it took two years to recover.

What do you think of the house? I hope you are putting your own stamp on it, but tread carefully: Rachel and Katie have had a lot of upheaval in their young lives.

I'm glad you have accepted the challenge to stay at Kilteelagh. Indulge me to write to you every now and again, to have a letter sent with my random thoughts. It's not meant as interference, you are now the owner of Kilteelagh House, but it is intended as a gesture of solidarity, to say I believe in you and what you can do for Kilteelagh. The days and months of each season and year at Kilteelagh I know so well. They are captured forever in my memory and to put pen to paper now to you is a real comfort.

Darling, I do not want to upset you, but I must tell you my reason for writing these letters – which I have arranged, through Sean Eager, to be delivered to you from time to time. I have been given two months to live. I didn't want to tell you *and I know you think I am just ill, like any old person could be. You, darling, have had enough to deal with. I have lived my life and I am tired. Cancer is creeping through me and, when the final sleep comes, I will be ready.*

My solace now is to return through my memories to the good days of Kilteelagh in these letters to you. My hope is that you too will gain comfort from this secret conversation.

Forgive me if I preach and go on about housekeeping, but for me writing these letters is an exercise in love, where I tell you about my life at Kilteelagh. Hopefully you will understand why I picked you as the person to carry the house into the future.

As I sit here writing, I am sustained by happy memories like just last week, Rachel and Katie in the kitchen, baking biscuits I had to pretend to eat, because my appetite is not good these days. The kitchen has always been the focal point of the house. I think when we moved in all those years ago, it was the only room with proper heating. That's why we picked the bedroom directly over it, because we got the warmth throughout a winter's night. The same range is still there. If it is temperamental, give it a good kick at the side. That usually works; look for the dent – it has been kicked many times before. If that doesn't solve the problem, Ray Fogarty in the address book will come out, but make sure he doesn't overcharge. Always query his first price and he will drop down pretty fast.

Thank you for reading these ramblings. It might be strange getting these letters, but I hope you will learn a lot about Kilteelagh and a thing or two about your grandmother, which in time you may like to pass on to your own children. See this as a big adventure, Marianne, but even when the responsibility weighs heavily on your shoulders, don't shut yourself away from love or the invitation to love.

Your loving grandmother,

Collie xx

PS I always think of something when I have signed off a letter, so there is another page here in a separate envelope. Open it when you are in the sitting room and when you have a moment of quiet. C xx

Katie came bursting through, her face full of anguish.

'Rachel said we might have to go back to Aunt Katherine's. I want to stay here.'

Rachel ran in after her. 'I only told her the truth, that you're trying out this life and we'll have to put up with whatever you decide.'

'Why did you have to bother Katie with this? She's too young.'

'No, I'm not,' Katie shouted.

Marianne stuffed the letter into her pocket and stood up. 'I'm not going anywhere. We're going to live together. This is our home. But yes, I have a year's trial to make sure we're all happy with this arrangement.'

Katie threw herself at Marianne, burying her head into her.

'I want to stay here – and I'm hungry.'

Rachel went to the window. 'I got them to deliver, so it shouldn't be long.'

'Where will we eat?' Marianne asked.

'Why? Grandma said we had to eat at the kitchen table,' Katie said, her voice low.

Marianne laughed.

'I think Grandma was good at saying things and doing the exact opposite herself.' She went behind the sideboard and fumbled around until she found the small foldaway table.

'When everyone was gone to bed, Grandma used to have

her tea and cake in here, her china cup, saucer and plate on this table, while she looked at the TV.'

'I want to use it,' Katie said.

Marianne set up the table and Rachel said she would walk down to the gate and wait for the takeaway delivery.

'She likes Tom, who delivers from the chipper, that's why she ordered from Greystones instead of Balgaddy,' Katie said.

After they had wrapped away the remains of their takeaway, Marianne suggested they make up their beds.

'Where are you sleeping?' Katie asked.

'For tonight, I was thinking of the room at the front, where I used to sleep when I came on holidays.'

'That's a junk room now. We don't really use it,' Rachel said.

'Oh, well, I'm sure I can bunk down anywhere.'

'There's my mummy's room or my grandma's,' Katie said.

'I suppose it will have to be Grandma's room then.'

Katie's face brightened and Marianne felt she had made the right decision, though a part of her baulked at sleeping in Collie's room.

'She died after Katherine had her transferred to hospital,' Rachel said, and Marianne tried not to show the relief she felt.

Upstairs, Katie pointed out the sheets she wanted, and they made her bed first. Rachel said she would make hers later and asked could she go for a walk to the lake. Marianne wanted to say something about smoking but stopped herself.

'It will be dark soon, so don't be long,' she said.

'I want to go for a walk. Grandma said a walk with Benji is always a good idea,' Katie said, jumping on her bed.

'Yeah, you two can, but not near the lake. I want some time on my own,' Rachel said.

'Meanie.'

Rachel made a face and backed out the door quickly.

Katie turned to Marianne. 'She goes smoking and she meets Tom, and she thinks I don't know. Aunt Katherine said Rachel is going to come to a bad end. What does that mean?'

Marianne swallowed hard. 'A stroll might be a very good idea.'

They decided not to use the overgrown track near the house and instead set off down the driveway to the path past the rhododendron grove.

Katie ran ahead with the dog. Marianne stood on the avenue and looked back at the house. It still appeared neglected, but with the shutters back and the windows open, there was a lived-in look she liked. She had to make a go of it here, she had no choice. She would have to find somebody to help tidy up the front and maybe paint the outside. That was the plan and she had to stick with it. Katie was waiting at the rhododendron bushes.

'I can see Rachel. She's going to be very cross when she finds out we followed her.'

'We're not following her. Let's look at the sheep in the field,' Marianne said as she took Katie's hand and guided her in the opposite direction to the lake. The little girl, if she minded, didn't say anything, and began to warn Benji not to jump and frighten the sheep.

'Who owns the sheep?' Marianne asked.

Katie looked at her in surprise.

'We do, and there are two goats to keep the grass down. Grandma says it's the only way to keep the fields right. We have a horse too, but he's over at Aunt Katherine's.'

FIVE

The house was quiet. Katie was finally asleep, and Rachel was in her room. Marianne reached into the cabinet under the kitchen sink, where she knew Collie kept her bottle of Jameson whiskey. She poured a generous measure. Pulling the ice tray from the freezer, she popped an ice cube into the glass. She walked to the drawing room and turned on a light beside the window. Pulling Collie's letter from her pocket, she began to read:

Kilteelagh House
Balgaddy
Co. Wicklow

My dearest Marianne,

I hope you are sitting where you can view my beautiful painting. How I loved that dress. I stitched it with my own hands. It was meant to be for the County Ball that Mike and I were supposed to go to at the end of April 1973, a few years after we moved in to Kilteelagh House.

Two months beforehand, I got the bus to Dublin and walked the city until I found a Vogue pattern for the perfect gown: off the shoulder, strapless with a button-through short jacket. I picked a sumptuous navy satin and velvet ribbon for a little bow tucked to one side over the high waistline. This dress, I knew, would be the height of sophistication.

When I showed Mike the pattern, he wasn't too happy. I knew it was the design. He thought it too daring, but he also insisted the navy blue was such a dull colour. I ignored him and spent my evenings working at the kitchen table, pinning down the pattern and cutting it out. I was very careful with all the panels, tacking every seam, before I ran the machine over it. I don't think I ever worked, before or since, with such intensity and concentration. When I slipped the dress on, even when unfinished, I didn't feel like Collie Keane any more. I felt like this exotic creature who should have diamonds to show at the neck to offset the darkness of the fabric.

As I walked, the dress swished around me, whispering promises into the air. I knew some would say it was over the top, but that's exactly what I loved about it. I had enough fabric to make the bolero jacket, as per the pattern, but in truth I wanted to wear the dress with a simple shawl. It was a pity I never got a chance to show it off at the County Ball. Mike came down with food poisoning and instead of dazzling the whole county, I was left cleaning up after my poor husband, who never seemed to make it to the bathroom on time.

When I slipped on the dress for the painting though, I can honestly say it was one of the happiest moments of my life.

Collie xx

Marianne stared at the portrait over the mantelpiece, trying to decipher the signature in the corner. Grandfather Mike had apparently never liked the work and always sat at an angle, so he didn't have to look at it. Marianne's mother said it was quite a joke in the house that Mike Keane couldn't handle his wife looking so devastatingly beautiful and so different. Chloe also said he was a simple, hard-working man who usually indulged the notions of his wife, and he probably found it hard to believe that any woman who could look like a film star in a long dress would be happy to live a relatively simple life at Kilteelagh. But Chloe also didn't remember Mike very well; he'd died when she was only four years old. To her, he was a tall figure who always smelled of tobacco smoke. She was too young to remember much else, but from what her sisters said, she knew at mealtimes he was served first, and on Sunday after Mass he sat in the parlour reading the newspaper until he was called upon to carve the roast.

Getting up, Marianne walked to the fireplace and, leaning on the marble mantelpiece, stretched onto her toes to examine the painting closer. The dress was exquisite; the look in her grandmother's eyes was soft, as if she knew and trusted the artist. Collie's hair was different, tied up in a loose bun with wisps framing her face. Her smile was wistful, maybe of long-ing. Thinking she was reading too much into the work, Mari-anne stood to view it from an angle. It was then she spotted something she hadn't noticed before. In the small mirror over the sideboard was the shadowy figure of a man. She peered closer, but she couldn't make it out. And yet, when she stepped back, she saw the faint traces of an outline; the artist perhaps leaving a reminder of his presence. Downing the last of her whiskey, Marianne suddenly felt tired. She had got this far and now she should prepare for the next round.

She couldn't face even going into Collie's bedroom. Instead, she cleared items off the single bed in the junk room. Taking fresh sheets from the hot press, she also grabbed the patchwork quilt Collie had always laid out for her. The room had not changed that much. There was still the gap where the curtains should have met when pulled across, and the piece of guttering which blew in the wind, knocking against the top left corner of the window. It was the plastic tapping on the window which woke her up shortly after dawn the next morning. Not wanting to disturb the girls, she slipped out of the house and set off down the avenue, along the path and across the soft, dewy grass to the gazebo. The birds called out to each other, and a heron flew slowly over the lake, dropping quickly into the reeds further down.

Pulling her cardigan around her against the chilly, crisp morning air, she wandered down to the old jetty. It had seen better days. Gingerly, she moved along, stepping over holes where the planks of wood had disintegrated. She had to stop three feet short of the end, which was dipping precariously below the water line. They had such fun here, the summer they stayed for two months at Kilteelagh. Collie had recently added the jetty, making the lakefront look like something out of a movie. Marianne used to run along and fling herself into the water, often making the ducks squawk and rise, flapping their wings in agitation. Collie laughed out loud and said she must get a small boat, but for some reason, she never did. Shivering from the cold, Marianne turned back towards the house. She had no idea where to start on her first real day at Kilteelagh House.

As she rounded the rhododendron, she saw Rachel at the upstairs window waving frantically at her. She scurried along, afraid something was wrong. When she got to the kitchen, Katie was sitting at the table in her pyjamas and Rachel was banging down a cereal bowl in front of her. 'You know I have to go to school; the bus will be passing the gate in half an hour. Katie has to be walked to her school.'

'Sorry, I was out looking at the lake.'

'Can I come with you tomorrow morning?' Katie asked. Marianne, grateful for the friendly voice, nodded as she reached into the fridge and took out the milk carton. She turned to Rachel. 'Go, get ready. I've got this.'

Rachel, the cereal box in her hand, sighed loudly before handing it to Marianne and making her way upstairs. When she came back down, her bag slung over her shoulder, Marianne noticed her skirt was too short, and her eyes were smudged with black eyeliner.

'Are you allowed make-up?' she asked in the most neutral tone she could muster.

'Nobody checks. Don't forget to pick up Katie from school at 2.30 p.m., and we need lunch.'

'You can get it at the school cafeteria, right?'

Rachel giggled. 'I'll take money to buy something, but Katie needs a proper lunch.'

'A sandwich, no crusts and a chocolate bar,' Katie piped up.

'She has another snack when she gets home and we usually eat dinner at 6 p.m.,' Rachel said, fixing her bag on her shoulder before leaving by the back door.

Marianne nodded, feeling as if she were the babysitter. Katie tugged at her skirt. 'Will you help me pick something red?'

'Why red?'

Katie was about to answer when Rachel ran in the back door. 'I need the lunch money.'

'I don't have any change. Shit, take my card.'

'I can't use it at school.'

'Can you go to the cash machine first?'

'I suppose.'

'Take out enough for the week, say twenty-five euros.'

'OK.'

'My number is 1210.'

Rachel scrawled it on the palm of her right hand, then tore out the back door and sprinted down the avenue. Marianne waited until after she turned the bend in case she came back and needed a ride to school; to her relief it proved unnecessary. Katie had already gone upstairs. When she heard Marianne on the first-floor corridor, she skipped towards her wearing a sparkly red dress.

'Can I wear this? Mummy bought it for me, but I haven't worn it yet.'

'I don't see why not, you look amazing.'

She tied Katie's hair back with a fancy scrunchie and then set about making a quick sandwich for her lunch.

'Don't forget to take off the crusts and also my something-nice,' Katie said.

Marianne looked in the food cupboard but could only find bourbon chocolate biscuits. Katie made a face.

'Why does Rachel get money for lunch, and I don't?'

'Rachel is a little older.'

'She only buys cigarettes; she doesn't eat lunch.'

Marianne didn't react but guided the little girl to the door. The dog lumbered after them down the avenue, turning back when they reached the gate.

At the bridge, Katie pulled Marianne aside. 'Me and Grandma always stopped here.'

'Shall we throw in a leaf?'

Katie quickly snapped a bunch of leaves from a butterfly bush and ran across to the other side of the bridge to throw them in the water.

'Grandma says they're our little boats battling their way through a storm.'

'Let's launch lots of boats,' Marianne said, and they threw some more leaves, watching them race past each other, carried by the fast water rushing over the rocks. When Marianne glanced at her phone, she realised they were going to be late and they beetled along, laughing at their own stupidity. At the school gate, everybody had already gone in.

'You're going to have to bring me in to class. Just tell the teacher I wasn't feeling well. She says we should stay away from the river; it's dangerous,' Katie said.

Marianne knocked gently on the classroom door. The teacher smiled and told Katie to take her seat, before turning to Marianne.

'Do you mind if I have a quick word?' she said, stepping outside the classroom and closing the door behind her.

'I'm sorry we're late.'

'That's perfectly all right. I realise it must be difficult for you. I wanted to offer any help I can with Katie. She's a strong-willed young lady.'

'Thanks, but we'll be fine, and Rachel is a great help.'

'Teenagers rarely offer their help for nothing. Katie needs a strong mother figure in her life, particularly now. You know where I am if you need me.'

The teacher had slipped back into the classroom before Marianne had a chance to reply. She wanted to say she had negotiated life in New York City, and she was well capable of bringing up two lovely young girls and the teacher could mind her own damned business. Instead she said nothing and felt angry and out of her depth – and it was only the first day. She quickly left the school.

On the way home she stopped at the bridge to take a breath in the hope it would help her calm down. It was 4 a.m. in Manhattan. She might be tumbling out of a taxi after a night clubbing with Jay and propping up the bar at Paul's Cocktail Lounge on Sixth Avenue. What was she doing here, pretending she knew what she was at and licking her dress-designing wounds?

SIX

Marianne got up early to tramp across the fields, steeling herself for Rachel to wake up. There had been almost total silence from Rachel since she had come off the school bus the previous day. Marianne and Katie had ambled along the avenue to meet Rachel. Katie ran ahead, twirling to make her red dress fan out and watching the light catch the sparkles.

'Why is she wearing that dress?' Rachel asked.

'She wanted to, and it's so beautiful. Why not?'

Rachel muttered something about Marianne not under-standing, and ran towards the house.

Katie began to cry. 'I wanted to pretend everything was fine and you were my mummy,' she sniffled as she ran into Mari-anne's arms.

'Sweetheart, there was nothing wrong with wearing the dress. OK?'

Katie pulled her head from Marianne's shoulder.

'There is, Mummy ordered it on Amazon and said it was my dress for when she got better. She said we would go to the city and have a day out with a fancy lunch in a place that deserved a dress like this.'

Marianne carried Katie back to the house, the dog keeping close and every now and again, sniffing and nudging at her shoes. Rachel did not join them for dinner and only appeared when her sister was getting into bed.

Katie was the first up once Marianne, her feet sodden, got back to the kitchen. When Rachel came downstairs, she didn't say anything, but Marianne caught her stealing glances at her as she plaited Katie's hair. When Rachel went for the bus, she made a big deal of saying goodbye to her sister, but she didn't even glance at Marianne.

An hour later, when both children had gone to school, Katherine drove up the avenue. She didn't say anything as she got out of the car and took a box from the back seat. Walking past Marianne, she placed the box on the kitchen table.

'Some home-made bread and the pizza dough the girls like; ye can make your own pizza. I have some sauce and toppings in tubs for you, too.'

'Thank you.'

Katherine looked directly at her. 'Don't read anything into it. My argument is not with those girls, who have lost so much. I know they love their home-made pizza.' Marianne nodded. Katherine stopped and stared at her. 'What's wrong, has Rachel been giving you lip?'

'No, but it's harder work than I ever thought possible.'

Katherine guffawed out loud.

'I did try to warn you. Word of advice, not that you're interested in my opinion, but when they're at school, you relax; you won't get another minute on your own.'

Marianne picked up the kettle to fill it.

'We're not friends, just related, so don't bother on my account. I'm off into Dublin for a few hours.'

When she was gone, Marianne felt strangely lonely. She

went upstairs to Collie's bedroom. Hesitating outside the door, she felt she should knock before going in. The room was bright, the sunshine falling across the bed, sparkling off the bottles of perfume on the dressing table. She didn't even know why she was here. It wasn't as if she'd ever spent any time with Collie in this room. Her grandmother was always up at the crack of dawn, with fresh bread in the oven by the time anyone else made it downstairs.

Marianne stood at the window which overlooked the back-yard, where Benji was lying out on the cobbled stones. This place needed her right now, but she worried that her grand-mother was expecting too much of her. She turned to the wardrobe. It wasn't closed properly, a bulge of clothes peeping through the gap between the two doors. Gently, she pulled one side open. The rail was dipping under the weight of the outfits hanging there and the interior smelled musty. She was about to shut the door when she noticed a hanger with a special cover at the back. Forcing her way past the bulk of wire hangers, which were almost collapsing under the weight of clothes, she managed to grip the one she wanted and pull it out, the long cover lurching from the wardrobe and sweeping across the bedroom carpet.

Her nose twitching from the pungent smell of mothballs and staleness, Marianne crossed the room and propped open the window to let the air circulate. She laid the hanger and cover across the bed and unzipped it. Folds of navy-blue satin tumbled out, the skirt spreading across the bed. In places, there were dustings of mould, but the dress still looked beautiful. The velvet ribbon was frayed and dulled in places where it had been pressed back for too long.

Holding Collie's dress up to her, Marianne looked in the mirror. When she moved, the light dazzled on the fabric, catching the pleats of satin. It made her look beautiful, even if her hair was long and frizzy because she had not brushed it yet.

She picked up the hem of the dress and examined the exquisite stitching of her grandmother, who had been as careful about the stitches that could not be seen as those that could. Grandmother Collie and this amazing dress were the reasons Marianne studied dress design. Over the years, Collie asked her to send sketches and photographs, and in return posted her old Vogue and McCall patterns, saying they might be of some help. They were an enormous help – not that she had ever fully admitted that to her grandmother. She twirled, making the skirt fan out. All these years later, the dress was still so glamorous and could rival anything at the Met Ball. Holding the garment at the waist, she let the fabric rustle back into place.

Collie, she thought, had exceptionally good taste and was an expert dressmaker. She remembered she started sewing with Collie, making gowns from spare pieces of fabric for her dolls. Her grandmother was so patient, always telling her it was the cut of the scissors and the stitching of the seamstress that made the difference between a garment that looked good and one that didn't. How she had enjoyed learning from Collie.

This ball gown was precious to Collie, Marianne knew that well. The fabric needed to be cleaned and the dress aired out, she thought. Quickly googling how to wash satin, she bundled it under her arm and went downstairs to stuff it in the washing machine on a gentle cycle. Watching the dress in the tub, she worried that her grandmother would disapprove. When Rachel walked in the back door, Marianne jumped.

'You scared me.'

'What are you doing?'

'I'm not sure, I put Grandma's ball gown in the washing machine. I hope I've done the right thing.'

'She'll kill you—' Rachel stopped herself, tears creeping down her cheeks.

Marianne reached out and caught her in a tight hug.

'Let it go, it will make you feel better.'

Rachel leaned against her, tears convulsing her body. 'I'm sorry about Katie's dress, Mum died and then Grandma, I didn't see why she had to dress up.'

'We all have our ways of coping,' Marianne said, rubbing her back.

'But you seem OK,' Rachel said, pulling away abruptly.

Taking her hand, Marianne said, 'I lost my mom and dad too, then Grandma and then my job. I'm a mess inside, but Collie believed in me and asked me to be here for you, and I am going to do my best. You guys are my family now; we can be strong together. I'm not planning to go anywhere. We will get through this, I promise.'

'Do you, though?'

'What do you mean?'

'What about in a year's time, after you've spent a winter in this old house?'

Marianne sighed. 'I want to be honest with you, Rachel. It won't be easy, but I'm going to give it my best shot. We're a family and I will do everything to make sure it stays that way.'

Rachel smiled and looked at the washing machine. 'Best not to let on to Katherine about the dress. She will only give you grief for something that's not even her business.'

'And I certainly don't need that,' Marianne muttered, checking the time on her phone.

'How come you're home so early?'

Rachel sat into the table and started to pick at the pattern on the tablecloth. 'I needed to come home, I feel safe here.'

Marianne plopped a mug and plate in front of her.

'It's nearly lunchtime anyway.'

SEVEN

May

Katie ran down the stairs pulling her rabbit behind her.

'I'm not going to school today.'

'Really, any particular reason why?' Marianne asked as she poured the cornflakes into Katie's bowl. She felt exhausted. Somehow over a month had passed since she'd taken on the house, but every day seemed to blur, just getting the girls to school, preparing meals and trying to navigate running a family.

'I don't want to dress up.'

'What do you mean?'

'Teacher told us all to dress up as our favourite character in a book.'

'She asked this when?'

'We got a note home.'

Marianne stared at the little girl.

'How am I going to rustle up an outfit in forty minutes?'

Katie shrugged and concentrated on gently pulling Benji's ears. Rachel zoomed through the room looking for her French book.

'Katie always forgets to hand up her notes, you should check her bag every evening,' she said as she pulled the book from under a pile of clothes on the table. Pausing to pat her sister on the head, she let out a sigh and said she had to go or she would be late.

Marianne rubbed her forehead with her fingers in an attempt to relieve the tension headache beginning to pulse in her head.

'We'll look through your books, I'm sure we can come up with something,' she said a little too brightly.

'I don't want to. Can't I just stay home with you today?'

'Sweetie, I'm sure we can do something quickly. We will raid Grandma Collie's wardrobe.'

Katie's face puckered, tears bulging in her eyes. 'I don't want to have a costume for silly book day, OK?'

Marianne's phone pinged with a text from Rachel:

FYI, Mummy did Katie's costume when the school last had book day.

'What costume did Mummy make?' Marianne asked gently.

The little girl smiled broadly.

'Elmer the Elephant.'

'I bet it was fantastic.'

Katie nodded, the tears rolling down her cheeks. She flung herself at Marianne.

'Sweetheart, I'm sure if we explain it to your teacher, it will be fine, and you can still go to school.'

Katie nodded and allowed Marianne to wipe away her tears.

'Also, I have a play date with Sarah today.'

'That's settled, I'll have a little talk with your teacher.'

.   .   .

Katie ran upstairs to get dressed, leaving her cereal untouched on the kitchen table. When she came back down, she asked could they take the car to school.

'Just eat something first, anything.'

Katie picked a chocolate biscuit from the packet Rachel had left on the table the night before.

'When can I visit Dolores, or maybe she can come here?' she asked.

Marianne, who was searching for her car keys, stopped to look at Katie.

'I will have to get to know this Dolores; you seem to like her a lot.'

'She's such fun, for a grown-up. Grandma said she was a little bit crazy.'

'Well then, I will have to meet her,' Marianne said, ushering Katie to the car.

In the schoolyard, the teacher was admiring the colourful outfits of the other children.

'Marianne, I was hoping Katie told you about our special project.'

'Yes, she did, but she didn't feel like dressing up. I hope that's OK.'

'Katie can help me inspect the other costumes,' the teacher said, taking the little girl's hand and leading her gently away.

Marianne did not go back to Kilteelagh House but decided to drive into Balgaddy town. She wanted to place a notice in the local post office saying she was seeking a handyman.

'You're the new owner of Kilteelagh House?' the post-mistress Bridie Murphy asked, looking her up and down.

'Collie's granddaughter Marianne, from the States,' Marianne said, extending her hand.

Bridie pretended not to notice. 'Katherine is well known and liked in these parts,' she said firmly.

'Excuse me?' Marianne said, slightly embarrassed. Bridie shuffled the newspapers on the counter in front of her and concentrated on aligning the edges, so the stack looked neat.

'I wanted to place a notice in the window,' Marianne said.

Bridie looked up. 'The window is closed to personal notices at the moment. Try the newsagent's down the street.'

Marianne stuffed the handwritten card in her handbag.

'Are you going to stay out there at Kilteelagh?'

'I live there now.'

Bridie picked up a bundle of mobile phone receipts and shoved them in an envelope.

'It's a lonely spot for a young woman.'

'There are three of us. Anyway, Collie managed just fine for decades on her own.'

'Yes, but nobody would mess with Collie Keane. She was one tough bird. When her husband died, she turned that place around, did whatever she had to do. No one had anything but a good word to say about her.'

'I know,' Marianne said quietly as she turned and left the shop.

She headed for the coffee shop on Parnell Street, choosing to sit outside in the morning sunshine and sip her cappuccino. Closing her eyes, she listened to the town; there was the odd car cruising past, the thud of the beer kegs as they were delivered to the cellar of the pub next door and a car alarm blaring in the distance, until it was suddenly cut off. This town was her base now, but she didn't know anybody and it made her feel awkward. She wasn't sure if she would ever fit in. When her phone rang, she was grateful for the distraction and that it was Jay. She couldn't face chatting to any of the others, who all wanted to talk her out of staying at Kilteelagh. 'I couldn't sleep, so thought I would call. When are you coming home to Manhattan?'

Marianne's face beamed with pleasure to hear the happy tone of Jay's voice.

'Why, do you miss me?'

'Course I do. New York needs you.'

'This is my home now.'

'You're going to have to sound more convincing, darling.'

'It's hard, Jay, no work; the kids, the house. I don't have enough time in the day, only snatches to myself.'

'Duh, says every mother.'

'Yes, but I'm not meant to be a mother, not yet anyway.'

'I guess you're going to have to find something to fit in with the schedule of the little darlings.'

'No kidding.'

'Anyway, I have landed a job – theatre design. Totally different to what I was doing, but I have a window slit over-looking Bryant Park!'

'I'm green with envy.'

'They're looking for another designer, I could mention your name.'

Marianne felt the pull of working in the city, but as quickly she shook away the longing.

'I have to stay here, Jay; I can't give up on Kilteelagh, but maybe I should give up dress designing.'

'Honey, get out there, make your own opportunities. Hell, stick to the designing. If I lived in that amazing house, the creative juices would be flowing. Let me arrange for delivery of your design gear from storage. Honey, I've got to fly. Talk soon.'

Jay had already rung off, but she still held the phone to her ear. A wave of loneliness coursed through her for the life she used to have, the easy city life, the easy life of an only child. Shaking off the memory, she walked to her car without talking to anybody.

When she turned in at the driveway of Kilteelagh House, Marianne felt tears rising inside her. How she wanted it to be summer again, when she was so happy here with her mother and father. She stopped the car after the rhododendron grove. The house still had the same feel about it. She had always believed there was a magical quality about Kilteelagh House. Her mother once said Collie was offered a lot of money to allow it to be photographed by a jigsaw company, but she had been horrified at the notion that Kilteelagh House would be cut into a thousand little pieces.

Marianne took in the sad spectacle before her. Would anybody want it now for a jigsaw image? It was a beautiful house in the spring sunshine, but the neglect of the past decade showed in almost every square inch, and in the garden, which was overgrown and, in places, smothered in weeds. She had some money; maybe she could do it up. She smiled as one particular memory flashed through her head. Collie at the kitchen table with a series of masonry paint colour cards. It happened every few years when the house began to look unloved from the outside. Collie examined every combination and colour and asked everyone's opinion. Once she said she wanted to paint it a dark purple or a bright blue, but nobody believed her. Marianne asked her to paint the house pink, but Collie laughed.

'I don't know why I even bother with this circus; I'm never brave enough to choose anything but boring white. White is such a safe colour. Safe will have to do.'

Marianne pulled the car to the side of the avenue, reversing into the grass and over a clump of fading daffodils in her hurry. She drove back to the town, anxious to buy the paint before she changed her mind. After parking outside the hardware shop, she marched to the counter, asking to see their range of masonry paint colours.

'Are you looking for white, or we have a nice cream in stock?' a man wearing overalls spattered in paint splashes asked.

'I want pink, light pink, please.'

'We have a lovely soft shell pink. How much do you want? Maybe try one can as a tester first?'

'No, I'm sure about the pink, I'm just not sure how much I need.'

'We can always order in more stock. Are you local, maybe I know the house?'

'Kilteelagh House, outside town.'

'Collie's place?'

'Yes.'

The man laughed. 'She dithered over the pink and a lot of mad colours many times herself, but in the end, she always stuck with the white. You'll need ten tubs, if you're doing the back the same colour.'

'Yes, I am.'

'Well, I have five in stock that you can be going on with. I'll have the others in for you on Friday.'

'Will you take cash now for the five, and I'll pay for the rest when they come in?'

'Cash is king,' he said, carrying the tins and putting them in the boot of the car. 'Kilteelagh is a fine house, it's nice to see the place being done up.'

Marianne didn't falter until she swung her car up the drive and saw Katherine parked out front.

'Where have you been? I have a few extras for the girls. This time, stuff they like from Marks and Sparks in Dublin. I left a box on the kitchen windowsill,' she said as she walked back to her car.

'I was buying paint for the outside of the house.'

'You needn't have bothered; Grandma overbought last time. Look in the old stables, there's probably enough to do the whole house if that stuff keeps.'

'I've picked a pink colour.'

Katherine sniggered. 'Well, well; the mouse that roared. Did my mother ever think you would turn Kilteelagh into a pink house? Even I, the daughter she could not trust with her precious abode, would not have done that to her. Collie must be turning in her grave.'

'I think it will look lovely. Grandma Collie only ever stayed with white because it was safe.'

Katherine guffawed and pointed at the house. 'She stayed with white because she thought it represented new beginnings. Not that anyone could ever get a new start with Kilteelagh House and its lands around their neck.'

'I didn't know.'

'Who cares, anyway. You need to reconsider. Don't waste your money on paint. You know that, even if you stay now, you'll be begging us to take it off your hands in a few months' time.'

'Thanks for the box of goodies. I don't want to argue, Katherine.'

'Just stating the facts. The box isn't intended for you. I did it for those poor girls. You can change everything for all of us by doing the right thing: turn over Rachel and Katie to me and let us put Kilteelagh up for sale. You certainly would be making it easier on yourself.'

'Collie entrusted Kilteelagh to me and I won't let her down.'

'That's right, honour a dead woman's wishes when your own flesh and blood are in front of you begging you to do the right thing. You're not doing those poor girls any favours,' Katherine blurted out as she stomped back to her car and jumped in.

Marianne bolted around the back, afraid Katherine would see her crying. Grabbing the box from the windowsill, she threw it on the kitchen table and made her way straight to the drawing room. Kicking off her shoes, she lay down on the velvet couch, taking deep breaths to calm down. A part of her wanted to leave Kilteelagh, but a bigger part of her wanted to stay and fight. She was scrolling through Instagram, trying to distract herself, when she heard someone tapping on the window. Hurriedly ducking her head, she sank further into the cushions to avoid being seen. It had been a difficult morning and now she wanted some time to herself. The person rapped again with a fist of knuckles, making the glass shiver.

'Yoo-hoo, anybody home?'

It was obvious the caller wasn't going to give up, so she went to the window and saw a woman in her early sixties, wearing a black trench coat and a wide-brim red rain hat. She waved and gestured that she was walking around to the back door. By the time Marianne got to the kitchen, her visitor had already made her way in and was taking off her coat.

'The beautiful granddaughter I have heard so much about. You must be Marianne. I'm Dolores O'Grady, Collie's best friend. I live across the way.'

She held out her hand, but quickly pulled it back and gathered Marianne in a tight hug.

'We're almost family, let's not bother with the formalities.'

'Pardon me, but I don't really know you, though Katie has talked about you.'

'Collie said to give you a few weeks to settle in. No point rushing in on top of you the minute you arrived. You were very young when I last saw you. And I always seemed to be out of town when you were visiting with your family. If you want to get to the sea, you must traipse through my land. That's why it's best to get on – my friendship is invaluable in the summer.'

Marianne wasn't sure whether to take her caller seriously or not. Underneath the trench coat, she was wearing a suit, the jacket nipped in at the waist, a lace blouse frothy around her neck. Her hair was swept into a loose bun at the back of her head, showing off her long, graceful neck.

'I thought we should get to know each other, you must be crying out for some company,' Dolores said, and then laughed aloud as if she had just made a joke. 'Who am I kidding? I bet I'm the last person you want bothering you now.'

'No, it's nice to meet Collie's friends,' Marianne said, pulling out a chair at the table for her.

'You're being kind and I like that,' Dolores said, flopping down on the seat. 'I felt the same about Collie when she came knocking on my door. But you know age is no barrier to a good friendship – if you click, you click. How are you finding Kilteelagh House?'

'Daunting, but I love it here. I hope I can live up to my grandmother's expectations for the place.'

Dolores guffawed out loud. 'Collie said you would say that. That's why I'm here, to tell you to do what the heck you want. God rest her soul, I loved Collie, we were like sisters, and she would want you to enjoy your time here.'

'She's writing me letters. It's as if she couldn't let go. I don't know where to start.'

Dolores reached out and pulled at Marianne's hand. 'Like any person with Irish blood, put on the kettle.'

As she filled the kettle at the sink Marianne saw Dolores loosen her bun and let her long hair swing down her back. With her hair down, she thought Dolores looked younger. 'You don't mind, do you? That hat might look good, but it couldn't even ward off a bit of mist.'

Marianne switched on the kettle and leaned against the counter, waiting for it to boil.

'Will you keep Kilteelagh, do you think?'

The direct question surprised Marianne.

'It's probably too early to say. I love the place, but whether I will be able to keep it is another thing. Dress designing is all I know. I don't know how I could do that from Kilteelagh, or if I even want to...'

'It will fit if you want it badly enough. Collie would be very proud, I know.'

Marianne shook her head and was about to answer when Dolores leaned towards her.

'There's a lot of people in these parts banking on you to fail so Katherine can place the house and land on the market. You have to prove them wrong.'

'Good to know, but why would anybody care so much?'

Dolores slapped the table, making Marianne jump. 'For God's sake, look around you, girl – it's prime land. If Collie had given in, it would be a sprawling housing estate by now.'

'I had no idea.'

'Collie was not a woman to be bossed around. They never could cop on to the fact that the only way Collie was going to leave Kilteelagh House was in a coffin, and that's what she did.'

'No pressure then,' Marianne said as she plopped a teabag into a mug.

Dolores stood up.

'You're not making tea with bags. Collie's granddaughter surely knows better.'

Delicately picking the teabag out of her mug with her long nails, Dolores threw it in the bin, a drip of brown tea flowing down the side.

'In Kilteelagh, it has to be Earl Grey tea – and no cheating with those Earl Grey teabags, they're nothing but dust.'

Opening the cupboard doors, she rummaged until she found the tea box.

'Surely you know where Collie kept her teapot.'

Marianne didn't object but fished in one of the bottom cupboards and produced a white china teapot.

'Two heaped spoons are my preference, though Collie always insisted on three,' Dolores said as she scooped the tea leaves in. 'Now boil that kettle again, tea leaves need the water to be spitting hot.'

Marianne could have protested but she knew, much as when her grandmother used to put her foot down, there was no point arguing.

'Pardon me if I'm overstepping the mark,' said Dolores, scrabbling around the top of the cupboard until she found a tray, 'but shall we have a tray of tea in the drawing room?'

'I'm not sure my mugs are good enough.'

'Nonsense, we'll use Collie's china tea set, I'm sure she would approve.'

Dolores grabbed the teapot and tea cosy and placed it on the tray. 'Lead the way; we'll use the tea set in the side cabinet.'

'Shouldn't we wash it first?' Marianne asked as Dolores took out the delicate cups and saucers.

'No need, we last used them when we waked Collie – there won't be a speck of dust on them.'

She handed a cup and saucer to Marianne. 'A wedding gift to Mike and Collie. She loved the grey leaves, the pattern of autumn set off by the gold rims.'

Dolores took a silver strainer from the cupboard before pouring the Earl Grey.

'Collie liked a single cube of sugar, how about you?'

'I'm good,' Marianne said as she tasted the tea.

Dolores sat into Collie's armchair. 'Your grandmother told me to help you out, so you must tell me where to start. I have time on my hands, and you need help turning this place around.'

'At the moment, I'm feeling my way.'

'Which is all well and good, but let's give those watching a run for their money and something to talk about.'

'I wanted to put a sign up in the post office looking for a handyman, but Bridie Murphy wouldn't let me. She suggested the newsagent's, but I don't remember the owner allowing anybody to do that. She was trying to fob me off, which really annoys me because I need the driveway tidied up and the house painted.'

Dolores guffawed loudly. 'I bet Bridie took great pleasure in turning you away. Silly woman, she should know not to take sides.'

'What do you mean?'

'Bridie and Katherine are as thick as thieves. Bridie is on the town council and owns half the businesses in Balgaddy. She would like nothing better than to see those fields out there churned up and as many houses as possible packed in.'

Marianne didn't say anything.

'More houses mean more business. You watch Bridie Murphy. She has her own reasons for wanting you out of Kiltee-lagh House.'

Marianne firmly put down her cup and saucer. 'I really don't want to get involved in the local politics, I just want to create a home here for Rachel and Katie.'

Dolores fussed about putting her cup and saucer back on the tray. 'Collie always did point out I'm too much of a straight talker, too much to say and not afraid to shout it. We can revisit this another time.'

'Don't go. Balgaddy seems such a great place, and I never realised Collie...'

'It's a grand spot, but every great place has its backstory,' Dolores said as she lifted the tray and carried it to the kitchen. Placing it on the table, she looked at Marianne. 'I see there is a letter from Collie in the hall for you. You should read it, sit in the parlour and take time over it, I'm off. I'll call by another day.'

'You know about the letters?'

'She told me about them and at times I helped. She dictated several to me, but she swore me to secrecy. I only did it when she was so tired towards the end. I always had to read them back to her. I'm not sure she fully trusted me not to add in my own words of wisdom.'

'She must have trusted you a lot.'

Dolores took Marianne's hands. 'She was my sister and I, hers. Those letters are her life story, you won't hear anything from me before Collie wants it revealed. But I'm here to help you every step of the way, and if you need a hand around the house, please call me over.'

'What will I do about the driveway? I ordered gravel to arrive today.'

'I will get Jack, who tips around my farm, to come over and bring a few men in for you. They'll have it finished in half a day. Anyone else would only make the job last weeks and cost you a fortune.'

'That's not Jack Farrelly, by any chance?' Marianne asked.

'Ah, he said he had met you; helped out with the gate. He's such a handsome chap.'

Marianne blushed. 'He thought I was breaking in.'

'Oh darling, he was only ribbing you. Jack can be quite the devil at times; always up for a joke and a laugh—' Dolores stopped when she saw Marianne's face. 'What's wrong?'

'You're being so kind to me. I already don't know how I could manage without you.'

'Come on, girl, it's nothing. Tell me, when am I going to see the famous New York toughness we've heard about?'

'I guess I'm just finding my feet.'

'You will. Trust in yourself,' Dolores said, lightly pecking her on the cheek before she left.

Marianne gathered up her post from the hall table, picking out the letter from solicitor Sean Eager. Strolling to the drawing room, she slit open the envelope.

Kilteelagh House
Balgaddy
Co. Wicklow

My dearest Marianne,

How have you settled in? I hope you have been brave enough to put your own stamp on Kilteelagh House. I am sure if you haven't already, you will very soon. I know you love the old place. If nothing else, it will give certain people in the town something to talk about. It must be such a transition for you from big city life.

I remember when your mam, Chloe, first went off to New York, she said the thing she missed the most was being able to walk up the avenue and have fields and trees either side. She missed the open space, something she never appreciated until she left home. I guess you miss your tall buildings and the noise of your city streets. When Chloe left here, I was so upset. Though I never let on to her, she had to forge her own way and she didn't need me piling on a whole load of guilt.

I didn't see her for five years and then after she met your dad, they were setting up home. It was hard to put the expense of coming all this way on them. But when they did, I fell in love with you. You took to the countryside like you had been born to it. This did not wane as you grew older, and for that I was very thankful. Remember the three months you came one summer. In the middle, Chloe and Brad took off to London and you stayed behind with me. We spent our days at the lake and by the bridge, mucking about. We dressed up to go into Balgaddy for coffee. Those are the type of things that make good memories. I realised then, age does not matter one iota.

I bet you found the dress after my last letter. I should have asked to be buried in it, but I knew Katherine would have had something to say about that. She certainly tried hard enough over the years for me to take down the painting. But I was not going to let that ever happen. We got the drawing room wallpapered about six years ago and I made sure the workmen had the chimney breast decorated before she even got to the house that morning. I knew if the picture ever left that hook over the fireplace, she would spirit it away and it would be found in pieces or on a bonfire soon after.

Every year, too, I fought her attempts to get rid of the velvet couch and armchairs. If Katherine had her way, a cold, cheap faux leather couch would have taken over my drawing room. She is so like her father. She has such a practical streak, which I have always found disconcerting.

When she and Steve decided to marry, I never saw a girl less excited and more practical, even about her wedding dress. I wanted her to go all out, buy something really stylish. It had to be a dress her children would find in the attic years later and look at, wondering about their mother as a young woman. But Katherine wasn't having any of it. She bought a simple polyester fabric and a nice pattern and had me make a panelled long dress. I couldn't bear that it was so plain, so I went to Dublin and bought lace for the bodice and front panel. She loved it when she saw it, but seemed most happy that she didn't have to pay for it. She wore my grandmother's veil. I washed the veil and put it on the clothesline, not knowing if the old lace would fall apart, but it turned out lovely.

You might not know this, but I actually offered Kilteelagh House to Katherine and Steve when they got married, just as long as I could continue to live here with them. I always thought she turned it down because they wanted to start off their married life with an element of privacy and a bit away from my gaze. But as the years went on, I realised Katherine was just different. She hated the farming, hated the old farmhouse, and yearned for a busy city life. What she was doing with Steve, I don't know, because that man was born wearing a pair of wellingtons. I just want her to be happy, and I reckon it is only when her children are grown up, or nearly there, that Katherine will seek out happiness for herself.

These are the good days in Kilteelagh House, Marianne. Enjoy the spring and summer months, so you have good memories to sustain you through the winter days. It is time now to start getting jobs done around the house and garden. Have you noticed the hawthorn hedge in the far field? If you stand at the landing window, the blur of white blossom is like a beacon on the horizon, a signal that summer is tiptoeing in on us. Remember, you used to call it the fairy place. We often went there, tramping across the grass early in the morning, in the hope of glimpsing the fairies at play. Those were good days, Marianne. Don't get bogged down with how much needs to be done to the place, but enjoy the treasures still at Kilteelagh.

However, I should acknowledge there is much to be done to keep the old house standing. Every window really needs replacing. If you can afford it, it should be a priority if you don't want gales whipping through the rooms in the winter months. A place like Kilteelagh could take every cent you have, so prioritise structural matters and insulation. Decoration, though it lifts the heart, can come later.

I hope you have managed to find somebody to help with the garden. The daffodils will be looking scraggly. Let them die back. Don't be tempted to tidy them. I always bunched the stalks together and tied them down with a band to let all the goodness go back into the bulb. I like to think that is what has kept such a good display all these years.

How are the girls? I imagine Rachel has begun to kick a little. That girl has a heart of gold, but she needs direction and you, a woman from the city who knows the outside world, are more than capable of giving her that. Don't be afraid to offer your opinion and don't mind her if she storms off; teenagers are good at that. I always found it best to let her cool down. In *her own time, she will return to the conversation. It will also give you time to look at the argument from both sides and be more prepared to meet in the middle.*

Forgive me if I'm going on too much. I hope what I write is some reassurance to you. You're doing fine, I just know it. Before I go, stop, and consider May. It was always my favourite month, a time of renewal, when the birds are busy lining their nests and loud in song, the summer flowers are beginning to slowly show and nature is loudly renewing itself. These are truly the good times.

All my love,

Collie xx

Marianne tossed the letter aside. Were these truly the good times? Surely, they were merely words on a page, but what did Collie know about her struggle here at Kilteelagh?

The dog was kicking up a racket outside, so she walked around to the front of the house. A truck with a heaped load of gravel was trundling up the driveway. The driver stuck his head out the window.

'Where do you want it, lady?'

Marianne hadn't a clue, but had picked a spot halfway down the avenue when a man in a Jeep sped up to the house.

'Hi again,' he said to Marianne before turning to the delivery driver. 'I didn't think I would make it in time. Can you tip it out at four different points on the avenue from top to bottom? I will leave the car here, because we start on it tomorrow.'

Jack swung around to Marianne. 'It's the incentive to get it done in less than a day, block in the car, only hard work will free it.'

She smiled uncertainly.

He laughed when he saw the surprise on her face. 'You weren't expecting to see me so soon again. But I do a lot of work for Dolores across the way.'

'I confess, yes. Dolores said you do odd jobs for her.'

'I've gone back to college – studying law – so working for Dolores is handy money. I try to do her jobs around my lectures. I'll see you bright and early tomorrow, I hope to be finished around two.'

He called out to the lorry driver to wait, and he jumped in the cab and was on his way down the avenue before Marianne had a chance to reply. He had a nice smile, she thought, and soft eyes. Not to mention, he was the only person anywhere near her age she had chatted to so far.

EIGHT

Marianne made her way to the dining room. She always liked this place tucked between the kitchen and the drawing room, with its long windows and view of the lake. She felt it was almost a secret room because it was used so rarely. The walls were a deep red colour, and the fireplace was painted black. Collie only ever used the room for formal dinners at night, so she'd felt dark colours suited it best. Maybe she should ask Jack Farrelly to staple cream calico cloth the length of the walls and paint the cast-iron fireplace white, so that light reflected into every corner.

Reaching into a basket, she pulled out a small bolt of silk. Jay, knowing how important it was to her, had pulled it from her desk on the last day in the office before they were all locked out. When it had arrived a couple of weeks ago, she'd run her fingers along the length of it, but the memories had overwhelmed her, and she had slipped it into the basket, not sure when she would return to it again. She let the shimmering blue silk skate across the mahogany dining table. It was soft, making fine dust puff up as it swept across the polished wood. It had been a present from Collie. She had arrived in the States for Christmas one year with the bolt under her arm.

'My best friend hightailed off to China for two months and I told her bring back the best silk for my granddaughter, who will be a famous dress designer one day,' she'd said, opening the bolt and letting the silk tumble across the carpet.

Marianne loved it, letting it run through her hands, holding it up to the light, watching the sun sparkling across the fabric, making it glimmer and shine. She loved that her grandmother knew she wanted to be a dress designer and took her ambition seriously. For a long time, she had the silk hanging in her room until she noticed that the sun had faded parts so that it was streaked a dull, dirty yellow colour. She had sliced off the half-yard that was faded and stored the bolt carefully in a cupboard after that. There were many times in the years that followed when she took out the silk and arranged it into a design around her hips and shoulders, but for some reason she was unable to pin a pattern to it and cut into the fabric with shears. She felt as though every dress she designed was for the blue silk, but she never could commit to a design that fully justified the beautiful fabric and Collie's faith in her.

Sweeping the light silk over her shoulders, she felt Collie watching her, willing her this time to find the perfect design for such a beautiful bolt of fabric. Twirling about so that the silk spread out like a cloak, she saw the old clock on the mantelpiece and realised it was almost time to collect Katie from school. Folding the silk back on the bolt, she grabbed her coat and set off down the avenue at a quick pace. At the school gates, she stood at one side of the other parents, not feeling part of this group who were chatting loudly about their children. Flinging her arms wide when she caught sight of Katie, she dropped them when she saw her small, cross face.

'I told you I'm going to Sarah's house today. Don't you remember?'

'Honey, I'm sorry, I forgot. Off you go, I will collect your later. Tell her mommy to text me the directions to her house.'

Katie ran off and Marianne turned away, strangely upset that she had got it wrong.

'You can't get it right, no matter how hard you try sometimes,' the voice said from behind her. Jack Farrelly was smiling broadly. Marianne was taken aback to see him but tried to hide her surprise.

'I'm actually Sarah's dad, so no worries, we can drop Katie back home.'

'I didn't know you had a kid,' Marianne hesitated. 'I mean, at this school.'

'I probably confused you with all the talk of me being a student.'

'Maybe.'

He laughed, explaining that he was a mature student. 'Don't worry, Katie has been over for a play date with Sarah before. It's the small house beside the church.'

His daughter called him, and he said he had better go.

'But what about your car, don't you need it?'

'It's only a short walk and I'm sure Sarah's mum, Aideen, can drop the girls back.'

'Oh, OK.'

Marianne felt put out and she wasn't exactly sure why. He was walking away when she called after him. 'Before you go, I was wondering whether, after the drive, you would be able to do some more work at the house for me?'

'You know me, I'm always willing to earn a few bob.' He laughed.

She didn't join in but asked him about hanging the fabric on her dining room walls and painting the fireplace.

'Sure, I'll have a look the next time I'm at Kilteelagh,' he said, before his daughter yanked his hand to drag him away.

Marianne strolled home, enjoying the soft breeze, and finding time to stop at the bridge and take a breath. In her head she reran the encounter with Jack. She knew his type so well; married but acting like he wasn't, and this guy was cheeky enough to do it outside the school gate. Pity, because he had a cute smile, she thought.

At Kilteelagh House, the flower beds at the front needed work. She thought she should put that on her list as a priority. Stopping to examine the silver-grey growth of lamb's ears, she heard Collie's voice. 'Don't be afraid to touch, dear. Sure, I talk to the plants, and I think it keeps them happy.'

Marianne stroked the silvered green leaves, luxuriating in the softness like the best velvet. It had spread and there were large tufts at one side of the driveway, which she must tell Jack to keep. Walking up to the front door, she examined it closely. It looked as if it had been locked a very long time and the brass had dulled, patching green. She took in the view. Collie was standing on exactly this spot on the top step the last time she saw her alive. It had been a short visit for a few hours. They had linked arms and walked down by the lake, had tea in the drawing room, chatting to each other non-stop. She heard Grandma Collie's loud laugh and it made her smile now. After they said their goodbyes at the car, Collie had stood on the top step and waved until the car had rounded the rhododendron grove. Her last image of her grandmother was Collie bending down to snip spent daisies from the pots on the front steps. Standing on this spot, Marianne realised now her grandmother did it to hide her tears and loneliness.

A few days later, she'd sent Collie a gift voucher for the fancy garden centre on the Arklow Road. Collie had phoned her up and given out yards about wasting her money, but the next week she had proudly sent her photographs of her new bed of roses under the parlour window. Marianne stopped to examine the bed.

Maybe Jack could advise on tidying up the rose beds when he was finished doing the avenue, she thought. Or maybe she could ask around the school mums for the name of another handyman. A cute married man was not what she wanted right now. Loneliness coursed through her thinking of Peter, lovely, kind Peter who'd promised to leave his wife. She had been the fool to believe him until she saw him in Brooklyn strolling hand in hand with her. At a loose end, she had gone to the Botanic Gardens to see the roses and instead found herself cowering behind a tree near the lake, watching Peter and his other half playing with their little girl. Peter looked happy. When she confronted him, he'd told her he loved his family and he also loved her. What they had was good, couldn't they continue? She broke it off and the next day her parents were killed when a tree fell on their car. It was as brutal as that, she thought.

Marianne woke the next morning to the sound of scraping on the driveway at the front, the shovels pinging as five men filled wheelbarrows and wheeled them to different parts of the avenue.

'How am I going to walk past all of them? I don't even know them,' Rachel said.

'They're too busy working; they aren't going to be looking at you.'

Rachel snorted and dropped her skirt an inch lower, slamming the back door behind her.

'I like Sarah's dad, you know. He's funny,' Katie said.

Just then, Dolores rang to ask her what was happening at Kilteelagh and told her to go out and offer the labourers some tea. 'You'll get a better job if you give them tea and biscuits, otherwise they might be tempted to cut corners,' she said.

Marianne called to Katie to get her school bag and they walked out towards Jack and the other men.

'I didn't realise you were going to have so much help,' she said.

'I have an assignment due in by this evening and it needs a final bit of polishing, so I want to get this job done pretty sharpish.'

'You could have rescheduled; I would have understood.'

'These're my brothers, so no big deal. I'll buy them a pint later in the pub.'

He lifted the shovel, and she wasn't sure what to say next.

Katie tugged at her sleeve. 'Remember the tea.'

'Oh yes, help yourselves in the kitchen. There's tea and coffee beside the kettle and milk in the fridge.'

'We couldn't find any biscuits,' Katie said, and Jack laughed.

'Coffee will be just fine in a while.'

'If you have time, would you remember to look at and measure the dining room?'

'It's next on my list,' he said.

Marianne nodded and moved away quickly.

Katie ran ahead, climbing the gravel hills on the driveway as they made their way to the gate and on to school.

NINE

June

'We always use the back door. Nobody would ever even think of walking up to the front. What's the point?' Rachel asked, making a face.

'It's silly not having the front door available to us, and it would be so nice.'

'But it's been like that for years.'

'Which doesn't mean it has to stay that way,' Marianne said as she searched through the drawer in the kitchen dresser. At the back, she felt the large iron key and pulled it out.

'That looks like a jailer's key,' Rachel said, trying to hide her interest.

'Can I have a go?' Katie said, snatching the key and running ahead of the others down the hall. She pushed the key in the lock and attempted to turn it. 'It won't turn,' she said, disappointed.

'Let me try,' Rachel said, shoving her sister out of the way. Katie ran off. Marianne wasn't sure if she was in a huff or bored, but she handed Rachel a tea towel so she could get a better grip.

'Did you ever think there was a reason why Grandma didn't use the door? Maybe she couldn't ever open it,' Rachel said.

'Oil should do the trick.'

Scuttling to the kitchen to find the canister of oil, she saw Rachel escape upstairs to her room. It was a Saturday morning and she thought she had found something they could tackle together. She felt cross that both children had disappeared, but knew she had no right to be. She let the oil gurgle into the lock, not sure if she was doing the right thing. Wandering into the drawing room as she waited for the oil to do its work, she noticed the armchair she had pulled to the side window the day before had been put back in front of the fireplace. She was tempted to change it back, but she stopped herself. Instead, she marched to the hall and yelled for the girls to come downstairs.

'What is it? I'm on the phone,' Rachel shouted out.

'Tell them you will call back.'

She heard Rachel sigh and come slowly down the stairs, Katie following behind, her toy rabbit tucked under her arm.

'I thought we could have a family meeting,' Marianne said, trying to keep her voice light.

'What do you mean?' Rachel asked.

'We could talk about what we want and how things are going, and if we need to change anything.'

'I want a tree house. Grandma said she would get one built, but...' Katie's voice trailed off.

Marianne took her hand. 'Let's sit down, shall we?'

The girls trooped in after her and sat on the couch. Marianne took Collie's armchair.

'You left, and I thought maybe you don't want to have the front door opened up.'

'Amy rang and I haven't spoken to her in months,' Rachel mumbled.

'I was playing with my rabbit, giving him quality time,' Katie said solemnly.

'All right, but maybe we could give some time to each other. You see, I want to ask your opinion on a few things. The first is the front door.'

'It's Grandma's house and she didn't want to use that door, but I don't really care,' Rachel said.

'I would like a front door for when people come round to play, so I don't have to explain,' Katie said.

'I would like when people call round that we have the front door working,' Marianne said.

'Grandma didn't want to have it open,' Rachel said.

'We're in charge now. OK, so are we all agreed on opening the door?' Marianne asked.

All three stuck their hands in the air. When Katie giggled and said it was like school, Rachel and Marianne joined in.

'This is a bit silly, but fun,' Katie said, and the others agreed.

Marianne straightened in her chair and looked very serious. 'Next on the agenda: this room. Should we decorate?'

She thought she had said something wrong, because neither of the girls laughed, but stared past her shoulder.

'Will I move to Number Three on the agenda?' she asked gently. They both nodded and Marianne pretended to consult a list.

'Ah, yes,' she was about to say more when she heard Dolores call out 'yoo-hoo' and make her way towards the back door.

Katie ran ahead of Marianne to the kitchen. Rachel disappeared upstairs once more. Dolores was standing with her arms wide as Katie ran towards her.

'Katkins, you must come over; my dogs are missing you. Surely old Benji can spare you.'

Katie pulled free. 'Can I bring Marianne? We can come after school on Thursday.'

'Of course, I've been meaning to invite you all anyway.'

Marianne smiled faintly and Dolores chuckled to see her discomfort.

'We're trying to open the front door. Do you know why Collie never bothered with it? She only ever used the steps when she wanted to see down the avenue.'

'No idea. Collie was tight on certain things. Now, I have to help Katkins with her work of art.'

Katie had already got out her crayons and a big pad. She turned to a page which had been mostly coloured in.

'We're determined to finish today, aren't we, Katkins?' Dolores said, picking an orange crayon.

Katie nodded and the two of them sat together, their heads touching as they became engrossed in their work.

Marianne stole outside, so she could sit and read Collie's latest letter. Benji followed her for a while but then turned back, his loyalty to Katie stronger. She walked down the narrow path, the ferns pushing against her legs, spilling water over her shoes. In the distance she heard the ducks on the lake, and she stopped, remembering all the times she had ambled down this path with Collie. She crossed the soggy grass to the gazebo. It was a cloudy, damp day and the gazebo looked worn and unloved. She made a mental note to ask Jack how much it would cost to restore it. She liked Jack and he kept his word. She trusted him to give her a fair price and do a good job. She saw the way he looked at her, tried to make her laugh, but she didn't react. She didn't trust him that way.

Sitting down, she closed her eyes, listening to the sounds of Kilteelagh. In the distance the faint hum of the motorway, the rippling of the water as the ducks pecked each other in their constant battle over territory. The birds in the trees calling to each other. Somewhere a dog was barking and Benji scooted about on patrol as if he had been sent a secret signal. It was easy to imagine why Collie had fought so hard to keep this place. There was something faintly magical about Kilteelagh; it wormed its way into her thoughts and cloaked her in a warm feeling, when all she thought she wanted was a busy city with sirens and traffic – a very different, other life.

She took out the letter and began to read.

Kilteelagh House
Balgaddy
Co. Wicklow

My dearest Marianne,

Today the words don't come easy. I am tired and even here at Kilteelagh House life seems to be dull. There are always days like this when you wake up and you take everything for granted. I am sure it has happened to you, and I hope, like me many times previously, you have managed to snap out of it.

Kilteelagh House, I always feel, is a way of life. I have my routines, and in those routines is a certainty that I can get through the day. Writing notes every day for inclusion in the final letters to you is one of my great pleasures. It means of course I can filter the information the way I want, but I suppose that is my privilege at this stage.

There are times when I wonder if all of this is boring you and instead of engendering a love of the old place in you, I am restricting you from going out and experiencing things your own way. My hope is that these letters lead you on a path where you begin to realise that my history of Kilteelagh House and my memories can be a backdrop for your own Kilteelagh story. When that time comes, it will be my pleasure to fade away, hopefully to pop up from time to time, when stories are being told about Kilteelagh.

I don't like to see the passing of May; it always strikes me so much as a month of great hope and renewal when the garden is happy to take to the stage again. In May, anything seems possible. Sometimes I have thought I could even hear the growth and renewal all around me as I set out along the avenue in the early morning, the birds flitting about and busy, the dog snuffling at all the new smells and the wisteria cloaked in flowers. Did I mention about the dahlia tubers in the old stables, to the right as you go in the door? They look like dead old tubers, but I think even now you will get away with it, if you soak them in warm water overnight before planting. The flowers will reward you throughout the summer days and well into autumn.

June is a more sedate month, when growth continues, and the birds have settled with their young. Have you seen the bird feeders around the garden? There is one outside the drawing room window, and it is such a joy to sit there and watch the blue and yellow tits, the bullfinches and chaffinches edge closer to it to nip at the seeds. The robin comes too, but in his own time. I get the impression he has rights to a different period, because none of the others join him there. There are always two magpies that frighten off the other little birds and try their luck, but they can only reach the cast-off seeds which have fallen to the ground. Every now and again I hoosh them off, though I'm not sure if that is very fair.

When Mike took over Kilteelagh House, it was in a decrepit state and looked as if it had trouble continuing after standing for over one hundred years. Mike was only really interested in the land around it and so he left the organising and the running of the house to me. The house seemed an over-whelming job and there were times I wanted to walk away, but there is a magic about the place too. Do you feel the pull of Kilteelagh House, the magic that cloaks you and makes you feel safe? I hope and pray you do.

At Kilteelagh, days can merge into each other beautifully. Before I had children and certainly before they went to school, time seemed a different thing and of course less demanding. To

live by the seasons has been a privilege, but you do it your way,
Marianne. To know the past is a good thing, to be tied down by
it is very different. Have courage and faith in your decisions.

Love,

Collie xx

Marianne held the letter close. What was it about Collie that
she always judged the mood right? The days were merging, and
she still had no clear idea of what she should be doing here. She
didn't hear Dolores approach, so when the other woman tapped
her lightly on the shoulder, she jumped.

'I got released early from colouring duty, and Katie has gone
upstairs to tidy her room.'

'Do you think she's OK?'

'I think she lost her mother and grandmother, and she's
trying to muddle through.'

'I don't know how to help her. Even though I lost my
mother and grandmother too.'

'Are you muddling through?'

'Honestly, I don't know.'

Dolores wiped some leaves off the seat and sat down beside
Marianne.

'Katie will be fine and so will you. Just give it time.' She
grasped Marianne's hand and squeezed it tight. 'You have
backup. I'm here to help.'

'I know, it's all so much, all of it.'

'I find it helps to take life in bite-sized pieces.'

'Except I can't do that, dealing with Rachel and Katie.'

'All you can do is to love them and be there for them.'

'I wish somebody could tell me how to do it. It's been
months now and I'm still on hot coals every time I talk to
Rachel. And with Katie, I feel I let her down so much. I don't

know how to be a mother. I am not sure I have a mother's touch; I never get anything right.'

Dolores sighed loudly.

'And you think that makes you so different to any other mum out there?' She squeezed Marianne's hand tighter. 'I once had a job and I was told the first day if the bosses said nothing, they were happy. "You will hear about it when things are wrong." Parenting is a bit like that. You're in at the deep end, trying to juggle a teenager and a little girl. Go with the flow and hopefully it brings you in the right direction.'

'I'm not sure Collie thought this through. If she had any sense, she would have let the girls stay with Katherine.'

'Your grandmother was very definite in her wishes. Collie thought the world of you, and she also knew how difficult you were finding it after losing your mum and dad.'

'So she gave me this project.'

'What if she did? It's not such a bad thing.'

Marianne got up and wandered to the lake edge. The ducks swam towards her as if they expected to be fed.

'So what's the deal with the front door really?' she asked Dolores, who had reached into her pocket and was throwing some sort of grain onto the lake water.

'You must think I'm a right bat, but I was feeding the chickens earlier. I always have a little bag of meal in my pocket.'

'There's something about the front door. I needn't open it up, but it would be nice to have the house functioning normally. What's the big secret?'

'No secret.'

Marianne clicked her tongue in exasperation. 'Jack starts painting the house this week and it would be great to have access to that door.'

'I thought you had cooled on Jack. Nice to know you still have him working for you,' Dolores said, giving Marianne a wide smile.

'Stop, Dolores, let's get back to the door,' Marianne replied, her cheeks turning pink.

'I'm not sure I can help you; Collie kept a lot of things under wraps, it was just her way. I only know a little from some of the letters she dictated.'

'I should have come to see her more often.'

'Guilt or looking back are not going to help you now.'

'I suppose. There must have been a very good reason to keep that door shut. I remember when we came from the States, we thought it was because she was always in the kitchen and could keep an eye on the comings and goings more easily.'

'That's a good one.'

'You really don't know?'

Dolores shook her head. 'I think you're attaching a significance to it that may not be there, and anyway, why should it affect your decision on the door now?'

Marianne shrugged her shoulders. 'I guess I'm still trying to please her.'

'Nuts to that. The approval of a dead woman is too much of a burden and not one your grandmother would have wanted to put on your shoulders.'

'It might as well join all the other burdens, including: how am I going to get Kilteelagh House back in decent shape before winter?'

Dolores laughed. 'Collie said you would analyse and worry too much. She was convinced it was your American side coming out.'

'I'm not so sure about that.'

Dolores took Marianne's two hands. 'Let's go back together and get that door open. I might not look it, but I have a good deal of strength in these arms.'

Marianne shook her head, but Dolores was insistent.

'Come on, it will be a bit of fun. I often wondered what it

would be like to stand in the actual doorway of Kilteelagh House and take in the view of the avenue.'

She linked Marianne's arm as they moved away from the lake and towards the house.

'With any luck, the oil will have done the hard work,' Marianne said as they made their way around the back and through the kitchen to the hall.

Katie, when she heard them talking, came running downstairs. 'Can I do it, please? I want to be first out the door,' she said.

'As soon as we get it open,' Dolores said as she twisted the key, the creaking of the lock making them stop and listen.

'Creepy,' Katie said, and Dolores hugged her.

'Go around the front and push from the outside on my count,' Dolores said, and Marianne did as she was bid. On the steps she waited until the count of three to push hard against the door as Dolores and Katie on the other side pulled with all their strength.

The door groaned and shifted a little, the paint cracking at the side. Spiders woken by the strong vibrations darted for cover; beetles and woodlice at the bottom of the door zipped in all directions.

'On my count again,' Dolores shouted. Marianne shoved her shoulder against the door and it gave way with a whoosh of dust, throwing her into the hallway. Katie jumped with delight and Dolores, who had fallen back against the wall, said it was time for a drink.

'Let it all settle and let the creepy-crawlies run for cover before cleaning up around there,' Dolores said, making straight for the cabinet in the drawing room. 'Time for a Baileys. I don't suppose you have ice?'

Marianne and Katie didn't answer. They were too busy sweeping up the dust and pushing the spiders out onto the steps. Marianne broke up the cobwebs high in the corners of the lintel and Katie wiped the dust off the outside.

'We're going to need hot soapy water to shift a lot of this dirt,' Marianne muttered as she went to the kitchen to put on the kettle.

'Get some ice while you're there and I'll fix the drinks,' Dolores called out.

When she came back along the hall, Marianne was holding a basin of water and had a glass full of ice tucked under her arm. Dolores took the glass and ducked back into the drawing room. Marianne handed a spare pair of gloves to Katie and the two of them started on the door, the water quickly turning dark brown as they washed off decades of dirt and grime.

'Will Jack paint it tomorrow?' Katie asked.

'I think he might get around to it later. He's got to do the walls first.'

Katie made a face.

'It's just that Sarah is coming on Thursday.'

'I can have a word with him, ask him to get the front done first,' Marianne said, and she saw Katie's face light up.

'What a grand view. Now, time for a break, ladies. Drinks on the top step of Kilteelagh House,' Dolores said in a hoity-toity voice. She was carrying a tray with three drinks: two Baileys and a Coca-Cola for Katie.

'To a new era at Kilteelagh House,' she said, raising her glass as the others picked up theirs. They clinked loudly, making Rachel hurry down the stairs to see what was happening.

'What about me?' she asked.

'Get a glass from the cabinet, darling, I'm sure you can have a sip of Baileys,' Dolores said.

Marianne shook her head. 'Afraid not, make it a cola, Rachel.'

They stood taking in the view from the top step as they waited for Rachel.

'What are we celebrating, the opening up of the front door?' Rachel asked as she came back into the hall.

'Much more than that: the start of a new phase for this grand house and all in her,' Dolores said, raising her glass high. They lifted their glasses to hers and laughed loudly, which made the dog run around the front, wagging its tail.

Marianne pulled out a stack of stools from the hall cupboard. 'I remember Collie used these for sitting on the front step. There was just room for the four of them, but we always hated having to haul them out the back door and around the house to the front steps.'

'It looks different from up here,' Katie said.

'Your grandmother used to say when things were wrong, she would sit out on the top step and it always came to rights,' Dolores said.

A quietness blew between them as each remembered Collie.

'I miss Grandma,' Katie said, snuggling closer to Marianne.

'We all do, darling, in our different ways,' Dolores said, and held her glass up high again.

'To Collie, one of a kind.'

They clinked again, but this time it was more subdued.

'Now, I must go home,' Dolores said as she downed the last of her Baileys. She made a big deal of going back in the front door to collect her things from the kitchen, then returned to the hall to exit by the front door. 'A generous lick of paint and some polish and elbow grease on the letter box and knocker, and this entrance will look very fine indeed,' she said, before heading off down the avenue. Marianne and Katie watched her go, waving when she turned around at the rhododendrons.

'Do I have to help clean the brass?' Katie asked, and Marianne shook her head, saying she could manage it on her own.

On the steps, she looked down the avenue, tidy and gravelled, the sheep huddling in the front fields and the bed of roses at the front which Jack had weeded and mulched, she did not know when. The grass and weeds which had threatened to strangle the rose bushes had been dug out. He said he had pruned a few dead tips as he was afraid to do too much all at once. Benji came and flopped at the bottom of the steps. Marianne stood savouring the moment. Collie was right: you had to stop and let Kilteelagh flow around you.

TEN

Marianne had the house to herself. Katie was on a play date and Rachel said she would not be home until later in the evening. Katherine had driven up to the front of the house earlier and parked outside for a few moments. Marianne was about to go out when she saw Katherine turn her car around and speed away. She was so fed up with Katherine calling over unannounced, and now this. Either Katherine had meant to intimidate her, or she had genuinely forgotten why she had turned in to Kilteelagh House in the first place. Marianne didn't want to know the answer; she was not going to let anything get in the way of her enjoyment of the quiet of Kilteelagh today. Finally Katie was sleeping through the night; her nightmares had disappeared and Marianne didn't need to sleep across the landing from Katie's bedroom any more. She wanted to move to a permanent bedroom of her own and had picked one at the very top of the house. It had the best view, with two windows overlooking the fields and the avenue. It had once been her grandfather's room but had always been out of bounds when she was young.

In all the years, it was surprising that Collie, who liked to sit at the front landing window and watch the avenue, had never moved into this room. The other day, Rachel had pulled up the windows to rid the room of the stale, musty smell, so when Marianne turned the handle and walked in, it was chilly. A part of her wanted to turn away and leave the room as it was, but she knew she had to make her own space in this house if she was going to call it home. Stepping inside, she skirted past boxes of books, old furniture stacked against the walls and clothes piled on the bed and spilling onto the floor. Lingering at the window, she surveyed the gardens and countryside. It was a bright morning, the blue sky pushing down on the trees, the hawthorn blossom dazzling across the horizon. There was a sense of quiet industry in nature under the calm exterior.

Benji was lying out on the gravel at the front of the house, beside the triangular flower bed where the rose bushes were sprouting buds and green leaves, and a swathe of pansies had begun to fade and looked scraggly. From here, she could see the sweep of the avenue down to the rhododendron bushes and the tips of the azaleas at the gate. The driveway looked cared for, with the potholes filled in with gravel and the weeds cleared away from the gate to past the rhododendrons. She hadn't seen Jack in a while, so when his Jeep came speeding up the avenue, her first thought was that something might have happened to Katie, and she automatically checked her phone in case of a missed call. There wasn't one, so she ran down the stairs and pulled open the front door.

'What's wrong?' Jack asked.

'What do you mean?'

'Your face clouded over, or are you just unhappy to see me?'

'No, I'm sorry. Can I help you?'

He jumped out of the car. 'So formal; I'm going for a coffee to the next town, and I thought you might like to join me? Give us a chance to chat, away from Kilteelagh. I really do talk about more than jobs to do around the house.'

'For a coffee?'

'Yes, would you prefer lunch? I can run to a sambo, I'm sure.'

Marianne felt an urge to giggle, but she stopped herself.

'Thank you, but I'm in the middle of something, and I can't leave it.'

'No worries, I was passing and thought I would chance it. Maybe another time?'

'I will ring if I have work,' she said, and she thought he looked put out at her reply. She rushed back to the house, determined to forget about Jack Farrelly. She had enough on her plate at the moment without complicating it with Jack. She made her way up to Mike's old room. Clearing out all her grandfather's stuff would nicely occupy her, and she wouldn't have time to think of Jack.

The room appeared to be full of junk. When she peeked into the top box of a tall stack, it was full of old *Time* magazines worn at the edges and faded with age. It had been a very long time since anybody had sat and flicked through any of these publications. Marianne moved to the writing desk in the corner beside the window. Ledgers and account books from when Kilteelagh House was a thriving farm covered the desk. Gathering them up, she stuffed them on top of the box of magazines. The desk was a simple roll-top, but with a clean and a polish, she knew she would like to use it.

The big, heavy mahogany wardrobe would have to stay where it was, taking up the far wall. When she pulled out the bottom drawer, the neatness of the contents was at odds with the rest of the room. Carefully, she lifted out crisply ironed tablecloths and linen. Linen napkins were folded small, round lace tablecloths creased with precision and rectangular striped tablecloths with faded stains that looked as if they had been used for picnics. In between the layers was a scattering of lavender, its aroma released by the disturbance now filling the air with a soft scent which made her sneeze.

Opening the wardrobe doors, she was surprised to find suits, trousers, shirts and ties as if her grandfather's clothes had never been cleared away. Gently, she took out the hangers, worried that she was the first to tamper with these items in decades. She laid the different suits across the bed. When she took out the last one, she wondered why Collie had kept them all these years and why the room, which had been her grandfather's, had never been cleared out and repurposed. When she saw one of his jacket pockets bulging, she reached for his pipe.

Her mother's abiding memory of her father was the aroma of his sweet tobacco. Sometimes, she had told Marianne, he liked to wander by the lake and pull on his pipe. This memory of Mike Keane was strangely disconcerting, and so, too, was the realisation that this man's presence had so quickly faded from Kilteelagh House, even though most of his possessions were still here. Flopping onto the bed, she moved a box from the bedside table. A photograph of Collie and Mike in a silver frame lay flat on the top. It could have been knocked down by a careless move, but Marianne wondered was it something that had been done a long time ago and never corrected. This bedroom had been abandoned, not as a shrine to Collie's dead husband, but almost because nobody cared enough to archive the little personal items that had made up Mike's life. Marianne's mother said they were never allowed in here after their father died, and over time the room was clearly all but forgotten except for the occasional hoover and dusting. None of her children ever dared ask Collie about it, as it was felt she could not face the removal of her husband's possessions.

In need of a break, she wandered down to the next landing and Collie's chair. The velvet chair was uncomfortable, the cushion lumpy in places. From here, though she had a good view of the avenue and front gardens. Collie in the last weeks of her life moved from this chair to her bed almost as if she were waiting for something on the avenue. She knew Katherine had complained that, even two days before she died, Collie had insisted on being carried to the chair and propped up to view one last time the avenue and fields that ran across to the lake. Katherine said Collie cried when she was taken back to bed, knowing she would never sit there again.

Katherine had made it clear to anybody who would listen that Collie had been beyond daft. In her last hours on earth, transferred to a hospital bed, she had fretted about not being able to sit looking out of her landing window at those bloody daffodils she had seen a million times before.

Marianne shook herself to remove the thoughts of the past, thoughts that brought their own kind of pain now that she was the only person in charge. Darting downstairs, she grabbed refuse sacks from the cupboard before returning to fold Mike Keane's life into the nondescript black bags. She had four bags full when she heard a car on the driveway. When she saw it was Katherine again, she was glad the back door was locked. Slowly, she pulled away from the top window and watched as her aunt got out of the car, shoved the dog out of the way and walked around to the back door. She felt slightly guilty when she heard Katherine rap on the door, before she dialled Marianne's number.

Quickly turning her phone to silent so it didn't give her away, she stuffed it under a mound of Mike's ties. She stood watching it vibrate as Katherine kept redialling. Katherine, when she left the message, sounded cross. Marianne stayed out of sight until she heard her car speed down the driveway. She checked the message.

'I am trying to keep my nose out, but you are leaving me no choice. You need to step up to the mark and sort out Rachel, before it is too late. If you don't do it, I will have to step in. This is real life, Marianne, not some make-believe.'

She listened to the message two more times. Katherine sounded more upset than cross. She should ring her, but what would she say? 'Help me, I haven't a clue what this is even about'? Rachel seemed fine, moody like any teenager, slightly resentful and sweet in so many ways. Marianne did have a feeling she was missing something, but she had no idea what. What was Collie thinking of, leaving her in charge of two young girls? Katherine was right, it was like she was playing house. She was marking out the rooms at Kilteelagh like she used to draw lines in the grass at home for her make-believe house. In the grass rooms she felt protected, living a fantasy life. Here at Kilteelagh, life was too real, too overwhelming, but she couldn't pull out now.

Soon, her belongings from New York would arrive and she would have to fully settle here. She had zipped back briefly to Manhattan to organise everything there after the reading of the will and now, finally, after delays by the shipping company, her shipment was to be delivered to Kilteelagh. She didn't want to ring Katherine back, but she figured she must talk to Rachel, find out what was going on. For now, she wanted to continue with the room. Grabbing a handful of tweed blazers, she stuffed them in a bag. There was a charity shop in Bray, or maybe the local amateur dramatics society would like the stash. That was something she could ask Dolores about, she thought, as she lingered over a hanger with silk ties which had only ever been put on for funerals and weddings. She was about to put all the bags in the front hall when she noticed the writing box.

Her grandfather had not struck her as a man who was given in any way to writing letters. The leather was worn away in places, she noticed as she opened it and took out a bundle that had been neatly stacked in one corner. It seemed to consist of correspondence with various banks, including statements, but one piece of paper poked out of a bank envelope as if it had been hurriedly shoved in. Marianne gently eased it out.

It was an undated letter from Mike to Collie, though she wasn't sure if her grandmother had ever read it.

Kilteelagh House,
Balgaddy

My Lovely Collie,

I came home from the doctor's today and told you I was OK. It was a lie, and I am not sure I will ever tell you the truth. I don't want to cause you pain. I already see in your eyes the distress of somebody who is haunted by loss.

I wish I could see the life return to your eyes. To see them dance with laughter again; if I could do anything, it would be whatever was necessary to restore that look.

In the last few years or so I have wondered what the matter is, though I haven't asked because at times you seem so preoccupied. I love you, Collie, and I know in your own good time you will open up to me. There is nothing you can tell me that would dent how much I love you.

I hope that comes before this cancer has time to spread too far. When we met, I always felt I was the more enthusiastic and, I suppose, I thought I could get you to love me. I thought we were doing fine, but you seem unhappy, Collie, and for that I am very sorry.

I know you love Kilteelagh, and it gives me some comfort to think that when I leave here, I leave Kilteelagh in your safe hands.

If you can, remember me well. Know me as the husband who loved you, though I am at fault for never really showing it. I am cursed with the reserve of an Irish man afraid to show his feelings. But I love you, Collie, and always will.

I treasure our three daughters and I hope you will keep my

memory alive to them, especially little Chloe, who probably
will not remember me at all. I am tired now, but I will write
again soon.

The letter wasn't signed, as if the writer intended to return to
that piece of paper. Marianne put it back in the envelope. It was
time to pick up Katie.

Rachel was due home at eight. Marianne stayed with Katie
until she fell asleep. They had both worked hard on the
bedroom once they got home from the play date, and they had
cleared the room, emptied the wardrobes and bedside tables,
and managed to store everything they'd gathered all in the hall
to be collected by the charity shop van. Marianne wandered
into the room now. She had taken down the heavy drapes and
rammed them in the washing machine, so the windows were
bare. Crossing the wooden floor, she thought she heard voices
through the open window. Stepping to the side, so she could not
be seen, she noticed two figures in the shadows of the rhododendron as if they were coming from the lakeside. The girl laughed
and ran up the avenue, the young man following her, grabbing
her by the waist. Marianne watched them kiss, not realising for
a moment it was Rachel.

She had no idea what to do. Run out of the house and
embarrass Rachel, or wait to speak to her when she got in? But
when she heard Rachel shouting, Marianne didn't stop to assess
the situation.

She tore down the stairs and bolted out the front door,
grabbing a support cane from a flowerpot on the way. Marianne's heart was thumping, anger coursing through her as she
ran in the half-dark down the avenue. Grabbing her phone
from her pocket, she put on the light and swung it past the
bushes towards the rhododendron. She heard the words 'get

off me' and the crunch of gravel, then the sound of someone panting as they ran. Rachel came into view and almost collided with Marianne. Tears streaming down her face, Rachel was clutching her breast and hiding a huge hole in her T-shirt.

'Where the hell is he?' Marianne shouted.

Rachel pointed further down the avenue. Marianne tore past the rhododendron, shouting at the top of her voice as if she were chasing a wild animal. There was no sound, only her angry words as they faded across the lake. Suddenly, feeling afraid and foolish as her adrenaline spike disappeared, she ran back towards the light of the hall and the open front door. As she banged the hall door shut behind her, she could hear Rachel sobbing at the kitchen table. Rachel, her breath short, stared at Marianne.

'I'm sorry, I'm sorry,' she whispered through her tears.

'What did he do to you? Who the hell is he? We must call the cops.'

Rachel jumped up. 'No, no – and I don't know who he is. I met him on the train from Dublin and we got talking.'

'What were you doing on the train from the city?'

Rachel snorted loudly. 'I went to Dublin for the day.'

Marianne didn't flinch. 'I think you had better start talking.'

Rachel leaned against the sink.

'I wanted to go to Dublin, where nobody knows me, and just hang for a bit.'

'Did you?'

'Yeah, I had a look around the shops for a while.'

'And?'

'And nothing. I had a burger at McDonald's, and I got the train home. I met this guy; he was really nice, and he said he was going to Greystones and getting the bus to Balgaddy too.'

Marianne sighed loudly.

'I know it sounds stupid now – he even said he lived on our

road. I was surprised because I know everybody around here, but he said he was a cousin of the Diamonds further along.'

'Did he hurt you?'

'He was lovely at first. He held my hand, and I liked that he got the bus with me. On the part of the avenue where we couldn't be seen from the house, he kissed me and said he wanted to see me again.'

'And the rest?'

Rachel fumbled with the basket of laundry on the worktop.

'He asked was anybody at home and I said no, so he suggested we go into the house. He became quite pushy. I don't know, I got afraid; he began to kiss me again, but this time he was rough, and it hurt and he began to pull at my top and put his hands under my T-shirt. That's when I started to scream and fight him off.'

Marianne stood up and dragged Rachel into a tight hug.

'Look at what he did to my T-shirt – he ripped a hole in it. And he twisted my breast. It hurt a lot,' she snorted into Marianne's neck.

'We should tell the police.'

Rachel shrank back. 'Please don't, everybody will find out and I'll be called a slag.'

'No, you won't.'

Rachel looked directly to Marianne.

'Please, please.'

'Will we check with the Diamonds in case he is over there?'

Rachel shook her head. 'I knew he wasn't living there. I thought he was so taken by me that he would say anything. I was a stupid bitch, I was flattered.'

'This is not your fault; he attacked you.'

Rachel snuggled further into Marianne. 'I'm sorry, can we just forget about it?'

'Darling, why did you go to the city? You told me you were—'

'I needed a break. It's hard being here, trying to think of everything, and Katie depending on me.'

'Which is why I'm here.'

'But you won't stay, will you? In the end it's going to be the two of us.'

'You don't know that. I'm putting a lot into living here, I am committed. I love you both very much.'

Rachel shivered with tears again. 'But you're not our mum are you, or Grandma Collie?'

Marianne paced the floor in frustration. 'I don't pretend to be, but I do love you guys. I don't have any family left either, you know. My mom and dad are dead, and I never even got to say goodbye to them, or to Grandma Collie. You are hurting, Rachel, but so is everybody else in this house. We have to help each other.' She gently stroked Rachel's head. 'Stop trying to take charge, it's time to trust me. It's time to be the fifteen-year-old girl you are.'

Rachel pulled away. 'Are you going to stay forever?'

'Nobody can answer that. I can only say I want to. Please give me a chance and let me take charge.'

Rachel allowed Marianne to grab hold of her again. Marianne felt her snuggle into her chest and she prayed she could keep her word.

'What do we do about what happened?' Rachel asked quietly.

'You learn from it. But from now on, you tell me the truth,' Marianne said firmly.

'OK.'

'And this weekend you help me pick paint for my new bedroom and some other rooms too.'

'Even the drawing room?'

'Especially the drawing room,' Marianne said, and Rachel giggled.

. . .

Marianne was still asleep when there was a loud hammering on the front door the next morning. By the time she had got downstairs and pulled back the door, there were stacks of cardboard boxes piled high on the top step. A delivery man waved, turned his van and left as Katie came rushing down the stairs.

'Is all this for us?' she asked, her eyes wide with excitement.

'It's my design stuff from the States.'

'Can I open it with you?' Katie asked, helping her pull the boxes into the hall. Katie began to pull at the flap of one of the boxes, but Marianne told her to wait until she got a knife from the kitchen. Once she had sliced through the tape, Katie dipped in, pulling out a bundle of trouser suits in dark blue and brown. 'Are these your clothes?' she asked.

Marianne picked up the outfits, which were part of an office-to-cocktail capsule collection. She should be glad to see them, and she knew Jay must have gone to some trouble to recover them for her. But, looking at them now, they seemed rather dull.

'This is lovely,' Katie said, pulling out a cerise chiffon scarf and draping it around her neck. She wore it as she helped carry in a big box of spools of thread and placed it on the dining room table.

One by one, they tipped the contents of the boxes onto the table.

'Ugh, I don't like this,' Katie said, picking up a chocolate-brown dress in jersey fabric. Marianne took it, rolled it into a ball and threw it into the far corner of the room. Rachel stuck her head around the door.

'What's with all the noise?'

'Marianne got a big delivery from America, her designer gear,' Katie shouted.

'Right, you believe that?' Rachel said as she ducked back upstairs.

Katie picked up a black silk skirt. 'Why so dark? Why can't

you design dresses that make it feel like summer all the time?
Everybody loves summer.'

'That's not a bad idea.'

'We can call them Katie's dresses.'

'For the Kilteelagh Collection. It has a nice ring to it.'

'Do you mean it?'

'If I go back to designing, yes.'

Katie beamed with pride as Marianne emptied another box
onto the dining table.

'Let's get started organising this lot,' Marianne said, and
Katie climbed up on a chair so she could reach the pile.

'Are you going to use Grandma Collie's sewing machine?'

'I have one of my own – it's in one of these boxes, I hope.'

'Can I use Collie's machine then? She showed me how; we
made a pink skirt together with a Hello Kitty badge on the
pocket.'

'Grandma Collie taught me how to sew too. We came over
every second summer and she always had patchwork pieces
ready for me.'

'Me too,' Katie giggled.

The little girl wrapped a piece of floral fabric around her
waist and threw the rest over her shoulder.

'We're going to have such fun,' she said.

ELEVEN

July

Kilteelagh House,
Balgaddy,
Co. Wicklow

My dearest Marianne,

Are you cursing me for putting so much on you? The gloss of adventure has probably worn off now and the sameness of life at Kilteelagh House is setting in. Well, I won't apologise; call it the privilege of a person near death. We tend to take liberties, step outside the social lines. I have taken a huge liberty with you, sweetheart, but please walk the road with me.

I never wanted to go quietly. What could be worse than to die without anybody bothering to fully consider the life lived? I know Katherine is probably furious with me. She will get over it, she is a woman who likes to be outraged, and no doubt something else will come her way soon and her focus will shift. Forgive me if I wanted you to see past the old woman I have become to the rich life once contained within the four walls of Kilteelagh House. Who knows, by exploring my life you may gain some insight into your own. I know I also run the risk you won't stay the course. I want you to know there is no shame in feeling a wobble; it would be strange if you didn't.

Why don't you do some of your dress designing? Sometimes, to immerse yourself in something you love can help deal with the strangeness of the present. If you want any help with sewing, Fiknete, who has an alterations shop upstairs on Parnell Street, is your woman. She has been a good friend to me, and I'm sure she wouldn't mind lending a hand. You have a huge talent. Try to make it work at Kilteelagh, darling; I know you can do it.

Have you come across my grand tea set yet? No doubt Rachel and Katie have pointed it out. It was a wedding present from Mike's Aunt Phyllis. At the time I thought it was rather sombre bone china with a slate greyleaf motif, but over the years I have come to appreciate that leaf tea from a china cup can upscale even the smallest of gatherings. Mike used to laugh at me when I set a tray of tea on Sunday afternoons for both of us in the drawing room, or as he said, the parlour. I always insisted we drink from my china cups. He was right to laugh at me, but sometimes it's the traditions we make and cling onto that give us hope all is well in a time of chaos.

The tea set arrived in a big cardboard box, each cup and saucer wrapped in newspaper. It came with the note: 'Leaf tea from a good bone china cup will sort any problem that a marriage encounters, and if it doesn't in the first cup, it will have to by the second. P x' What Phyllis said was true, and that set with all its delicate strength has brought me through thick and thin.

I never got to meet Aunt Phyllis. The old dear had sent the tea set ahead and boarded the Tralee train to visit us when she had a heart attack and died. The train was between express *stops and the only way they had of calling for help was to drop a note at a station to ring ahead for an ambulance and I suppose a hearse. Poor Phyllis died on her first trip away from home in ten years. Her demise and exit from this world, which merited two paragraphs in the next day's Irish Times and almost half a page in the local newspaper the following week, is what made her stand out. But for me it's the tea set; the generosity of her gift; the accuracy of her advice which stayed with me and ensured she was forever remembered at Kilteelagh House.*

We all wish to be remembered, isn't that what life is about, setting up our legacy for those left behind? Think of me kindly, Marianne, and if in this act of remembrance I have made you smile, then my work here is almost done.

But before I go, did you do the lake walk yet? To think of you treading in my footsteps is such a huge comfort now. I remember fondly the fields around Kilteelagh, the cowslips steadfast against the bold red poppy in the far corner where the grass and wildflowers mingle and the cornflowers, which from a distance looked like spots of blue dancing in the air. The yellow yarrow stood tall like soldiers on guard. No doubt there is the clash of gaudy red and orange nasturtiums too, from the time you enthusiastically threw a seed packet down there. Little did we know that the nasturtium would run rampant and self-seed for every year thereafter. I have, in the past, pulled it out, but it always bested me; its return is a reminder of the little girl with the seed packet and a silly grandmother who indulged her. In later years, I appreciated the streak of colour in the meadow, much as you have brought so much colour to my life, especially in the stories your mother told me when we used to chat once a week on the phone.

Marianne, you remind me of myself when I was your age; outgoing, full of ideas and fun, and why wouldn't you be? Please don't ever lose your beautiful qualities, not even with the prospect of parenting a teenager and a young child, as well as running Kilteelagh. When I list it like that, it sounds so much, but I trust in you, and I trust you to bring up Rachel and Katie in the values instilled in you by your own parents.

Take charge, darling, and when times get tough, you will find the tea set in the right-hand cupboard of the bureau in the drawing room. Sip Earl Grey and remember the advice of Aunt Phyllis.

All my love,

Collie xx

Marianne stuffed the letter in her dressing gown pocket when she heard Katie on the stairs. Katie pressed the kitchen door open a little.

'I can't sleep; I don't feel well.'

'Have you a fever?'

'What?'

'A temperature. Just let me check. Where did Grandma keep her medicine box?'

'Nana only ever used her hand; we don't have a medicine box.'

'You're not burning up,' she said, touching Katie's forehead.

'Grandma always said we would wait it out a bit before calling the doctor.'

'And how do we wait it out?'

'Ice cream and a movie, maybe?'

Marianne took a tub of cookies-and-cream ice cream from the freezer. 'I think this will go down very well,' she said.

'Can we snuggle up on the couch together? Grandma always rubbed my forehead.'

Marianne grabbed a rug from the chair beside the Aga and two spoons from the cutlery drawer. 'Let's do it.'

Katie led the way up the hall, skipping along happily.

'Can I pick the movie?' she said, jumping onto the couch.

'Aren't you feeling too ill?'

Katie stared at Marianne.

'There's nothing wrong with my brain,' she said, flicking on Netflix and calling up *The Devil Wears Prada*.

Marianne sat on the couch beside Katie, throwing the rug over their knees.

'Do you think, if we woke Rachel, she would get cross?' Katie whispered.

'I can go check; she may not be asleep yet.'

Katie pressed the pause button and Marianne climbed the stairs to Rachel's room. She was standing outside, wondering if she should knock, when suddenly the door was pulled back.

'Jesus Christ, what are you doing here?'

'Katie and I—' Marianne knew she looked guilty and the upbeat tone to her voice didn't help.

'Were you spying on me?'

'No.'

'Do you do that every night, loiter around my door? Weirdo.'

'Rachel, I wondered if you were sleeping, and I wasn't sure whether to wake you.'

'What's wrong?'

Rachel pushed past Marianne and raced into Katie's room. 'Oh God, where is she?'

Marianne took a deep breath. 'Downstairs, watching a movie; do you want to join us?'

'What?'

'Come on, it will be fun.'

'It's almost midnight.'

'So?'

Marianne continued down the stairs. She didn't look back, but she heard Rachel's light footfall behind her.

'Where were ye? I don't like being on my own,' Katie said as they joined her on the couch.

Rachel jumped up as Katie pressed play.

'Can I get the bottle of Coke from the pantry?'

'I'm not putting it on pause again,' Katie said, her voice high-pitched with frustration.

'I'll go grab it,' Rachel said, jumping across her sister and running down the hall. When she came back, Rachel was grinning.

'Grandma sometimes let us use her tea set, why don't we?'

'The fancy one in the bureau, are you sure?' Marianne asked.

'It's not as if she would know, is it?' Rachel said.

'She might haunt us,' Katie piped up and Rachel giggled.

'What if she does? Grandma could never stay cross for long.'

Marianne got up and tried to open the bureau doors.

Rachel gently nudged her out of the way. 'You have to press first, then pull,' she said, neatly releasing the door.

They took out the cups and saucers. Katie got Grandma's little table and they arranged three sets, letting Rachel pour the Coca-Cola.

'Cheers to us,' Katie said, holding aloft her cup, which was filled to the brim. They clinked the china gently, then delicately sipped their drinks.

'Will somebody press play already?' Marianne said, and the others laughed as they scrunched up on the couch together.

TWELVE

The following week Marianne stood watching the water gurgle from the pipe under the bathroom sink and flow across the floor.

'Do something, the place is getting drenched!' Rachel shouted.

Marianne pressed her hand against the rush of water, only managing to slow it. The water pummelled against her skin, looking for a weak spot.

'Ring somebody, get it to stop.'

'Yeah, let me reach for my phone. Oh, I forgot, my hand is plugging this leak,' Marianne replied, her voice heavy with sarcasm.

'I'm ringing Aunt Katherine.'

'No, we can handle this.'

'The place is bloody flooding.'

Katie popped her head around the bathroom door.

'Sarah said her dad will be here in a few minutes.'

'Ask him how we stop the water; there must be a faucet somewhere.'

'Faucet?' Katie giggled.

'Tap – ask about a tap.'

'I did, he said to turn it off from the outside.'

Marianne pushed harder on the water fountain. 'Where outside, there are acres out there?' She shifted and a spurt of water shot past her and hit Katie in the face.

'Honey, I'm sorry. Rachel, you take over here.'

'But I'll get wet, and what are you going to do?'

'Rachel, please, can we discuss the ins and outs of it later and you just do as I ask?'

'OK, but I'm not being late for work over this crap.'

Rachel squatted down and placed her hand over Marianne's. 'Don't move until I say so.' When she gave the word, Marianne pulled away her hand, massaging where it was cold and numb.

'Sarah's dad says try down at the gate. Can I go and get dressed now?'

'Marvellous, I'm bloody left in the swimming pool,' Rachel said.

Marianne turned to say something, but when she saw Rachel smiling, she didn't make any comment. Rushing down the stairs, she grabbed her raincoat from a hook on the hall, jumped into the car and drove quickly down the driveway. She had no idea what she was looking for, and was checking under the overhang of bushes and weeds by the gate when Jack's car pulled up. He took out a crowbar and marched over to the left of the gates, pushing branches and bushes out of his way. 'Got it,' he shouted as he bent down to scrape the muck and moss from a square on the ground. Using the crowbar, he manoeuvred the water tap shut.

'OK, that's done it. Now we must sort out the bathroom. Will I follow you up to the house?

'Please.'

Rachel was already in her room when they got back. Pushing her head around her door, she said she had thrown towels on the floor to soak up the water.

'Can you bring me to work? I'm going to miss the bus, and Mrs Simons will kill me as this is my first week helping out at the florists.'

Jack said he had a bit of time and would get on with sorting out the bathroom, if Marianne could ferry all three girls to work and summer camp.

Katie tugged at Marianne's arm and pulled her down to whisper in her ear. 'I was supposed to draw a picture and bring it in, and I forgot.'

Jack tipped Marianne's elbow. 'You go, I have it from here.'

She realised she was still in her pyjamas and pulled her raincoat tighter around her as she went downstairs to get the snacks ready. When Katie followed her to the kitchen, she looked unhappy.

'What's wrong, sweetie? I'm sure we can explain you forgot, or you had to have an early night.'

Katie pulled out a chair and slumped at the kitchen table. 'I don't want to go to summer camp today.'

'Why, are you feeling sick?'

'I just don't want to go.'

'There must be a reason, sweetie.'

'I don't want to, all right?'

Marianne sat down at the table beside the little girl. 'It's not all right, there's something wrong. You can tell me, Katie.'

'Mummy said I have to learn to deal with things myself, that nobody should be allowed to bully me.'

'Is somebody bullying you?' Katie shrugged her shoulders. 'Maybe I can help, sweetie.'

Katie turned her head away from Marianne and concentrated on Benji, who had brushed up against her knees.

'Did another kid say something to you?'

Katie didn't answer.

Rachel rushed into the room and grabbed a yoghurt drink from the fridge.

'I have to go, are ye ready?'

'Give us a minute, we have to sort something out here,' Marianne said, raising her hand to hush Rachel.

'What's wrong?'

'A kid is causing a bit of trouble for Katie at summer camp.'

'Who?'

'I don't think who is so important,' Marianne said, but Katie looked at her sister and mouthed Ava Henderson's name.

'You tell that little witch to piss off,' Rachel snapped.

Marianne stood up. 'Has this sort of thing happened before?'

'Like, every month. Grandma was so fed up going into school complaining about her, but Ava Henderson is a teacher's pet. She's never done summer camp before, so rotten luck she decided to do it this year.'

'So you're saying there is no point me going in to complain.'

'Doh.'

'But we can't just let this go on. And Katie, you know you would be sad to miss it.'

'What am I supposed to do?' Katie asked solemnly.

'What did this girl say?' Marianne asked gently.

Katie took a deep breath. 'She said Grandma Collie was gone to hell, that she and Mummy were having a party there.'

'That sounds like adult talk to me,' Marianne said as she hugged Katie tight.

'Grandma and Mummy are not in hell, are they?' Katie asked.

'Is there such a thing as hell? And even if there is, those two beautiful women wouldn't be anywhere near a place like that,' Marianne said.

'I have to get to work,' Rachel said, lifting up her rucksack.

Marianne ran upstairs to change into jeans and a top. When she got downstairs, both girls were waiting in the hall.

'Katie and me had a talk and she's going in today. I gave her a few pointers on how to deal with the bully,' Rachel said.

Marianne looked from one to the other. 'OK, are you happy about that, Katie?'

She nodded and they went to the car. They didn't talk much during the journey to drop off Rachel. Outside the hall where summer camp was taking place, Katie said she wanted to go in on her own.

'Are you sure? What about Ava Henderson?'

'What about her?' Katie answered, before she skipped off. Despite her apparent confidence, Marianne couldn't help feeling apprehensive.

When she got home, the house was closed up and Jack had left a note on the kitchen table: *All sorted. I threw the dirty towels in the washing machine but wasn't sure how to turn on your fancy one.*

She dialled his number and was disappointed when he didn't answer. She switched on the kettle; Dolores was due in the early afternoon. She turned the washing machine to a 90-degree wash before going upstairs to check the bathroom. The wooden floorboards still looked sodden, and she opened the bathroom and landing windows to help dry them out. Lingering on the landing, she sank into Collie's velvet chair. The roses were blooming; the agapanthus was tall, holding up its dusky blue blooms for all to see. She wasn't sure if she had enough done at this stage; it all seemed to take so much time. The jetty and gazebo had to be her next priority. Maybe she shouldn't put them before new windows, but somehow Marianne knew it was right for her family to do it this way.

Dolores had promised to bring some plants for the pots at the front door today, and maybe then she could knock another thing off her list. She sank back in the chair. There was no reason to have it here now, it blocked the way into Rachel's room, but she didn't want to move it. That would be an acknowledgment that Collie and her ways were completely gone, and Marianne wasn't ready for that just yet. Why her grandmother insisted on sitting here, she wasn't very sure, only that the view of the estate was spectacular. From here, she could see the whole driveway to the top of the gates at the end. Was it that Collie was waiting for that one main event to transform her life, and it never ever happened?

Marianne sat for over an hour in Collie's chair enjoying the peace of Kilteelagh House.

Reluctantly, she moved when she saw Dolores driving up the avenue. She went into the bathroom and slicked some lipstick on before going downstairs. Dolores was already tipping pots of flowers onto the front steps when she pulled back the front door.

'I went for colour over substance. Nice hardy annuals. You couldn't keep anything on this step over the winter anyway. But this lot might just hang in there until the start of October,' she said as she closed the boot of her car.

'What do we do now?'

Dolores threw her eyes upwards. 'We arrange the pots nicely, water them and congratulate ourselves on a job well done, of course.'

'We don't have to repot them, or anything like that?'

'Darling, if you're getting an easy way out, take it. How about the two of us set off on a little spin? We could drive to the mountains and take in the views.'

'I don't know, Dolores; I like to be here in case anything happens with Katie, or Rachel comes home early.'

'Cluck, cluck, you're worse than Collie. Come on then, I'm wearing my gardening clothes, we could get a start at the gazebo; cut down the brambles and hack away the nettles.'

Marianne went inside to get her gardening gloves, while Dolores walked around to the stables where the tools were stored. Dolores was already swiping at the nettles when Marianne reached the gazebo. 'Come on, girl, there's a lot to be said for this type of gardening. Get stuck into those briars. You won't know what needs to be done here until it's cleared, and no point paying anyone to do it.' They worked side by side, hacking and cutting and tearing weeds from their roots. Neither had time to talk.

At one stage, Marianne stopped when a briar curled around her, the thorns sticking into her forearm. Swiping it away, she saw it had snagged a thread on her cardigan. Tired, she backed away and wandered down to the lake to take a breather. Dolores followed her. 'I reckon we've done enough here for now. Collie always said we should just attack it, but somehow, we never got out to do it. Her heart was willing in the last years, but the physical body couldn't manage much.'

'Why did she stay here? There's so much upkeep to Kilteelagh.'

Dolores looked all around her as if she were afraid somebody might be listening. 'She wouldn't be happy if she heard you say that; that's more like Katherine-speak. But yes, in the last five or six years, it was a huge burden to her. If things were different, she may have let it go, but that was not to be.'

'What do you mean exactly?'

'Collie had to keep Kilteelagh going. and that's why she asked you to step in. I'm sure when she's ready she will explain it all through her letters.'

'You know something, but you're not telling me.'

Dolores smiled and looked out over the water. 'It's not my story to tell, Marianne.'

'It's dumb. It seems to have been madness to keep the old place, lovely and all as it is.'

Dolores put a hand on her shoulder. 'All in good time. Collie always got the timing right in life. I don't suspect she will be any different in death.'

'Do you think she was right to leave me with the kids? I'm not a mother. At least Katherine knows how to be one.'

Dolores clicked her tongue against her teeth. 'Would you please stop comparing yourself to high-and-mighty Katherine. There's no comparison, and I mean that as the biggest compliment to you. She is not as lily white as you imagine.'

'What do you mean?'

Dolores looked worried as if she had said too much, but then ploughed on, 'I've started, so I'll finish. Don't you ever wonder what she is doing, gadding off to Dublin all the time?'

'She likes the city, I guess.'

'And what's in it and what it offers her. There is a certain class of person who craves the anonymity of the city more than others.'

'Dolores, what do you mean?'

'My girl, nothing is what it appears from the outside.'

'What are you saying exactly?'

'I'm not sure it's my place.'

Marianne looked at Dolores. 'I thought you were my friend. And if you are, you wouldn't be talking in riddles.'

Dolores sighed and pushed her hands deep in her pockets before she spoke. 'I should not have started this, but there are rumours out there in the ether.'

'Out in the ether?'

'Darling, there has been talk.'

Marianne picked up a stone and skipped it across the lake. 'I don't want to know, but at the same time I do want to know. There's a lot about Katherine I don't understand. I never really knew her. She and my mother didn't really get on, and now we're stuck fighting it out and it's exhausting.'

'I shouldn't have brought it up. I'm sorry, I spoke out of turn.'

Marianne swung around to Dolores. 'You're only warning me, I know that. So, you'd better tell me everything you know.'

'She has been seen in Dublin with some man and... she has been seen in pubs, drinking. Katherine drinks a lot.'

Marianne stared out across the lake, watching the ducks as they squabbled over a piece of rubbish bobbing on the water. 'Is it any business of mine? If this is even happening, she may have her reasons. I won't be her judge.'

'But she's quick to judge you, did you ever think of that?'

Marianne shook her head and walked away. Dolores followed at a slow pace. 'Katherine has yet to realise you can't be throwing the first stone if you live in a glass house.'

'It's why my mother hated Ireland: the constant gossip.'

'You asked me, Marianne, and I'm telling you what everybody is saying.'

Marianne placed her hand on Dolores's arm. 'I wasn't including you in that. I know your reason for telling me. It's the motives of others I question.'

She felt Dolores relax.

'I never wanted to overstep the mark, but Collie asked me to watch out for you and I think you should know this.'

'Collie knew?'

'Yes, but she said it was Katherine's business and only hers.'

'Which is the position I shall adopt.'

Her phone rang and Marianne wandered across the grass as she answered it. When she came back, her face was pale. 'That was the summer camp. Katie punched another girl on the nose. I'm going to have to go there.'

'It must be the Henderson girl – and if so, it's nothing she didn't deserve.'

'Katie said the advice from home was to tackle this girl and punch her. I never told her to do that!'

Dolores looked at Marianne. 'But Rachel probably did. You go, I'll close up the house.'

Marianne sprinted across the grass and up the avenue to her car.

THIRTEEN

'I just did what Rachel said to do. I didn't mean to hurt her or to cause blood,' Katie said as she ran to Marianne and buried her head in her jacket. The camp leader beckoned to them to follow her into the office, where Ava Henderson and her mother were sitting down. Ava was sobbing as her mother held a tissue to her nose.

'Look at what that wild child has done to my girl. She should be thrown out of the camp.'

Ava Henderson's mother made to stand up, but the camp leader asked her to stay sitting.

'I'm sure Katie is sorry for what she has done—' Marianne made to say, but Katie stepped forward.

'I didn't mean to cause blood, but I'm not a bit sorry. My mummy and my grandma are not in hell and you can't say that.'

'Excuse me, young lady, Ava would never say such a thing,' Mrs Henderson snapped as she straightened up in her seat.

The camp leader rapped on the desk with her knuckles as if she was calling order at a meeting. 'Throwing around accusations is not going to help the situation. Why don't we find out why this has happened and work towards getting the girls to, if not make friends, be able to tolerate each other for the duration of the camp.'

'That girl has no mother and has gone wild. I'm not one bit surprised with that slip of a thing playing house and mummy,' Mrs Henderson said.

Katie tugged at Marianne. 'Tell her to stop. She can't talk about us like that.'

Marianne swallowed hard. A tension headache was settling in; the woman's voice needlessly loud. The camp leader was saying something, but she could hardly make it out. Katie squeezing her hand made her realise she had to act. Without thinking too much about it, lest she lose courage, Marianne spoke.

'I apologise for my youth; I apologise for what Katie did, but I want to tell you, Mrs Henderson, you and your daughter are reprehensible. And from this day on, Katie will not be bullied. I will not have you say anything about Katie's beautiful mother or our wonderful grandmother. If you do, or your daughter does, you will be hearing from our attorney. I hope you take what I have said seriously, and I hope I have made myself perfectly clear.' Gently, she tugged Katie's sleeve and they moved towards the door. As she reached the knob, Marianne turned to the startled group. 'I never condone physical violence, but I can see, in this instance, Katie had no choice. This will not happen again. And may I suggest, Mrs Henderson, that *you* go to hell.'

Katie flung back the door and they walked out, striding down the corridor, their backs stiff, waiting for someone to call them back. When they got outside, they rushed to the car. Marianne was fumbling so much with her keys that Katie took them from her and pressed the button to unlock the car.

'Are you all right to drive?' she asked.

Marianne nodded, starting up the car and sweeping out of the gate. They were a mile down the road when she pulled into the side. 'Did I really say all that?'

'You did; you told Mrs Henderson to go to hell! You were perfectly clear,' Katie giggled.

Marianne feigned shock and then laughed, tears of relief streaming down her face as they hugged each other tight.

'I don't think anybody is going to bully me from now on,' Katie said, her face bright with excitement.

'I must ring the poor lady from the summer camp to apologise. She didn't deserve that outburst.'

'But the Hendersons did.'

'You know, I think they did,' Marianne said, slapping the steering wheel.

Her phone rang. 'Where are you? I'm at home and there's nobody here,' Rachel said, her voice indignant.

'We were sending the Hendersons to hell,' Katie shouted.

'We're on the way home. Will I get a takeout on the way?' Marianne asked.

'Pizza, I've gone off fish and chips,' Rachel answered.

Katie giggled. 'You mean you've gone off the delivery boy from the chipper.'

'Shut up, Katie,' Rachel snapped, ending the call.

'How do you know that?' Marianne asked.

'Sure, I know everything that goes on,' Katie said, and Marianne thought she sounded way older than her years.

FOURTEEN

August

Kilteelagh House,
Balgaddy
Co Wicklow

Dear Marianne,

How I loved the sunshine and warm summer days when we would take the old rucksack from the back hall and fill it up with bacon butties and bottles of orange squash and head down to spend the day at the sea. I always sneaked in a hip flask of coffee laced with brandy, and fig rolls for dipping. You kids hankered after ice cream and complained bitterly that our little bit of coastline was never going to be on the route of the ice cream van.

Your mother once offered the Mr Whippy in the town what she called fifty bucks to drive out and surprise you guys, but he was a hard-nosed businessman and said to make it worth his while at least three hundred bucks would have to be on the table. When the milk of human kindness was flowing down the road, Mr Whippy was hiding behind the wall. Chloe resented the way he spat out the word bucks as if her money was somehow dirty. Your mother would never be beaten. She had Brad drive into town and come back with a few blocks of raspberry ripple and umpteen wafers, plain and ribbed. By the time we had served it all, it was dripping almighty, but that added to the fun.

Those were the times when summer days were long and lazy, or maybe time has distorted my memory. I shall never forget the squeals of delight as you learned to skim your first stone, the wonder in your eyes as it bobbed across the surface of the sea.

When I woke up this morning, the air was cool and damp. I so want to feel again the warm sunshine, the feeling in Kilteelagh when the windows are thrown open and the outside is invited in. I relish the memories of those days of freedom, when the dog could wander in and out, but preferred to flop under the shade of the butterfly bush, not far from the gazebo. My greatest delight on a hot day was to walk barefoot, skipping across the cobbles and tiptoeing along the stony path to the lake and the smooth cool of the jetty walk. Those were such good days, when the daily routine was replaced by a casual picnic attitude that recharges the brain and is good for the soul.

What am I rambling on about? Well, when I woke up this morning the day was grey and cold, the air damp and I pulled on my wool shawl. I wanted to stay in bed, but I forced myself downstairs to make a pot of tea and sit at the kitchen table and write this letter. There are the sunny days, Marianne, and there are days like this, when it is an effort to do anything at all or work up any kind of enthusiasm. Life, when it offers you the sunshine days, is handing out a special gift. This should not be taken lightly, because it is the sun-filled days that bring us through the grey ones.

As I sit here, I know that in the later afternoon at Kiltee-lagh, the sun will break through and for one hour and maybe two, all will be right with the world. The flowers in the garden will raise themselves to the sun and the animals in the fields will wander to graze apart. Inside the drawing room, it will be too hot by the window, and you will have to angle the chairs at the fireplace to escape the glare.

At Kilteelagh, like life, there are the grey hours and the sunshine days. Make sure you cherish the warmth of the sun and let it heal you when you need it most.

All my love,

Collie xx

Marianne pushed the letter onto the bedside table and pulled the duvet over her head. The rain pelted down outside, drumming out a symphony of sound on the stable's corrugated roof. The house was quiet, as if the intensity of the rain had drowned out all possible sounds. Giving up on a lie-in, Marianne got up and pulled on Collie's velvet dressing gown. On the first landing, she stopped to peek into Katie's room, smiling when she saw her fast asleep, the rabbit squished under her head. When she saw the light under Rachel's door suddenly go out, she tapped lightly and looked in. 'Can't you sleep either?' she asked softly.

Rachel, her head under her pillow, didn't move or answer. Marianne knew she was only pretending but she retreated, making her way downstairs to the kitchen. The house felt damp and chilly; three days of rain had chased the summer away. Scrabbling around the food cupboard, she took out the hot chocolate, put a pan of milk on the hob, spooned in the chocolate and stirred. When she heard Rachel come downstairs, she reached for two mugs.

'It's August, but more like December out there; hot chocolate should make things better.'

Rachel slipped in to sit at the table.

'You don't look well. Are you feeling all right?' Marianne asked quietly.

Rachel shrugged her shoulders and cupped the mug of hot chocolate Marianne slid across the table. They sat opposite each other, sipping quietly until Rachel took out her phone and began to scroll Snapchat.

'You know you can talk to me. I might be able to help,' Marianne said.

'Who says there's anything wrong?'

'You came home from your day out and went straight to your room. It might be best to talk about it.'

'As if you would have any answers.'

'That's true, but I've been told I'm a good listener.'

Rachel slurped her chocolate and continued to scroll on her phone. The dog whined to go out and Marianne got up and opened the back door. The rain whooshed in by the wind swirled around them, making Rachel hunch her shoulders more. The dog ran under the table.

'Darned dog, I never get it right with him,' Marianne said.

'He's showing you up because he can.'

'That leaves me with a warm, fuzzy, good feeling for sure.'

Rachel shrugged. Marianne pulled over the biscuit tin and took out a packet of chocolate fingers and pushed them across the table.

'We have hot cocoa and chocolate biscuits, and I'm ready to listen.'

Rachel pushed back her chair and stood up. 'Why can't you stop being so damn nice? You're here, my mother isn't. Nothing is going to change that.'

Rachel made to walk past Marianne, but she jumped up

and blocked her way. 'Rach, I thought things were OK between us, and even if they aren't, I want to help.'

Rachel shoved lightly against her and Marianne, grabbing her chance, caught the young girl tightly around both arms. 'I know it sucks, but I'm all you've got. I'm here and it's bloody raining outside, so we might as well be doing something.'

'You don't give up, do you? You need to take a hint,' Rachel said, gently pulling away.

'Grandma Collie gave me a job to do, and I'll be dammed if I don't do it. Besides, you guys are my family. What am I supposed to do, walk away and pretend everything is hunky-dory?'

'I can sort it out myself. You don't have to jump in and solve everything for me.'

'I don't, but I want you to know I'm here whenever you want to talk.'

Rachel grabbed some chocolate fingers from the biscuit tin then muttered that she was going back to bed.

Marianne headed into the dining room. It was her haven away from the teenage angst and small-person problems. Picking up an ochre yellow silk, she wrapped it around the mannequin to make a tight, ruched bodice with tiny straps and a long flowing A-line skirt. She pinned it into place and took a photograph with her phone to send to Jay. It would be so good to talk to him right now.

It was only 10 p.m. in New York, so she dialled his number. When Jay answered, she heard chat and the hum of a busy bar behind him.

'Marianne, it's so good to hear from you, but I'm out with clients – we're waiting for a table at Le Bernardin. Can I call you back tomorrow?'

'OK. I just wanted to chat, maybe run a few ideas by you. New design ideas.'

'Girl, you need to come back to Manhattan before you

change even more. There's still time to dump it all over there in paradise and come home to work for a living. I still think it was a mistake to write off your office-to-cocktail collection, and if you feel like a change, Richard, my boss, is looking for somebody just like you. In fact, he was asking about you the other day.'

'Very funny, but I'm not going to uproot these two girls. They need to stay here, and that means I stay here too.'

'Darling, can we talk about this another time? They've called us to our table and I'm going to have to be on my best behaviour. I can just about pass this off as a business call, but not for much longer. Richie is giving me dagger eyes.'

'OK, talk soon.'

Marianne knew that before she'd finished her sentence, Jay had already cut her off. Pushing the phone into her dressing gown pocket, she felt tears rise up inside her for the life she had left behind, the conversations, the arguments, the chat and the gossip.

'Can we talk a little bit – but I don't want to be cross-examined.'

Rachel was standing in the doorway, her voice high-pitched with nervousness.

'Sure, sit down.'

'Who were you talking to?'

'My friend Jay in the States.'

'A guy?'

'Yeah.'

'Is he your boyfriend?'

'Jay? No, he's gay and a colleague. Well, he was a colleague in my old life.'

'Do you miss it?'

Marianne sat down. 'I do, sometimes.'

'I know where I'd rather be. It's a no-brainer.'

'But this is home, Rachel, and that means something.'

Rachel got up and poured a little milk in the dog bowl.

'It's easy for you to say because you know New York. You've lived there. Us, all we know is Balgaddy and Greystones and a few other towns and, every once in a while, Dublin. It's all pretty crap.'

'Is that what's wrong – that everything's crap?'

Rachel didn't answer at first, but stroked Benji gently as he slurped the milk noisily.

'I want to go out with a group of girls. Their parents are allowing them. We want to go shopping and have pizza.'

'Who are these girls? Are they your friends?'

'Yeah, it's Dublin tomorrow. Can I go?'

'You have to be careful in the city. You know what happened last time.'

'We know and we will be home by six, I promise.'

'Maybe I could talk to one of the other parents.'

Rachel jumped up. 'Please don't embarrass me, I want a day out with some friends, that's all. I will keep in touch, I promise.'

'What time are you thinking of leaving?'

'Does that mean I can go?'

'Who else is going?'

'Ella, Dearbhail, Megan. They all live in Greystones.'

'I haven't heard you mention their names. Are they new friends? What about Laura?'

'Laura doesn't want to be friends with me any more. I like these girls, they're cool.'

'Are they nice girls?'

'Yeah, I think so.'

'As long as you're home by six, I suppose it's OK. You must keep in touch. I'll text you a few times to see how you are doing.'

Rachel's face brightened. Reaching over, she hugged Marianne lightly. 'Thank you, you really are the best.'

'I'm not sure Grandma would have allowed it. but I'm trusting you, Rachel. Do you understand?'

Rachel nodded and asked could she go back to bed. As she listened to her light footsteps on the stairs, Marianne worried that she had given in too easily. She turned off the kitchen light and locked the door so the dog wouldn't sneak upstairs and get on the beds. The rain had stopped and the house was quiet, the stillness that comes when a storm has passed. Maybe Collie wouldn't have allowed Rachel into the city, but Marianne put the thought out of her mind. It somehow felt right, and she hoped by tomorrow night she would feel the same way.

FIFTEEN

Marianne dropped Katie at Sarah's house, then drove Rachel to Greystones DART station to meet up with her friends.

'If you're not happy, ring and I can collect you.'

'We're only going shopping; I hardly think I'm going to hate that.'

'And watch your money and your phone, you don't want to lose either.'

She knew Rachel was humouring her when she promised everything would be OK.

'You're just going to drop me, right? I don't want you getting out or thinking you can wave at the train or anything,' Rachel asked anxiously as they drove down Greystones' main street to the station.

Marianne guffawed loudly. 'Hey, it wasn't so long ago when I was your age myself and mortified if my mom tried to strike up a conversation with my friends.'

Rachel, she could see, was agitated or excited or maybe a combination of both, so she concentrated on the driving. When she pulled up outside the station a group of about four girls all squealed and waved. Rachel jumped from the car, not bothering to say goodbye. Her step was light and her back straight as she skipped across the road to the group. She flinched when she saw Katherine approach the girls and talk for a few moments to Rachel, before making her way towards Marianne's car.

Katherine rapped on the passenger seat window.

'Hardly any of my business, but is it wise to let Rachel high-tail it off to Dublin with that lot?'

'They're her new friends, and it might be nice for her to get away from home for a while.'

'Really, is that your attitude?'

'Katherine, I don't mean to be rude, but this is none of your business,' Marianne said, glad her voice was stronger than she felt.

'She is flesh and blood, Marianne, and if you don't care about the girl, I do. That lot are bad through and through. She's a changed girl since she hooked up with that crowd.'

'She is keeping in touch by text with me and will ring if anything is the matter.'

'Fat lot you can do stuck at Kilteelagh, but as I say, none of my business.'

'Exactly, Katherine, it's not.'

Marianne revved up the car and pulled out into the traffic before her aunt could reply. The elation of getting one over on Katherine was short-lived. Her mother had always said the two people in the family you never fell out with were Collie and Katherine, because both had a capacity to harbour a long grudge. Feeling nervous and anxious to make amends, she stopped the car and dialled Katherine's number but there was no answer. She decided to go home and drive around to Katherine's before lunch. Back at Kilteelagh, she couldn't settle. Maybe she was wrong to let Rachel off to Dublin with those girls, but she wanted to see her happy face and give her a little bit of independence.

To take her mind off things, she sat with a small piece of

charcoal and began to sketch a summer dress. She imagined it in Collie's blue silk, the folds of the skirt wafting in the light breeze, the only embellishment the small ruffle at the end of the short, straight sleeves.

When she saw Jack park his car, she waved and beckoned to him to come into the house. He was already in the kitchen when she made it down the hallway.

'I found a coffee machine in an unopened box and wondered would you like a cup? It won't take long to brew.'

'Are you sure you're not in the middle of something?' he said, his voice flat.

'I also meant to say thanks for helping with our flood in the bathroom last month.'

'No need.'

She felt uncomfortable. 'Jack, it's hard becoming a parent at a moment's notice, as well as running Kilteelagh and trying to work out what my future is. I'm sorry about my reaction back when you asked me out for coffee.'

'Water under the bridge,' he said, and sat down at the table.

She busied herself filling the machine with ground coffee and water, then sat opposite Jack at the table.

'How are things going?' he asked gently.

Marianne sighed deeply. 'You'll think I only asked you in to unburden myself.'

'And didn't you?'

'Maybe.'

'There's nothing wrong with that; we all need to talk at times.'

'Is Sarah your eldest?' she asked as she took two mugs from the dresser and checked the machine.

'My eldest, but I know what it's like with teenagers. Sarah's half-sister is eighteen years old.'

'I let Rachel go off to Dublin with girls I haven't even met.'

'Does Rachel know them?'

'She calls them her friends, but I've never heard her talk about them before.'

'Keep in touch with her, and hopefully everything will be OK.'

'It's just Katherine saw her at the DART station and made a big deal of me letting her off on her own with a bad lot.'

'These days Katherine would make a big deal of anything.'

Marianne took the coffee pot and poured hot coffee into each mug. 'It sounds like you've heard things about me.'

'Nobody is listening to Katherine. She's bitter that you have Kilteelagh and the girls.'

'I should make my peace with her, but I don't know how.'

'Katherine is the type who won't make any peace until it is on her terms.'

'Does she expect me to walk away from Kilteelagh, Rachel and Katie?'

'That's exactly what she wants, and make sure you don't give in to her.'

'Easier said than done. Bridie Murphy in the post office still won't talk to me, and I noticed my post is only delivered on a Monday and Friday, and I know from the number of letters she is letting them pile up.'

'She wants you to go in and complain, so she can have a go at you. Bridie has a sharp tongue, so best avoid that. Go over her head, raise it with the district office in Bray. That should put manners on Bridie.'

'I should talk to you more often about my problems in Balgaddy.'

'So, let's set a date for another coffee,' he said, and immediately shook his head. 'I didn't mean a date as such...'

Marianne didn't say anything at first, unsure how she should react. When she saw he was waiting for her answer, she mumbled that she would ring him.

'I look forward to that call,' he said.

Marianne sighed loudly.

'You're worried about Rachel?' he asked.

'Would you have let her go to Dublin?'

'It's not going to help to know what I would've done. She's gone now, and you will have to hope she uses her common sense if anything arises.'

'I hope you're right.'

Jack took Marianne's hand. 'You worry too much. Trust in yourself and in them. You're doing an amazing job. Don't let Katherine pull you down.' She didn't take her hand away; she liked his gentle touch.

'It's easy for you to say, but I have Collie on my shoulder. If I mess up, she'll probably come back and haunt me.'

Gently, she pulled her hand free.

Jack laughed nervously and slurped down the last of his coffee.

'I'm hoping to get a start on the gazebo today. If you need me, just phone or come out on the top step and shout,' he said. He hesitated before leaving the kitchen, but Marianne's mind was full of worry, and she barely noticed.

There was no point tiptoeing around Katherine any more, she realised; it was time to confront her. Without thinking too much about it, in case she backed out, she got in her car and drove the short distance to her aunt's house. Hesitating when she saw Katherine in the kitchen, she noticed her aunt didn't bother to look up from what she was doing when she heard the car approach. When she opened the door, Katherine had a glass of wine in her hand. 'The weather is so piss awful, there's only one thing to do: drink enough so we don't notice. What do you want?'

'We need to talk.'

'Talk, talk, what's the point of talk? Unless – are you giving up on Kilteelagh at last?'

Marianne felt like shouting at Katherine, but instead she shook her head.

'We have nothing to talk about then,' Katherine snapped.

'We are family. We can't ignore that.' Marianne moved closer to her aunt. 'Do you think Chloe or Collie would like what is going on?'

'Mother could have prevented all this shite if she had done the right thing in the first place.'

'I feel we're going around in circles. I'm here to stay, Katherine, and it would be so much better for our families if we could get on.'

Katherine banged her glass of wine on the table, making the liquid plop across the tablecloth.

'Easy for you to say when you're holding all the cards and the keys to Kilteelagh House. I worked hard for Collie, especially the last months, looking after her. I don't understand why she left me out like this.'

'But she didn't leave you out entirely.'

'Sorry, I forget the four fields with the damp scutch grass that is worth nothing to no one and a bunch of share certificates. Am I supposed to be grateful?'

Marianne turned to the door to leave.

'Sit down, I'm not finished yet,' Katherine said gruffly.

Marianne hesitated, her hand on the doorknob. Katherine got a glass down from the dresser. 'We can at least try to be civilised. Do you want a drink?'

'I'm driving.'

Katherine spun around, one hand on her hip, the other waving the glass of wine about like it was a torch. 'Aren't you the party pooper?'

'I'm sorry, Katherine, I really can't drink. I promised Rachel, if she needs me, I'll drive to collect her—'

'And you wouldn't have this problem if you hadn't let her go in the first place.'

Katherine reached for the bottle of Chardonnay and topped up her glass. Opening the fridge door, she took out a bottle of Pellegrino water. 'Sparkling, I'm afraid.'

'That's fine.'

Katherine poured the water into the glass and handed it to her niece. Marianne twiddled with the glass stem, keeping her eyes on the flowery tablecloth. Katherine sat opposite, arranging her kaftan as she did.

'You were a silly girl ever to leave New York. If I had a chance of living there, I would grab it with both hands.'

'I wanted to honour Grandma's wishes.'

Katherine got up and pulled down her packet of cigarettes from the top of a kitchen cupboard.

'No brownie points for honouring the wishes of a dead woman. Collie wasn't all she was cracked up to be. It might be best if you didn't idolise her so much.'

'She was always good to me and my family. She was a good grandmother. Anyway, New York didn't hold much for me after losing my mom and dad.'

'And you think living at Kilteelagh will be any different? You've jumped from the frying pan into the fire. You can change your mind; those girls will be just fine right here.'

Marianne stood up. 'Is this what it's all about? You want Rachel and Katie?' Katherine stared at her, but said nothing. 'I am Katie and Rachel's guardian. I don't intend on reneging on that any time soon. I wish you wouldn't be like this, Katherine; it makes it difficult to be friends.'

Katherine tipped a cigarette from the box and lit it with a lighter she took from inside a cup on a top shelf. Tipping her head back, she pursed her lips and blew a smoke ring to the ceiling, before she answered Marianne.

'When it comes to family and land, there is more war than peace.'

Marianne opened the door and was about to go out when she turned back to Katherine. 'I have always admired you, particularly as a mother. I don't want it to be like this.'

'It needn't be. What am I asking you to do? Go back to the most amazing city in the world and live your young life. What's wrong with that?'

'Collie wanted me to take over Kilteelagh and that's what I'm doing, like it or lump it.'

'You're being stubborn, just like Collie. She refused to get rid of Kilteelagh when it was falling around her ears and only adding to her health problems. That house will break you, Marianne. Best to sell it now and reap the benefits.'

'I don't want to quarrel, Katherine. You and the girls are all I have left of the Keane family.'

'Life is hard, and sometimes we have to make decisions which will put us in conflict with those we once loved. Think long and hard about what you're doing.'

'I want to become friends, but I'm going to go now,' Marianne said as she stepped into the yard.

Gesturing for her to wait, Katherine went to a bureau beside the window and pulled open a drawer. 'I have something here I've been meaning to give you, but I keep forgetting. It was Collie's. I borrowed it and only wore it once. It's yours now, like everything else at Kilteelagh.'

Katherine scrabbled around in the drawer and took out a small ring box.

'You don't have to do this, Katherine. I don't want it.'

'I do. It's not mine and was never intended for me. I don't want anyone implying I took it from my mother when she was on her deathbed. It's yours, you have it,' she said, her voice sharp.

She looked directly at Marianne. 'Those tough days when Collie was so ill, it was hard sitting in that room. She liked to have the curtains drawn back and, no matter how bad she was, if you touched them, she rose up like a dragon. I was always the fidgety type; I used to pace the room and one day, I opened the drawer in her dressing table. It was a right treasure trove. I was surprised to find this box. I never knew Daddy bought it for her. I was going to Dublin the next day, so I took it. I wore it and, boy, did it make me feel good. You and your mother were always her favourites. She obviously wanted you to have everything, and it's best if you have this too.'

'It hardly matters now.' Marianne pushed Katherine's hand away when she reached over with the box. 'I doubt Grandma would mind you having it. She was always so generous.'

Katherine laughed, her face twisting into a sneer. 'She was generous when she wanted to be, but mostly she was a stubborn old bat who never knew when to give in and when not. That's why she left you that heap of a house and me out in the cold.'

She pressed the box into Marianne's hand. 'I never saw her wear it. I don't know if it meant anything to her.'

As Marianne carefully opened the velvet box, Katherine leaned forward. 'I don't expect it's worth much, and the purple stone is sort of gaudy. Collie was never that flash.'

Picking up the ring, Marianne turned it over in the palm of her hand. A gold band with alternating white and purple stones, it glinted in the light. 'Could those be diamonds?'

'I will eat my hat if they are. What would Collie be doing with a diamond ring my father could never have afforded?' Katherine said.

Twisting the ring, Marianne examined it closely. On the inside of the band, the name of the maker: Tiffany and Co. 'I think we can take it that these are diamonds. It's a very beautiful ring.'

'Can't say it does anything for me – and what did Collie

need it for anyway, stuck in a dilapidated mansion in County Wicklow?'

Marianne didn't answer, but carefully returned the ring to the box.

'Keep it, Katherine,' she said.

'I don't want her stupid ring, it's yours,' Katherine said, pushing Marianne's hand and the box away.

Back at Kilteelagh, Marianne opened the ring box again. Katherine spoke a lot of nonsense at times, but she was right that this ring somehow did not fit with Collie. Walking to the drawing room, she left it on the mantelpiece. She must remember to ask Dolores if she knew its backstory.

In the meantime, she couldn't get Rachel out of her mind. She checked and rechecked her phone. She was annoyed at herself for letting her go to Dublin. To take her mind off her worry, she picked up a piece of charcoal from Katie's stash and began to sketch another summer dress on a spare piece of paper. As she smudged the lines and drew a figure-hugging dress that flowed from the waist down, for a few moments she felt like herself again and not the anxious, doubting guardian who never seemed to get it right.

SIXTEEN

Marianne was in her favourite place at Kilteelagh – the dining room she secretly called her design studio – when her phone rang. Absent-mindedly, she answered it, though she didn't recognise the number.

'Is that Marianne Johnson, the guardian of Rachel Keane?'

'Yes, is something wrong?'

Fear streaked through her and she strained to listen as Garda Michelle Downey introduced herself.

'I'm at Dundrum garda station. Rachel has been arrested after taking a sandwich from a shop in the town.'

'Are you sure? Rachel was in Dublin, shopping with her friends.'

'She was on her own at the time of her arrest. Can you come to the garda station to collect her? Do you need directions?'

'You're not going to press charges, are you?'

'That will be a decision for the DPP.'

'DPP?'

'Director of Public Prosecutions. We can talk about it in a while. Can you come straight away?'

'You will have to give me the Eircode and GPS co-ordinates.'

Marianne grabbed a pen and wrote down the address. Her head was thumping, but she walked around the house, making sure windows and doors were locked. Grabbing a blazer from the wardrobe, she tied up her hair, thinking she should look business like. She phoned Jack.

'I have an emergency with Rachel. Can Katie stay the night at yours with Sarah? She asked me earlier and I said I had to talk to you.'

'Is everything all right?'

'Yeah, it's stupid girl stuff.'

'No problem, Katie is having a lovely time and she's already borrowed Sarah's PJs.'

'Thank you so much.'

'Take your time and ring me in the morning. There's no rush.'

Marianne drove to Dundrum in thirty minutes. She didn't rush from the car, because she knew that once she got inside, life would become very difficult. She wished Collie were here, but maybe she didn't, because Collie would never forgive Rachel for having her summoned to a garda station. Slowly, she walked up the steps and into the public office. She gave her name and was told to wait.

The garda who walked into the public office and called her name was tall and broad with a smile on his face. 'I bet this is the last place you want to be,' he said.

She smiled, unable to speak. He buzzed her through and led her down a corridor and into a room where Rachel and a female garda were sitting at a desk. Marianne saw that Rachel had been crying.

She sat down beside her and took her hand gently.

'Rachel here was caught leaving the shop in Dundrum with a sandwich which she didn't pay for.'

'Was it some mistake, can I pay for it? Maybe she didn't have enough on her, though my card is on her phone.'

'There may be more to it than that,' the garda said as she shuffled the papers on the desk in front of her.

'We have explained to Rachel that as this is her first offence it may be that the DPP will give permission for it to be dealt with under the Garda Youth Diversion Programme, where it won't go on her permanent record.'

'Diversion Programme?'

'Everybody is entitled to a chance, and Rachel here, from what I've heard, sounds like a good candidate.'

'How do we get her into this?'

'Rachel must wait to see what is decided in her case. If she is accepted into the scheme, she will be invited back to the station and formally cautioned.' She turned to Rachel. 'Those kids aren't your friends, and you should stay away from them. They're trouble.'

Marianne edged forward in her seat. 'What happened exactly?'

'I'm giving you a copy of Rachel's statement and I'm telling her to talk to you about it.'

'I should never have let her go out with those girls.'

'Sometimes we can only try our best. It's not easy raising teenagers. We'll be in touch but, just so you know, there's a backlog, so it could take months.'

She opened the door and Marianne tugged at Rachel to follow her. They didn't talk as they walked down the corridor to the outside. On the steps of the garda station, Marianne turned to Rachel. 'What the *hell* were you thinking? What's going on with you?'

Rachel didn't answer. Marianne walked ahead. At the car she stood and waited for Rachel, who walked slowly behind her.

'Get in,' Marianne said. She had already started the engine when Rachel climbed into the passenger seat. Afraid because she felt so angry, Marianne turned the classic hits radio station up high so neither of them could talk.

Rachel sat with her head back and her eyes closed for most of the journey. When the car rumbled over the cattle grid at Kilteelagh, she shifted in the front seat.

'Do we have to tell Aunt Katherine?'

Marianne hit the brakes. 'Is that what you're worried about? You're arrested for shoplifting and all you can say is, "Do we have to tell Aunt Katherine"? It's a bit more serious than that, don't you think?'

'I know how serious it is.'

'Do you, Rachel?'

'Why did you come and collect me? I didn't ask you.'

'Would you have preferred a ride in the back of a police car?'

'I don't care.'

'Rachel, you do care. Cut the crap.'

Rachel opened the car door. 'You can't talk to me like that.'

Marianne put a hand on her shoulder. 'Oh yes, I can, and I will. What you have done is totally unacceptable and unbelievably dumb.'

'I don't care what you think. Katherine is telling everyone you are only playing house here. As if you really care; you can always go back to New York.'

Rachel got out of the car and banged the door before running across the grass to the gazebo. Marianne sat for a moment and watched her as she stood at the lake's edge, a lonely figure, her shoulders hunched against the damp chill of the evening. Slowly, Marianne got out of the car and tramped after her. The ducks streamed across the water towards her, gathering in the shallows, hoping for breadcrumbs. Rachel was kicking the soft ground at the edge of the water to frighten them off. Marianne reached into her jacket pocket and grabbed the crumbs she always carried these days and threw a handful far out, so the ducks would follow.

'Rachel, we need to talk,' she said.

Rachel said nothing, pulling her jacket tight around her.

'Can we start over, talk this through?'

In the distance they watched Steve walk across the field to check on the horses.

'Will I go to jail?'

'I hope not. I don't think so.'

'Can we talk here? I don't want to go into the house, it's almost like Grandma Collie can hear me in there.'

'Did the others leave you?' Marianne asked.

Rachel dipped her head, tears rolling down her cheeks. 'They said I had to do it, to show I deserved to be in their group. They said they had all done it and now it was my turn.'

Marianne grasped Rachel's hand and squeezed it. 'Why didn't you ring me?'

'I thought I could handle it; I wanted to get everything over and done with.'

'They have cameras everywhere.'

'The owner shouted at me and I put my hands in the air and the sandwich fell out from under my top and...'

'Anything else?'

'There was a bottle of Coke. I put it back on a shelf, but he said I wasn't getting away with it.'

'How long have you known these girls?'

Rachel's cheeks puffed up and she exhaled slowly. 'I knew them all along, but Grandma said I must stay away from them.'

'Ah Rachel, I should have been left a handbook on yours and Katie's friends. Grandma was a good judge of character.'

'I know that now.'

'You need to stay away from them. Do they go to your school?'

'No.'

'Well, at least there's that.'

'I'm sorry I said mean things to you.'

'We will have to get through this. I think it's best Katie doesn't know – or Katherine.'

'Yeah.'

Marianne caught a stone and skimmed it across the surface of the water, watching it skip five times before sinking.

'This is my fault, I should have done better,' she said.

'You weren't the stupid idiot who stole a sandwich. I don't even eat sandwiches.'

'Hopefully you'll get a second chance and not a record.'

'I've messed up big time, haven't I?'

'We both have. Now, let's get indoors. We'll just have to pray what the garda said would happen, happens.'

As they walked across the grass, Rachel caught Marianne's hand.

'I'm sorry, I'm so sorry.'

Marianne squeezed her hand. 'I know,' she said.

When they got to the house, Rachel asked could she go to her room. Once she had gone upstairs, Marianne went straight to the cabinet in the drawing room and took out a bottle of whiskey. Pouring a large measure, she sat on the velvet couch. Uncomfortable sitting across from the painting of Collie, she moved to the fireside chair favoured by Mike, where she did not feel so much under Collie's scrutiny.

She felt foolish for ever allowing Rachel to go to the city with those girls. If Collie were here, she would have created blue murder and grounded Rachel forever. Marianne had even forgotten to ground her for a day. She downed her whiskey in one. She needed to get lost in the fabric and the colour for a while. She needed to grab some time for herself, to recharge and gather strength. The road ahead was going to be long and lonely, but she had made a start by handling the latest drama on her own.

In her design room, she took out her machine, threaded it with cotton thread and placed the A-line skirt seam under the foot. As she pressed the pedal and fed in the fabric, letting the machine run down the long seam, she felt in control again. She pulled the second side seam together and ran it through the machine. Shaking the skirt out, she held it up to her waist. It was light pink cotton with the hint of a deeper pink stripe. The fabric required a simple design. This was her design, a dress for walks by the sea and in the countryside for sure, but somehow she also knew it would stand out in Manhattan.

SEVENTEEN

September

It had been a lovely summer getting to know the girls when they were not tied down by a timetable. Rachel kept busy with her part-time job and Katie was at Marianne's elbow, helping with the sewing, offering to water the roses and persuading Marianne to spend long days on the beach. It was a special time that Marianne, like the girls, used to recharge for the school year ahead and the start of the September rush to the year's end.

She was still in her dressing gown when she saw a car drive up the avenue. Alone in the house, she shrank back from the drawing room window, hoping to view the visitor unnoticed as the car swept up to the front steps. She was a little disappointed when she saw Dolores get out; she had hoped it would be Jack. She waved, forcing a smile on her face. Dolores, already at the top of the front steps, waved back and stood expectantly at the door. By the time Marianne opened the front door, her neighbour was already talking. 'Still in your dressing gown? Lucky for some. Do you mind if I come in?'

Dolores had this way of presenting herself as if everybody

had been waiting for her arrival. Stepping into the hall, she stood looking around as if she was passing the time until invited in further. Marianne fumbled with her dressing gown. 'I'm only just up. I went back to bed after the girls went to school.'

'Are you ill?'

'I needed to rest. I'm finding it hard to get back into the school vibe.'

'Well, there's no time for that. I hear Bridie down at the post office has taken it upon herself to visit you this morning, so we had better spruce up the place. Best foot forward, and all that.'

'What?'

'I told you, Bridie and her committee are all interested in Kilteelagh House. They will start by trying to be friends—'

'Dolores, I just want to go back to bed.'

'And give them the satisfaction of saying you are a lazy layabout? Not on my watch.'

'This is dumb, I'm not putting myself out for these people. Please, Dolores, you're going to have to leave.'

Dolores reached over and gripped her tightly by the shoulders. 'There's no need to get upset, best let them in when you have me here to back you up.'

Marianne pulled away fiercely. 'Best that everyone realises I can fight my own battles. And I say it kindly, but that goes for you too.'

Dolores didn't look a bit put out but clapped her hands in excitement. 'That's it, that's the spirit I've wanted to see for a long time.'

'And now that you have...' Marianne swung back the front door.

'What are you doing? Now is the ideal time to meet these ladies, when you are well capable of showing them what you are made of.'

'Dolores—'

'You know you won't get back to sleep anyway. They'll plague you, if you don't hear them out.'

'Like you are plaguing me now. Why would I want to meet Bridie or anyone associated with her? They're definitely in Katherine's camp.'

'Exactly why you should meet them and put them firmly in their place.'

'All right, but nobody is staying here for long. Let's get this over with.'

'I'll boil the kettle and make some coffee. You go and get dressed,' Dolores said, immediately taking charge.

'You're worse than my grandmother,' Marianne said as she stomped up the stairs.

'I'll take that as a compliment,' Dolores called up the stairs after her, then added: 'Hurry, girl, we don't want the women from the town committee thinking you stay in bed all day.'

Marianne found she wasn't actually unhappy at the turn of events. Sometimes she was lonely when Rachel and Katie were out, and Dolores had a way of buoying her up without delving too deep into the reasons why. She heard the ping of dishes being put in the dishwasher, the cereal boxes being cleared away and the milk cartons put back in the fridge. Marianne sat on her bed. She could hear the murmurings of Dolores to the dog, who was at her feet, monitoring her every move and hoping for a titbit. She listened intently. It was as if she was back in the days when Grandma Collie would let her lie in, saying teenagers needed their sleep. Usually, when she wandered downstairs after noon, the lunch and dinner would be cooked and simmering in large pots on the stove. Often, too, the cooling grids would be spread across the kitchen table and scattered with brown bread and white fruit scones, just out of the oven. She savoured the memory for a moment, the memory of good times at Kilteelagh. When she heard Benji set off out the back door barking, she quickly pulled on her jeans and jumper and tied back her long hair. When she got downstairs, Dolores was sweeping the tiled floor.

'Isn't all this over the top? I really don't know why we're doing it,' Marianne said.

'Because we can't have this lot getting one over on you, can we? They would be only too delighted to spring a surprise on you.'

Marianne poured a coffee from the pot.

'What do I care what they think? All that matters to me is Rachel and Katie.'

Dolores took off her jacket and hung it on the back door hook. 'Exactly, isn't that why I'm here?'

'I don't follow.'

Benji was barking and kicking up a racket down at the gate. Dolores caught Marianne by the arm. 'That'll be them, we'll act surprised, pretend we're having a chat.'

'We are having a chat.'

'They're here on a reconnaissance trip to see how you will take to the idea of selling up. They want to see you under pressure, and this is their way of finding out. We need a show of strength and a very definite and emphatic no from you, to selling.'

'Jesus, Dolores, what business is it of theirs?'

Dolores exhaled loudly.

'Remember, I told you Collie resisted advances from developers. Bridie owns half the town and every shop she has in her name would prosper if the Kilteelagh lands were built on.'

'But isn't it all zoned agricultural anyway?'

Dolores shook her head. 'It was, until Bridie became a county councillor. Now, under the development plan, the land around the town, including Kilteelagh, has been zoned residential, which means if you sell up, it's only a matter of time before the whole place is built on.'

Bridie's BMW zipped into the backyard, Benji following behind, barking and growling.

'You tell them where to go. That's what Collie did every time.'

'She ran them from the door?'

'Good Lord, no; she invited them in for tea, got all their plans out of them and then let them down ever so gently. They were always a bit afraid of Collie.'

They saw Bridie step out of the driver's seat and look up towards the roof. The other two women, Marianne did not recognise. They shooed away the dog and walked smartly to the back door.

'Did you see Bridie eyeing up the house? No doubt she will have a thing or two to say about the changes,' Dolores wittered as Marianne opened the back door.

Bridie rushed over, grabbing Marianne's hand.

'You are an absolute tonic; look what you have done for the old place. It's looking so well. Pink is such a brave choice.'

Bridie called over the other two women.

'Let me introduce Rita and Olive. Rita owns the flower shop on Parnell Street and Olive is the secretary at the school. You might know her already. Is it all right if we come in?'

Marianne stepped back and the three women trooped to the kitchen. Bridie hesitated when she saw Dolores.

'I'm sorry, we didn't know you had company.'

Dolores sat back in her chair. 'Now, Bridie, we're not strangers. We can all have a chat and a catch-up.'

'You have a new motor, Dolores, very fancy.'

'You know me, Bridie. Fancy is my middle name.'

The women stood awkwardly in the middle of the kitchen as Marianne skirted around them.

'We should go to the drawing room, there's more space there,' she said, directing the women along the corridor.

'Should we have come to the front door? Have you opened

it up? It's just Collie always said come round the back. She was nearly always in the kitchen.'

'We have opened up the front, but you weren't to know,' Marianne said, ushering the women into the drawing room and towards the couch. She sat on a velvet armchair and stared at her guests, who were sitting primly on the edge of the couch, waiting for her next move.

'This room hasn't changed a bit. I would have thought a young girl like you would have wanted to throw away all this old-fashioned stuff,' Bridie said primly.

'We like it as it is. Collie loved this room, and so do we.'

Dolores strolled in and said she had put the kettle on, then settled herself into the other velvet chair.

'You ladies are so kind to call on Marianne. She needs all the friends she can get in Balgaddy as she takes on Kilteelagh House.'

Bridie made to say something, but she stopped as Marianne coughed to clear her throat before she spoke.

'Ladies, I'm so happy that you have dropped by. My grand-mother told me all about the committee and all her dealings in the past.'

'Collie was quite a force of nature, and we didn't always see eye to eye, but I think we could have said we were friends,' Bridie said.

'Is that what you call it?' Dolores snapped, then she jumped up and said she would make the tea.

Once Dolores had left, Bridie sat forward in her seat. 'Thank you for making us so welcome, Marianne. I was afraid we had got off to a bad start.'

'When you refused to let me put a notice in the post office window?'

'A mere misunderstanding. I'm sure we can get past it. Katherine is a very good friend of mine, but I'm sure we can all be adults about the situation.'

'I'm glad you think so,' Marianne said, her voice frosty.

Bridie shifted uncomfortably in her seat. 'You're very like your grandmother. My granddaughter was telling me you're a dress designer. Quite a jump to leave such an exciting city career and come here to...'

'Look after Kilteelagh and my cousins.'

'Well, yes. It's a huge responsibility on such young shoulders.'

'I don't think my grandmother would have asked me if she didn't think I could do it.'

Bridie waved her hands around in agitation as the other two women sat further back in the couch, reluctant to join the conversation.

'I was suggesting nothing of the sort. Collie never did anything without having a good reason for it, and I'm sure she thought long and hard on this particular situation.'

'I'm very glad she picked me. Coming to Kilteelagh has opened up a new world for me. I love it here. I couldn't imagine living anywhere else now.'

'Well, isn't that something. I do believe you sound exactly like your grandmother,' Bridie said, her mouth set as if she was having difficulty getting the words out. Rita sniggered and the other woman tapped her lightly on the knee. Marianne barely noticed; it had just dawned on her that what she'd said was true: she couldn't imagine living anywhere else. A warm glow crept through her. Maybe this whole adventure was going to end well after all.

Bridie sighed and twiddled a thread the dog had pulled on the couch armrest. They could hear Dolores being busy in the kitchen. Rita nudged Bridie with her elbow. She shook her shoulders and beamed at Marianne as if she had just noticed her sitting there.

'Thinking of Collie made me nearly forget why we came here today.'

Marianne smiled, signalling clearly to Bridie that she was aware of her unease.

'We were hoping you would join our town committee. I know it may appear stuffy for a young person like yourself, but it's a good way to get to know everyone. Balgaddy is small but the Balgaddy Town Committee is really quite powerful.'

'I'm not so sure I'll have time.'

'You will be able to fundraise for charity, at least. Collie always made sure to do her bit, even when we were at logger-heads on other matters.'

'I should be happy to fundraise, though I'm not sure what's involved. As long as I don't have to bake.'

'There's one thing you could help with straight away. Could we have the front field for our Christmas market weekend? There's quite a following, and we get a chance to show off the best of Balgaddy.'

'Sounds like a fabulous event, but how many are expected to attend?'

'Obviously, the more the merrier. We would need the front field, and if those attending could use the front sweep of the driveway for parking and turning around...'

'I've only just had the driveway done; I'm not sure I want a lot of cars parking there, or the foot traffic across the fields. Isn't there somewhere more central this could be done?'

'We've used the town hall in the past,' Rita piped up, and Bridie hushed her.

'We were thinking of a winter wonderland theme, which is really more suited to the outdoors. We won't be a Christmas market like you see in Berlin, but I think it could be rather special.'

'There are animals in that field, and I'm not sure I want the disruption of a lot of people milling about. Steve looks after the animals and he wouldn't want them disturbed either.'

'But it will give you such standing in the community.'

'Are you trying to persuade Marianne to allow all and sundry in on top of her for a Christmas market?' Dolores asked as she walked into the room, carrying a tray of tea.

'Dolores, I didn't realise you could hear us.'

'I bet you didn't. You damn well know Collie would never have let a Christmas market be set up outside her front door.'

'Marianne can make her own decisions; she doesn't have to follow her grandmother slavishly.'

'You're right, she has a good head on her. Marianne knows well what is right for Kilteelagh.'

Ignoring the sharpness of the exchange, Marianne got up and poured the tea, handing a teacup and saucer to each woman. The service of the tea brought a moment of contemplation. There was surprise when Marianne's low but firm voice broke the silence. 'I realise I'm new to the area, but Dolores is right, I've known Kilteelagh all my life and only want the best for it. I'm sorry the Christmas market isn't a good fit. If I can help in any other way though, please don't hesitate to ask.'

Bridie put her cup and saucer on the coffee table. 'Of course, we find it very disappointing, but we respect your opinion and thank you for reaching the decision so promptly. It gives us time to look for an alternative venue.'

Dolores laughed out loud. 'What are you talking about? Balgaddy never had and never will need a Christmas market. It's a load of old balderdash.'

Bridie looked severely at Dolores as she edged herself forward on the couch so she could address Marianne directly.

'I know you have only been here through the summer months, but the winters at Kilteelagh are hard. I hope you know what you are letting yourself in for.'

'Can't be as bad as minus three in New York and several inches of snow. I'm good.'

'No underfloor heating at Kilteelagh. Let's see what you

have to say, come January,' Bridie replied in a lighter tone, but Marianne thought she detected a hint of bitterness.

Suddenly tired of having visitors, she stood up and extended her hand to Bridie. 'It was so good of you to come by, but I need to take a call from New York shortly. Regrettably, I will have to bring this meeting to an end.'

They walked slowly from the room. 'The front door is really quite lovely, maybe you could exit that way and walk around to your cars. I'll keep the dog inside, so he doesn't bother you,' Marianne said as she directed her visitors to the left.

'Oh, we've never had a reason to use the front door before,' Rita said, pushing Bridie in front of her.

Marianne turned the key and unlocked the door.

'There are going to be a lot of new things at Kilteelagh. You should come by again soon. It was so lovely having time to chat.'

When she shut the door as they made their way down the granite steps, Marianne was doing her best not to laugh out loud.

'Bridie can put that in her pipe and smoke it,' Dolores said as she leaned against the fireplace in the hall.

She winked at Marianne. 'It's around 5 a.m. in New York. Am I right?'

Marianne giggled, pulling a face to copy Bridie. Dolores joined in, her shoulders shaking as she laughed. 'There's a lot of Collie in you. If the old dear is looking down, she's one proud lady,' she said.

'I don't like Bridie, but do you really think she is after the land?'

'That lot have been after it for years. Bridie is money mad. She would throw you under a bus real fast.'

They heard the car rev around the corner of the house and go down the avenue. Benji, who had zoomed out the back door, followed for a while, but stopped at the rhododendron to bark before giving up and returning to his spot at the bottom of the steps.

'They're not dangerous though, are they? I mean, they won't do anything silly?' Marianne asked.

'Dangerous, no. Silly... that I can't guarantee.'

'No worries then.'

'Mind you, rows over land bring out the worst in us. You should know that from all this stupid business with Katherine, who no doubt was behind this little escapade. She just wants to show she has the powerful people on her side.'

Marianne dawdled in the doorway of the drawing room. Dolores was such a kind woman, and savvy too, but at this moment, she wanted to be on her own, to gain some peace in her head away from Kilteelagh. 'I think I might go into Dublin for a bit today, while the girls are at school.'

Dolores reached for her coat and handbag, which were thrown on the mahogany chair in the corner of the hall. 'I can take a hint; you go off and buy something for yourself. Take a break from this life and be a young woman in the city again. You owe yourself that at least, after putting up with Bridie and her pals.'

'You don't mind if I rush off?'

'Why would I? But remember, this is only the start from that lot. Now she's got a foot back in the door, Bridie will never give up. She's always wanted this land.'

'She should give up right now. It will always be a no from me. I don't intend to throw my grandmother's lifetime's work down the drain just like that.'

'Which is exactly why she didn't leave the place to Katherine. That madam would have sold it for a few crates of Prosecco.' Dolores blushed at the venom in her own voice and glanced quickly at Marianne to see if she had noticed. Marianne pretended she had not heard, preferring not to get drawn into a conversation about her aunt. The dog scooted into the hall, jumping up at Dolores and trying to snap at her hands.

'That Benji needs to get some manners. He would never have done that to Collie,' Dolores said as she made her way down the steps, holding onto the handrail in case the dog forced his way past her.

Marianne waited until Dolores was well gone before she made her way to her car. She drove through Balgaddy, waving to Bridie, who was back standing at the window of the post office, and Rita, who was brushing the path outside the church. She was stopped at the lights when the postman pulled up in his van.

'There's a letter for you. Can you take it? It would save me a trip out,' he said, handing over a white envelope.

Marianne threw the envelope on the front passenger seat, then steered onto the N11 link road. Turning up the radio, she was determined to forget about Kilteelagh for a little while.

EIGHTEEN

Dublin city was quiet. Marianne strolled past the horses and carriages near the top of Grafton Street. She stopped to pat one of the horses, who was feeding from his bucket. All the times in New York she had hurried by the corner of Central Park, afraid to get trapped in conversation.

'Any chance you want a turn of the Green?' the driver asked as he polished the brass on the carriage.

'No, thank you. We have these in New York too.'

'All the more reason to compare the experience; have something to tell when you get back home.'

Marianne shook her head and laughed. 'This is my home,' she said, sliding quickly away in case she was subjected to any more questioning. Strolling down Grafton Street among the shoppers, she let herself be seduced by the friendly atmosphere. Leaning her head back, she took in the height of the buildings, none more than three storeys over the ground level. She missed the skyscraper shadows of Manhattan, everybody rushing along, heads down in the knowledge that there were people above them in another world living their lives, laughing, being greedy or making love. Here, she walked along the street, the sky open overhead. She joined a group of people standing watching a street artist, but moved away quickly when a man wearing jeans and a hoodie asked her had she the price of a bus fare.

She wasn't sure why she had come to Dublin, given that she didn't want to shop. Maybe she'd needed to get away from Kilteelagh to understand how much she really missed it. She bought a takeaway smoothie and walked back up the street and crossed over to St Stephen's Green, where she sat on a park bench directly inside the entrance. Pulling the envelope the postman had given her out of her pocket, she turned it over in her hands. She knew it was another letter from Collie.

Kilteelagh House
Balgaddy
Co. Wicklow

My dearest Marianne,

Have you ever completely loved one person? If that has not yet come your way, I wish it for you. What I am about to tell you now, I have told no one: not Mike, my husband, not my daughters, and not even my best friend, Dolores. There are some secrets we need to shutter inside us, because to share them would mean an invitation to seek the input of others, and that is something, in my case, I could not bear.

I want to tell you first that I was happy with Mike. We had a strong bond, and when he died and he left me with my three young children, I thought my life would never be the same again. You are expecting me to tell you of someone I met after Mike's passing; please don't immediately judge me, but hold any criticism until you know the whole story contained in this letter. I am here today to tell you of Lucas, whom I met one glorious weekend at Kilteelagh. We were together for such a short time, but my love for him is eternal. I say that with utter conviction and a belief that Lucas was the love of my life, and I was his. Maybe we didn't get a chance to move on to the next stage of our relationship, the stage where a level of ennui is accepted. Or maybe for us, we put so much into those few days together, it could sustain us forever.

I loved Lucas with all my heart, and I still do. But when he literally walked into my life, I was not to know he would so tear my heart apart. It was before Chloe came along, and Mike had taken our two girls to see his parents in Limerick. I never really got on with his mother, and I made excuses so I could stay on my own at Kilteelagh that weekend. Mike knew I was looking forward to being on my own. He understood I needed a break from my daughters, my family and just about everything. I think these days women call it 'me time'.

Mike was a good and understanding man. What happened had no reflection on my relationship with him, but it has haunted me that I could never tell him, though I suspect he knew something had happened, because after that weekend I was a changed person. I wish I had something grand and romantic to tell about the first time I ever saw Lucas.

I was doing a bit of gardening, as much as you can when you have a field to contain. I was slashing back the nettles so they wouldn't crowd in on my daffodils. I had also picked a lovely bunch of daffs for the hall table. I didn't pay much attention when I heard the rattle of the cattle grid. Next thing, this man wearing a suit came up the avenue asking the way to the nearest train station. I told him he had a few miles walking ahead of him to Greystones, and he asked me what I was doing. He pointed to my bunch of flowers and said I shouldn't have picked them.

I had a few choice things to say to him, and nicely told him to mind his own business. He must have liked my spunk because he laughed heartily. Turns out he was from Holland;

he was a businessman and his car had broken down on the
Balgaddy Road. He intended to go back to Dublin and get a
mechanic to collect the car after the weekend. I couldn't leave
him stranded like that, so I rang our local garage and they
towed away the car for repair. Lucas couldn't believe my kindness and insisted on paying me back by taking off his jacket,
rolling up his sleeves and getting dirty, slashing away at the
remaining nettles for me.

We worked solidly together for about an hour. Then we got
a call from the garage to say the car needed a part and it
couldn't be fixed until late on Sunday. I was enjoying his easy
company. He made me laugh and, boy, did he listen. You know
when you feel that you are a right fit for a person? He wanted
to stay at La Touche Hotel in Greystones, but I told him to
save his money and stay at Kilteelagh. That was the start of it,
and not for one minute do I regret any of it.

When I look out at those daffodils, I remember the warm
feeling of companionship, the great laughter between us and
that this ridiculous man did not mind that his beautifully
pressed trousers got wet and muddy. I have never known such
complete happiness. I didn't think of Mike or the kids. I was
Collie Keane, and this man who had walked into my life made
me float. You're thinking I'm mad, or I was mad. But that is
what it felt like. I floated on a cloud of happiness. At first, I
offered him a room in the house and some food. We laughed
and talked as I led the way up the avenue. His suit was ruined,
so I got some of Mike's clothes and sent him off for a bath
while I got dinner. When he walked back into the kitchen
wearing Mike's corduroy trousers and check shirt, he looked so
different and so handsome, as if he should always be like that.
It was as if he belonged with me at Kilteelagh House.

We had two nights together and two-and-a-bit complete
days. Marianne, I have never been so committed to someone; I
have never, before or since, thrown myself with such wild

abandon. It was so freeing and so beautiful. For those days, I felt so loved, so unrestricted and so free. A strange thing to say, but with Lucas, I felt at home in a way I never did with my husband. Know this: I have never felt guilty for what I have done. This was not a fling. I would return to those days in a heartbeat.

I look back now and marvel at that weekend and wonder what could have been for us. Sometimes I worry – it was so long ago, was my love for Lucas a figment of my imagination? At least I have the painting to prove otherwise. I wore the ball gown on the second night. He cooked up a feast for us. He made me sit in front of the fireplace and he pencilled a few sketches. I didn't take it very seriously until a few months later the painting was delivered to Kilteelagh.

Mike was never happy with it. I had told him I had let a Dutch man stay. I had to, in case anyone from Balgaddy let slip he had been seen at Kilteelagh. I passed off the painting as Lucas merely repaying a kindness. Mike, to his credit, accepted the explanation. If he wanted to know why I was wearing the ball gown, he never asked. Possibly, he did not want to know the answer, so he avoided the truth by deliberately not asking the question. Mike was a gentleman and he continued to love me. I loved him, but what I felt for Lucas was a passion that I can hardly explain to this day. All I know is, if he were to walk in here as I write this letter, I would throw myself at him, because I have yearned for him and loved him all these years.

Please don't think any the less of me; my husband and children did not suffer because of me. If anything, I am the one who suffered, not being able to be with Lucas. There are days still where I feel a pain run through me that I don't know him any more. There are days here at Kilteelagh when the rooms even smell of him. I will love him forever; I can say no more.

All my love,

Collie xx

Marianne folded the letter carefully. Turning her face to the sun, she let the warmth of the rays wash over her. An overwhelming sense of sadness seeped through her. There were so many questions left unanswered, and there was nobody to ask. If she approached Dolores, she would feel that in some way she was betraying Collie. And to discuss it with Katherine would be to draw down the ire and outrage of a child. When a young couple sat on the bench beside her, Marianne got up and walked away. Sneaking back a look, she grinned to see them cuddling and kissing, oblivious to anybody watching.

No longer wanting to be confined in the city, she yearned for the quiet of Kilteelagh so she could process this latest news from her grandmother. Hurrying along, she crossed the road near The Shelbourne Hotel and made her way to the car park. Somehow, she felt this love affair confided in one letter was not yet finished in the telling. Her grandmother had never even hinted at another love, never let anything slip about the origins of the painting, though her insistence on keeping it over the drawing room fireplace was beginning to make more sense.

Traffic was heavy and she made it back to Katie's school just before the children were let out.

Katherine, who was talking and laughing with a group of other mums, excused herself and came to stand beside her.

'Look, I don't want a scene or anything like that, but Marianne, I seriously want you to reconsider staying on at Kilteelagh.'

'Not this again, Katherine, not here.'

'I have made an appointment with a solicitor in Greystones. I want you to know.'

'OK.'

Katherine took out her car keys and rattled them loudly.

'No, it's not OK. I shouldn't have to go legal. I don't want to, but you are giving me no other choice.'

'I'm not having this conversation with you, Katherine.'

Katie ran to Marianne and pulled at her cardigan.

'I need to write a long story tonight.'

'Oh, OK.'

She turned to say goodbye to Katherine, but she was already walking back to her car.

'What will I write about?' Katie asked excitedly.

'Anything you like, I guess.'

'Teacher says it has to be something about our family.' Katie was quiet for a while, before she piped up. 'I know, I could write about Grandma and the painting. Would she mind, do you think?'

'I don't think so. Why do you ask?' Marianne looked in the mirror at Katie in the back seat. 'And what do you know about that?'

'Grandma told me a famous artist broke down on the road near Kilteelagh and she had let him stay while his car was fixed, and he painted the picture to say thank you. I wish that could happen to me.'

'It sounds like a fine story.'

'But Grandma said it was our secret.'

'I don't think Grandma Collie would mind. I think she would be very proud you wanted to write the story of her painting.'

Katie, she noticed, was smiling and happy as they turned in at the gates of Kilteelagh House.

NINETEEN

October

Katie threw herself at Marianne, blubbering into her shoulder at the school gates.

'Darling, what's wrong?' Marianne asked, holding Katie close and walking quickly towards the car. Katie burrowed into her shoulder, unable to speak. At the car, Marianne unfurled the little hands around her neck and sat Katie on the bonnet.

'Sweetheart, what's the matter? Was somebody unkind to you?'

Sniffling, Katie shook her head.

'Whatever it is, I'm sure we can sort it out,' Marianne said.

'It's Aunt Katherine. She told Hetty and Molly they can have a big Halloween party, and everybody will go there, and nobody will come to our party. We always have a Halloween party at Kilteelagh. Aunt Katherine knows that.'

'Maybe she forgot. I'm sure we can sort this out,' Marianne said, opening the car door and persuading Katie to get in. Anger bubbled up inside her that Katherine could be so mean.

'In fact, why don't we go straight away and sort this out,' she said as she revved up the car. Katie sat quietly in the back seat as they drove through Balgaddy town. When they turned in to Katherine's, Katie began to cry again.

'What is it, darling?'

'I'm afraid Katherine is going to get very cross at us.'

'Not if I get cross first. I think maybe it's best if you stay in the car.'

Katie nodded, taking out her lunch box to eat some leftover biscuits. Marianne stomped across the gravelled backyard to the kitchen door. Not bothering to knock, she marched straight in. Katherine was sitting, a glass of whiskey in front of her on the table.

'So, you heard then?'

'I don't care what you think of me or what you say about me in the town, but how could you do this to little Katie?'

'How could you steal Kilteelagh House from me?'

'Katherine, I know you are angry at me, but this is really low, hurting a little girl like this.'

Katherine jumped up. 'What about what you have done to my children? We could have been well looked after, you too, if we sold Kilteelagh House, but no, the Yank wants to pretend she can do it.'

Katherine, who was still in her pyjamas and dressing gown, swayed and stumbled against the chair, making it screech along the tiles.

'You do know your two girls will be here shortly. Do you want them to see you like this?'

'Giving parenting lessons now, are we?' Katherine cackled loudly and refilled her glass from the bottle of whiskey on the worktop.

'I'm not going to argue with you when you're in this state. Clean yourself up; get yourself together and come around at seven to collect the girls. I will bring them back to mine; I should get to them on the road before they reach here.'

'I don't need saving, Saint Marianne. You're getting more like Collie every day that passes. And I can look after my own kids. I will give them the best Halloween party ever.'

Marianne took out her phone, found Steve's number and texted him:

> I'm taking the girls back to Kilteelagh; can you come and look after Katherine?

'Did she give you lessons? That's exactly what Collie liked to do too, creating a wedge between myself and my husband,' Katherine shouted.

'Get some rest,' was all Marianne said as she went out the back door, pulling it gently behind her.

Katie was sitting in the driver's seat waiting for her. She looked at Marianne's face and tears welled in her eyes.

'She got cross, didn't she?'

'Aunt Katherine isn't feeling well, so we're going to talk later. We will have Hetty and Molly back at our house for dinner.'

'I don't want them coming back to Kilteelagh.'

'Katie, don't be unkind. This is something that can be sorted out and we are not going to take it out on the girls.'

Katie frowned and unbuckled her safety belt.

'Well, I'm riding shotgun, I don't care about them,' she said, and Marianne smiled, allowing her to take the front seat on this occasion.

By the time they had collected Hetty and Molly and driven back to the house, Rachel was already there doing her home-work at the kitchen table. Marianne put down breadsticks and cheese and told the other girls to get on with their work while she sorted out supper.

'What's the choice? Our mum usually has a choice of three meals to heat up,' Molly said.

'It's Spaghetti Bolognese, and it's home-made,' Marianne said. 'I'm afraid no choice, but there's garlic bread too.'

She started chopping the onions. When Steve rang, she walked to the drawing room to take the call.

'I'm sorry, Marianne, that you had to see Katherine like this. I try my best to get rid of all the alcohol in the house, but when I'm out on the farm she runs into Balgaddy and buys more.'

'Has she been drinking like this for long?'

'For two years now. Between that and going off to Dublin to drink during the day, she's quite a handful. The girls are the ones who are suffering.'

'They can have their dinner here. Do you want me to drop them back later?'

'Please. Thanks, Marianne.' He hesitated and she could hear him swallow hard. 'I'm sorry about all the other trouble with Katherine too. She's taken the whole will thing badly.'

'I didn't ask Collie to leave me the place.'

'I know. She's not herself. And all this palaver with her pushing to take Kilteelagh from you is only stoking up more trouble for us.'

'OK. Well, I'll drop the girls back around seven.'

When seven o'clock came, Marianne left Rachel in charge of Katie while she drove Hetty and Molly back home. She thought of dropping the girls off and driving away, but Steve came out to the car and invited her in.

'I can't stay long. I've left Rachel in charge at home, and Katie can be quite a handful when it's just the two of them.'

'Katherine wants to talk to you.'

'Are you sure it's a good idea?'

'I hope so. I want to put all this behind us, and I hope I have persuaded Katherine to do just that.'

Nervously, Marianne followed Steve and the girls into the

kitchen. Katherine told the girls to go watch a movie and leave the adults to talk. Steve pulled out a chair for Marianne. She sat on the edge, conscious that Katherine was watching her every move.

'Katherine and I wanted to thank you for what you did today,' Steve said.

He looked at his wife, who muttered, 'Yes.'

He pulled out a chair for Katherine and asked her to sit down. She sidled into the chair. Steve nudged her in the side, but she pulled away from him. 'Come on, Katherine, we talked about this.'

'What do you want from me? To say it's hunky-dory that she got Kilteelagh and I got almost nothing from my own mother? I appreciate what you did today, Marianne, and it shows you have a kind heart, like Chloe, but I can't pretend I'm happy about the will. That's never going to happen.'

'I think I'd better leave,' Marianne said.

Steve made to stop her, but Katherine went to the door and opened it.

'Katie can have her stupid party,' she said, her face turning red. 'Now please leave.'

Marianne ducked out the door and jumped in her car.

When she got back to Kilteelagh, Katie was waiting in the kitchen for her.

'Did she get cross?'

'No. She said she's sorry she forgot about your party, and Molly and Hetty will be happy not to compete with yours, because it's always the best party at Halloween.'

'She said all that, did she?' said Rachel, walking into the room.

'Not in so many words, but Katie can have her party.'

'Can we have toffee apples and carve pumpkins and everything?' Katie asked excitedly.

'Nice to see my old Katie back. And yes, we can,' Marianne said.

'Every year Grandma let us have a big party. It's my favourite time of the year.'

'Oh, I never knew that.'

'How could you, living in America?' Katie said, her tone matter-of-fact.

Marianne looked at the date on her watch. 'It's only two weeks away, though. How are we going to get everything done?'

'You'll work it out. Can we go up in the attic and get down the Halloween decorations? Grandma never wanted to spend too much on new decorations; she said they were a waste of money.'

'She's right; it really is only a day or two at most.'

Katie's face fell. 'But I thought in the States, Halloween is a big deal?'

Marianne laughed out loud. 'I don't know anything about how you guys celebrate Halloween.'

'We always have the party around 2 p.m. for a few hours till it starts to get dark, and then everyone goes trick-or-treating around the town and in the housing estate at the far side of Balgaddy. I love Halloween. Can we get the decorations down now?'

'No, it's bedtime. We'll tackle all of this tomorrow.'

Katie pursed her lips. 'Please, please. It won't take long and then I'll go to bed, I promise.'

'OK, but it better not take too long.'

Katie jumped up and down and snatched a torch from the dresser.

'We have to get the ladder from the stables. I'll help carry it,' Katie said, bolting out the back door.

Marianne knew there was no point arguing. They carried the ladder between them and set it down in the hall. 'I suppose you know where the attic is?' she asked.

'The landing on the top floor. I'm not allowed on the ladder, but I'll hold it while you go up in the attic.'

'Marvellous. It sounds like I've got the short straw on this one,' Marianne said.

'I don't know what that means, but can we just do it?' Katie said, making Marianne smile.

They hauled the ladder up two flights of stairs, stopping for breaks every few steps. On the top landing, they set it up to reach the attic hatch.

'Do we need the torch?' Marianne asked uncertainly.

'No, silly, there's a switch on the right when you push up the cover,' Katie said, getting increasingly impatient to get on with the job. Gingerly, Marianne climbed the ladder and pushed at the hatch door with two hands until it released.

Feeling around the space, she brushed off some cardboard boxes before coming across a plastic switch and turning on the light. The attic was low and dark, the light only illuminating a small part of it. Luckily the box nearest the attic opening had 'Halloween' scrawled on the side.

'Found the box,' she called out, but Katie was quick to come back with an answer.

'Grandma always brought down two boxes; look around again,' she said.

Marianne pushed a few other boxes around. She saw the second box, just under her grandmother's tin sewing box, which she also grabbed, then made her way down the ladder carrying the Halloween boxes. She went back up to turn off the attic light and, holding the sewing box under her arm, she climbed carefully onto the ladder, making it wobble.

'Hey, are you holding it for me?' she called out to Katie.

Red-faced, the little girl scurried back to the bottom of the ladder. 'Sorry, I was opening the boxes looking for the spider Rachel hates.'

'Let's carry everything to the drawing room and you can have a good root through the decorations while I have a look at Collie's sewing box,' Marianne said.

She could see Katie was thrilled to have a free run on the decorations, so she went back to the dining room and cleared a space on the table for the sewing box. It wasn't anything special; an old USA Assorted biscuit tin, which had rusted over time. Prising open the lid, she smiled at the neat row of spools, mainly in dark colours. Satin ribbon and little bits of lace were folded neatly in one corner. A navy velvet ribbon was wrapped in tissue paper and separate from the rest. Her grandmother must have squirrelled it away in case she had to replace any of the velvet on the ball gown. In the middle was the red and green pin cushion Marianne remembered from childhood, the straight pins arranged in a circle on one side, the sewing needles on the other.

Carefully taking it out, she balanced it on the small table beside her mannequin and pinched out a straight pin. Being here at Kilteelagh with Collie's tools felt so right now.

She was about to return to the sewing box when Katie ran into the room with a huge Happy Halloween sign.

'We always put that over the painting, though Grandma said we should get a witch's hat for her instead.'

'I think we will leave the painting well alone. Grandma might come back and haunt us if we ever did anything to it.' She laughed.

'I put the spider on the bathroom door,' Katie said.

'OK, but aren't we going to decorate outside as well?'

Katie looked around her. 'When we're finished in here, we won't have anything left.'

'Oh ridiculous, we just need a few empty rubbish bins and brushes and white sheets.'

'Can it be like the three of us, a tall mama ghost, a teenage ghost who smokes, and me?' Katie asked, jumping up and down with excitement. Marianne hugged her gently.

'And we can put lights around the door. I'm sure I'll find them with the Christmas decorations.'

Katie clapped her hands. 'I know we will have the best Halloween house. What party games will we have?'

'I bet you didn't have Grandma Collie trying to organise party games.'

'Of course I didn't, she would never have done that in a million years. We always had snacks and we fed and petted the sheep and the horses in the fields – which was OK when we were very young, but not now.'

'You want a more sophisticated party?'

'Yeah, because I'm older now,' Katie said.

They heard Rachel cross the first-floor landing. Katie gestured to Marianne to hush. 'Let's see if she finds the hanging spider.'

There was a loud shriek from upstairs. Marianne ran to the hall.

'Who the hell put that spider there? Katie, I'll kill you,' Rachel shouted as she rushed downstairs looking for her sister.

Giggling, Katie bounced up from behind the couch. 'Fooled you, Rachie, Happy Halloween.'

Rachel threw her hands in the air. 'You know I'm afraid of spiders,' she said, then stomped back up the stairs.

Marianne followed her and knocked gently on her bedroom door.

'I don't want to talk to anyone, go away,' Rachel shouted.

'Can I have a quick word?'

'Whatever,' Rachel said as she opened the door and let it swing back.

'Look, I know it was a cheap shot, but to be honest, that's the first time I have seen Katie laugh out loud since I moved in here. I'm sorry if it's at your expense, but I'm not sorry it happened.'

Rachel flopped on the bed. 'OK, I get it.'

'So, will you come down and help us make three ghosts for the front steps?'

'We never put anything out the front.'

'Well, we're going to this year.'

Marianne turned to go downstairs, but Rachel called out to her.

'I'll be down in a minute, but Katie has to move that spider. She can put it somewhere else, but not there.'

'OK.'

'Promise?'

'Promise.'

Katie had already moved the spider. 'OK, I was listening on the stairs,' she said as Marianne walked by. A few minutes later, Rachel appeared.

'I found a few old white sheets for the ghosts.'

'We can use the recycling bins in the kitchen and the sweeping brush, though we will need some long sticks as well,' Katie said.

Marianne laughed and said they had better get on with it before she changed her mind. Rachel got two long sticks from the stables, and they set to work, balancing them against the front railing for support.

'We'll have to secure all three to the railings with rope otherwise they may blow away,' Marianne said.

Katie ran off and came back with a roll of ribbon.

'Heck, Katie, that is for the dresses; we will have to get something else,' Marianne said as she went into the kitchen and rummaged in the drawer until she found a roll of parcel cord.

'I thought the ribbon was pretty,' Katie said, her voice shaky with disappointment.

'Jack will be back working on the gazebo tomorrow, so I'll

ask him. I'm sure he'll come up with some idea to make sure they don't end up in the field.'

'But can't we put them out tonight? I found some battery-operated lights we can use as well,' Katie said.

'No thank you, we're not fumbling around in the dark,' Marianne said firmly. She looked at Katie. 'It is definitely past your bedtime. Upstairs, please, and I'll follow in a minute.'

TWENTY

Marianne was up bright and early and in her design studio. She loved the quiet time of the morning when the light bounced across the room and was reflected in the folds of mellow cream fabric, which Jack had erected on a series of curtain rods. He had said it was so she could easily remove them if she wished, but Marianne wasn't going to do that. She intended this to be her design hub, a place where she could turn Katie's idea for Kilteelagh summer dresses into a collection. Katie was right: the world needed the Kilteelagh summer dresses collection.

Jay, when he'd rung, had been a little disappointed when she told him she was abandoning her earlier capsule collection. 'Darling, I went to so much bother to get that back for you. Don't tell me it was for nothing.'

'Things have changed – *I've* changed since I came here, Jay. I can't see how designing cocktail dresses and business suits is the way forward for me.'

'But you know you have a market in office and going-out clothes.'

'I have this idea and I want to run with it as far as I can go. I want to bring summer to people's lives. They may be living in the city, but they can have some of that carefree, country feel with them all the time.'

'Well, that does sound lovely. Email me a sketch or two and let me have a look.'

'I really believe in it.'

'I've been making some great contacts in the fashion magazines. Get something together and you never know. If they buy this touchy, feely countryside summer feel, you might be on to something.'

Marianne walked over to the mannequin, which was now adorned with a light pink dress with a flowing skirt under a delicate-looking bodice with a square neckline. She wasn't sure whether to let the sleeves fall in folds to the elbow or gather them into a narrow band of deep pink velvet. Tacking the velvet in place, she stood back to inspect the design. Placing a little ribbon on the neckline, she fashioned a small bow. The dress should be worn walking across the fields and down to the sea. There was a faint floral pattern which would catch the light as the fabric moved with the wearer. Katie had suggested a patch pocket, but she hoped that she would be distracted enough by the velvet to forget.

Suddenly today it felt like sketches were becoming samples. Her favourite was the dress that Katie called a big bunch of flowers. Covered in wildflowers including daisies, poppies, cornflowers, cowslips and pink harebell, the light chiffon fabric was gathered at the waist from a bodice with an off-the-shoulder neckline; the billowing sleeves were long and collected into a frilly cuff. Sweeping the ankles, the dress had to be worn barefoot, the chiffon fabric backed with a light cotton lining to keep the wearer cool.

Last night she had worked up a sketch for a more formal dress in soft turquoise silk. It had a long skirt with a stiff high waist into which a pleated blouse was tucked. The deep V neckline with small, covered buttons down each side complemented the long, straight sleeves tied into one covered button at the wrist. She might just have enough to send to Jay, she thought as she moved out to the kitchen to get breakfast.

She saw Jack already hard at work at the gazebo. He waved across to Marianne and she sent a text inviting him to come up to the house for a coffee when he was ready. Making her way to the kitchen, she called the girls for breakfast. She was surprised when Jack appeared so promptly at the back door. 'I'm badly in need of caffeine; there wasn't any milk at home, and I miss my morning cuppa,' he said.

'I'm afraid we only have instant; I haven't had time to put on the coffee machine this morning.'

She had no idea why she was apologising.

'As long as it's coffee, it will do,' he said, pulling out a chair.

'What do you think of the gazebo, will it take long?'

'It's going to take another week or so. I'm stripping it right down and replacing most of the timber. I was looking at the carvings on the seat. Would it be all right if I cut them out as squares and set them into the new seating?'

'Is it that bad?'

'Worse. I'm surprised nobody has fallen through either the seating or the floor. Most of the wood is sodden and rotten.'

'Collie wasn't that good with the upkeep of Kilteelagh over the last few years. She did well to hang onto the place, and that was probably enough. I was thinking it would be great for a fashion photoshoot by the lake, whenever I have enough pieces ready. I will have to get the jetty finished as well.'

'Pieces?'

'I'm forging ahead with the dress designing, and hoping to get a collection together.'

'Wow, that's something.'

Katie, who was moving her cereal around her bowl, piped

up: 'We're going to be famous, even in New York, we're going to have fashion shows and everything.'

'Well, I'm glad I'm getting to know you now.'

Marianne looked embarrassed. 'It's early stages. Let's see how it goes,' she said.

'If there's anything I can do to help, just ask,' Jack said as he shovelled three spoons of sugar into his coffee.

Picking up his mug, he said he'd better get back to work. Rachel hurried through the kitchen, saying she was going to be late.

'Can we make our Halloween costume this year?' Katie asked.

'I'm sure I can run up something or other. What do you want to be?' Marianne asked, ushering her to the back door.

'A helicopter.'

Rachel sniggered. 'And I want to be a Concorde.'

'My little sewing machine will have to run overtime,' Marianne said.

Katie caught her hand. 'I'm serious about the helicopter. I'm fed up with being a witch.'

'Fine, as long as you accept my version of a helicopter.'

'Here we go, something really arty nobody can understand,' Rachel said, diving away from Marianne, who had reached over to nudge her waist.

Marianne couldn't wait to get back to her studio. Several hours later, after pinning her finished sketches to the wall, she stood back and looked at the five nearly completed summer dresses, the colours of sunshine. Each design was different, but each gave the impression of carefree summer days when the living was easy. She would have to dress them up and down to convince the city girls they could get away with such simple lines in a city setting. The Kilteelagh Summer Collection, she thought, by Kilteelagh Design. It had a nice ring to it, she mused, and the garments looked young, fresh and pretty. With a lot of luck, it could even be featured in a magazine.

Looking out the window, she saw Jack on a ladder working hard dismantling the gazebo roof. Someday soon, she would have beautiful girls wearing her summer dresses wafting about that same gazebo, paddling in the lake as a photographer snapped pictures. Up until now, she had been fumbling along, worrying how she could make Kilteelagh work for her, when she should have been thinking how she could work for Kilteelagh. Every new collection needed a backstory. She went straight upstairs and pulled Collie's ball gown from the wardrobe.

Hanging it up on the curtain rail, she examined the detailing of the gown and the neat stitching of the seams. If Collie could produce such a gown at her kitchen table, then her granddaughter could make her collection of summer dresses a success.

Taking the dress from the hanger, she carried it downstairs to the drawing room. If she cleared the furniture away, she might just have enough space for a runway. Holding the dress up to her, she sashayed around the velvet couch and towards the bay window. It might be time to think of introducing Kilteelagh Design to the world.

Dolores was on the avenue, but Marianne continued to strut like she was in front of an admiring audience. When her friend saw her inside the window, she hurried along.

'That dress was made for you,' she said as Marianne opened the front door.

'Come in, you can tell me what you think of the Kilteelagh Design idea!'

'Hey girl, what has happened since I saw you last? The years have slipped from your face.' Putting her hand out to touch Collie's gown, she ran her fingers along the folds of satin. 'I didn't know she still had this dress; it's so beautiful.'

'And it will be the centrepiece and inspiration for the collection.'

'You're going to make ball gowns?'

Marianne laughed and told Dolores to follow her. She opened the dining room door and invited her friend in.

'So, this is where you have been hiding away,' Dolores said as she walked over to view the sketches. 'It's not as if it hasn't been done before in one way or another, but there's something timeless and other-worldly about these floaty dresses. You're on to something here, my dear.'

Marianne pulled two mannequins into the centre of the room.

'Still at a very initial and rough stage,' she said, arranging the chiffon fabric across one of the mannequins to show a flimsy, floral dress which floated gently. The sleeves were not yet attached, and one side of the hem had been tacked up as if the designer was unsure of the final length. The other mannequin was draped in a sky-blue silk from when Marianne had been trying out different ideas the night before.

'Where did you get this printed chiffon, it's quite beautiful.'

'I used to know a lot of suppliers, and I just googled to see if I could find their European counterparts. This cottage garden chiffon is one of my favourites; they sent a sample by courier.'

'But who will make these dresses for you?'

'I can manage the samples myself, but I'll have to set something up long-term if I'm to fulfil orders.'

Dolores looked at her. 'Darling, you will have to set it up long before that, because the orders will come flying in from all over.'

'I'm not so sure, but thank you for your confidence in me.'

Dolores went over to the sketch of the more formal dress marked out in turquoise silk.

'Please can I have this dress? I have a wedding next year and

I want to wear it.' She made a face. 'That is, if you don't think I'm too old for one of your designs.'

'Don't be silly, I would be honoured.'

Dolores did a slow, reverential clap. 'The Kilteelagh Design Collection, I can see it now.'

'What would Grandma think?'

'She would be more than proud, but you really have your work cut out for you.'

'I've been sketching, so it's a matter of a lot of hard sewing work. I'm thinking of holding a proper fashion show, something small in the new year, to launch my designs.'

'You will have the show at Kilteelagh?'

'I'm not sure how I will do it, but my friend Jay in the States is going to help, and this house is such a beautiful setting.'

'But won't you need a whole team working for you, to get the best show and the best samples out there?'

'Although by the time I have trained somebody to the standard required, I won't have any time to design.'

'Sounds like you need somebody straight away who can do all those things and train a few seamstresses to do it right. You need to be free to design.'

'That would be ideal, but I can't see how it will happen.'

'You need someone who can sew and cut a good pattern...'

'Someone who can work to the standard required.'

Dolores cleared her throat. 'I can help.'

Marianne took her friend's hand. 'No offence, but this type of work is specialised.'

Dolores put a finger to Marianne's mouth. 'Hush. Before I moved to Balgaddy and the children got in the way, I worked in the atelier of a wonderful designer in Paris. I think I can find my way around a pattern and a sewing machine again.'

'Wow, for real?'

Dolores stood up and twirled.

'You may not like my taste in fashion, but I made all of these beauties myself. Here, pick up my skirt hem and look at the finish on the seam.'

She edged closer to Marianne, so she could pull up the hem of the flared and panelled poplin skirt and examine it.

'It's beautiful. I had no idea.'

'I often fancied being a designer myself, but my ideas are too far out. Who would want to buy anything I put my mind to? Neither can I sketch like that,' she said, pointing to Marianne's work.

Dolores pulled Marianne to her in a hug. 'Your grandmother loved sewing, too. It's how we first got to know each other, exchanging patterns and sometimes sewing together. Whenever things were down for her, she turned to her sewing to help make things right. In spring, she made a lot of outfits. Strangely, it must have been her dark time of year; I never really knew why, but once the daffodils showed their heads, Collie got sewing, often staying up half the night to finish a garment. Most of what she wore, she'd made herself.'

'I knew she had a sewing machine, but I never realised she made so many clothes.'

'It was like therapy for her, I think, although she would never talk about it. Boy, she was so proud of you, though. She had a big scrapbook of all your drawings since you were a kid, she said you were going to be a glamorous dress designer someday.'

'I wish.'

'Wishes can come true, but with a lot of hard work.'

Marianne got up and hung Collie's gown on the window shutter. 'Dress designing will have to wait for another day; first I have to make Katie's Halloween outfit. She wants to be a helicopter.'

'Has Katie played that old helicopter trick on you?' Dolores chuckled.

'What do you mean?'

'Every year she told Collie she wanted to be a helicopter, and every year Collie had the huge job of persuading her to be anything but a helicopter.'

'She's so keen on it, and I don't want to disappoint her.'

'Rather you than me, Ms big shot designer. Now, I must leave you to the helicopter dilemma. My book club is meeting to revisit the old classics. *Pride and Prejudice* this month. I had a look at the movie, couldn't face the book, but I won't be admitting that to anyone else.'

'Any ideas on the helicopter?'

Dolores turned around in the hall. 'That's easy. I always said to Collie, get the old top hat in the attic, clean it up and stick the propellers on it. Lots of bright colours, and run up a cape to match. Collie was dead set against indulging fancy ideas for Halloween. She insisted if she gave in to the helicopter, she would be asked for the Eiffel Tower next.'

'I think your idea might have saved my life.'

'If you say so. When will we sit down for a proper chinwag about your designer plans?'

'Let me get the Halloween party on Friday over and done with and I'll be able to concentrate properly on Kilteelagh Design.'

'Sounds like a plan. See you Monday, darling, and don't forget to send over the kiddies for their candy.'

Marianne was about to close the door when she saw the postman on the avenue.

Dolores stood and watched as he pulled up at the steps and rolled down the window.

'Letter for you, Marianne, with Mr Eager's handwriting on the front,' Dolores said, taking the envelope and handing it to her.

'You enjoy reading it dear; you can tell me all about it some other time. I will get a lift down your long avenue from Mr Postie,' Dolores said as she got in the passenger seat.

TWENTY-ONE

Marianne sat on the velvet couch to read Collie's letter.

Kilteelagh House
Balgaddy
Co. Wicklow

My lovely Marianne,

My favourite time is when the garden is quiet and at rest after thriving all through the summer months. A few flowers are still bold enough to try and bloom, and the dahlias especially may try a late last show. The yellow dahlia in the front bed hangs on for as long as it can and stands tall once the brazen annuals have passed.

Fill up the feeders for the birds again. In September, they ignore us as the chicks grow up and learn to fly, but in October my little friends return to peck and feast from the feeders. Spring is seen as such a time of renewal, but for me October is the key month, the bridge to winter and beyond.

It is time to tidy up the garden for winter, otherwise come spring there will be too much to tackle. But the cool chill of autumn is also a good time for the physical work outside. It's a good tonic too to clear the head, getting ready for the short winter days when the grey darkness comes in on top of us.

You must have been shocked when I wrote about the man I loved. I suppose I have to continue to address this now and tell you how I lived my life once he was gone. I missed him so much. There were days I thought I could not go on, and days I thought I should make my way to Greystones and get on a train. I had this crazy idea that I would go to the airport and buy a ticket to Amsterdam and go to him. I never thought it completely through; I was never going to rock up to his address and knock on his door or ring his bell.

But I am jumping ahead. I must return to the pain of him leaving Kilteelagh that weekend. I stayed in the drawing room, watching from the window as he walked down the avenue to meet his taxi at the gate. I felt my feet twitch, wanting to run after him, shout at him to come back to me; come home to Kilteelagh. I wanted to take his hand and let us walk back up the avenue together.

But my love for my family and my loyalty to our family unit kept me rooted to the spot. There was also my deep love for my children and the realisation that Lucas also had those same responsibilities. Before he left, we sat on the velvet couch and he told me if his circumstances ever changed, if he ever became free, he would come looking for me. He pushed his address into my hand and said I was to do the same. That if I ever called him to come, he would drop everything and be at my side.

I remember his words so clearly. 'This is not a fling; it is not an affair. I am whole when I am with you. I will love you forever. I will be in Dublin one more time. It is entirely up to you, but if you want to see me, I will be staying at The Shelbourne Hotel. Shall we say noon on 11 June? If you don't turn up at the Lord Mayor's Lounge, I will understand. If you decide to come to meet me, we can, for a few hours, be together and free of our burdens. It is for you to decide. I understand if you won't or can't. Nothing is going to change the way I love you.'

He kissed me lightly on the top of my head as I blubbered. I grabbed his hand and kissed it. After he rounded the bend in the avenue, I stood inside the bay window until the evening began to draw in and the light at dusk began to play tricks with my eyes, so that on more than one occasion, my heart skipped as I thought I saw his shadow flitting between the trees.

A weekend that was so perfect, it still makes me feel warm inside that I was so... loved. He wrote to me before 11 June and asked me to please meet at The Shelbourne. I decided to go. I felt in the Dublin hotel we would have the peace and anonymity that the city brings, and who the hell from Balgaddy would be loitering around there anyway?

I wore a purple dress I'd made from a Vogue pattern. It was floaty with a skirt that fell to mid-calf from a high waist. The bodice had a V neck, and it was sleeveless, with one-inch straps under a bolero jacket. Mike didn't pass comment when he saw me heading off wearing the dress hidden under a raincoat and carrying my high sandals in a plastic bag, so I could change on the train. He trusted me so much.

I was nervous walking into The Shelbourne on my own, but Lucas was there waiting. He stood up as I walked towards him. He was dressed up too, wearing a shirt and tie and a smart linen suit. I was so anxious I didn't know what to do, or where to look, but as always, his presence was so calming. He took my hand and kissed it gently, then led me to sit beside him on a small couch set into the window.

He never let go of my hand and I liked that. With him I felt complete; with him I felt like a woman again. I know in this day and age that all seems quite sedate, but I was soaring with happiness. I think for that hour I allowed myself the freedom to think that it could always be like this. I didn't consider the details, nor did I want to.

I don't remember talking a great deal at the start. We were happy in the hum of the lounge, just being together. Lucas ordered a whiskey, but I stuck to Earl Grey tea. When the silver pot was put down, he placed the strainer and poured, popping one cube of sugar in the cup, as I liked it. When he handed me the china cup and saucer, I remember wishing it could be like that every day for us.

That's what I like to remember from that meeting, not what followed, when I had to say goodbye forever, and walk alone from The Shelbourne back to the train station.

Neither of us had a choice. We both were married and had children. I wasn't brave enough to walk away from my girls. I could have walked away from Mike in a heartbeat, but my girls were part of me. Lucas said he wanted me to leave Kilteelagh later that night and sneak away with him, and maybe I should have. My heart wanted to do that, but the practical brain told me otherwise. Mike didn't deserve it either.

I remember looking around the Lord Mayor's Lounge at the beautifully dressed women, thinking any of them would be braver than I. I felt like a coward for not being able to step into the unknown.

Lucas was prepared to move to Ireland. He said he would find a job here. He was prepared to leave his wife and arrange to go back and forth to see his two children. He said we could work something out with Mike. God love him, Lucas had no idea what the word marriage meant in Ireland. I was sentenced to life, and no love affair was going to change that.

He knew me, though; he understood that I couldn't even consider his proposal. He didn't push me. He told me that one day he would come back to me; that one day we would both be free and when that happened, he would seek me out. It was ironic that only a few years later Mike was dead and I was on my own bringing up my girls at Kilteelagh House. I could have written to Lucas – and believe you me, there were many times I sat down to do that. But something inside me was afraid he had forgotten me. What would be worse than to spill my heart onto a page to find he didn't answer, or he did with so much regret, it would ruin what came before. There was also the fear in my heart that if I followed him and showed up on his doorstep, I would have to break up his marriage and tear him away from his children. I don't know if I was ready to take on that great burden.

He pledged that if he became free, he would come back. I trusted him to do that and as the years passed, I yearned for it more than anything. I clung to that promise all these years. I imagined a moment like in a movie, where he would come up the driveway and I would run to him. It became almost an obsession as my life here at Kilteelagh became smaller and lonelier. It became a pastime, much as others resort to knitting. Today, I asked Katherine to help me to my chair by the landing. To her credit, she didn't sigh, complain, or give out, and for that I am eternally thankful. But he didn't come. Maybe there is a way he and I will meet again in the next world. I certainly hope so, because I know it won't happen in this one.

As the years went by, I realised I had made a big mistake in not taking a chance on a great love. I have suffered for that, and poor Mike did too, which is my shame.

The only thing I did for Mike was not to tell him, and maybe that wasn't a mercy at all, because I know he was lonely, but there was nothing I could do for him.

My heart was with somebody else, and I never wanted to change that.

I will leave you for now.

All my love,

Collie xx

Marianne sat, the quiet of the house all around her. None of them had known. How had Collie kept it secret all these years? Was she waiting for him even as she neared death? Marianne's heart ached for her grandmother. She felt an overwhelming sense of sadness for Collie, waiting her life away at Kilteelagh for a man who never returned. Anger bubbled up in her too, that Lucas had not come back. Picking up her sketch pad, she climbed the stairs to sit in Collie's chair.

Carefully with her charcoal, she sketched out a woman wearing a simple shift dress. The sleeveless dress was above the knee. She wrote down the possible colours: ochre yellow, white or light blue. Pushing the sketch pad to one side, she decided to make her way to the attic and find the top hat for Katie's costume.

She dragged the ladder into place and climbed into the attic.

It was freezing cold, mouse droppings all over the floor. In one corner were boxes labelled with heart stickers, chronicling a family's life: 'Photographs Summer 1962', 'Christmas 2001', 'Photos 1991 to present'. Shifting boxes out of her way, she saw several suitcases marked 'Collie's stuff'.

Unzipping the nearest case, she peered inside. It was full of remnants and leftover pieces of fabric, which had once been carefully folded and stored. A deep green fabric grabbed her attention. Reaching in, she could smell sandalwood from a sachet Collie had placed there many years previously.

She pulled out a tight roll of light green silk, the fabric unfurling across the dusty floor. There was enough for a summer dress, which had been thought of but not stitched. A crimson-red heavy satin had been stuffed in a bag, long forgotten and never opened out. Marianne felt sad looking at the fabric that was never cut and stitched, the forgotten cloth representing dreams that had never been realised and were destined to be locked away in the dark.

There were three other cases, all with the same label. Behind them a sewing machine and another sewing box on legs. She remembered the sewing box, how it opened in a concertina of drawers each with different threads and needles. The white satin pin cushion was called the fancy one and contained the best straight pins with the multicoloured heads which Marianne always liked to arrange in the shape of the letter C. Tears rose up inside her, but also a resolve to make this new venture work for her and for Kilteelagh.

Dragging one of the cases to the attic door, she realised she would not be able to manage them on the steps on her own. She dialled Jack.

'Fancy a break? I could make a sandwich and a coffee. I might also ask you a favour to help get a few things down from the attic.'

'Give me five.'

'Come on up to the top floor – you'll see the ladder on the landing.'

As she waited for Jack, she unzipped another case. Luscious soft silks in bright colours fell out, showing different shades of taffeta underneath. Picking up one of the silks, she threw it across her shoulders, drawing it into her waist inside her jeans. When she heard Jack on the stairs, she pushed the cases to the hatch opening.

'There are a few cases, a sewing machine and a big sewing basket. And a top hat!' she said, as he began to climb the ladder.

'Don't you think you're a bit overdressed for a rummage in the attic?' he said.

'Oh this,' she said, pulling at the fabric. 'My grandmother kept lots of different fabric, and this is silk.'

'The pink and blue colour tones suit you,' he said as he pulled the first case towards him and heaved it out of the attic.

She handed the rest of the items to him, and he stacked them at the top of the stairs.

'Let me help you down,' he said, holding out his hands.

'I should be fine,' she said and stepped onto the ladder.

She wobbled at the top step, and he called out, catching her two ankles first and then climbing the ladder to steady her at the waist.

'Now, will you let me help you?' he asked.

Marianne nodded and he gently led her down the steps to the landing.

'Next time you want anything taken from the attic, call me and I'll go up,' he said, reaching to take a stray hair from her face.

She stood and waited for him to kiss her. She couldn't help but be disappointed when he didn't try.

'Where shall I take them?' he asked.

'What?'

'The cases and bits and pieces?'

'Oh, the old dining room to the right after the drawing room,' she replied as he set off, a case in each hand. She followed, stopping in the hall to look in the mirror. Her hair was a mess and she had mayonnaise on her shirt collar from when Katie got her aim wrong trying to squirt mayo on a bagel.

'You've picked a beautiful room to work in. You can see right down to the gazebo – or rather, you could when it was still standing,' he said.

Marianne looked towards the lake. Her heart lurched to see the empty space where the gazebo had been.

'Give me a few days and you will have the outline, I promise,' he said gently.

She didn't answer, but led the way to the kitchen, where she made grilled cheese sandwiches.

They were sitting at the table, eating, when Jack put down

his coffee cup and looked at Marianne. 'So, do you think you will stay on after the year?'

'I hope so, it's my intention to stay here with the girls, develop my design business and bring the house back, slowly but surely. Why do you ask?'

'Katie has told Sarah she prays every night to her mother to make you stay. I don't even know if I should be telling you this, but sometimes, as a parent, it's handy to get the inside track.'

'They know the deal; I've been honest with them.'

He pushed back his chair as he stood up.

'That all sounds very logical, but little kids need to be reassured a lot, particularly someone like Katie, who has lost so much.'

Marianne shook her head and sighed deeply. 'I never seem to get it right.'

'Look, I didn't mean to cause offence or butt in where I'm not wanted. Katie raves about you all the time. I think whatever you're doing, it's working.'

'Thanks. On this same note, you should know that Sarah has been talking about you and your wife to Katie. She says you're getting back together. It's made her so happy. That's so great for all of you.'

'What do you mean?'

'Sorry, have I put my foot in it? I was just repeating what Katie told me.'

He sat down at the table again.

'We're separated, nearing the finish line on divorce. It's all amicable; we just want to do the right thing by Sarah and her half-sister.'

'So why does Sarah think you're getting back together?'

'I don't know. We've been separated the last few years, and we've never told her anything else. In fact, the girls know the divorce will be going through soon. Maybe that's where this is coming from.'

'Kids. She must have got her wires crossed.'

'Yeah. Look, could I have another coffee for takeaway? It's hard to get my head around this.'

She switched on the kettle. 'Maybe I shouldn't have said anything.'

He took the mug of coffee, lightly brushing against her fingers as he did.

'I'm so glad you did,' he said.

He walked to the door but turned around before stepping out into the backyard. 'Marianne, it never seems to be the right time; we will have to work on that.'

She smiled and he laughed. His eyes were soft and warm, and she wished he didn't have to go, and that she didn't have to rush off and collect Katie.

TWENTY-TWO

November

Dolores arrived carrying a huge tote bag. 'I thought I would bring a few bits from my old life. All you need to do is clear some space on a table for me and I'm grand.'

Marianne took her friend's hand. 'I think we can do better than that.'

She led Dolores into her design studio and to a small desk set up at one of the windows.

'For you, the desk with the view.'

Dolores sat down.

'You're kind, Marianne, but can I change the aspect?'

'I thought you would like this spot.'

'I do, and it is indeed splendid, but if I stay here, I will have to swivel around every time I need to talk to you. My old neck couldn't put up with that.'

They each took one end of the desk and lifted it to the corner near the fireplace.

'Could I possibly stay here? There is such a lovely outlook on the whole room.'

'If you're sure.'

Dolores pulled her chair over and sat down. Taking a calendar from the tote bag, she placed it at the centre of the bureau.

'Nothing wrong with having a reminder of how many days we have till the new year and soon after, hopefully, the showing of the Kilteelagh Collection.'

'When you say it like that, it's a bit scary.'

'Nonsense. You're well able; I heard you had twenty-five kids for the best ever Halloween party, and you even managed to make a helicopter costume for Katie. After that, a fashion show should be easy-peasy.'

'I wish.'

'I think you should go for it. How many pieces will you have to show?'

'I'm hoping to have twenty or more samples.'

'Not near enough.'

'But there's just me and you – how can we produce more, or fulfil orders if we get them?'

'You should plan for up to thirty pieces, maybe twenty-five, and the same dresses in two different colours works very well too. And you will need your showstopper at the end.'

'I haven't fully decided, but I'm not going over twenty pieces.'

'Anything else?' Dolores asked, hoping to change the subject.

'Collie's ball gown; we could have the story of it printed on the invites.'

'The one in the painting? What condition is it in?'

'It's a gorgeous dress, beautifully made.'

'Agreed, but does it dazzle?'

Marianne walked over to the window where the dress was hanging, and she lightly ran her hand over the satin.

'Maybe if I used it as an inspiration; they could go down the catwalk together.'

'A nice way to pay homage to the dress that started it all. I can be your PR person, too, if you like.'

'Are you sure you can juggle all the different roles?'

Dolores pointed at Marianne. 'Don't mind me. I have kept a hand in the fashion world these last years with freelance consultancy work. I still know who to ring. But the pressure is on you because you will have to come up with a design to rival Collie's satin beauty.'

She reached out to touch the ball gown. 'I actually saw this on Collie once.'

'I thought she never got a chance to wear it,' Marianne said.

'Maybe it was when she was making it and trying it on for size. The funniest of things it was, when she answered the door. I was doing my rounds...' She tapped Marianne on the hand. 'I know you're busy, but this won't take long. It was back in the seventies when I used to call at every house, collecting donations for the church roof fund. I know I was stupid; the bloody priest drank most of it. Anyway, it was a Saturday, around seven, and I knocked on the front door. When there was no answer, I tapped on the windows of the drawing room. Next thing, Collie appeared wearing that stunning gown. She had the envelope ready for me. I whistled when I saw her, but you know Collie, when she didn't want to talk, she just ignored it and handed me the envelope. Only Collie could make it look perfectly normal to be answering the door in a ball gown.'

'No explanation at all?'

'I knew Collie well enough back then not to ask anything. I was a fool to think she might say something about the dress. Collie always kept her own counsel.

'It was only years later, when we became firm friends, that I saw the portrait and recognised the dress. I never let on to Collie, though.'

Marianne gathered up the silver-grey silk and pinned it onto the mannequin. Methodically tucking the silk into the waist, she crouched down to make sure she had a straight line. When she was finished, she looked around.

'What do you think?' she asked.

'It looks clever and beautiful and needs a very simple bodice and neckline to set it off, or maybe consider going sleeveless.'

Marianne gave Dolores the thumbs up.

'If I were a bit younger, I would go for that design myself. I could imagine wearing it to stroll through St Stephen's Green and down Grafton Street.'

Dolores seemed lost for a moment in her dream, before grabbing her handbag and car keys from her desk.

'Silly me, I have a hairdresser's appointment in Greystones, I had better get going.'

Marianne walked over to the ball gown and slipped it off the hanger. It was heavy. She was about the same size as Collie had been back then. Unzipping the zipper, she stepped into the folds of fabric and pulled it up over her T-shirt. It was a snug fit, but that suited the design. Pulling off the T-shirt, she fixed the bodice in place before zipping up the dress and dropping her jeans to the ground.

Automatically, she coiled up her hair in a small bun. Swishing the skirt of satin from side to side, she felt herself walk taller. How disappointed Collie must have been not to show the dress in public, and how happy she must have been to wear it for Lucas. The velvet bow needed replacing. When she moved, the heavy folds rustled and the satin glinted according to the light. A knock on the studio door made Marianne jump. Thinking Dolores had forgotten something, she laughed and shouted, 'Come in.'

'Wow, you look stunning,' Jack said.

'Oh, I didn't realise it was you,' she said, scrabbling to throw some spare grey silk over her shoulder to cover the front of the dress.

'I'm sorry, I met Dolores on the way out and she said to go straight through. I didn't mean to intrude.'

'No, not at all, it's just me being silly and trying on my grandmother's ball gown.'

'Did Collie ever have a place fancy enough to wear a dress like that?'

'As it turns out, no,' Marianne said.

She noticed he had pushed his hands in his pockets and was making a big effort to appear nonchalant, which struck her as rather sweet.

'Do you want me to come back later?' he asked.

'No, don't be silly.'

He scratched his temple and cleared his throat.

'I had a bit of time on my hands last night, and I fashioned the seat for the gazebo with the carving inserts. We could go down and have a look, whenever you have a chance.'

'How about now?'

'Not dressed like that. You don't want to ruin that dress.'

'You're right, but it's the sort of dress that, when you try it on, you don't want to take it off.'

'I feel that way about all my clothes,' he said drily, and she giggled.

'Do you want to wait in the kitchen while I change back into my jeans?'

'OK,' he said, fumbling with the brass doorknob and making it rattle loudly as he left. Unzipping the dress, she heard the screech of a chair being pulled out from under the kitchen table as Jack sat down. When she hurried down the hall a few minutes later, he was hunched over his phone, his elbows on the table.

'Ready when you are,' she said, and he jumped up. He opened the back door for her, and they walked across the yard to the lake path. Jack went in front, every now and again shoving old briars and bushes out of the way. She could see one side of the gazebo had been erected.

'Were you working in the dark? That wasn't here last night.'

'It felt like the night, but I was very early. I thought you would get a better idea if I got a side up. There's no problem if you're not happy with it,' he said nervously.

She walked over to the wooden seat, and as she ran her fingers along the initials carved on a carefree summer's day by her mother and father, she felt tears rise up inside her. She shouldn't be here; they should be taking on the worry that was Kilteelagh House. Roughly, she swiped away the tears, mumbling sorry over her shoulder. In two strides, Jack was beside her.

'Please, don't apologise. I understand how emotional this is for you.'

'You've done such a good job. Thank you.'

He didn't answer, but gathered her into his arms. She sobbed and he held her tighter. After a few minutes she pulled free.

'If the law doesn't take off, you could set up a carpentry business.'

'Then I would never enjoy it as much; this is my hobby.'

'You have done such a beautiful job, it's like they came along and carved their initials here and we never had to replace it.'

'I am so glad you like it.'

'I don't like it; I love it. Thank you.' She patted him gently on the arm before heading off in the direction of the lake. He followed, reaching out to take her hand. They stood for a few moments hand in hand until she said she had to get back to the house. He held onto the tips of her fingers before releasing her, and she liked that. She started to move away.

'I'm hoping your gazebo will start looking itself at day's end,' he said, and she turned and smiled at him. Marianne continued towards the house. She felt happy for the first time in a long time. She stopped and lingered on the avenue, gazing at Kilteelagh House, where the sunshine was washing gold across the top windows.

TWENTY-THREE

Kilteelagh House
Balgaddy
Co. Wicklow

My dearest Marianne,

I would so love to know how you are getting on.

It's best to have a project to garner the mind and propel you through the chilly, harsh days of November. The days are short, and here in Kilteelagh there are parts of the land that never get a chance to warm up in the hours of daylight. The ice around the hazel trees can stay for days on end, and the ground is hard and unyielding. The watery sun has no heat in it and the ice builds up in pockets in the grass. Nice to crunch underfoot, but only if you are wearing waterproof shoes.

The November days at Kilteelagh can merge into one another, the sun checking out too early, the birds tired of scrabbling around unyielding earth and practically hopping into the kitchen to be fed. When the days were like this, there was a temptation to sit indoors beside the Aga, but I forced myself out the door to walk the land to see the daffodils begin to push small shoots through the hard earth. For me, it was a signal that times of darkness too will pass. It doesn't matter what the wind and rain throw at them, the bulbs send their shoots upwards, giving us hope that spring can't be far behind. Try and set a deadline for yourself, it focuses the mind and, like the daffodils and the crocus, you can cling onto the certainty that better times are only sleeps away.

It is strange that in November I always felt such hope, something that is hard to muster in the gloomy days of December and January. There can only be hope when we see the growth against the odds, and for me personally, it is always another year in which there is a possibility that Lucas may come back to me. That was one way of thinking about it, and the other was the heartbreak of another year without seeing him. I never went searching for him, and maybe I should have, but I knew if he could have come back to me, he would. I knew in my heart, if he were to show up, it would have to be when the daffodils were in bloom, when the avenue was lined with yellow flowers, all gently swaying in the breeze as he walked by. The emergence of the daffodil shoots each year, therefore, brought an overwhelming sense of hope for the future; a sense of hope that life would change and be far better.

I may never see a full spring from start to finish again but, Marianne, I know when I am gone, the daffodils will continue to bloom each year and life, as it should, will go on at Kilteelagh. It warms my heart to know you will be at the helm.

It was always in the dark days of winter that I wondered, will it be in spring when he comes back to me?

And what if it is? What would that say, having waited all these years, if we missed each other by only days or hours? All the years I could have gone looking for him. Regret is deep in my heart. Why am I telling you all this? Maybe at some level, I'm hoping you can learn from my mistakes, to grab every *opportunity, big and small, to treat every winter as the precursor of a fine spring.*

No doubt you will have decided on your course now and the girls too will have settled into a routine. I rather imagine you are managing everything splendidly. I know I have left Kilteelagh in good hands. Katherine was no doubt outraged, but I am sure now, even she realises the future of Kilteelagh could not have been secure with her. Kilteelagh needs someone who is going to put the work in, with little tangible reward. It needs a person who can look to preserving it for the future, without resenting it.

There are those who will never understand that a house which has seen the troubles and joys of a family must be allowed to stand. It has earned its place in our history and our future.

No doubt Bridie has made herself known at this stage. She and her committee are very good for Balgaddy, but there are times when she loses the run of herself. Towards the end of the year, she usually looks for help with her crazy idea for a Christmas market. I have never entertained such a notion. Bridie always did have notions above her station. I always think to give in to Bridie, even in the relatively small things, could boost her confidence to push for more. I have often wondered what her fascination is with Kilteelagh. Yes, she would love our land and would build in every last patch of it, but I have also felt she was drawn to Kilteelagh House for some other secret reason. Maybe I am indulging a flight of fancy in that one, but Bridie when she is at Kilteelagh always seems to be different to the interfering busybody she is every time we try to do business at the post office. For some reason, Kilteelagh brings out her soft side, but it is no reason to trust her. I'm sure Dolores has alerted you to her shenanigans.

How are you managing with the garden? It is such a challenge in November. The wind buffets the house looking for weak spots and the rain leaves puddles all over the yard. I usually tie supports on the cherry blossom and magnolia trees. The small eucalyptus at the side of the house may also need a bit of help. It is still young, and while the roots are strong, the wind can be quite worrisome around it. It has survived, though, these last few years, despite the fierce winds which blow in across the Irish Sea. Don't move the pots with the bay trees. That corner tucked in at the side of the steps at the front door offers the best shelter for them. To move them would be to risk losing them.

I wondered would you, or have you, or will you open up the front door? We always used the back. I don't know why, but once Mike died, I didn't want to use the front door any more. I stood behind his coffin as he was taken out of Kilteelagh House and gently down the steps to the hearse. From that day on, I never walked through the front door. It didn't seem right to be pulling back the door and doing everyday things, when Mike had made his final exit from there. I loved Mike in my own way, and I missed him. I never cleared his clothes from the front bedroom either. I think guilt kept me away from any reminders of him. Ours was a loving but strange relationship.

Did I love Mike? I can honestly say I did. He was a kind and gentle man, and I feel guilty that I could not give him more of myself. When he was ill, I looked after him every day. One day not long before he passed, he caught my hand and told me I was not to remain a widow.

'There is so much love in you, Collie. You need the support and strength of a good man. I give you my blessing,' he said. We held each other and cried. It's strange; wouldn't you think, with Mike's blessing, I would have looked for Lucas? Something held me back, the fear of failure, the fear of rejection. Maybe to live with hope and dreams is best after all. The love I had and still have for Lucas was and is perfect. To have acted upon it would only have been to invite in the imperfections.

I did what I needed to do. Sure, I have regrets, but my life at Kilteelagh has been good. This house has sustained me, occupied me and helped me feel at home when all around me, life was changing. I hope it does the same for you.

To some a house is just that, four walls and a roof. But Kilteelagh to me was a home first and somewhere where our history as a family was made; somewhere I could entrust my deepest secrets. This is why, even when times were tough and I came under pressure to sell, I wouldn't.

Don't get me wrong, what Bridie and her family were offering was exceedingly generous, but I couldn't leave Kiltee-lagh. What if Lucas came looking for me, and also, where would I go that would make me feel so right with myself? Kilteelagh is in my blood and until my heart stops beating, it is part of me. I want to be part of Kilteelagh in death, to nourish the fields and the lake water; to be part of this land.

I want to do that with my Lucas, because I know in my heart that if he does not make it in this life, we can be reunited in death. But enough of me. Marianne, I hope you are begin-ning to prosper at Kilteelagh, and beginning to enjoy the house. Sometimes, it can appear an uphill struggle, and the house wins a lot of the time. But in these cold winter days, think of the past sunshine days when you could walk barefoot, the windows stayed open all night and the birdsong was so early, it was practically dark when the first bird opened the dawn chorus at only a tiny chink of light in the sky.

Savour these times, darling, and let them carry us through the hard times.

All my love,

Collie xx

TWENTY-FOUR

Marianne was still in bed the next morning when Katie ran upstairs and pulled at the duvet, whispering that one of Grandma's friends was at the front door.

'But it's so early, did she say what she wants?'

'I didn't ask, Collie said never keep somebody at the front door talking, get an adult.'

Marianne tied her dressing gown tight around her as she made her way downstairs. The woman was standing on the top step looking out across the fields.

'Can I help you?' Marianne asked loudly.

The woman didn't turn around immediately but waved her arm towards the horizon.

'It is so beautiful here; you must pinch yourself every day.'

'Excuse me?'

The woman swung around.

'I am sorry, I had forgotten how beautiful Kilteelagh is.'

'You know the house?'

'When I first came to Ireland as a refugee, your grandmother had me here a few times a week. She taught me how to sew.'

'And you are?'

'Fiknete, I live in the town. Dolores said you may require help sewing, and she said you are very fussy.' Marianne didn't know what to say. 'I have surprised you too early in the morning. I am up at six, and for me eight o'clock is coffee break time. I run the alterations business Bobbins and Bows in Balgaddy, but if you are interested, I could do some sewing for you, too.'

'I haven't fully decided what I am going to do.'

'I am hoping when you do decide, you will have room for me in your sewing circle?'

'What?'

Fiknete took a bag which had been on the ground beside her and handed it to Marianne. 'Some samples of my work, for your consideration,' she said, thrusting the bag towards Marianne.

'Thank you. I'm not sure if I can take on anyone just yet. It's not really a sewing circle, I might be looking for someone long-term who would undergo certain training.'

Fiknete blushed and she pulled at the collar of her blouse.

'You can ask Dolores about me and look at my work. Call in to my place on Parnell Street if you want to talk some more.' She smiled brightly and Marianne couldn't help smiling back.

Fiknete had walked down two steps when she turned around to Marianne.

'You're so lucky to be here at Kilteelagh, and Collie would be so proud that it is going to become a centre of dress design.'

She hopped into her Mini and revved down the avenue, making the blackbirds around the gazebo fly into the air. Katie called from the kitchen that she needed help. Marianne dropped the black sack in the corner; it would have to wait until the girls had gone to school.

It was two hours later when Marianne carried Fiknete's black bag into the kitchen and tipped the contents out onto the table. There were four patterns and four summer dresses. In each case, the pattern envelope was neatly pinned onto the back seam of the dress. She shook out a simple cotton dress made from a Simplicity pattern, a panelled, slightly flared skirt, a short puff sleeve with a round neckline with three buttons, which had been covered in a contrasting fabric spaced down the front bodice.

A Vogue Nina Ricci pattern was pinned to a royal blue wrap-over dress with a deep front neckline, cap sleeves and buttonhole pockets. Marianne held the soft silk dress to her. She loved the swish of the skirt. The seams were expertly finished. Running her finger across the bottom of the skirt, she felt the hand of Collie in the blind hem. Checking the seam, she found the tiny tag Collie always insisted on inserting to date the garment. Collie had once shown her how she had added this individual touch to each of her creations. Marianne needed no further proof that Collie had indeed trained the dressmaker. She glanced at the other two dresses, before folding them back in the bag. Rather than phone, she drove into town and parked near Parnell Street.

Fiknete had a small upstairs place, a tiny sign on the first-floor window saying she was offering alterations. Marianne climbed the steps, dithering at the glass door.

'Come in, please, I don't bite,' Fiknete called out.

Marianne stuck her head around the door.

'I was hoping we could have a chat.'

Fiknete, who was threading her sewing machine, looked like she was in her sitting room. There was an armchair beside the open fireplace where a gas fire was inserted and a television in the corner. The walls of the room were covered in shelving, holding spools, patterns and baskets of fabric remnants. Off the room, Marianne could see a small kitchen.

'Welcome to my home and business,' she said, waving her hand to show off a tiny flat.

'I didn't realise you lived and worked in the same place.'

'Yes, it saves money because I only have to pay one lot of rent, and mostly people in the town don't mind.'

'Mostly?'

'Mrs Murphy on the town council used to complain that I shouldn't be living here, but I alter her outfits for free. She likes to buy a lot of oversize clothes in the sales and have me cut them down to size.'

'I'm not sure she should be taking advantage of you like that.'

Fiknete laughed. 'I ran with my family from Kosovo and ended up in a refugee camp in Macedonia and finally got refuge here; altering a few items of clothes for free is no big deal.'

Marianne didn't know why, but she felt uncomfortable because she didn't know what to say. Fiknete flicked the sign on the door to closed and offered her guest a chair.

'Have you come to talk about the dresses?'

'They're so beautiful. Collie taught you well. I recognise her handiwork.'

'Your grandmother and Dolores O'Grady have been my angels. Collie took me in when I was only seventeen years old with no education, and told me I had to learn a trade. It was so difficult for me in Balgaddy; my English was not good back then. Nobody was going to hire me. Collie had me out at Kilteelagh every day. I started with the basics and she never let me advance until I passed her test.' Reaching for a photograph over the fireplace, she handed it to Marianne. 'My very first piece, a skirt gathered at the waist. I thought I was a dress designer.'

'That's taken at the gazebo.'

'Yes, with the lake behind, so beautiful.'

'My grandmother never mentioned anything about this to me,' said Marianne, replacing the photograph on the mantelpiece. 'We were back in Ireland every two years when I was young, but since I grew up, my visits haven't been so frequent.'

'She loved you dearly, and was always talking about the fact that you were the one person who appreciated good design. I should have called on you earlier to see how you were getting on, but I figured you had your hands full.'

'I think Collie is the reason I'm a dress designer.'

Fiknete switched on the kettle. 'Would you like tea?'

'No, thank you, but could we talk a little about you doing some work for me?'

'I would be more than happy to sew dresses. You just need to give me your pattern or your sketch and I can take it from there.'

'That sounds good, but how would you fit it in with your work here?'

Fiknete shrugged. 'I am busy at back-to-school time when they want the uniform skirts turned up, and maybe around Christmas. I do some wedding dresses as well. There is enough to keep ticking over, but that's it. I couldn't keep this place on if it were not for Mrs O'Grady.'

'Dolores?'

'Yes, she owns the building and she set me up here for free and told me it can stay that way until she decides to sell. That was several years ago. I look after the place for her.'

'What a gesture.'

'Like Collie, Mrs O'Grady has been more than a friend. I couldn't stay in this country but for her.'

'I still don't know how you can keep both strands running. I will make demands on you.'

'The alterations shop opens on Thursday and Friday mostly. I can do that work at night and I can come to Kilteelagh during the other days and the weekend, if you allow it.'

'Are you sure? Maybe we should have a trial first?'

'I can start tomorrow. Give you two days; show you how I work and then we can discuss payment.'

'Fiknete...'

'Call me Fi, everybody else does – it takes less effort.'

'If you don't mind.'

Fiknete threw her eyes to the ceiling. 'Do you really think Irish people were going to bother to learn the correct pronunciation of my name? I don't include Collie or Dolores in that, but it keeps it easy for everyone else.'

'When you say it like that, I want to call you Fiknete.'

'I think we are going to be the best of friends,' Fiknete said, reaching over and grabbing Marianne in a big hug. Marianne pulled herself free and said she had better get back to Kilteelagh.

'I will call by tomorrow early,' Fiknete said.

'Not too early, maybe around nine thirty; I'll be back from the school run at that stage.'

'Coffee time then,' Fiknete said, and she stood at the top of the stairs to see Marianne out.

On leaving Parnell Street, Marianne decided that rather than go straight home she would call on Dolores. Her friend was in her front garden as she pulled in at the house.

'Well, hello there, how nice to see you calling on me, Marianne,' Dolores said as she ordered her dog to heel. 'Let's walk through to the kitchen. We can sit out on the deck; it's quite sheltered, with a view to the sea.'

Marianne took in the modern kitchen and deck. Dolores burst out laughing.

'You've never actually been in here, have you? You thought I lived in a tumbledown house. My husband died a few years ago, but he left me well provided for and I've invested well. My consultancy work has also brought in a pretty penny.'

'It's so wonderful. If I had a view and a kitchen like this, I don't think I would ever leave the house.'

'Ah, but you have magical Kilteelagh. Collie always told me

I could spend all the money I liked on this place; it would never stand up to the mystery and magic of Kilteelagh.'

'I don't know, in the dead of winter, I would pick this house any time.'

'Certainly, with my underfloor heating, I think you might.'

They sat on the deck where Dolores had coffee already brewing,

'It seems sensible to have the coffee machine working overtime. When one is out on this deck it is either a whiskey, champagne or a coffee which is required.'

She poured the coffee into two china mugs and handed one to Marianne.

'Now, what brings you to this side of the road? I take it you have met Fiknete?'

'Yes, I called in on her place this morning. Her work is really exquisite, and she tells me you are her angel, as Collie had been.'

'Yes, Fiknete is a dear friend. A beautiful young woman who was lucky enough to come across Collie.'

'I wanted to ask you about that. Maybe it was at a time when I was busy setting out in life, but I don't remember Collie talking about her.'

'You were at college and living away from home, and I don't think you had much communication with your grandmother at that time.'

Marianne felt uncomfortable thinking back to the missed phone calls, the letters left unanswered as she at first enjoyed student life and then fell madly in love.

Dolores reached over and touched her hand. 'Collie understood that you were finding your way, she knew you would come back to her when you were ready.'

'I did, about three years later when my boyfriend dumped me, and I came to Kilteelagh for two weeks.'

'I remember that. Fiknete had moved to Waterford at that time, but returned almost as fast as she went.'

'How did Collie get to know Fiknete?'

'It was the time the government decided to take in Kosovan refugees and three families settled here in Balgaddy. Fiknete was with her mother and father and her brother. Collie sent some old suits belonging to your grandfather to help the family. Next thing, there was a knock on her back door and Fiknete's father was there. It turns out he had found a wedding band in the pocket of one of the suit jackets and had made enquiries as to who was the donor, and walked out to Kilteelagh. Collie was very touched by the gesture; the ring had been her grandfather's and also Mike's wedding ring. It had been lost a year before his death. Seemingly, there was a hole in the lining of the pocket, and it had got wedged in a seam.'

'I know that ring, I heard Collie talk about it before.'

'She was so overcome when she saw the ring that she began to cry, and the poor man escorted her into the kitchen and poured water into a glass from the tap for her. His English was not so bad, and they chatted, and she offered him work tidying up the gardens at Kilteelagh.

'As she got to know Fiknete's father, Collie asked about his family. There was his wife, a younger son and Fiknete. The poor man was worried for Fiknete, so Collie invited her to Kilteelagh and offered to teach her how to sew and help her with her English. The girl was hesitant and quiet at first, but soon they were getting on like a house on fire. If you don't mind me saying, Fiknete filled the gap when you were enjoying yourself in the outside world. Collie took her under her wing and for a while the two of them were inseparable. Katherine wasn't too happy, always suspicious Fiknete and her father had an ulterior motive, but even she calmed down eventually.'

Marianne looked out to sea, attempting to hide the hurt she felt that her grandmother had chosen someone else. It's not that she hoped Collie had pined away because her granddaughter had drifted out of contact, but that she found such an interesting replacement. The waves were curling into shore driven by a light wind, making her shiver.

'Have I said too much?' Dolores asked.

'I should not have expected Collie to put her life on hold because I wasn't here,' Marianne said, making a big effort to keep calm.

'It was never intentional. Sometimes people are drawn to each other for reasons nobody can explain.' Dolores topped up the mugs of coffee. 'Fiknete was good for Collie too. She was having a hard time from Bridie and her sort, and it was good that she had another focus. We both became quite attached to Fiknete.'

'She told me you let her have the flat rent-free.'

'She looks after the building and small garden for me. It's easier for me to have somebody living in the place, than have the hassle of renting to people I don't know. Besides, when she came back from Waterford, she needed somewhere to stay urgently, so it worked well for both of us.'

'She's coming to Kilteelagh tomorrow and we can start work.'

'Fantastic, I'll be over around eleven. I have an appointment in the town earlier.'

Marianne got up to go.

Dolores stepped in front of her. 'Don't be upset by the relationship Fiknete had with Collie. I can tell you Collie loved you so much and she never stopped talking about you. Fiknete will tell you that too. When you came back into the Kilteelagh fold, there was nobody happier than Collie.'

Marianne, when she got back home, stopped at the gazebo. Almost four years of barely any contact had passed before she'd rung her grandmother in tears. She remembered Collie had spoken in a soft, warm voice and told her to get on a flight.

'I will book it here, dear, just turn up at the airport. You need the quiet of Kilteelagh now.'

She heard her voice as if she was back in that time when her boyfriend, the man she thought she was going to marry, walked out on her. She had come to Kilteelagh and stayed two weeks; the embrace of Collie and Kilteelagh House had helped mend her broken heart and she never let her relationship with her grandmother fracture again. Sitting and leaning against the new wood of the gazebo, she could hear Collie.

'The day will come when you meet somebody, and you will know that person is for you. That is the relationship to cherish and never let go. You will know him when you meet him, maybe not immediately, but when it happens and it is both ways, there is no better entanglement.' Marianne at the time had presumed she was talking about herself and Mike, and asked her grandmother to tell her more about the man she loved.

'He was kind and gentle and treated me like I was a princess. He believed in me and in our love. We worked together and were good together,' Collie said, before clapping and saying they couldn't spend the whole day gassing on about love.

Marianne returned to her car and drove up to the house, where she went straight to the design studio and the stack of cases from the attic. Opening all the cases, she let the fabric tumble out onto the floor. There were bright colours here Collie would never have worn. Marianne took out a length of deep red velvet.

There was just one which was two metres long, but she thought enough to cover the cushion of the armchair in the hall, which looked faded and sad.

She draped the velvet over the chair, letting it crumple onto the seat. When she heard a car on the driveway, she thought it must be Jack. She opened the front door, but the car had already gone around the back. Marianne quickly checked her appearance in the hall mirror and tied her hair in a tidy ponytail before making her way to the kitchen. Her heart sank when she saw Katherine get out of her car.

'Can I come in?'

'You don't have to ask, Katherine.'

'It's not my home any more, is it?'

Marianne didn't rise to the bait but switched on the kettle.

'I won't be staying for tea; I have come to tell you I'm going to my solicitor about the will.'

'You do what you have to do, Katherine, but Collie was very clear in her will what she wanted to happen.'

'But it's not right, is it? She must have known I wouldn't take this lying down. You can fix this, Marianne.'

'What do you mean?'

'Collie was my mother and by rights, you know I should have been left Kilteelagh. I have already told you I won't see you left out. I am willing to give you fifty thousand euros, which is a hell of a lot of dollars.'

'You're forgetting my commitment to Rachel and Katie.'

Katherine, agitated, began pacing between the table and the sink.

'Collie has created this situation, and somewhere she is sitting back and enjoying the spectacle. Do you want to see us debt-ridden for life because we had to fight you in the High Court?'

'I am not asking you to fight me; I'm asking you to accept your mother's will.'

'Easy for you to say, when you end up with everything.'

Marianne slapped down two mugs.

'Do you think I asked for this, Katherine? I would turn the clock back in a nanosecond if I could. I've lost all my family and I was not even able to be here for Collie taking her last breath. Do you think I want to be in Balgaddy for the rest of my life, trying to eke out a living dress designing, when I could be trying my hand at it in New York?'

'I'm giving you an out; go back, we won't think less of you.'

Marianne was reaching for the carton of milk in the fridge, but instead she banged the door.

'You don't get it, do you, Katherine? I would think less of myself. Collie had her reasons for leaving Kilteelagh House to me and I won't let her down. I am not going to let Rachel and Katie down either.'

'You're leaving me with no choice but to start legal proceedings, and that will put us in a potential quagmire which could ruin the family.'

'I am giving you a choice, Katherine, but you are choosing to be stubborn and pig-headed and stupid. Collie would never have wanted it. Please don't do this.'

Katherine stared at her. 'You should have stayed in America. You will never be accepted around here, not when they realise what you have done to me.'

Marianne opened the door. 'You should leave now, Katherine.'

Katherine swept out the door and Marianne heard her get in her car and speed down the avenue. Sitting at the kitchen table, she put her head in her hands, tears wetting her cheeks and fingers. When she heard Jack walk across the yard, humming a tune to announce his presence, she swiped away the tears. He walked in the back door and stopped in his tracks when he saw her sitting at the table.

'Do you want me to come back later?' he said.

'No, please come in.'

Jack looked uncomfortable. 'I was only trying to cadge a cup of coffee, which seems irrelevant now.'

'No, please, I need a coffee too. Is everything all right?'

She got up from the table and busied herself with the coffee machine, but her shoulders hunched and shook as tears over-whelmed her again.

'Marianne, what's wrong?'

'Everything is wrong,' she said.

Unable to stop herself, she started to cry again. Jack ran to her and led her to a chair. 'Let me put on the coffee,' he said as he helped her to sit down. He put the filter in the machine, the coffee on top and poured the water from a jug before switching on the machine.

'It's probably none of my business, but do you want to talk about it?'

'It's Katherine! She's *still* threatening to take me to court over the will. I don't know why she keeps doing this. She goes silent, and just when I think things have calmed down, she goes crazy again. But she always hated this place.'

'The word in the town is she wants to sell Kilteelagh to Bridie, who is planning a new housing estate. With Balgaddy within commuting distance of Dublin, who wouldn't want to bring up their kids here?'

'You think it's a good idea?'

'I didn't say that.'

Marianne banged the table with her hand. 'Are people really talking about this? I suppose everybody wants me to fail and go away and give Kilteelagh to Katherine.'

'Most people want to stay out of it, but Katherine and her cohort want to make a lot of money.'

'But she has so much, and a lovely husband and children.'

'Did that ever stop anyone?'

Marianne's shoulders slumped, her hair falling around her eyes, as tears took her over again.

Jack got down two mugs and put them on the table.

'Where's the sugar?' he asked.

'Top cupboard to the right,' she whispered. Without asking,

he put a heaped spoon of sugar in her coffee and pushed the mug across the table.

'A court action will take a very long time and bags of money. I don't think Katherine knows what she's talking about,' he said.

'She doesn't care, you mean.'

'I reckon she's hoping to frighten you away, so if you want this place and to make a go of things, you have to sit tight.'

Marianne pushed the hair out of her eyes and sipped her coffee. 'Easier said than done. Is it ever going to end with Katherine?'

Jack stirred his coffee with a spoon, the clink of the metal against the side of the cup loud in the quiet of the kitchen. 'It's not going to end until you stop it,' he said.

'She's a woman with a mission, I can't stop her.'

'But maybe you can outwit her.'

'What do you mean?'

'If this goes to court, it's in nobody's interest. Katherine is going to look like a selfish land grabber; you're going to look like an imposter who came here to do her out of her inheritance—' He stopped when he saw Marianne's face. 'Steady on, that's not the way I see you. I'm thinking aloud here in relation to both sides and how a court might look at it.'

'So, you're judge and jury now.'

'There won't be a jury. I'm a law student, remember?'

Marianne threw her hands in the air. 'So, tell me what to do.'

Jack traced the pattern of the tablecloth with his finger.

'There won't be any winners if you go to court, so you have to avoid it at all costs. If it were me, I would offer Katherine something she couldn't resist. Even if you go all the way to the court, you will have to enter negotiations and you will be advised to offer "go-away money", rather than incur the costs of an action that could last days.'

'Even though I've done nothing wrong?'

Jack shook his head. 'It's not about who is right and wrong, it's about mitigating your losses.'

Sighing loudly, Marianne pushed herself away from the table and headed for the back door. Jack followed.

'I know you don't want to hear this, but you have to do something now, because when solicitors get involved, it could drag on for years. It could ruin all of you financially and emotionally.'

'She wants me to give her Kilteelagh.'

'But maybe she would accept something that it wouldn't hurt you too much to give.'

'Like what?'

Jack pulled Marianne to sit on the stone block at the back door which the morning sun had left comfortably warm.

'There's the field with the road frontage at the other side of the lake. You could give it to Katherine with a promise you wouldn't object to planning there for one house.'

'And what do I get?'

'Do you know the field?'

'I knew there were lands at the other side of the lake, but I've never been over there.'

'Exactly my point, it can't hurt that much then. And Katherine already has two fields there.'

'But how much is it worth, money-wise?'

Jack got up and kicked at the moss on the cobbles.

'Does it matter? It's peace of mind. Whatever it's worth, it will be a lot less than four or more days in the High Court, which is what you are looking at for any case involving a will.'

'I don't know if Collie would be happy.'

'You own Kilteelagh, Marianne; this isn't about Collie any more.'

Marianne pushed her head back and let the winter sun warm her face.

'I don't see why I should give in to Katherine. She's being a bully.'

Jack flopped down beside her. 'If you can get her to stop and she's happy, then maybe you can concentrate on what is important: your life here, the girls, your business. At the moment, Katherine is sucking every bit of energy you have, and if she really goes down the legal route, that will intensify to the point you might end up having to walk away from Kilteelagh.'

'You're saying I have to lose a field I didn't even realise I owned, so I can keep Kilteelagh?'

'Exactly.'

'But what if Katherine doesn't want the field, or laughs me out of it?'

'That will all be in the presentation.'

'What do you mean?'

'Katherine was here this morning ranting and raving. She won't listen to reason today, but ask Steve if they will both come up to the house next week. You can have had the field valued by then and present them with a folder giving all the details. Steve will want an end to the aggravation and Katherine will want the field so she can sell it to Bridie, who will no doubt try to put not one, but two houses on it.'

'Won't it impact on Kilteelagh?'

'It's the far side of the lake. You won't see it from the house, and we can plant a windbreak, so you don't even see what is going on.'

'But couldn't I sell it?'

'You could, but then she would go to court for sure. We will have a document drawn up where she agrees to renounce any claim over Kilteelagh.'

'There's so much to think about.'

'And a gazebo to be painted.' He placed his empty coffee mug on the windowsill. 'Let me know what you want to do, and I will help with the paperwork.'

He kissed her on the cheek before walking off towards the lake. Marianne sat in the sunshine. His touch was gentle and it made her feel good. She had expected, when she was invited back for the reading of Collie's will, to end up with a smattering of jewellery, at most. She had quietly hoped for some memento or the painting, but she had never imagined she would be left with Kilteelagh House and lands. Part of her still felt cross at her grandmother for leaving her with the responsibility of Kilteelagh, which she loved and hated in almost equal measure at this very moment. And there were the girls; she loved Rachel and Katie with all her heart. Gathering up the mug from the windowsill, she dropped it in the sink before moving on to her design studio.

Here among the silk and Collie's sewing things, she could relax and think clearly. She sat at Collie's machine, remembering the first time Collie had let her sit down and thread the needle. She smiled, thinking how nervous she had been, her hand shaking as she pulled the thread from the spool and gently guided it across the top of the machine and through the little eyelet hole, before tackling the difficult manoeuvre of twisting the thread down to the needle. At one stage when she had let the thread go and said she couldn't do it, Collie had reached over and guided her until, suddenly, Marianne noticed her grandmother was no longer helping her and she was doing it on her own.

She was alone now, and she prayed that Collie would guide her to make the right decision for her family and for Kilteelagh House. All she could do was make the offer of the field to Katherine, but she decided to do it in an email, because she couldn't face her aunt's anger any more.

TWENTY-FIVE

Fiknete arrived at the back door carrying a large tray covered in a tea cloth.

'Collie always loved my biscuits, so I baked these for you this morning.' She pulled off the tea towel and placed the tray on the kitchen table. 'We can have coffee before we start, please? I was up extra early getting my other work done.'

Marianne, who had already set up the coffee machine, switched it on. 'Tell me how you got on with my grandmother?'

Fiknete laughed out loud. 'She was so bossy, and everything had to be perfect; I didn't even like her at the start, and I don't think she liked me either. My father told me if I did not come here and be polite and learn how to sew, he would marry me off to the first man who asked.'

'Did he mean it?'

'No, but it showed how serious he was that I learn something that could help me in the future. I was lost at school and I didn't have friends either. The only ones who wanted to make friends with me were boys, and I knew what they were really after.'

'But you and Collie, you became friends?'

'Eventually, I baked a lot and sweetened her up.'

Marianne smiled as she poured the coffee.

'Please try my choc chip biscuits. I baked them especially for you because they are American.'

'Tastes just right to me,' Marianne said, biting into one of the biscuits. 'Shall we bring our coffee into the design studio?'

'You are like your grandmother, she never wanted to waste time chatting either.'

Marianne didn't answer but led the way to her studio. She opened the door and let Fiknete walk in first.

'Amazeballs. This room is so different; what have you done? Mind you, I don't think Collie would like it.'

'It needed a makeover.'

Fiknete, who was fingering the cream muslin fabric, sounded giddy when she spoke next. 'This is a space to be creative. How lucky are you to be in Kilteelagh and able to do what you want!'

When Marianne cleared her throat, Fiknete straightened up and saluted. 'Present and ready for work, Captain.'

Marianne was slightly irritated at Fiknete's attitude, and she imagined Collie had been too, but there was something sincere about the woman which she liked. 'I've set up Collie's machine on the dining table and I thought you could work there. Here is the sketch of what the finished dress should look like, and I've pinned the cut-out pattern pieces to the fabric.'

Fiknete took one of the pieces and turned it over so she could see the fabric. 'Such wonderful colours, it will be a joy to sew this dress.' She ran her hand across the machine. 'Collie never let me sew on this; she had a very old machine for me which she borrowed from Dolores. At the end, she said I had graduated to sew on a really good machine, and she bought me one. It is the one I use for my business, and she also gave me my first order: the new curtains in the sitting room.'

'They are wonderful.'

'Very difficult, with lining and pencil pleats; they almost took over my flat. I didn't want her to pay me, but she insisted I charge the full rate or she said I would never get my business off the ground.'

'How did you get more work after that?'

'I was lucky – the seamstress in town retired and so people had to come to me. I also made sure to charge lower than anybody in Greystones; Irish people always like to think they are getting a bargain. Also, I suppose people talked about my work after that.'

'I know Collie always liked to think she had got the best deal.'

'That is because she always did. Collie was somebody nobody wanted to question. You will have to be like that now.'

Marianne was about to answer when she heard Dolores call from the kitchen. Fiknete began to thread the machine. 'I can't have Mrs O'Grady seeing me chatting and not working. She is depending on me to help you.'

Moving her fingers expertly across the machine, she threaded the blue thread and already had a sleeve under the foot of the machine when Dolores opened the design studio door.

'I like the look of this. Fiknete, it's a pleasure to see you sewing once again at Kilteelagh,' she said as she made her way to her table. 'Today, Marianne, I'll be sending out feelers to the people I know in the business for help as to when is the best time to have a fashion show and what exactly we need for it. It's a while since I left the fashion world, and I need to get up to speed.' She took out her laptop and arranged a notebook and three pens on the table. 'Don't mind me, if I need to make a call I will go to the kitchen,' she said.

Fiknete reached for her phone and attached her earphones. 'I like to get lost in my music. I hope that is all right?'

Marianne nodded and was herself soon lost in pinning the tissue-paper pattern pieces to the fabric she had laid on the other half of the dining room table.

TWENTY-SIX

December

Kilteelagh House
Balgaddy
Co. Wicklow

My dearest Marianne,

There used to be so much about December I liked, loved in fact. We always made a big deal about the run-up to Christmas at Kilteelagh. Aisling led the charge and we happily joined in, enjoying her infectious enthusiasm. She kept all the old traditions, getting the girls to stir the pudding ingredients with the battered wooden spoon and make a wish; organising a bit of illicit poitín to add a special flavour to the Christmas cake, and bringing the girls around the kitchen table to cut out the old-fashioned garlands from multicoloured tissue paper.

Somehow, when Aisling was around, it all seemed so special and magical. I think when their dad walked away to start another life with his new family, she was desperate to make good memories for the girls. I found myself looking forward to each weekend, when she always had activities arranged for us. It was murder standing in line waiting for Santa in Dublin, but with Aisling there was no opting out, and in truth it was worth it to see Katie's beautiful face light up with excitement. Rachel of course was a pain, but even she knew there was no getting out of a family Christmas that started with the opening of the first window of the home-made advent calendar. For goodness' sake, even Benji the dog had an advent calendar. It was on the mantelpiece over the Aga and every morning he sat and wagged his tail, looking up at it, until he was allowed to have his treat.

Before Aisling came to stay, things had been quiet around Kilteelagh for a while, but when my own three girls were young, I went all out. It was the one time of the year I let the purse strings go and, in a way, I threw caution to the winds. The rest of the year I saved the pennies, but in December, it felt like an investment in the family. Funny, it was often the activities which cost nothing that were the most fun, like when we tramped in the frosty cold across the fields down to the boundary with Dolores' farm. We pulled enough holly from the tree to fill the house. Dolores always insisted we took the best branches with the berries, that the holly her side never grew as well. She complained, but she never let us home without a cup of hot chocolate in her fancy kitchen and cinnamon biscuits delicately iced to look like snowflakes.

One year, Katie, the silly girl, forgot her gloves and Dolores gave her a leather pair lined with cashmere. She always had a soft spot for Katie, and of course Katkins had to be the one to carry the holly home. Katie loved everything about Christmas.

It was why Aisling tried so hard for her last December. But the fatigue came over her every time. There would be fleeting moments of happiness and endless times when we tried not to catch her eye, pretending and then abandoning our plans and heading home, helping her up the stairs. She never cried out in pain, even though we all could see it on her face. The worst part was the silence afterwards; none of us articulated it out loud, but celebrating Christmas was the last thing we wanted to do that December. Our impending loss was all around us. Christmas, Aisling's last December and all the things that came before it, was a reminder of how much we were going to lose. Christmas that year was cruel and set to get much worse.

Aisling died, as you know, on 21 December. Our hearts were shrivelled with grief and loneliness. My poor darling tried to stay longer. For a woman who'd never prayed in her life, she prayed and begged to be allowed one more Christmas with Rachel and Katie, but death never listens or makes bargains. That December was a cold and harsh month which extinguished the light in all of us. As Aisling lay barely hanging on, I found a handwritten letter from Katie to Santa asking for her mother to be allowed to stay with her and to please make her mummy better. A desperate little girl tried to bargain, writing in capital letters that she would never ask for anything ever again.

To my shame, I never brought up the letter with Katie, and I should have, because after Aisling had taken her last breath, I knew that our precious Katie not only had lost her mother, but her innocence had also been cruelly shattered. All too young, Katie had been forced to grow up and inhabit a real world. How could I bring any magic into her life after that?

Two days before Christmas, we buried Aisling. Katie on Christmas Eve refused to leave out any food or drink for Santa or even a carrot for the reindeer. She was showered with presents, but it only brought her and our loneliness into sharp focus. We made some attempt, and even though I did not want any Christmas lights to be turned on, I switched them on in the hope it might brighten little Katie's eyes.

In truth, I had to stand idly by and watch my grandchildren suffer. There was nothing I could say or do to lessen their pain. After that, Christmas for us became something to endure and, yes, for me to pretend everything was all right. Kilteelagh looked magnificent all lit up. My heart wasn't in it and their hearts weren't in it. We went through the motions, putting the lights up, making the cake and the pudding, but none of us had the inclination to even taste them. Our hearts were broken into tiny pieces.

I was at a complete loss as to how to drag us up from the black pit where we had settled.

I have tried, but you can't draw up what isn't there. Katie, who usually could get excited at the drop of a hat, I know humoured me and I took that as a sign that in time, the wound of grief would heal, but in truth, I hadn't the energy to deal with it.

When Aisling died, I wanted to go in on myself, to move away from the world. I did it for about five days. Dolores held the fort and then she kicked me out of bed and told me very firmly I had two girls who had lost their mother and been abandoned by their father, and they couldn't afford to lose their grandmother as well. She was right, of course, and I put everything into helping the girls. But no matter what, in December I lost the will. They saw it in my face, and I certainly saw it in theirs.

Katie refused to visit Santa or to believe in Santa again. It was heartbreaking at her age. It was so difficult the next Christmas because other mothers tried to avoid her in the weeks leading up, in case she said something their children should not hear.

So, we had a little girl who did not have any play dates in the school holiday period, where she could have done with any diversion. I did my best and I tried to surprise her on Christmas morning, but the light had gone from her eyes. She saw her mother die at Christmas time and nothing could obliterate that. I probably should have put the girls into counselling. God knows it was suggested to me, but I honestly thought we could muddle through. We were a good team, but somehow in the last December around her death we had fallen apart.

I am sure you are wondering how you can make it different. I think the only thing to do is move away from Kilteelagh for a little while. I have asked the solicitor to include a cheque here so the three of you can go to New York. The excitement of such a trip would be incredible for the girls. Take them out of school early and go for a week. Make new December memories for them. I hope and pray you will show them New York.

Am I dictating too much? I hope not, but I do believe they need to forge new Christmas memories, special moments between the three of you. New York at Christmas is magical. I know, because I went once to visit your mum and dad, when you were a little baby. I really came over to help with you and give Chloe a break, but there were days I went into Manhattan on my own and I loved to stroll along the streets and avenues and wander about, happy to be part of something so big.

I even went ice skating in Central Park. I never let on to Chloe; she would have gone mad and turned it into a big deal amid a huge worry about me hurting myself, if I had fallen. It was the most magical time for me. Take them skating, Marianne; they have to go on the Central Park rink surrounded by the park and the skyscrapers; it's so wonderful. Have a hot chocolate with marshmallows on top afterwards. Go to Tiffany & Co. on Fifth Avenue – it's only a short walk from the ice rink.

I laugh when I think now how I rocked up to Tiffany & Co. in my heavy coat and snow boots. I thought they might not let me in, but the Americans are not at all stuffy and they don't judge an ability to spend by your appearance. I looked at everything, even the outrageously expensive pieces of jewellery

I had only ever seen on a magazine page. I went up in the lift, so I could walk down the lovely sweeping staircase. I was dazzled by the chandeliers, vintage and modern, the diamonds so beautiful they made me gasp. I was never a fan, though of that modern cuff bracelet they brought out, but there was plenty else for me to admire. In Tiffany, I felt like a queen. They were also kind enough to find me a seat in the cafe, where I spent a fortune on a coffee and cake. The glory days of Tiffany & Co. may be in the past, but being there gave me the sense of a world I'd never known before or since.

Maybe the girls would like a necklace from Tiffany. Remember for your eighteenth birthday I had a sweet silver necklace with a Tiffany heart sent to you. New York has such a special place in my heart. In Manhattan, I felt I could conquer the world. It was so different to my life here at Kilteelagh.

Marianne, please show Rachel and Katie your New York. I believe it will instil in them the confidence they need right now. However, you are in charge, and you must do what you think is right.

I have spoken so little about Kilteelagh in this letter. The hard days of December must be getting to you; another reason to jet off to New York. Go and make new and cherished memories with Rachel and Katie, and maybe for yourself too. I wish you luck and lots of fun. Remember, when winter comes, spring can't be far behind. I so selfishly wish for myself that I will get to see one more spring in Kilteelagh, see the rhododendron in all its glory and the daffodils bloom for me one last time.

Love,

Collie xx

Marianne looked at the date, 3 December. She didn't know if she wanted to return to New York, though she knew the girls would enjoy it. Collie usually got her way, and she knew this letter was not so much a request as an order to make Christmas a happy time again for Rachel and Katie. A part of her resented her grandmother's interference. She stuffed the envelope behind the clock on the mantelpiece and went to the design room. Fiknete and Dolores were due any minute. She switched on the heater because the central heating radiators were not enough to keep the high-ceilinged room warm. Dolores had brought the electric heater the day before, because she said their toes were turning numb as they carried out the close work on the blue chiffon dresses. Fiknete had elaborately coughed to show her breath could be seen, and she insisted there was ice on the inside of the window glass. Marianne knew she wasn't wrong. In her bedroom upstairs there was a light film of ice on the inside of the bay window. She would never admit it to Dolores, because she knew she would mock her for spending a fortune on the restoration of the gazebo instead of ploughing her cash into heating and insulation in the main house.

Marianne laid out the pink silk fabric and was pinning down the pattern pieces when she heard Dolores come into the kitchen. Huffing and puffing loudly because of the cold wind outside, she called out to Marianne.

'I'm going to put the kettle on, do you want a coffee?'

Rather than shout back a reply, Marianne joined her in the kitchen.

'Is everything all right?' Dolores asked.

'Collie sent a letter suggesting I take the girls to New York for a week later this month.'

'Oooh, nice for some.'

'She said since Aisling died, the girls haven't enjoyed Christmas.'

'Are you surprised? They loved their mother so much, and

what a rotten time of year for it to happen. There's nothing worse than death, a wake and a funeral right before Christmas Day.'

'I wish Collie had told me how to deal with this.'

'She has. Go to New York.' Dolores looked straight at Marianne. 'You're going to have to make the decision for the girls. Be firm. Katie didn't want the lights back on the Christmas after losing her mum, but Collie got tough and said it was happening. Even when Rachel backed up her sister, Collie held tight.'

'I'm not sure I'm that strong.'

Dolores flicked a dog hair from the cushion on the armchair beside the stove.

'That poor little girl needs something to pull her out of herself. I never knew how they got through these past few years. We all got Katie the best presents, but nobody could soothe the hurt in her heart. My theory, for what it's worth, is that she thinks she can't enjoy Christmas any more. She feels guilty.'

'But will bringing them over to New York really make a difference?'

'Who knows, but it might be a lovely distraction.'

'It would be nice to show them my home city, but—'

'But what? It can't be any worse than the last three wretched Christmases they had. You have a chance to make real memories with them and give them a respite from Kilteelagh. Show them there's a big world out there. And let's face it, most of it is in New York.'

Marianne was about to answer when they heard Fiknete's Mini pull into the cobbled backyard. A whoosh of cold swept through the kitchen as Fiknete pushed opened the door and staggered in, carrying a big saucepan.

'Vegetable stew for all of us; central heating for our bellies in this old house,' Fiknete said, placing the saucepan on the Aga.

She got herself a mug and waited for Dolores to pour the coffee.

'Have you heard? Bridie in the post office has retired.'

'She threatens that every year.'

'Well, I have heard more; should I tell it?'

'Go on, it's not so bad if we're gossiping about Bridie. She's said enough about all of us in the past.' Dolores laughed.

Fiknete touched the large bun at the back of her head as if she was preparing to go on camera. 'She has resigned because she has had to. There is talk about money missing.'

'How could that be?' said Marianne.

'That's not good,' Dolores said.

'She was made to resign, and the running of the post office is being handed over to somebody else.'

'Well, I hope this affects her position on the town council, too,' Dolores said.

Marianne put her empty mug in the sink. 'Time to stop the gossip and get on with our work,' she said, and Fiknete and Dolores looked taken aback by the sharpness in her voice.

Fiknete, who was never a woman to back down, turned to Marianne. 'I would never gossip about you or Kilteelagh, Dolores knows that too, but Bridie has brought this on herself. She has a vicious tongue about most people in this town, and especially people who have moved in recently.'

Dolores put her hand up to stop Fiknete talking. 'Marianne, remember, is like her grandmother. Collie never wanted to hear gossip about anybody either. She always said we all lived in glass houses and she didn't want to draw any stones her way,' she said as they made their way to the design studio.

At the door, Marianne stopped. 'It's OK, but no gossip interfering with our work in this room,' she said, and the others nodded in agreement.

Marianne took the shears and began to slice along the edges of a pattern as Fiknete set herself up at her sewing machine.

The sound of the shears as they scraped across the table slicing the silk, and the machine whirring as Fiknete rang down a long side seam, filled the room. Dolores walked out to the hall a few times and they heard her on the phone, talking about the collection and the fashion show. After the final call, she rushed back into the room, her face red with excitement.

'That was my old friend, she's a buyer with a major department store and she's very interested in seeing your collection, Marianne.'

Marianne, who was trimming the collar pieces, stopped what she was doing. 'Which store?'

'I won't say yet, but she wants to come to the show.'

Fiknete raised her head. 'Do you want me to leave the room?'

'Don't be silly; it's just best not to know at the moment. Nerves are high enough as it is,' Dolores said.

'Can we have a hint?' Fiknete said.

'No, I don't want to know, I have too many butterflies in my stomach already,' Marianne said, her voice shaky.

'Well, I would like to know where my fine stitching is going to end up,' Fiknete said, her voice betraying her annoyance.

'Fiknete, it's not happening, all right,' Marianne snapped.

Dolores threw her hands in the air in frustration.

'Marianne, it's a real opportunity. The collection deserves this and so does the designer. Have faith, darling, and trust me.'

Muttering that she needed a break, Marianne pushed past Dolores and dashed up the stairs. She went to her bedroom on the second floor. Shaking, she marched to the window and pressed her forehead against the cold of the glass. Taking deep breaths, she concentrated on the view.

Outside, the clouds were huddling over the distant trees. The wind was whipping around Kilteelagh, and it was about to rain. It was a dull, miserable day, and she felt every bit of it. She was afraid of the next steps, because if they went wrong, so too would her life here at Kilteelagh. There was such love and loyalty for this old place in her heart, it sometimes frightened her. She longed for spring, when the garden would begin to bud and the birds would start to sing and fuss about, making nests. She must get Jack working on a wild seed bed in the front paddock, she thought, and mentally chastised herself because Kilteelagh House had got so under her skin. When there was a tap on the door, she knew it was Dolores.

'Have I done or said something wrong? I certainly never intended that.'

Marianne clenched her fists, her nails digging into the palms of her hands in an effort to stop the tears rising inside her.

'I feel a fool, Dolores. Don't think of me as ungrateful, please. Somehow, I like it the way it is, working together in my studio, and the department store step sounds so big and into the unknown and—'

'Is that all it is, girl? You had me worried,' Dolores said, sitting on the edge of the bed. She tapped the duvet beside her, and Marianne sat down.

'What would you be if you were not frightened and over-whelmed right now? But that doesn't mean you can't do it. Your designs are amazing, and we want a wide audience to appreciate and buy them.'

'But what if the department store buyer actually *likes* my pieces and the orders come flooding in? I'm not set up for that. That scenario would be a death knell for me as a designer...'

Dolores shushed her loudly, like you would a child who was overreacting.

'You are jumping ahead of yourself. Right now, we concentrate on putting on the best show ever. Your designs will wow, I just know it.'

'I wish. But what if they do and I can't deliver?'

Dolores caught Marianne's hands and squeezed them gently. 'Remember, I have done this before, and I have done consultancy work for a few Irish designers on a freelance basis over the years too. All I'd need is a few weeks to get a bigger operation set up.'

'I'm scared, Dolores, I don't want to jeopardise our future here at Kilteelagh. I've worked in the industry long enough to have heard all the warnings about expanding too soon.'

'Hush, you're putting the cart before the horse; let's take one step at a time.'

Marianne shivered. 'Suddenly, this has gone from the three of us in one room at Kilteelagh, hoping to have a fashion show and a few orders, to having the potential for something so much bigger.'

'Dream big, and let's work hard and see where we go.' Dolores got to her feet and held out a hand. 'Come on, we need to go down and try Fiknete's stew or she'll get in a strop.'

When they got to the kitchen, Fiknete had laid the table and was hunched over the stove, ladling stew into a bowl.

'Is everything all right?' she asked, without raising her head from her intense stirring of the pot.

'Yes, I'm sorry,' Marianne said.

Fiknete handed the bowl of stew to her.

'No need to apologise, you have a lot riding on this, and we understand. Collie would have been climbing the walls by now.'

Dolores giggled and the mood in the room lightened.

Fiknete ladled stew into the other two bowls and sat down at the table. 'Anyone in a mood for another story from our great town?' she asked, then suddenly her face darkened. 'It involves Katherine, and I don't think I should tell it,' she added, grinding pepper into her stew.

'You've started, so you should finish,' Dolores said.

Fiknete looked to Marianne, who pretended to be concentrating on cutting a hunk of beef. 'If you don't mind, Marianne?'

'Just get on with it,' Marianne said, her voice cross.

'Everybody is saying she is going all out to win Kilteelagh

back—' She stopped when she saw Marianne frowning. 'I'm sorry, but people talk when they come in for the alterations. I hear everything.'

'What are they saying about me?' Marianne asked.

Fiknete's face went red. 'You don't want to hear any of that.'

'Is it that bad?'

'No, I don't feel comfortable telling you. You're my boss,' said Fiknete, lowering her eyes and pushing the stew around her bowl.

Dolores, who had been eating, wiped her mouth with a cloth napkin. 'Maybe we should talk about the weather. It's always a good fallback.'

Marianne shook her head. 'I'm sorry, but sometimes I get so tired of people talking behind my back. I would like to know what they're saying.'

Fiknete put her spoon down on the table beside her bowl.

'OK, they say you are having an affair with Jack, and he is only after you to get his hands on Kilteelagh House. He only rents the place beside the school, and they say Katherine is going to bring you to court and take Kilteelagh back and when that happens, Jack will leave you high and dry.'

'And what do you two think?' Marianne said, leaning back in her chair and folding her hands.

'I don't believe any of it. I never talk about you. They ask me about what you are doing here at Kilteelagh, but I say I have signed a confidentiality clause,' Fiknete said.

Marianne burst out laughing. 'Fiknete, what have you done? Now they'll think I'm a right prima donna.'

Dolores looked at her two friends. 'Nothing wrong with a bit of mystery. I've heard the same stupid stories, most of them put out by Bridie – not that anyone will listen to her now. You plough your own path, dear. That's what Collie did, and it worked very well for her.'

'There are times I would love to return to my anonymous, boring old life,' Marianne sighed.

'But you would miss us too much, not to mention you would definitely miss everything about Kilteelagh,' Dolores said, and the three of them returned to their food.

'Seriously though, do you miss New York?' Fiknete asked after a while.

'All the time, and especially this morning, I guess. Don't get me wrong: I love it here, but it would be so neat to meet up with friends downtown or in Central Park.'

'Go there and bring the girls; enjoy city life. You deserve it,' Dolores said.

'I don't know, there are so many memories of my parents there, especially around Christmas. New York is a different place for me now, but yes, I think the girls would love it.'

Marianne looked at her phone.

'Time to get back to work.'

Dolores gave a small clap as Fiknete looked from one woman to the other, chortling happily.

TWENTY-SEVEN

Two days later, Rachel came home and stomped upstairs to her room, banging the door behind her.

'She's in a mood,' Katie said.

'Get on with your homework, I'll be back in a minute.'

'Why do I have to miss all the fun? Can't I come with you?'

She picked up Katie's maths copy and handed it to her.

'Please, sweetheart, give me a break.'

Katie sighed. 'OK, but when am I going to be let in on what's really going on around here?'

Marianne had to hammer loudly on Rachel's door to be heard over the sound of music.

'Are you OK? Can I come in?'

Rachel didn't answer but unlocked the door.

'Please turn down the music so we can talk.'

Rachel did as she was asked and sat on the bed.

'I'm all right, you didn't need to check on me.'

'Is that being OK, slamming doors and not talking to anyone?'

Rachel shrugged her shoulders. 'What do you want from

me? There's nothing wrong with banging a door every now and again.'

'True, but it isn't really your style. Let's talk it out.'

Rachel went to the window and twiddled with the blind cord. 'Can I say anything?'

'Yes.'

'You're not going to like it.' Rachel looked away for a few minutes, before turning towards Marianne. 'You got post this morning, and I read it.'

'What? Was it a mistake?'

Rachel shook her head.

'I knew it was from the gardai and I wanted to know what was in it.'

'And?'

'I'm getting that Garda Diversion thingy. I have an appointment in the garda station the third week in January.'

'OK, just give me the letter.'

Rachel took it out of her pocket and handed it over. Marianne scanned it.

'At least that's turning out right for us,' she said, stuffing the envelope in her jeans pocket. Walking quickly out of the room, she leaned over the banisters and called out to Katie to come upstairs.

'Am I in trouble?' Katie yelled back.

'No, come here. I need to talk to you and Rachel.'

Katie ran up the stairs.

'Can we talk in your room?' Marianne asked Rachel.

'Yeah, but I thought I wasn't in trouble.'

'You're not.'

'Are you selling Kilteelagh?' Katie mumbled, sitting on the bed beside her sister.

'Oh God, no! Do you guys want to go to Manhattan for a vacation?'

'New York?' Rachel asked.

'Will we be home in time for Christmas?' Katie asked.

Marianne indicated for the two girls to make room for her on the bed and sat down.

'But what about Mum's anniversary?' Rachel said.

'We'll leave in a few days and fly back in time for the twenty-first, so we can be here for Aisling's anniversary. What do you guys think?'

'Grandma wouldn't be too happy about this,' Katie said.

'Collie isn't here; but actually, it was her idea. She knew we all needed a good break.'

Marianne expected excitement, chatter and planning, but instead the girls were silent.

'What's wrong?' she asked. Rachel shook her head.

'Nobody has ever offered us a way of being away from Kilteelagh around Christmas. It's all we ever wanted. The pain was unbearable those days coming up to Christmas the last two years, but we don't want to forget our mam either,' Rachel said.

'I never want to do school plays again when everyone has to bring their parents to watch – you know what I mean?' Katie added.

'I do,' Marianne said gently.

'Are we really going?' Rachel asked.

'But what about all the designing and the dresses?'

'We will have the show in the new year, but I might try to fit in a few meetings with the New York buyers while we are there. We will go for ten days. But most of the samples will be well on the way by then, and Dolores and Fiknete will keep everything going for me.'

'Are you going to use local girls as models?' Rachel asked.

'I'm not deciding that tonight. No more talk about that; let's chat about New York.'

Katie pulled at her sleeve.

'Can we go ice skating? Grandma said if we ever go to New York we had to skate in Central Park, but I also want to skate at the Rockefeller Center like in *Elf*.'

'I think we could fit in both as long as it isn't the same day.' Marianne laughed.

'Can we buy Christmas presents for each other over there? Where are we going to stay?'

'Yes, we can do all our shopping, and I think I should be able to arrange an apartment.'

'Like we're living there?' Katie asked.

'It would be in Brooklyn, but that's where Dyker Heights is, and it's famous for having the best Christmas lights in the world.'

Katie snuggled in close. 'But what about Benji? He can't come with us.'

'I'm hoping we can persuade Dolores to let him have a vacation at hers.'

Rachel got under the covers.

'I'm glad we're going to New York, but can I have my room back, please?'

As Katie and Marianne went downstairs, Rachel stood on the landing and watched. She called Marianne when they reached the hall and silently mouthed thank you.

'We're going to make a list of everything we want to do in New York,' Katie said, hurrying off to get her best notebook and pen, but turning after a couple of steps to hug Marianne around the neck. 'This is going to be the best holiday ever!'

The next day Marianne was up extra early in her studio. She had cut out the latest design after Katie finally went to sleep the night before, and now she had to create a dress to match Collie's navy satin gown. She intended to sew it herself and wanted to have it done before they flew out. Collie's dress was big and heavy, the satin adding gravitas. By way of contrast, she wanted her showstopper to reflect the wispiness and lovely lightness of the collection dresses. It would be the design that was going to make the collection stand out. Reaching up to the top shelf of the cupboard, she pulled down a bolt of printed silk which she had found in one of Collie's attic cases. It had a cream background with gold and cream roses interspersed with brown and light green foliage. It was so opulent she knew her design needed to be simple and chic. As she unfolded the bolt, a small bag marked 'Clones lace border' fell out from between the folds of the fabric. It was vintage lace which had been delicately crocheted with a fine hook. There were different motifs: a clover circle and flowers arranged in two repeating rows along the scalloped border. Marianne held it up to the fabric and she knew immediately what her design should be. Getting out her tape measure, she measured the lace to make sure she had enough for a full skirt.

Taking out her sketch pad, she quickly drew with a pencil a simple V-neck dress with wide straps at the shoulders, a silk lace slip bordered with the lace falling below the hem. Dolores called out as she came through the kitchen. She gasped when she saw the fabric.

'I remember when Collie ordered this from a new fabric shop in Dublin. Every year she took it down but was afraid to cut into it. She said it cost her so much, she was terrified she would make a very costly mistake. She would be so proud that you're not afraid of it.'

'I've decided I'm definitely going to take the girls to New York. We fly out on the eleventh and return on the twenty-first. I've cut out all the dresses, and I should have this one finished myself before I go.'

'You want to know if we can manage?'

'It's ten days, but can you?'

Dolores smiled. 'Everything will run like clockwork; you have left it all in the hands of two bossy women. Let's hope Fiknete and I are still friends when you come back.'

TWENTY-EIGHT

A few days later, Marianne was in her bedroom, ironing clothes to put in the suitcases when she heard a car come up the avenue. Thinking it might be Jack, she glanced out the window. Fear swept through her when she saw Katherine in the driver's seat. What if she had come to stop the girls going to America? She considered hiding, but she knew if Katherine had something she needed to get off her chest, she would not leave until she'd had her say.

It would be so Katherine, she thought, to create a fine mess and stop them going to New York, leaving her to pick up the pieces and tell the girls. Shuddering because she felt cold, Marianne walked down the stairs as Katherine pulled up at the front.

She heard Katherine run up the steps and bang loudly on the door. Marianne paused, wondering if she should ring Jack or Dolores, but when Katherine knocked sharply again and called out her name, she took a deep breath and opened the door.

Katherine looked excited and was smiling when she stepped into the hall. 'I heard the girls are off to New York and I wanted to give them some money. You can't have enough spending money in a big city,' she said.

'They're at school; we don't leave until tomorrow.'

'I know, but I was hoping to talk to you as well.'

Marianne stood back as Katherine made her way down the hall to the kitchen as if she were a welcome guest. 'I have so much to do for our trip away. I don't have the energy to fight with you, Katherine.'

'I know,' she said as she pulled out a chair at the kitchen table and sat down. 'Sit and hear me out, please.' Marianne reluctantly sat down. 'I don't blame you for being hesitant, I have not behaved very well in the past. You haven't heard from me in a while because I've been getting help. I know I was on a slippery slope with the drink, but I'm fourteen days off it now and counting. I was hoping we could work things out.'

'I never wanted to fall out...' Marianne said, but Katherine motioned to her to stop talking.

'Hear me out and let me tell you, please. I've got help for my drinking and, with Steve's support, I'm doing fine. The truth is that I always hated this house, and the way Mother would never leave it. I resented it, but when she left it to you, I guess it awoke something in me. Yes, I wanted to sell it and make money, and maybe because my relationship with my mother was never the best, I wanted to destroy what she held dear. I don't mind admitting to that now. I'm sorry you got caught in the crossfire. I know you have enough on your plate.'

She sighed loudly before continuing. 'Steve wants me to take the offer of the field. A part of me wants to continue the fight for Kilteelagh, but Steve has made it clear what will happen if I do. He has been pushed too far, and I know he will leave and take the girls if I continue with this fight for Kilteelagh.'

She swallowed hard. 'So, I will take the bloody field – not because I want to, but because I have to put my marriage and my family first. If my mother had left enough to me in the first place, and been half-decent about everything, we could have got off on a better footing, but Collie only ever cared about Kilteelagh.'

Katherine shuffled and pushed her hair out of her eyes. 'Collie should have left that field to me anyway. It does round off our farm nicely, and we're hoping to build a house there we can rent out until the girls are older. Eventually, one or both of them may want to live there, or we can sell it to finance their dreams.' She clenched her hands tight and looked at Marianne. 'I have been rotten to you, and I have had a big mouth, spouting on what I thought of you, and I regret that now. You and the girls are family, and I can only apologise for behaving so badly.'

Marianne was silent for a moment as Katherine looked at her anxiously.

'Are you sure? You seemed so set on Kilteelagh House and lands,' Marianne said.

Katherine threw her eyes to the ceiling. 'I have made a goddamn fool of myself. Everybody knew how much I hated this place. I was hurt, and I was lashing out at you when I should have been examining myself. Collie knew I would sell up if she left it to me, and she did the right thing securing the future of Kilteelagh with you. Steve said if we go legal it will destroy all of us. We're family, and that's what is important.'

'We will have to get solicitors involved in the transfer of the field.'

'I know, and I know I will have to pledge to have no further claim on Kilteelagh House or lands.'

'Something like that.'

'I will do it – if you're happy, that is.'

Marianne looked at Katherine. 'I never wanted any of this aggravation, I'm glad we can put it behind us.'

'Me too,' Katherine said, reaching across and grabbing Marianne's hand and squeezing it tight. 'Collie made the right choice; I'll give her that. We're proud of what you have done here, Marianne.'

'You'll come to the fashion show?'

'Front-row seats, but before I go, can you please tell me what Fiknete is doing back at Kilteelagh? She and Collie were as thick as thieves.'

'Collie taught her how to sew and now she's helping out, sewing samples for the show and the buyers.'

'Collie would be chuffed. I have to go, but let's talk when you get back from New York. We must have a get-together over Christmas.' Katherine reached into her handbag and took out two envelopes. 'An early gift for each of the girls. Just do one favour for me in New York, OK?'

'Do you want something brought back?'

'God no, there's nothing worse than relatives and friends who hand out shopping lists.' Katherine pulled another envelope out of her bag and handed it to Marianne.

'I went online, and I have taken the liberty of booking an ice-skating session at the Rockefeller Center for the three of you. Please take a lot of photos.'

'Katie really wants to go there.'

'I know.'

'This is so kind of you—'

Katherine looked embarrassed as she sprinted for the door. 'Nonsense, it's nothing really.'

She rushed to her car, sounding the horn and waving as she went down the avenue.

Marianne watched her go from the front door. After the car had disappeared from sight, she lingered on the top step. Breathing in deeply, she smiled to herself that things were starting to change. Suddenly, she felt the true and proper owner of Kilteelagh House. She called the dog inside and closed the door.

TWENTY-NINE

January 2019

Kilteelagh House
Balgaddy
Co. Wicklow

My dearest Marianne,

How I hope you took up my suggestion of a trip to New York for all three of you. There is something about Manhattan that gladdens the heart and makes the spirit soar. Lots of the hustle and bustle also makes one appreciate the beautiful peace we have here at Kilteelagh. I feel now my days are running out; I know that I no longer will feel the freedom of a summer day at Kilteelagh, or the warm sunshine on my back, or the smell of the sea as I sit out on a picnic blanket, my shoes thrown off and my toes bare towards the waves. These are memories now, like when the warm breeze blows in the windows of the drawing room and somewhere along the hall a door bangs shut. So too are the doors shutting on the life that has been lived. What is to come, who knows?

I am certain of two things. I will be ready for death when it knocks on the door. When that time comes, I want in death to be with Lucas. I am hoping you can make that happen.

In the last weeks I have been left with time to think back on my life here and I can say without any regret that I love Kilteelagh, every brick in this house, every blade of grass in the fields and every drop of water in our lake.

As anyone who has pencilled in a date with death will tell you, my thoughts now are occupied with how I have lived my life, and wondering could I have done anything differently. The answer of course is yes, but how easy it is with hindsight to think up different scenarios. We can only do our best at the time. I feel that I wronged Mike and did not give much thought to righting that. With Lucas, did I put too much reliance on the fact that someday we would be together? Should I have gone looking for him when Mike died? What exactly held me back?

I loved Lucas all my life. I clung to the hope that he would one day be able to return to me. Mike was my rock, and when he died, I thought I could not go on. The fact that Lucas might someday return to me sustained me, but now I wonder, did it equally trap me? Lucas did not make it back to Kilteelagh. I was free, but in my heart, I knew he wasn't. What was I to do: haul three young children across to The Netherlands and upset his family life? If I waited for him, I would know that if he did come back to me, he was really free to love again. That is the only way we could enjoy any future happiness. It wasn't meant to be, and I can only hope now that if there is an after-life we can meet and at least nod in passing, knowing that at one time, we meant a great deal to each other.

It is still my hope that if Lucas were to walk up the avenue to Kilteelagh, you would welcome him. Speak fondly of me to him. I meant to include a special ring in a black velvet box, but I can't find it. I had Dolores go through the drawer and it wasn't there.

Maybe when there is the clear-out, after I have departed, you will find it. The reason I want you to have it is twofold. You have lovely long fingers, and the ring would sparkle beautifully on your ring finger. Lucas gave it to me that first and only weekend we spent together at Kilteelagh. It was so sweet. He woke before me on the Saturday morning. When I opened my eyes, I was terrified he had slipped away without saying goodbye, but he had left a sweet note on the dressing table saying not to worry, he would be back. When he strolled up the avenue about an hour later, my heart skipped for joy. He said he had gone to Balgaddy to find a florist where he could buy a bouquet of flowers, but as he passed Maurer's jewellery shop he saw the most beautiful ring on display. He said it sparkled in the morning sunshine and that reminded him of me. Lucas presented the ring to me and told me every time I looked at it, it would remind me I was very much loved.

Of course, I could never wear the ring; it was so beautiful and a rather extravagant piece of jewellery. There were days I got up early to try it on, for a short time before anybody at Kilteelagh woke up, and days when everyone was out, and I could play pretend and wear it. Funnily enough, it was always your favourite piece, and when you were young you used to beg me to be allowed to wear it for dress-up.

The strange thing was, when Mike died, I surely could have worn it all the time, but somehow, it felt strange and disloyal to Mike to do so. If I have a regret, it is that. I should have looked for Lucas, but the fear of rejection was so great, I remained at Kilteelagh pining for his return.

I ask you now, Marianne, to please wait to scatter my

ashes at Kilteelagh until Lucas can join me. He has not come back to me, but it is my fervent hope that in death we can, even if only in a symbolic way, be united. He told me when he was free, he would come looking for me to persuade me to be with him. We also pledged in death to find each other by leaving instructions in our wills as to what to do with our ashes. I leave this request with you now. Please keep my ashes at Kilteelagh until Lucas arrives.

It is my last hope as I look down the avenue that, in death, he will come back to me and that maybe he has made arrangements for such. I can only pray he has, and my devotion all these years has been to someone who loved me as much as I loved him.

Have I learned anything from this? I have, and it is pretty simple. Love in the now, and love big.

Thank you, dearest Marianne,

Love,

Collie xx

Marianne checked to see if Collie's urn was still on the mantelpiece. Katie and Rachel had picked that spot beside their mother's urn. She shivered; the room was cold because they had not bothered to light the fire in the fireplace in a few days. The kids usually had dinner in the kitchen, before Katie joined Marianne in the studio and Rachel went to her room to listen to music. The drawing room never got warm enough with just the heat from the radiators; it was bloody freezing in here. Walking towards the window, she saw there was ice on the wallpaper in the far corner and she thought she must get Jack to dry-line this room at the same time as the bedroom.

She had left the ring in the drawer of the mahogany table in the design studio. Walking to the old dining room, she thought back to Collie getting up early to try the ring on and wear it for a few minutes, enough time, she guessed, to dream of what might have been and sustain her for another day at Kilteelagh.

The ring was in its velvet box. Taking it out, she held it up to the light. Daggers of colour flashed across the diamond.

Slipping it on, she moved closer to the window. She noticed the intensity of the purple changed, depending on which way she moved her hand. She saw Jack get out of his car and make his way around to the front of the house. She was still wearing the ring when he knocked on the door.

'Hey, the designer buys her own jewellery. Where did you get such a beautiful ring?'

Embarrassed, Marianne put her hand behind her back. 'It was Collie's. I was trying it on.'

'It suits your long fingers. Come on, give me a look,' he said as he reached and gently took her hand from behind her back.

'Vintage, that's not from around these parts.'

'Like you would know.'

'I confess I don't know very much, but I like to think I know a nice piece of jewellery when I see it. I imagine something more refined and simpler would be to your taste.'

She didn't answer, and he appeared flustered and hurriedly started to talk about dry-lining the bedroom walls.

'I'm going down to the hardware shop; I thought I would measure up the bedroom today.'

'Can you price out the drawing room too? It's like a fridge in there.'

He took out his tape and made for the stairs.

'You can help, if you like.'

She laughed.

'After New York and then Christmas I have a lot of catching up to do in my studio. Best I get cracking on the work in there.'

She was only in the studio a few moments when Jack

tapped lightly on the door. She called out, but he had already opened the door.

'Would you like a coffee?' she asked.

'Sure,' he said, a little too quickly, and she looked at him.

'Is there something eating you?' she asked.

He swallowed hard.

'I have tickets to see a band at Vicar Street tonight – the first gig of the new year. I wondered, would you like to come along? It's short notice, but maybe Dolores or somebody could look after the kids?'

When she didn't answer immediately, he looked upset, and she wanted to laugh out loud.

'Give a girl time to think. I have to look at my day.'

'Sorry, I wasn't thinking.'

She dug him lightly in the ribs. 'I would love to go, if I can get a sitter.'

'OK! Great news! Well, I'm going to finish here around four, go home and change and pick you up at six. Maybe we could have a bite to eat before the gig?'

'This is beginning to sound like a date.'

'I jolly well hope so! What else would it be?'

It was Marianne's turn to feel embarrassed. 'I'm not sure,' she said.

He stepped closer to her. 'Look, I may be the gardener and handyman and not-yet-qualified legal adviser, but I hope I mean more than that to you.'

Reaching out, he pushed her hair gently out of her eyes. Feeling nervous, Marianne giggled. He smiled at her, before kissing her gently on the lips.

'Now, I think I had better make a start on the work before the boss fires me,' he said, pulling away from her.

When she heard Jack walk across the bedroom floor upstairs, she smiled. It had been a long time since she went out on a date, and even longer since she was kissed. She thought of all her dirty laundry piled up in a corner beside the bay window in the bedroom, and she cringed to think that was the wall showing the most damage from the damp and cold. No point thinking Jack wouldn't notice, because he was the sort of person who took in everything and made deductions even from what was hidden or unsaid.

She picked up the photographs Fiknete had left on the table for her. They were photographs of the three dresses which had been sewn, finished, pressed and stored. Marianne liked that Fiknete had taken various close-ups of the seams in her bid to impress her. Dolores had left a note saying the dress samples had been dispatched and received by the department store buyer before the Christmas holidays, and the buyer had indicated she would like to see the whole collection. Marianne thought again how lucky she'd been in having these two to step in and take care of everything. It had left her free to focus on the girls, helping them make lots of wonderful memories in New York.

On their return, she'd worried how they would get through Aisling's death anniversary. The three of them had agreed that on the morning of the twenty-first they would walk down to the lake and light Japanese memorial candles for Aisling, Collie and Marianne's parents, then let them slip away on the water. Katie and Rachel had huddled close to Marianne as they wandered back to the house to have hot chocolate, then they'd all gone to bed to sleep off the jet lag.

After that, buoyed up by her Manhattan experience, Katie had wanted to prepare for Christmas by baking, the way she had done when her mother was alive. Marianne indulged her, baking cookies, icing a Christmas cake nobody managed to eat and making home-made garlands to drape across the drawing room ceiling and over Collie's portrait.

It was all they had to do, because while they were away Fiknete and Dolores had cleaned and polished the whole house, put up a real Christmas tree, strung up lights outside and inside and left a special box for Katie marked 'Christmas tree', so the young girl could decorate the tree. Katie had jumped for joy and insisted nobody would go to bed and rest until Kilteelagh was ready for Christmas. They added decorations they had bought in New York, with Marianne holding Katie up high to place a special star they bought in Macy's the day they visited the Empire State Building.

Afterwards, she found Katie looking up at the star.

'Did we get the angle wrong, sweetie?'

'No, I was thinking it's a beautiful tree and the best star we have ever had,' Katie said, rubbing her eyes with her fists and yawning.

Marianne had pushed her up the stairs to bed. Later, she herself stood looking at the tree. It was the best tree she had ever seen, and it was their Christmas tree at Kilteelagh House. From that moment on, she knew that Christmas at Kilteelagh was going to be very good. When she tried to thank Fiknete and Dolores, they had brushed her away, saying it was easy. 'We were both in a decorating mood, doing up our own places, so it made sense. We thought it would be a nice surprise.'

'The best,' Marianne said.

She sat down at the table and smiled to think the last time they had sat here was on Christmas Day, when she insisted on inviting Fiknete and Dolores for Christmas dinner. She had not intended to do so, but Dolores let it slip her son would not be able to make it home and she would be on her own. Fiknete asked her to the flat, but they had laughed and said they might kill each other in such a small place, or even in a big place if it was just the two of them. They both needed the distraction of more company, having spent so many days working in close quarters.

Fiknete had arrived on Christmas Day with plates of food they had never heard of, and Dolores brought a box of booze, the bottles rattling as she carried it from the car into the house. They had presents they put under the tree and insisted that everybody play charades after dinner. The two women had also organised the biggest surprise for Rachel and Katie: a coal-black kitten with a red ribbon around his neck.

'We are sure Marianne won't mind,' Dolores said anxiously.

'Kilteelagh has to have a cat of its own,' Fiknete said, and Marianne smiled and said it had better be a good mouser.

It was, Marianne thought, the best Christmas Day she ever had. When Katie was tucked into bed that night, she said she wished Fiknete and Dolores lived at Kilteelagh all the time.

Downstairs, Fiknete poured Baileys for all three of them and they sat, their feet stretched towards the last of the fire in the open fireplace of the drawing room.

'You must miss your family at this time of year,' Marianne said.

'I miss them all the time, but we talk a lot on the phone and we FaceTime.'

'Why did they go back to Kosovo?'

Fiknete took a long slurp of her drink.

'When we came to Ireland, we didn't have anything. We had fled for our lives. We literally had the clothes we were wearing. Here, everybody was good to us, but my mother never could settle. My father knew that learning to speak English was key and he did, along with my younger brother, but my mother never would. When, after a few years the Irish government gave us a choice of to stay or return to our homeland with a few thousand euros to help us start again, my mother and father decided to return. My younger brother went with them.'

'You were left alone?'

'I was twenty-one years of age and I wanted to stay here. I had met a man and I thought I was in love. We moved to Waterford, but that relationship fell apart soon after. I arrived back at Kilteelagh and had nothing, but Collie and Dolores looked after me.'

Dolores held up her glass to the portrait. 'To Collie Keane.'

Fiknete and Marianne did the same. Fiknete looked at Marianne. 'If your grandmother and Dolores had not helped me, I honestly don't know what I would have done. I stayed here at Kilteelagh helping out, until Collie and Dolores came up with a plan for my alterations business and Dolores gave me my little place in Balgaddy.'

Dolores sat out on the edge of her chair and poked the fire, making sparks flit up the chimney.

'Fiknete, you deserved our help. You are an expert at the alterations and now at sewing designer clothes.'

'None of which I could have done without you two.'

She pointed out the drapes on the drawing room window. 'I made those; I remember Collie never bothered with curtains. She said who would be looking in at Kilteelagh House, and if they bothered to tramp up the avenue, they deserved to see something. But of course, once I set up in business, she had me make drapes for most of the windows here. And Dolores suddenly developed a liking for buying long skirts she had to have altered. They told a lot of their friends too, because soon my business was ticking over nicely.'

Dolores smiled. 'Equally we were lucky to meet Fiknete. It suited us all perfectly.'

They stayed in Kilteelagh that night but insisted on leaving early the next morning.

'You need time with your girls. We'll see you after New Year,' Dolores said firmly.

When Marianne waved the two of them off from the front steps, she thought she was very lucky to have these women in her life. Together they were just a little bit crazy, and that's exactly what Marianne loved about them.

Marianne shook herself back to the present and wandered to the kitchen and made some coffee. She heard Jack come down the stairs and she stepped out into the hall to intercept him and chat about the Vicar Street gig.

'There's coffee in the kitchen.'

He followed her and took the mug of coffee she offered. He took a sip, but quickly put the mug in the sink.

'No time, I am afraid. I have a lot on today and I had better get going if I am to be back in time to collect you. Are you good to go?'

She could see he was nervous because he kept putting his hand up to his fringe as if trying to arrange it and it never stayed where he wanted it to be.

'Yes, I am good to go,' she said shyly.

'Great, can I pick you up around five?'

She nodded and he dawdled awkwardly before gathering up his tools bag from the hall and leaving by the front door. She heard him shout hello to Dolores, who had pulled up in her car, and she quickly checked her face in the mirror because she didn't want Dolores detecting any changes and cross-examining her about whether Jack was 'the one'.

When Dolores let herself in a few minutes later, she was all smiles.

'I wonder what has come over Jack, he seemed so happy.'

'Was he? I asked him to dry-line the drawing room along with the bedroom, so maybe it is the thought of extra work and making more money.'

'Jack would never be so crass. No, definitely there was a spring in that man's step. I think it's lovely,' she said pointedly, but Marianne pretended to be interested in Fiknete's photographs and studied them intensely. She continued to keep her head in her work when Fiknete bustled in soon after.

'Let me put a few dishes in the fridge and grab a coffee,' she said as she hurried down the hall.

When she came back, Fiknete was beaming.

'I saw coffee mugs in the sink, and I know Dolores only likes her coffee after eleven. Have you been entertaining this morning, or maybe even late at night?'

Marianne didn't say anything; Dolores dug Fiknete in the ribs. 'Love may be in the air, methinks,' she said.

'How wonderful. Please, Marianne, brighten a dull January day and tell us all about it.'

Marianne, who was hand-stitching a velvet trim on a chiffon sleeve, put down her work.

'If I didn't like you two so much, I might get very cross,' she said.

'So, it's true – you guys are an item?' Fiknete said.

'An item?'

Dolores guffawed out loud.

'Fiknete, here is more Irish than the Irish themselves, and this proves it. Translation: together, boyfriend-girlfriend. Maybe more.'

Marianne put down her sewing.

'We like each other, and he asked me to go to Vicar Street with him tonight.'

'And you said yes?' Fiknete said.

'Yes, but I have to find a babysitter.'

'I will,' both Dolores and Fiknete said at the same time.

Marianne grimaced. 'He is great at doing work for me and helping me out, though. What if this spoils the easy friendship we have?'

'Pooh, what stupidity,' Dolores said as Fiknete caught both of Marianne's hands and twirled her around the room.

'Here you are, a young woman tucked away in Kilteelagh House. No offence to this beautiful place, but you must celebrate and go out and enjoy yourself. If you were in New York, wouldn't you be going out every other night?'

'Maybe, but my life was different there.'

'But you are so young, you need to enjoy yourself, have a drink, listen to music, dance, definitely kiss.' Fiknete closed her eyes as if she were conjuring up the different moments. When she popped her eyes open, she laughed and clapped her hands.

'Your hair needs to be done. Darling, you need a makeover, and what are you going to wear?'

'He said it's only a bite to eat and a gig.'

Fiknete looked at Marianne aghast. 'And you believe that, silly girl?'

'That is what he said.'

Dolores looked at Marianne. 'I despair at the younger generation sometimes. Surely, if it is a date, you dress up, put your best foot forward.'

Marianne shrugged. 'I don't think it's that much of a big deal.'

'Nonsense,' Fiknete said. 'You have been asked out on a date.'

'I suppose,' Marianne said reluctantly.

'Well then, what are we waiting for? You need a cut and blow-dry, and you are in luck because my second skill is hair and make-up.'

'Not now, we have so much work to do. I can't let it interfere with our schedule. I have decided to have the fashion show at the end of February. It is when some of the Americans from the fashion magazines and the buyers will be in Dublin, and I think we can persuade a few of them to come to Kilteelagh for a show. Jay says the Americans are on holiday here, and they will love to get an invitation to a house like Kilteelagh. He is organising all of it for me.'

'He is a good friend if he can pull it off, but don't you think that is going to take a bit of planning on our side as well?' Dolores said, sounding a bit miffed.

'It is, but we have several weeks and we are good at working hard together,' Marianne said as she reached out and hugged Dolores tight across the shoulders.

She turned to Fiknete. 'I would like my hair done, but can it wait until lunchtime, or something like that?'

'I suppose,' Fiknete sighed.

Marianne took a large notepad from the mantelpiece.

'I thought if we could have a quick meeting to find out where we are and to bounce ideas about the show.'

Dolores sat down at her desk but didn't say anything.

Marianne sighed. 'Dolores, I didn't mean to upset you. I was genuinely giving us all a break, because once we put our heads down for the show, it will be work, work, work.'

'It would have been nice to get a heads-up, but yes, let's get on with things,' Dolores said in her marbles-in-the-mouth voice.

'Come on – let's plan the show,' Fiknete said, her exasperation showing as she flopped down on her chair.

Marianne opened her notebook and looked at the two women.

'I want us to plan a fashion show for the drawing room,' she said.

'Here in the house, are you mad?' Fiknete asked.

'No, she's not, it's a bloody brilliant idea. Like the way fashion shows used to be, in a salon,' Dolores said.

'Exactly. I have to ask Jack, but he may be able to build some sort of a runway. We have to decide if it is going to be an exclusive show specifically for buyers, or will we invite local people? Really the collection samples will not be on sale to the public,' Marianne said, her voice loaded with excitement.

Dolores took out her pen and pad and arranged them on the desk before she spoke. 'Personally, I think it would be good to do something nice for the community. What if we put on an afternoon rehearsal-type show for local people, and the fancy do in the evening, would that work? Kilteelagh House would look amazing with lots of lights and candles.'

'We charge an entrance fee for the community show to fundraise for local charities. I think you're right: if we do it in the afternoon, it will serve as a rehearsal for the evening show,' Marianne said, and the other two women nodded.

'Who are going to be the models?' Fiknete asked.

Marianne threw down her notepad. 'That's the biggest problem – I just don't know.'

'We could ask local girls to model the dresses,' Fiknete said.

'And have every mammy in town complaining! It will be a headache, but maybe we can work something out,' Dolores said.

'Good. I suppose you know who we should invite to the evening show as well.'

'It's my job to know that, leave it to me.'

Fiknete put her hand up before she spoke. 'I was wondering if there is going to be food and drink.'

'Prosecco for the fancy evening show, and we should have nibbles,' Dolores said.

'I make delicious mini cupcakes, bite-size. I would be happy to do it with KD for Kilteelagh Design on each one.'

Marianne rubbed her hands together and laughed. 'I should have told you guys to just go and organise a fashion show, because you have everything covered.'

'We are rather good at what we do,' Dolores said as she took out her large contacts book. 'Might as well get started now. Do you mind if I take over the kitchen table for a while?' she asked. She was out the door before Marianne could give her answer.

Fiknete began to thread Collie's sewing machine.

'The turquoise silk dress, it is quite slippery, so I want to work on it slowly over this afternoon. I don't fancy having to unpick any stitch on that fabric.'

'I'm torn between leaving the sleeves long and straight or just to the elbow.'

Fiknete pushed her hand through the sleeve that was

already tacked in place. 'I don't like a long, straight sleeve. What if the sun shines hot? A sleeve to the elbow can look quite chic.'

Marianne examined Fiknete's hand and turned up the sleeve to her elbow. 'I think you might be right; you have a good eye.'

'Collie always said that, but also that I had a big mouth and terrible taste in men.'

'Sounds like my grandmother. Diplomacy was never her strong point.'

Dolores stuck her head around the door.

'I have a photographer friend who will get press shots ready for us. It will cost a little, but he will give me mate's rates. What do you think?'

'Photographs to send out in the hope the magazines or newspapers use them?'

'Yes. He's a press photographer working on the side, so they will be good.'

'OK.'

'I have a good feeling about this fashion show,' Fiknete said, placing her fabric on the machine. 'I think you are going to put Kilteelagh on the map, something your grandmother always wanted.'

'Let's not put the cart before the horse – that was another of her sayings,' Marianne said, turning away to drape a new ochre-coloured silk over the mannequin.

Fiknete took the hint and soon the whirr of the sewing machine could be heard. They worked side by side, each absorbed in her own tasks until Dolores burst back in. She pinned a big poster to the wall.

'I stole one of Katie's blank bits of paper,' she said. Taking a ruler, she pointed at a column on the left. 'Do you see all these things, ranging from models, chairs, a carpenter to build the catwalk, stylists to manicurists, parking attendants and invitation designers, media and social media support? These are all the things and people you will need to stage a fashion show. There's a long road ahead, so I will take any help I can get.'

Marianne swallowed hard.

'Are you sure we can do this, Dolores?'

Dolores stood at the fireplace, hands on hips.

'I damn well know we can,' she said, and Fiknete clapped excitedly.

THIRTY

Later that day, Katie dropped into the studio, as she often did, to help out.

She would arrange the different spools of thread and ribbon and gather up any stray straight pins, pushing them deep into Collie's red and green pin cushion. This time with Katie was Marianne's favourite part of the day. Rachel was usually busy elsewhere or in her room, so she and Katie had their special hour together. This was the time she did the slow, delicate work, like attaching the ribbons onto a dress, sewing on buttons and pressing seams. Katie examined every detail.

'I wish I could be a model for you and wear one of these dresses,' she said.

'They're meant for adults, I'm afraid, and anyway, you're the designer and the inspiration. That surely is an awful lot better.'

Katie didn't look convinced. 'Do you think I could walk down the catwalk at the fashion show?'

'You mean, if we even have one in the fashion show. I'm not sure we will. I was thinking of the floor in the drawing room.'

Katie looked disappointed. 'We have to have a runway, and

Sarah said her dad will build it for you and Dolores says he's a diamond and he will do it, and I agree.'

'Did she indeed?'

'Yeah, Sarah's dad said it wouldn't take much work and he could do it, so it could be one you can take away from the room and store until the next fashion show.'

'I think I should employ you as my event organiser – Dolores might be out of a job.'

'But I could walk down the runway, throw flowers on the floor like a flower girl or something?'

'Do you really want to?'

'Yes, of course I do.'

'I suppose we will have to get a job for you then. Maybe at the end when we're showing Collie's ball gown and the long dress I am designing.'

'Rachel will come too.'

'Where am I going?' Rachel asked, strolling into the room.

Katie caught her hand. 'Come on, we have to practise the walk. Marianne said we can be models on the catwalk for her show.'

Rachel pulled her hand away. 'No way. I'm not doing that.'

'You have to. Ava Henderson said her sister is going to be modelling.'

'Who?' asked Marianne.

'Ava Henderson.'

'The girl who bullied you?'

Rachel pulled Katie's hair and told her to shut up.

'Will somebody please tell me what has been going on?' Marianne asked.

Rachel pushed her sister and gave her a fierce look.

'Everybody is talking about the fashion show. They say you'll be auditioning for models.'

'I haven't fully decided yet. But Ava Henderson is not welcome here, nor any of her family.'

Katie looked at Marianne in surprise. 'But we're friends now.'

Exasperated, Marianne said she was finished for the evening and needed to get ready to go out.

Fiknete, who had come in and taken her seat at the sewing machine after her break, announced she was going to help Marianne get ready.

'I think I can get dressed for a date, Fiknete. I love what you've done with my hair, but I don't need your input on my outfit.' Fiknete's face fell but Marianne remained unmoved. 'I'm going upstairs to have a shower and get dressed, and nobody is allowed to follow me,' she snapped, as Dolores came up the hall.

'Sounds like I've missed something interesting,' Dolores said as she led Fiknete into the kitchen.

When Marianne came back downstairs wearing her Levi jeans, a silk shirt and a denim jacket, Fiknete threw her eyes upwards. She made to say something but Dolores elbowed her in the ribs.

'You look beautiful, darling, and perfectly dressed for a concert,' Dolores said, making sure to stand in front of Fiknete.

'But there is so little make-up, please let me do it for you,' Fiknete said.

'No offence, but I like a more natural look,' Marianne said.

'Are you really going out with Sarah's dad?' Katie asked.

'Yes. I'll be back later.'

'I am going to wait up for you.'

'No need, darling. I'll come and kiss you goodnight once I get home.'

'Sarah says her dad really likes you.'

'And you have to stop gossiping about us,' Marianne said as she tickled Katie on the nape of her neck.

'We're going to catch up on all that gossip, while you head off to Dublin,' Dolores said, as she took Katie's hand to let Marianne slip out to the hall.

She was standing on the top step when Jack pulled up.

He jumped out and went around to the passenger door and opened it for her.

'Your carriage awaits, madam.'

Marianne was a little embarrassed because she knew without looking that Dolores, Fiknete, Rachel and Katie were hiding behind the drawing room curtains and watching.

'Don't mind the audience, let's get out of here,' he said, striding quickly to the driver's side. He beeped as he turned the car and sped down the driveway. When he was sure they could not be seen any more, and they had rounded the rhododendron bend, he pulled over to the side.

'How are you feeling?' he asked.

'It's ridiculous, I'm worried about leaving Katie.'

'You're basically their mum now, there's nothing strange about that.'

He kissed her cheek and she giggled.

'Well. Please tell me what's so funny,' he said.

'I was just thinking this is so like my first date with Harry Bennett in high school. Once we moved away from my house, he pulled over the car and we had our first kiss.'

Jack took her hand and kissed it.

'I would love to kiss you on the lips right now, but I'm a coward and afraid that Katie or, worse, Fiknete will appear out of nowhere.'

'That fear I understand,' Marianne said, and they laughed as they set off to the city.

Marianne was buzzing. Jack was attentive, the music loud. Jack held her; they swayed together to the music and he kissed her tenderly on the lips. After about an hour at the gig, he asked her did she want to slip away for some of the best fish and chips in town. He held her close, his arm around her shoulders as they walked up to Christchurch and queued outside Burdock's.

'There was a time it was wrapped in newspaper; that doesn't happen any more, but it's still the same taste,' he said as he led her back to the car.

'Aren't we going to eat now?' she asked.

'It will keep hot, let's head out to the sea.'

He drove to Sandymount where they got out and found a spot to sit and open up their fish and chips bags.

'When you go back, please pretend we were at a fancy restaurant, or Dolores will kill me,' Jack laughed as they dipped their chips in tomato sauce.

'And if Dolores doesn't, Fiknete and Katie definitely will.'

'I guess we had better synchronise our stories,' he said.

They sat watching the comings and goings of the harbour.

'How does this compare to a New York date?' he asked. When she didn't answer immediately, he shifted uncomfortably. 'Sorry I asked,' he said.

She took his hand. 'In New York I wore shoes that were too high and uncomfortable, got wasted on cocktails that cost too much, and went clubbing with people I barely knew. To be honest, I don't miss any of it. I love my life now at Kilteelagh. Though I think I am now really quite boring.'

'And I brought you on a boring date.'

'I didn't say that!'

He reached down and kissed her. 'I'm glad you moved to Kilteelagh,' he said.

They kissed passionately until she felt the chips carton slide off her lap. He lunged forward to catch it but missed, the chips spilling across the ground.

'Well, this is a first! I've never ended up picking fries off the ground on a date.' Marianne laughed.

'An unusual five-star experience, my dear, courtesy of Jack Farrelly,' he said, scooping the chips from the ground to a bin.

When he'd finished, he pulled Marianne into his arms.

'Shall we go back and face the inquisition at Kilteelagh?'

'I like it when it's just the two of us.'

'Why don't I take Dolores and Fiknete home, then come back to you at Kilteelagh?'

'You will wait for the all-clear from me?'

'Of course.'

'What about the car? Katie gets up very early – she will surely see it.'

'Not if I park it down by the gazebo.'

Dolores and Fiknete were in the kitchen pretending to be reading the newspapers when Marianne arrived home.

'Where's Jack?' Dolores asked.

'He said to go on out, he'll take you both home.'

'Oh, I thought I might stay the night? After all, I am back here at 8 a.m. anyway,' Fiknete said.

Marianne shook her head. 'Sorry, Fiknete, but I don't want Katie's morning routine interrupted.'

'I imagine she'll sleep late; she only went to bed an hour ago,' Dolores said, but she leaned over and pulled Fiknete's arm. 'You can stay at mine, darling; let Marianne have her beauty sleep.'

Marianne didn't say anything as she watched the two women go out the front door to the car.

She slumped at the kitchen table. She had no idea what she was doing. Jack wasn't even divorced yet.

What would Katie and Sarah think?

She got up and pulled the bottle of whiskey from the cupboard under the kitchen sink and poured a large measure into a cup.

Gulping the whiskey, she was about to text Jack, when there was a light tap on the kitchen window.

'Is the coast clear?' he asked as he stepped into the room.

He grabbed her to kiss her, but she pulled away.

'I'm sorry, Jack, it's too soon; your divorce isn't officially through yet.'

'But—'

Marianne sighed. 'I should never have let you kiss me before. We have to wait.'

'It will be through very soon.'

'I have to think of Katie, and you have to think of Sarah.'

He sat down.

'Ah, Marianne.'

'And I have to get my collection together.'

He grabbed her hand, but she moved away.

Jack stood up. 'Marianne, I respect your decision. Just promise, when you are ready, you will tell me, and can we please stay friends in the meantime?'

'I would like that.'

He moved to the back door.

'You did enjoy tonight, didn't you?'

'Very much,' she said.

She was going to kiss him on the cheek, but she heard Katie's step on the stairs.

Jack rushed out the door as Katie, rubbing her eyes, hurried down the hall.

'Rachel is coming downstairs too; we have something for you. You came back so late,' she said.

Rachel, yawning, joined her sister in the hall. 'Let's go into the kitchen,' she said.

'We have a card for you,' Katie said.

'It's not my birthday or anything. What a lovely surprise.'

Rachel was grinning broadly as Katie handed over the card. It was home-made, with a hand-drawn picture of Marianne telling off what looked like the red-faced Hendersons. A bubble from her mouth said, *Go to hell!*

Marianne smiled. Slowly, she opened the card.

We love you. Can we call you Mum?
Katie and Rachel

She read the words, tears rising inside her.

When she didn't say anything, Rachel pulled Katie to her. 'Is it too early?' she asked Marianne.

'God, no. I can't believe it. Are you sure?'

Katie ran and embraced Marianne tight, Rachel following, wrapping the three of them into a big hug.

'I guess I should tell people to go to hell more often,' she said, and they laughed out loud, making the dog jump up to join in the fun.

When Marianne pulled away, she looked serious. 'Are you sure? I would never try to take your mummy's place.'

'We know that; it feels right. You fight for us like a mum. Mummy would be happy, and Grandma Collie would too.'

'I am honoured,' Marianne said, her voice low and emotional.

'Can we celebrate?' Katie said, running to the pantry and pulling down a heavy bottle of Coca-Cola. 'Coca-Cola ice-cream floats – our mum always said they were for a celebration.'

'And so they should be. Let's continue the tradition.'

Rachel got the ice-cream tub, put it in the microwave for thirty seconds to soften it, while Katie ran upstairs to get the decorative umbrellas and Marianne found crystal champagne glasses at the back of the cupboard.

'Let's always celebrate with mini ice-cream floats in champagne glasses,' she said, and the others agreed as they clinked together at the kitchen table.

'To hell and the Hendersons,' Rachel said, and the others chortled.

THIRTY-ONE

The holidays were over, and both Rachel and Katie were back at school. All three of them were finding it hard to get back into the swing of the school routine.

Jack texted Marianne early.

Can I call in after I drop Sarah to school? Want to talk to you about something.

She answered: *Sure.*

It was all she could do to hide her excitement as she helped Katie finish the last of her homework before going out the door.

'Why didn't you tell me you couldn't do it? We would have had more time yesterday afternoon.'

Katie scowled. 'Because then we would have wasted time on this boring word search instead of being together in the design studio.'

Marianne didn't say anything, but she smiled as she pointed out another word on the grid.

'I'll drive you to school, we won't have time to walk this morning.'

'I don't mind,' Katie said, and they pored over the book to finish the search.

By the time she had dropped off Katie and negotiated her way through the traffic in the town, Marianne was late getting back to Kilteelagh House. Jack was leaning against the back door, his hands in his pockets.

'How come you got here before me?' she asked.

He pointed to his bicycle parked up against the stable door. 'Sarah cycles to school these days. I nipped by you when you were parked in Balgaddy but you didn't notice.'

She blushed as she unlocked the kitchen door.

'Coffee?'

He followed her in and sat at the table as she set up the coffee machine.

'Did Katie tell you the whole town is talking about your fashion show?'

Marianne swung around. 'What is this town like? I have barely even discussed it with anyone, but everybody appears to know.'

'What about your new friend Katherine?'

'I mentioned it in passing, that I was considering it.'

Jack laughed. 'She's been going around the town boasting about her niece the designer and how you two are the best of friends all of a sudden. I think she's trying to make up for all the bad things she said.'

Marianne scowled. 'I don't want to hear any of it. It's in the past.'

Jack took the mug of coffee she placed in front of him.

'So, is the show happening?'

'My friend Jay in New York has persuaded me to have a show, and he's pretty sure some important magazine editors and buyers who are going to be in Ireland at the time will attend. So we're planning a show at Kilteelagh in about five weeks or so to fit in with their schedule. Even though it's a crazy idea and we don't have enough time.' She saw him straighten up in his seat before he spoke again.

'I was hoping my carpentry skills would be good enough to help you stage the show.'

'I heard from Katie that you might be able to build the runway for me.'

He smiled. 'I was working up to that, but I see my daughter has got in there before me.'

'I would pay you, of course. Would you consider it?'

'I'd be honoured. It's not every day I get to work for a big-time designer.'

She giggled and told him to follow her to the drawing room, where she set about trying to push the velvet couch out of the way. Jack picked up an end.

'Where do you want it?'

'Back against the wall for the moment. I'm thinking as far back as possible. The runway goes down to a small stage at the bay window, and we will have rows of chairs two deep either side.'

'I could do something you could take up and store afterwards.'

'If there will ever be another time.'

Jack stole a look at Marianne as he measured the length of the room.

'You should have more faith in yourself and your work. From what I hear, it's exceptionally good.'

'I think Katie is more than a little biased.' She laughed.

'Draw a sketch of what you want, and I should be able to do it, though you will have to allow a few days. I can buy the wood for you as well; I should get a good deal from the building suppliers in town.'

'Dolores is right, you're a diamond.'

She strutted along the imaginary catwalk towards the window. When she turned around, Jack caught her as she tripped over the footrest Katie had pushed there the week before, so it didn't get in the way of her practising her Irish dancing.

'Maybe stick to the dress designing and leave the catwalk to others?' Jack said as he caught her gently. Slowly, he pushed her back on her feet. 'Although, do you think before you become a household name we could go out on another date? I know the concert was packed, but I'm pretty sure you enjoyed it.'

'I loved it. Maybe Friday?'

'It's a date.'

Playfully, she batted him on the head, and he grabbed her hand, pulling her into an embrace. Slowly he kissed her, and she responded.

'The divorce will be finalised very soon,' he whispered.

She dipped her head, and he planted another kiss on her hair.

Luxuriating in his embrace, she closed her eyes and enjoyed the smell of him.

He whispered so low in her ear she barely caught the words and she wriggled so that he let her go. 'Did you hear me?'

'No, sorry.'

'I said that I want us to get to know each other better.'

'I do too, Jack, but we have to be careful around the girls.'

'Sarah has already suggested I ask you out again.'

'And Katie keeps telling me how wonderful you are.'

'Good girl, Katie. I hope you believe the same thing.'

Marianne moved to the window. 'It's hard, Jack, I'm trying to get my collection out, to keep Kilteelagh going, and I have to try and be a mom to Rachel and Katie. And until your divorce comes through...'

'Not long now. I need to be able to see you, to hold you at least.'

'I hardly get time to eat these days.'

'I'm here to help, Marianne.'

'I just need to get on with the work. Meet my deadlines.'

'OK, no date, but you have to eat. Can I at least bring dinner around on Friday night?' When she didn't answer immediately, he shrugged his shoulders. 'Friday night it is, you have to eat, Marianne.'

She laughed and said yes, making him beam with delight.

'Vegetarian OK for you? All the recipes I can cook are veggie.'

'Sounds good.'

She walked him to the door. Before he left, he turned to face her.

'I am glad we're friends, Marianne,' he said, reaching over and kissing her lightly on the lips.

'Me too,' she answered, allowing herself a little time on the top step to watch him drive away.

THIRTY-TWO

It had been a hectic few days, with Fiknete and Dolores arriving at Kilteelagh shortly after eight every morning. Often Fiknete and Marianne did not switch off the sewing machines until nine at night. They mostly worked quietly beside each other, except when Fiknete had what she called her 'recharge hour', when she insisted on singing at the top of her voice.

'Darling, you have to tone it down,' Dolores snapped one evening, but Fiknete said she needed it to clear the mind and recharge the brain.

'In that case, please don't be offended if I decamp to the kitchen, so that my brain isn't assaulted by your amazing singing,' Dolores said.

Fiknete, who either ignored the sarcasm or did not spot it in the first place, opened the design studio door as she jived to her own voice. Marianne, also unable to take the noise, followed Dolores to the kitchen.

'That gal can sew, but she sure as heck can't sing,' Dolores said, as she switched on the kettle for a cup of tea.

When Marianne didn't answer, she swung around.

'What's the matter? Has she got inside your brain too?'

Marianne sat on the armchair beside the Aga. 'Dolores, what if I've got the mood all wrong and the dresses are duds? What will we do? This is all Katie's idea; what was I thinking?'

Dolores sighed loudly.

'First, you haven't got those dresses all wrong, and secondly, it's natural to feel this way. Putting on a show here at the house is a big deal; it's a statement that you are a confident designer who shows her collection in her home, her own salon. It's really breaking all the rules.'

'What rules?'

'The ones that say you have to show in the big cities; you have to have an enormous budget; the ones that say only the very big designers can do it. Well, Marianne Johnson, you are doing it and it's going to be bloody fantastic.'

'Have you got any RSVPs back yet?'

'Some, it's a little early, but don't worry, I'm going to do a lot of arm-twisting, and everybody is going to be delighted to be here and they are going to be wowed.'

'I can't sleep at night, and every time I see the invitation my stomach feels sick, and I don't know what I was thinking.'

Dolores turned off the kettle and instead reached for the bottle of whiskey under the sink and poured a measure into two glasses. Handing a glass to Marianne, she told her to drink it.

'We don't gain anything in this world by playing it safe. You are being bold and brave, and that's to be commended. Your talent is such that this show will only be the start of many more. You're on the cusp, darling, whether you want to believe it or not. Concentrate on the garments and leave the rest to me.'

When the back door swung open, the two women jumped. Jack walked in carrying a large cardboard box.

'I'm here to cook dinner.'

Marianne jumped up. 'Gosh, I completely forgot, I'm sorry.'

He put the box down on the table and started to take out various vegetables and two bottles of wine.

'Don't worry, as long as you didn't promise a date to anybody else,' he said. He pulled out the pan drawer under the hob and began scrabbling around for the right saucepan size.

'Jack, we're frightfully busy and under pressure—'

Dolores put her hand on Marianne's arm.

'What she's trying to say is this is perfect timing. We are all nearing the end of a very tiring week.'

'I'm sure I can rustle up a few more servings if you and Fiknete care to join us.'

'And ruin a romantic rendezvous? It's Friday evening and I'm sure I have plans, and Fiknete too,' Dolores said. Her voice became a little sterner when she turned to Marianne: 'You should go have a bath and change out of those jeans.' She motioned for Marianne to go upstairs, as if she were sending Katie to get dressed for dinner.

'We still have an hour left. Fiknete wants to finish the skirt for the opening outfit tonight.'

'For God's sake, go – a fine-looking man wants to cook you dinner. Live a little,' Dolores snapped.

Flustered, Marianne made for the door to the hall.

Dolores followed her. 'I'll tell Fiknete to get a move on. We can regroup in the morning. An earlyish night wouldn't hurt any of us.'

Jack, who was setting up a chopping board, repeated his offer to cook dinner for four.

Dolores stopped in the doorway.

'Are you mad? I'm sure Fiknete and myself can find something more useful to do with our time than play giant gooseberries,' she said before she tramped down the hall.

As soon as she was gone, Marianne slipped back into the kitchen.

'I'm sorry, Jack, I was actually looking forward to tonight, but so much has happened all week and there has been so much pressure, I just forgot...'

'Hey, no need to apologise, I understand,' he said as he reached for a bottle of wine and uncorked it.

'Chardonnay, I had it chilling in my fridge, so it should taste good.'

He reached for two glasses, poured the wine and handed one glass to Marianne.

'Take your time, soak in a bath, have your wine and, when you're ready, we will eat,' he said, lightly clinking her glass.

'You're a star,' she said, and headed for the stairs.

Dolores and Fiknete were in the doorway of the drawing room, smiling like two kids who had stuffed their pockets with lollipops.

'That man is a keeper,' Fiknete said.

'She might be right. The big dress designer and her lawyer-cum-handyman lover. I can see you in the tabloids now,' Dolores whispered.

'Stop, Dolores, that's too much. Jack is... I'm not explaining anything,' Marianne said, and hurried up the stairs before they could say anything else.

'You can do the explaining tomorrow,' Fiknete called as Dolores opened the front door and guided her friend outside.

'Bright and early tomorrow, Marianne, and we will want all the details,' Dolores whispered as she tugged the door shut behind her.

Marianne heard the two of them giggling on the steps before they got into their cars and drove off. She crept back downstairs and into the studio. How could it be that from this former dining room they planned to launch a design collection? What they were doing was audacious and brave and maybe a little bit naive, but it also felt right. Fiknete had put the finished skirt on the mannequin, ready for Marianne to fit the bodice. She was tempted to continue working, but she heard Jack humming a tune in the kitchen and felt guilty.

Maybe one night off would be a good thing. Fifteen designs

were ready, with copies in different colours of each one. She had insisted on eighteen pieces, along with the final one, the showstopper to match Collie's gown. It wasn't a huge number for a fashion show, but it was a big number for the three of them. Already, Dolores was expert at cutting out and tacking, and Fiknete had taken over the sewing as if she were preparing for battle. She had a seam count each day and would not finish until she had achieved it or surpassed it. As a result, they were further on than Marianne had expected at this stage.

Very soon, they would know whether the gamble had paid off and if the fashion show had generated enough orders to sustain the business. Jay had rung her in great excitement to say he was confident that two American journalists and three international buyers would make it to the show. She jolly well hoped so, as it was being staged to coincide with the American journalists' and buyers' stopover in Ireland.

A tension headache nagged in her head and she slurped her wine. She didn't hear Jack enter the room. When he spoke, she jumped, spilling some of her wine on the table.

'I'm sorry, I didn't mean to startle you.'

'I was only standing here worrying that it could all go wrong.'

'But it probably will go right.'

'You are the glass half-full type of guy.'

'I suppose I am. You're talented, and you have a good team with you. This is a fantastic location, and your designs are supreme, so with a sprinkling of luck, everything should go great.'

'As if you know.'

'True, but I know you will have the best runway this side of Dublin.'

She laughed, and she thought he was going to kiss her, but he heard the sizzle of something boiling over on the hob and dashed from the room.

'I'll go upstairs and get ready,' she called after him. Snatching a spare dress sample from the shelf in the design studio, she ran upstairs.

When Marianne strolled into the kitchen almost an hour later, Jack whistled.

'You look beautiful. Is that one of your designs?'

She did a twirl.

'What do you think, it's one of my first samples. A shift dress cut on the bias. It's simple but I think it works.'

'It definitely works,' Jack said as he turned on the music and put his hand out to ask her to dance.

She laughed nervously and let him lead her across the kitchen floor until Benji, feeling jealous, jumped up to push them apart.

'Everyone around here seems to love you, including the old dog,' Jack said, laughing and turning to take his tomato and aubergine casserole from the oven.

'I think you have your own fan club, especially my Katie. She thinks you were fantastic to arrange a sleepover for her tonight. Funny that it coincided with Rachel staying over at Katherine's.'

'Found out,' he said, putting his hands in the air.

He placed the casserole along with rosemary roast potatoes and a mixed salad on the table.

'Am I being selfish that I wanted time with you, where we could be Marianne and Jack who like each other and who want to get to know each other better, not a mum and dad from the school run?'

'I don't know exactly how you pulled it off.'

'Our wonderful daughters might have had something to do with it. But that's enough chat about them. I want to get to know *you* better.'

Marianne smiled. 'I think you know a lot already. Jobless and without a family, I end up inheriting this old pile, and now

I'm trying to reinvent myself as this famous dress designer while at the same time playing mom to two girls who deserve better.'

'Right, now that you've got that out of your system, can the real Marianne please stand up?'

She looked at him and realised he was serious.

'Honestly, I don't know who the real Marianne is any more. If you'd met me a year ago, I was designing cocktail wear in stretchy fabrics and going out on the town every night. I spoke a lot of bullshit and my aspiration was to have my own place in the village.'

'The village?'

'Greenwich Village.'

'Right.'

'Now, even if I get into Dublin for a few hours, I miss Kilteelagh. This place has wormed its way under my skin, and I think I'm turning into Collie.' She sounded hysterical and he started to laugh. 'I'm glad you find all this amusing,' she said.

'Yes, I do, because when you drink wine and articulate your worries, your cheeks blush red, and your nose twitches a bit like a rabbit.'

Self-consciously she touched her face. He reached over and brushed his hand along her cheeks.

'It's beautiful; it's not meant as a criticism. I think you're fantastic, and when you tell it like that, I think it's making me fall in love with you.'

She reached for her wine and took a big gulp.

He was about to say something else when her phone rang, the noise twirling around them.

'I'm going to have to answer that,' she said, picking her phone up from the worktop.

She shook her head as she listened to the caller.

'I'm afraid I've had some wine to drink, so I can't drive. Let me see if Jack's OK to drive, if not I'll get a taxi.' Marianne put her hand over the phone so the caller wouldn't hear. 'It's

Aideen. Katie has a pain in her stomach and wants to come home. Have you had much to drink?'

'Aideen? Only a sip, I was too busy cooking.'

'Can you drive me there to collect her?'

'Sure.' He sighed and got up to get his jacket and car keys.

Marianne reassured Aideen they would be there in ten minutes.

'I'm sorry, I imagine Katie is a little bit homesick,' she said to Jack as she got off the phone.

'No bother, let's get going. Maybe we can continue with the food once she's sorted.'

'I don't know, Jack. One thing I've learned is that when Katie is sick, she needs me there all the time. I'm sorry.'

He opened the back door for her.

'No need, you know how to read the situation. Pop mine in the fridge and I'll have it for lunch tomorrow.'

'Tomorrow?'

'I'm here bright and early to start the runway. The wood should be delivered at eight in the morning.'

'Oh good,' she said as they got in the car and drove into the town to Aideen's place.

Katie was very subdued in the car. When she got into the kitchen and they could hear Jack drive away, she hugged Marianne.

'Rachel is going to kill me. She told me I wasn't to ruin your dinner.'

'You haven't ruined anything, sweetheart.'

'I have. We all want you guys to be boyfriend and girlfriend, and now I've messed it up.'

'I doubt if you being sick has ruined anything. Now, let's get you to bed and check if you have a fever.'

Katie pulled away from Marianne. 'Don't bother, I'm not sick. But please don't tell Rachel.'

'Aww, darling, I'm not going to tell anyone.'

'I messed it up though, and you're wearing one of our new dresses.'

Marianne went to the fridge. 'We hadn't got as far as dessert, and there's a wonderful Baileys tiramisu. I think you're old enough to have a little.'

'Oh yes, please.'

Katie ran and got two bowls and spoons while Marianne took the tiramisu from the fridge.

'Will Jack mind that we're eating it?' Katie asked.

'I think he will understand, he's Sarah's dad, after all.'

Katie looked happier and sat close to Marianne.

'I wanted to come home; I wanted to be here with you,' she said quietly.

'I know,' Marianne said.

THIRTY-THREE

February

The next few weeks passed in a blur of exhaustion. Fiknete arrived earlier each morning and stayed until late every evening; hunched over, hand-finishing every seam; an Ikea desk lamp lighting the way so she could follow the needle as she deftly pushed it in and out of the fabric. Marianne learned not to interrupt her when she was at this final stage of a garment. Once, she had brought in a cup of coffee and a few biscuits and started to chat as she placed them on a small coffee table beside Fiknete. Fiknete stopped what she was doing and looked directly at her.

'No offence, but I didn't ask for these and now you have upset my concentration. Please don't do it again.'

Marianne had nearly burst out laughing because at that moment, Fiknete sounded so like Collie. Instead, she apologised and swept away the coffee and biscuits to the kitchen.

Dolores too worked later at her desk, each evening having more than thirty emails to send out or answer.

'What if everyone you've invited turns up? There won't be room for them,' Marianne said.

'Darling, we have to over-invite, the death knell to a show is an empty seat. It's my job to ensure there aren't any vacant seats.'

Marianne looked out the window, to where Jack was cutting the grass around the gazebo. He had completed the runway in three days, working round the clock. She brought him coffee from time to time, and once she'd asked him to stay for dinner, but he'd said he had to study. She wasn't sure if he really was very busy or if he was just staying out of her way.

Dolores looked out the window as well.

'Maybe after this, bring him down a cuppa. He might be happier out of earshot of others,' she said kindly.

Marianne nodded and turned around to face Dolores.

'I know I was insistent on just eighteen pieces, along with the finale including Collie's dress, but do you think I was right about that?'

'You're the designer; you tell me why you chose that number.'

'I wanted to have fewer pieces than the usual show to allow each person in the audience more time to take in all the little details. As it's a smaller, more intimate setting, I wanted to take advantage of that.'

'Good point, I'm going to write it down as a quotable quote from the designer.'

Marianne hesitated and Dolores shook her head.

'I need everything to sell this show, and key phrases, especially catchy ones from the designer, always help. Now, give me more.'

'I can only say what I feel. I don't want a whole load of designs thrown at people. I want to present my creations; a way of life as seen through my garments. This collection brings the countryside into the city, where I hope it can hold its own.'

Dolores was writing furiously and Fiknete stopped what she was doing to listen.

'When you see too much, you lose interest, you don't pick up on the vibe. And I think in this age of social media, key pieces that spark something in the viewer or the customer are far more important than churning out a lot of different designs and styles, and hoping one of them strikes a chord.'

'You have put into words what I have been thinking all along,' Fiknete said, and Dolores nodded in agreement.

'Don't get me wrong, I want to show off these clothes. We didn't put our blood, sweat and tears into all this for nothing, but I want it to be a special experience, intimate and memorable. I suppose I want to create a show that I would like to go to,' Marianne said, her voice quivering with emotion.

'If you talk like that at the show, you will have everybody in tears,' Fiknete said, wiping her eyes.

'Yes, you stop right now because we don't want Fiknete to get too upset or she won't be able to finish number eighteen on the list,' Dolores laughed.

Marianne muttered that she needed to take a break and the two women watched her, moments later, stroll across the grass, where Jack was still tidying up around the gazebo.

'It's been a bit crazy around here; we haven't properly talked since Katie interrupted our dinner.'

'I figured you had enough on your plate. We have plenty of time after the show to get to know each other better.' He lightly tugged at her hair. 'That's if you will want anything to do with the handyman after your huge success.'

'Stop!' She slapped him gently across the shoulder. 'I don't want you to jinx it. I'm nervous enough as it is.'

'Have you a few minutes now? I know just the thing to clear the head and make you forget, for a little while anyway, what's going on here in the next few days.'

She looked uncertainly at him. 'Is it something I'm going to like? You're not suggesting a swim in the lake, or anything? The water is bloody freezing!'

'Good God no, but you will like it,' he said as he took her hand and led her down the path away from the gazebo and into the trees.

'I found a carving on one of the trees a while back. I wasn't sure if anyone from the house knows about it.'

They walked side by side across the hard ground. The ducks, who had been sheltering in the reeds around the lake, began to swim towards them.

'It's down at the far trees, I reckon it must be from years back.'

'I haven't been this far in so long; I always stay around the jetty and the gazebo, within running distance of the house in case one of the girls calls me.'

'I was clearing away the nettles with the strimmer; there are some nice specimens of trees and a lovely view of the water. Benji surprised a few squirrels there last week, and now he makes it part of his daily tour.'

He stopped at a large horse chestnut tree. 'Are you ready to climb?'

'Sure.'

Swinging off a low branch, he pulled himself up into the tree, before dropping his hand to help Marianne scramble up. She remembered it now, hiding out here with Collie on a hot summer's day, the leaves providing shade. Collie had a little ladder hidden in the undergrowth to make their climb easier. There was a real feeling of hiding away from everybody else. They sat on a little platform and munched custard creams and drank Miwadi diluted orange from the bottle passed between them, like two farmers taking a break from saving the hay.

Collie said this was their secret spot. 'A very good friend made this hideaway for me, and when days get me down, I come here, look out over the lake and think about him. He was a good man and a good friend.'

Jack nudged her.

'You were miles away.'

'Sorry, I remember Collie bringing me here when I was a kid.'

'Let me show you the carving.'

'I know it,' she said, and she reached across, feeling along the bark for the carving her grandmother had shown her. She always thought it was from a time when two young sweethearts marked their spot, but now she knew it was Collie and Lucas entwined in a heart. They pushed the branches out of the way to get a better look.

'I know the C, but who is the other initial? Wasn't your grandpa named Mike?'

Marianne hesitated. 'No idea who it is,' she said a little too quickly.

'A mystery. We don't expect our grandparents or parents to have secrets, do we?'

'Everybody has secrets.'

The breeze wrinkled the leaves, making them gently rustle. He reached over to kiss her, but she turned away.

'I think I had better get back,' Marianne said.

'Have you gone off me?'

She shook her head. 'Jack, I really like you, and the fact that you brought me here is lovely, but my brain is full of this show and what can go wrong and...'

Gently, he hushed her lips with his finger.

'I understand, forgive me for being so demanding. Of course you're caught up with all that's going on and how important it is to you and Kilteelagh. Forgiven?'

She smiled and nodded, and he beamed back at her.

'Let's get you back to the house before Fiknete launches a

search party,' he said as he jumped down and held out his hands so she could drop into his arms.

'Please don't worry about the show. The runway is secure, the models will know what they're doing. Dolores has thought of everything, and we're all behind you. Most importantly, your designs are bloody amazing.'

She looked at him. 'As if you would know.'

'That's true, but in this case I do. I have enough women in my life, thank you, to know these things.' He laughed, and said he had better get back to work.

She walked up the little path. From here she could see to the design studio windows, where Fiknete and Dolores were working away, Fiknete bent over the sewing machine and Dolores standing at the window on her mobile. Benji saw Marianne and ran over to her, nipping playfully at her hands as she made her way around the back of the house. When she got into the kitchen, Dolores was waiting for her.

'You are going to love this.'

'What?'

'American *Vogue* just called. They literally love the dresses, and they want to do a photoshoot here at Kilteelagh.'

'You're kidding?'

'Your friend Jay put me in touch with somebody there. They love the idea of a young, beautiful, emerging American designer, locked away in an old mansion in Ireland, just making beautiful clothes.'

'Mansion? And I'm hardly locked away!'

'I might have oversold it a bit, but hey, they will love Kilteelagh when they arrive.'

'Dolores!'

Dolores did a little dance. 'I know, isn't it fantastic?'

'But how are we going to get this place looking good enough for *Vogue*?'

'Pooh, you worry so much about the details. And, you know what, I reckon I'm going to be able to use this whole *Vogue* thing to get Irish TV down to film here too. This is so unbelievably exciting,' she said as she stepped out into the backyard to answer her phone.

Marianne sat with her head in her hands. Her stomach was heaving, and a tension headache was stabbing through her temples. When Dolores came back in, she poured a glass of water and placed it beside Marianne.

'You're going to have to get used to the attention, darling. That was the *Irish Times*, they want to interview you with photographs for the weekend magazine.' When Marianne didn't respond, Dolores sat down and in a voice that sounded deflated she said: 'Thank you, Dolores. Wow, American *Vogue* and the *Irish Times*, I couldn't have done any of it without you. You're the best.'

Marianne peeped through her fingers at her friend. Dolores looked old and sad; the sparkle was gone from her eyes and her shoulders were slumped. Marianne sat up straight and pushed the hair out of her eyes.

'I'm sorry, Dolores; I was selfishly only thinking of myself. None of this would be possible without you and Fiknete. You're right, I couldn't have done any of it without you. I would be sitting here, sewing dresses nobody was going to buy, because I would not have known how to get the word out, and for that, I will forever be in your debt.'

Dolores patted her hair and batted her eyelids as she enjoyed the praise coming her way. 'I'm only keeping my word to Collie to look after you. I'm thrilled this is working out. We can do this, though. Sure, we have to.'

Marianne pushed the glass of water away.

'It might be the occasion for something stronger, Dolores.'

'Way too early, but I'm not telling if you're not,' Dolores said, taking the bottle of whiskey and three glasses from under the sink.

'We had better call Fiknete, or we'll never hear the end of it. Although, maybe pour half measures,' she said.

When Fiknete came to the kitchen, she looked flustered. 'I was trying to finish a neckline.

What is the matter, you know I don't like to be interrupted?'

Marianne handed her a glass.

'So early, what has happened?'

'Sit down, darling, we are going to be world-famous, and all thanks to me and of course your amazing handiwork and Marianne's designs,' Dolores said.

THIRTY-FOUR

Dolores had insisted on asking Katherine and her friends for help. Marianne hadn't wanted to, but Dolores said they would never have the house and grounds ready for the photoshoots and show if they did not enlist their neighbours.

'We can't afford a cleaning company, and with the best will in the world, we will never get it all done ourselves. I'm sure Katherine would be only too thrilled to make amends and be part of something so big,' Dolores said, and handed the phone to her. Reluctantly, Marianne rang her aunt.

Katherine was excited. 'Bridie is great at this sort of thing. Do you think I could ask her and Olive? I'm sure we could make it up to you by this afternoon.' Marianne had no choice but to thank her aunt profusely.

Fiknete was not happy with the development. 'They are busybodies, and they will try to take all the credit, just you wait and see.'

'As long as Marianne has orders from the right people, what does it matter what Bridie and Katherine think? Now, let's make a long list to keep them busy and turn Kilteelagh House around,' Dolores guffawed.

They had no sooner finished the list and were sitting having a coffee at the kitchen table when Bridie's BMW pulled into the backyard.

'Will you look at the get-up of Bridie! I've never seen her wear jeans in her life. Who does she think she is, a farm worker? But then, since her fall from grace, she has a lot of spare time on her hands and nowhere to wear a suit.' Dolores sniffed as she looked out the window.

Marianne pulled back the door and called out a welcome as Katherine caught her in a tight hug.

'We're thrilled you asked us to help out. It doesn't matter what needs doing. The A-Team have arrived,' Katherine said at the top of her voice.

All the women except Dolores laughed, and Marianne stood in front of her so the visitors didn't notice. Katherine carried a big box from the car. 'Everything for home-made pizzas when we're done,' she said.

Dolores, who had borrowed a clipboard from Katie's room, said they had better get a start before the children got home from school. Each of the women stood and waited to be assigned a task and handed the cleaning utensils. Bridie was thrilled when she was given the drawing room to clear of cobwebs and wash the chandelier.

'I'm not great on a ladder, but I will do my best,' she said, scuttling off.

Fiknete said she was going back to the studio, as she had specialist work to do for the show and she didn't want to fall behind. Olive volunteered to help Jack tidying up the garden, while Katherine offered to clean the hall and stairs. Marianne concentrated on the front door and polishing the brass.

'The chandelier I can understand, but believe you me, they will be too busy looking at your designs to notice a few old cobwebs in the corner,' Bridie muttered, but when Marianne made to answer, she laughed. 'Girl, you should know me by now, I give out about everything.'

'I don't want to leave anything to chance, that's all. Americans can be very critical; I don't want anything to take from the dresses.'

'You're right, and don't worry, we won't let you down. Who's cleaning the windows?'

Dolores stuck her head around the door. 'I'm not sure I can manage the stretching with my arthritis, but you and Katherine should be able to reach them,' she said.

'You will need to serve a lot of pizza at the end of this, and some good wine,' Bridie said, as she concentrated on the high architraves around the bay window.

Marianne moved out the front to polish the bay window glass. Jack, who was tidying up under the magnolia tree, motioned to her to come closer.

'Try and tell the ladies and the kids not to walk on the runway. I have a last coat of polish to put on it tonight.'

'Will do. I hope you're going to stop by for pizza at the end of the day?'

'Ah, sadly I can't, I have to do a few things study-wise until about eight, but I will call back to put down the last coat of polish. It should dry overnight.'

'The magazine people will be here first thing in the morning, will it be dry by then?'

'I thought they were mainly going to be photographing outside?'

'I suppose I'm just trying to think of every eventuality.'

He reached across and took her hand.

'It is exciting and overwhelming now, but it's going to be great. I just know it; we all know it.'

'I wish I felt the same, but thank you.'

He kissed her hand lightly before giving it back to her.

Bridie stopped what she was doing to look at them. 'Aren't you the lovely pair?' she said through the open window.

Jack quickly pulled his hand away and Marianne pretended to be examining the flowerpots on the steps. Bridie waited until Jack had got in his car and was driving down the avenue to call out to Marianne.

'You couldn't pick better, Marianne. That Jack Farrelly is a good man,' she said through the open window.

'So, you don't think he's going to "stick with me so he can get his hands on Kilteelagh, but will probably eventually leave me high and dry"?'

Bridie put down the brush she had been using to catch the cobwebs and leaned out the window. 'All right, Marianne, you've had your say. I'm guilty as charged, but the fact that I'm here surely signals I am trying to make amends. I let my loyalty to Katherine get in the way, but I've known her a long time and we are the best of pals and I stick by my friends. I am hoping we can be friends too, despite what has happened.'

'Of course we can, now let's take a wee break,' Katherine said, carrying a tray of coffee into the room and placing it on a small side table.

'Oh, I always wanted to walk down the runway,' sighed Bridie. She was about to step on it when Marianne, who had walked back into the drawing room, put her hand up to stop her.

'Jack says not to walk on it; he still has the last coat of polish to put on.'

Katherine made a face and kicked off her shoes.

'Sure, I'm not causing any harm now, am I? Don't tell him though, just in case.'

Bridie slipped off her shoes as well and the two women walked down the catwalk in an exaggerated, silly way.

'Come on, Marianne, you might as well get a practice in for

when you go down the runway after the show is finished and everybody is on their feet clapping,' Bridie said.

Realising that she was well and truly beaten, Marianne took off her slippers and joined Katherine and Bridie.

Dolores, when she walked into the room with a large vase of roses in her hand, stopped to watch the three women.

'Thank God you three are not modelling the designs,' she said, a little too sharply.

'Come join us,' Katherine called.

'No, not for me, I am strictly a behind-the-scenes person,' Dolores answered in a firm voice which made the others giggle. Then Katherine jumped down off the runway and headed to the design studio. She called to Marianne to follow.

'I had a peek in here, and I thought wouldn't it be fantastic to frame all your beautiful designs and hang them around the hall?'

'Yes, but how would we get it done in a day?'

'Bridie's son runs the framing business in Greystones, and I'm sure she could make a call.'

'Already doing it,' Bridie said as she took her mobile phone from her pocket. She wandered down the hall as she spoke on the phone.

'OK, he said he will drop over in an hour or so and it should be no problem. He'll have them back to you by early afternoon tomorrow.'

Marianne looked at Bridie. 'That is so kind, and it's a brilliant idea, but won't it be very expensive?'

'He's giving you the family rate, which means you pay the trade price for the frame and glass and the labour is free.'

'I can't ask him to do that.'

'You're right, you can't, but his mam can, and I have. We'll leave it at that. Are we friends now?'

Bridie laughed. Marianne shrugged her shoulders. 'Maybe,' she said, and the others chuckled.

'God, the American is finally able to join in the craic,' Bridie said, moving the ladder under the chandelier so she could reach the crystals and wipe them with a damp cloth.

Each went back to her own work. The sound of spraying and the smell of polish were thick in the air. Katherine put on some music, and they turned it up high to drown out the drone of Fiknete sewing on the machine. Annoyed by the loud music, Dolores turned it down when she thought nobody was looking, but Bridie rolled it back up.

Just before six, when the girls came home from study and after-school clubs, Katherine suggested they knock off.

'There's only the hoovering left to do and we're there. Mari-anne, you do that, and we will assemble the pizzas,' Katherine said.

Fiknete said she would continue until nine so to count her out of the food.

'Can't you take a break and then go back to it, fresh and with good food in your belly?'

'Where I am from, we do not call pizza good food.'

'Fiknete, get over yourself! You'll change your tune once you've tasted our home-made pizza,' Katherine said.

'I still have to work until about nine. I am finishing the last garment and I have to press it. Best get everything done and then we can tidy the studio.'

'What does it matter how the studio looks? Sure, isn't it a centre of creativity?' Bridie said.

'It matters to me, Mrs Murphy,' Fiknete snapped.

'All right, but for God's sake will you call me Bridie?'

Fiknete turned back into the design studio, a deep scowl on her face. '"Call me Bridie"!' she said to Dolores quietly. 'Not so long ago, it was "Mrs Murphy to you, dear". What has happened to the woman?'

'Bridie does everything to suit herself, so who knows?'

'I know they're helping Marianne, but I still wouldn't trust her.'

'Me neither,' Dolores said, closing the studio door to drown out the noise of Bridie and Katherine laughing in the kitchen.

Marianne was making breakfast for Rachel and Katie when Katherine's car pulled into the backyard the next morning. Katherine and Bridie got out.

'We didn't want to miss the photoshoot, I hope you don't mind,' Bridie said as they made their way in the back door.

'Are the Americans here yet?' Katherine asked.

'I told them nine thirty, because I have to get the girls off to school first.'

'Oops, we're in your way. Will we go away and come back later?' Bridie asked.

'No, make yourself tea and take it easy. I'll have the girls out of the house in the next thirty minutes – Jack said he will drop them both to school.'

Bridie looked a little embarrassed, but Katherine set about making tea.

'We can leave, it's no bother,' Bridie muttered.

Marianne smiled. 'To be honest, it's lovely to have the company. Sitting here on my own, I was only beginning to worry. Dolores will be along in a while, and I'm sure she will organise us all.'

Her words seemed to placate Bridie, who plopped two sugar cubes in her tea. 'It's great to be part of the excitement; we don't often have something like this in Balgaddy. God knows, I have tried to bring the razzmatazz with the Christmas market every year, but there is such a resistance.'

'Come back to me for next December,' Marianne said, and Bridie rubbed her hands together with satisfaction.

When Dolores came in the back door ten minutes later, she frowned when she saw Katherine and Bridie.

'If I hadn't seen you with my own two eyes leaving after midnight, I would have said you had stayed all night.'

'Aww, Dolores, we didn't want to miss any of the fun, give us a break,' Bridie said.

'Now that you're here, you can make yourselves useful. I'm sure there's something that needs doing.'

'No doubt if there isn't, you will find something for us to do anyway,' Katherine said, and Dolores, annoyed, whipped off to the studio.

Marianne saw Rachel and Katie off from the front steps, but not before Sarah jumped out and ran from the car to hand her an envelope. 'Special delivery from the postman – he was at the gate when we were coming up,' she said.

THIRTY-FIVE

Marianne waited until the others were well down the avenue before she ducked into the drawing room to read Collie's letter.

Kilteelagh House
Balgaddy
Co. Wicklow

My dearest Marianne,

How are you? When did I last ask that? I've been so caught up with myself and telling you about Kilteelagh that I have barely given any recognition to the job you have taken on and what you have had to leave behind.

I can only pray and hope that I did the right thing by asking you to take over Kilteelagh, and that my selfish motives have not caused you pain. I am sure Katherine lashed out at the start, but if I know my daughter, hopefully she has come round by now.

Yes, I wanted somebody to take over Kilteelagh who would learn to love it as I have done. Katie and Rachel also needed a strong role model, and I'm sure you have risen to the occasion there. The one thing I never had any doubts about was your ability to mother those two girls who so desperately needed a ray of hope in their lives.

I know you have been just that for them, Marianne, because you have been my beacon of hope too. With you guiding the Kilteelagh ship, I am sure there are many years of adventures ahead. I won't say enjoy it; there are times Kilteelagh is such hard work – even I began to question the logic of keeping it on, but all you need is one more time when everything is right at Kilteelagh to sustain you through all the other times.

You may not remember this, but you were actually very young when I first told you I wanted you and your family to take over Kilteelagh when I was gone. You see, your mother Chloe always loved the place, and I believed she would honour my wishes. It was a complete surprise to me when she wanted to emigrate to America and, to be honest, I prayed for her return. But even before she met your father, she loved New York City. Kilteelagh, in a funny way, had prepared her for the world. When you can handle the solitude and the solitary life that Kilteelagh forces on you, you are ready to take on the world.

Chloe wasn't afraid to be alone, and not afraid to take on any stresses of the city. Kilteelagh set her up for the world but let her be taken away from me. Katherine stayed here, even though she fought the solitude of Kilteelagh with every fibre of her being. God has a funny way of making us pay for our sins. I know now I put Kilteelagh before everyone and everything. I don't regret it, but I guess I should have put more of a balance into my life.

I wouldn't let any of the Kilteelagh lands go, even when I could have sold off fields at the far end of the lake, and the money would have certainly made the house and my life more comfortable. Lucas probably had something to do with that. I always wanted Kilteelagh to look the same and I didn't realise that, as long as I was here, that was all that would have mattered. When I think how I tended to the daffodils so that in spring they'd be there in glorious yellow to greet him, maybe I was a little mad in my longing. Maybe I still am.

I am not going to write any more in this letter about Lucas. It makes me so sad that I failed myself in not seeking him out when I was free, and it makes me so lonely to think he didn't seek me out, or was unable to. There are times I wonder, am I deluding myself that we could be together in death, but it is all I have left now. To take that away would make the next last days unbearable. To die well, I need to know I am going to meet him.

Marianne, learn from my mistakes. Love well and keep a whole world going outside Kilteelagh and the children. That will ensure as you get older and Rachel and Katie make their own way in life, you won't be left behind.

Are you going to stay at Kilteelagh? My gut says if you've made it this far, then you will. But I want you to know you must follow your own heart. I hope you have used the time at Kilteelagh to find out what you want from life and where you want to be.

My heart hopes that it is Kilteelagh, but I am saying to you now, I respect any decision you make.

You have been nearly a year at Kilteelagh. I bet you can tell if it is going to rain, and you can smell the damp and cold in the air. I bet when you see the birds fly low, you take the clothes in from the line and when the weather is bad and Benji stays inside, you burrow into your duvet. At Kilteelagh, we live close to nature because the seasons and the weather dictate our lives. I often forgot what day of the week it was, and the date of the month never seemed to matter, particularly once the kids were at school.

If I have any advice left to give, it is to do it your way. Not the Collie Keane way but the Marianne Johnson way – only then will you be truly happy. I want you to be happy at Kilteelagh and every bone in my body says you will. But I want more than anything for you, Rachel and Katie to be happy.

Only you know how to achieve that – and I urge you to go for it, girl.

I want to think I will be happy if in death I have some way of reuniting with Lucas. It gives me hope at a time when there is none, and it still gives me a tingle of excitement that there may be more to come.

Indulge your old grandmother, who loved and loved and now wants to finally be with the man she has adored for so long. I said I wouldn't talk about Lucas again, but I can't help it. These days it is what sustains me. Our spirits, I hope, can float together as we roam through another world hand in hand.

Stay well, Marianne, and do what you want to do and what is right for you and the girls.

All my love,

Collie xx

Marianne, standing inside the drawing room window, folded the letter carefully and slipped it into her pocket. She couldn't imagine being anywhere else but Kilteelagh. She knew Rachel and Katie felt the same. The *Vogue* photographer had arrived with three different models. They parked a camper van on the avenue, which Marianne presumed the girls would use to change into Kilteelagh Design dresses. The photographer was wandering around down by the lake and Marianne thought she was scoping out the best locations. The models were huddled together at the gazebo sharing a cigarette, passing it from one to the other.

The model wearing the floral chiffon broke off from the others to stroke Benji, who had been idling around the jetty. Marianne noticed the dress floated gently around her as the cool breeze whipped in from the lake. Another model was wrapped in a warm coat, waiting for her turn to reveal the blue silk dress with the long skirt and sleeves.

'I'm going to send down a tray of tea and coffee. They must be frozen stiff,' Dolores said.

'Good idea, and give them some of Fiknete's biscuits, though I suspect as models, they won't touch them. Is the journalist here yet?'

'She rang; she came off the N11 five minutes ago, so she should be here in fifteen minutes or so.'

'Doesn't she want to know what photographs have been taken?'

'She can have a look afterwards and pick the best ones. They asked if we had a boat to go out on the lake, but I said it wasn't possible at this late stage to arrange one. We don't want any stupid accident happening and ruining our publicity.'

Marianne smiled at Dolores, who told Fiknete to make the coffee and the tea.

'Do you think the *Vogue* people like the designs?'

'They love them – and so they should, they're beautiful.'

Marianne should have known better than to ask Dolores, who she knew would have defended her designs even if they were dreadful.

'I had another letter from Collie. I think this one was in your writing, though.'

'Ah, you must be coming to the end of them and her grip still on Kilteelagh. I'm not sure Collie's obsession with this place was good for her in the end. She should have got out more.'

'Maybe she had almost everything she wanted here.'

'Now you're beginning to sound like her. Come on, we will bring down the trays. They might want to ask you questions.

Always helps to get the photographer on side. No doubt she will make more of an effort as a result. With any luck Katherine and Bridie will be bored at this stage and head for the hills. They look like a pair of groupies standing there, gawking at the models,' Dolores said.

When the journalist arrived at the gate in her Mercedes hire car, she introduced herself as Kate Reilly. She was wearing a tight trouser suit and high heels.

'Can we go in the house? I will never get across to the lake in these heels,' she said, when she pulled up her car after coming across the cattle grid. She had taken one look at Katherine and Bridie and said she would like to conduct the interview in private.

'We want this to be as natural a chat as possible,' she said, ignoring the huffing and puffing of Bridie.

'We can go to the design studio or the drawing room,' Marianne said, sitting into the passenger seat of the Mercedes before Kate roared up the avenue.

'We have to have shots in front of the house,' she shouted into the phone to the photographer as she parked at the bottom of the steps. Ending the call, she turned to Marianne. 'I love it here. I'd prefer to carry out my interview in the kitchen. There's something so authentic about sitting in somebody's kitchen. Don't you think the kitchen is the real heart of the house?'

Without waiting for an answer, she hopped up the steps. Marianne followed behind, directing her down the hall where Benji was sprawled across the kitchen tiles. She was thankful that Fiknete had insisted last night that the kitchen get a deep clean. After she had finished the last dress in the collection and eaten cold pizza, she said she was going to spring-clean the kitchen.

'It will help clear my head, and my brain is like a marshmallow after all that slow, close work with the needle,' she said, refusing any offers of help.

'Get a good night's sleep and wake up in the morning to a sparkling kitchen and the promise of *Vogue* coming to the house,' Fiknete said as she led Marianne to the door leading to the hall.

The journalist looked around the room. 'So lovely and quaint. I adore this place,' she said, pulling out a chair and sitting at the table.

Marianne turned on the coffee machine.

'Goodness, no coffee, I am in Ireland after all. Do you have tea?'

'My grandmother always preferred Earl Grey leaf tea in a china cup. Would that suit?'

'Oh, yes please,' Kate said, rubbing her hands in anticipation.

Dolores set off to get the tea set, while Marianne made a pot of medium-to-strong tea.

'So tell me, how did you come to be here, and what are your plans for the future?'

Marianne sighed.

'I hope you're ready for a long story.'

The journalist set up the voice recorder on her phone and sat back to listen. When Benji came sniffing around her knees, she shuffled uncomfortably, and Marianne pushed him out the back door.

Dolores set the teacups and saucers with side plates on the table and the teapot under a new cosy Fiknete had magicked from somewhere. As Marianne told her story, the journalist listened intently.

'And your aunt, how did she react to the American coming in and taking over the estate?'

Marianne hesitated. Dolores, who was loitering out of sight in the doorway, gritted her teeth.

'Katherine has her own home on Kilteelagh land, and she was only too happy to have her niece take over Kilteelagh

House. Her husband looks after the animals here, and she was here until near midnight getting everything ready for today. We're in and out of each other's houses all the time. It's reassuring to know they're always there.'

'You are so lucky. It could have been very different,' the journalist said. Marianne laughed and Dolores mopped her brow and headed back out to watch the photoshoot. 'So tell me, what's in the future for you and Kilteelagh?'

Marianne took a sip of her tea. 'My grandmother loved Kilteelagh and entrusted it to me. I intend to honour her trust, and I'm thrilled to be able to work from here and reach the rest of the world. What I'm doing with my collection is bringing a little of this magical place to the world. Kilteelagh is sewn into every seam of each dress. The inspiration for my collection of summer dresses came as I walked across the fields of Kilteelagh to the sea. The floaty summer garments came to mind as my daughter Katie – and she is my daughter now – said, 'Wouldn't it be lovely if we could wear summer dresses all the time?' She's right, too: walking down a street in New York wearing one of these dresses teamed with a denim jacket, and you have the best of both worlds – the magic of a summer's day at Kilteelagh and the buzz of the city.'

'Magic.'

'Yes, it is magical being here. Don't get me wrong, there are hard winter days, but I have family and friends who are behind me all the way. I have two special friends who helped bring this collection to where it is today: a former refugee named Fiknete, and my grandmother's wonderful friend, Dolores. Women of different ages, and from three countries, but we make a great team.'

'Would you ever come back to live in the States?'

Marianne thought for a few seconds before she replied. 'No. New York was my home for my whole life, so it will always have a special place in my heart – I took Rachel and Katie there for a pre-Christmas vacation, and we loved it. But Kilteelagh is home now.'

The journalist sat back in her chair and turned off her phone.

'That's the interview. I'm so glad Jay persuaded me to come over. This is a beautiful story. I'm planning an evening in Dublin tonight, but can I come back for your show?'

'That would be wonderful. I'm sure we can find you a front row seat.'

'Thank you. I'm not promising anything, but I am hoping for a lovely big spread in the magazine. If the shots in front of the house are good enough, who knows, we may make a mention on the cover.'

Marianne felt her stomach heave, but she smiled, afraid to say anything, because she could not trust herself not to throw up. Dolores came in on the pretence of offering more tea.

'Would you like a little tour of the gardens?' she asked, but the journalist said if they didn't mind, she might wander about herself in the hope of scouting out some more locations for photographs.

'We have to get it right. Marianne, you are on to something really big here, I hope you know that.'

'It's the stuff of dreams, I have to say.'

'Hell yeah, once this goes out in our magazine, all your dreams are set to come true. I think your grandmother would be very proud.'

Dolores, realising that Marianne was dumbstruck, ushered Kate to the drawing room. 'I want to show you a very fine portrait of Collie Keane herself, wearing the dress you will see in the show. Collie has been a huge influence on Marianne's life.'

Alone in the kitchen, Marianne sat with her head in her hands. She needed to get away from everything; she needed to take a breath. Without saying a word, she slipped out the back door and across the far field away from the house to a small stile in the stone perimeter wall.

Walking along the road, she longed for a normal quiet day at Kilteelagh House again. Before she got to the Kilteelagh gates, she saw Katherine and Bridie leaving, sweeping out onto the Balgaddy Road.

Jack, who was leaning against the gate, straightened up when he saw her and fell into step alongside her.

'Do you fancy a bit of company? I feel a bit like a spare part here. They asked me to stay on in case I'm needed, but other than showing them the carvings on the gazebo, there has been nothing the last few hours, only watching these girls shiver their way through the shoot.'

'I thought I'd walk to the bridge. Collie always advised a walk to the bridge to clear the head. I really need to do that right now.'

'Do you mind if I tag along? I have something to tell you.'

'No, just don't expect much from me, Jack, I'm completely overwhelmed right now.'

He took her hand and they walked on in a companiable silence together.

At the bridge, she didn't resist when he put his arms around her waist.

'May I introduce myself: Jack Farrelly, divorced?'

'Really?'

'As of today.'

She felt the anxiety slide away as she enjoyed the warmth of his embrace.

He kissed her and she kissed him back.

'Does this mean we can tell Sarah and Katie?' he asked.

'Yes,' she said, and they walked back hand in hand to Kilteelagh House.

THIRTY-SIX

Kilteelagh House was moving into a new phase where Kilteelagh Design took centre stage. It was the evening before show day, and Marianne had sent everybody home early to get a good night's sleep. Fiknete wanted to stay on, but both Dolores and Marianne had insisted she get some rest.

'You'll be no good to us if you drop down with exhaustion,' Dolores said, and Fiknete relented.

Marianne moved around the studio now. All the show dresses were hanging up, with a pair of sandals or shoes under each. Fiknete had placed a cover over the sewing machine on which she had worked so hard. Dolores' desk was a riot of Post-it notes, colour-coded according to importance. Pink Post-its required urgent attention; yellow could be overlooked; orange not even considered.

Enjoying her moments of solitude, Marianne ran her hand along Collie's ball gown, which was hanging from a special hook near the window. Fiknete had pressed it and the velvet bow had been replaced with an exact replica. She took the dress from the hanger and slipped it on. Walking to the drawing room, she stepped onto the catwalk. Sashaying down to the end of the runway at the drawing room window, Marianne felt the eyes of Grandma Collie on her, but she no longer worried. Circling at the top of the runway, she let the satin dress fan out before folding in around her. Closing her eyes, she imagined the room full and hopefully some applause for the Kilteelagh Collection. She bowed shyly, a glow of excitement rising through her to think of what was to come.

Dolores had taken on the lion's share of the organisation and on the morning of the show was at Kilteelagh at 6 a.m. When she knocked on the door, Marianne ignored it and turned over in bed, but Dolores was persistent. She tried scrunching her pillow into her ears, but there was no stopping Dolores. After five minutes, she stomped down the stairs and angrily wrenched back the front door.

'What the hell is wrong? It's so damn early.'

'Good girl, go and get some clothes on, we have a ton of things to do,' Dolores said, oblivious to the cross demeanour of her friend.

'What could we have to do so early?'

'We need vases of fresh flowers all over, and the only place to get the best choice is the market in Dublin. We'll drive there.'

'I don't need all those flowers.'

'Oh, but you do, my dear. Bunches of lilies, we have to do everything to impress.'

'I thought my designs were supposed to do that.'

Dolores rolled her eyes to the ceiling. 'Of course, your dresses are the stars of the show, but we need the sweet aroma of lilies to fill the rooms and roses to bring the romantic inside.'

Marianne knew there was no point arguing and she went back upstairs to pull on her jeans, runners and a hoodie.

'I'll drive, but you'll have to listen to my choice of music. No talk radio today, please.'

'Anything to get us on the road,' Dolores said, making for the passenger side of the car.

It took them forty minutes to drive into the city and onto Moore Street, where the flower sellers were displaying their wares. Dolores made a beeline for a stallholder halfway down the street.

'Five big bouquets of lilies, and we want something that is cheaper but will definitely cheer the crowds,' she said.

'I don't have anything cheap, but I do have good value,' the woman said, fixing her apron.

Dolores picked a mixture of greenery and roses and armfuls of lilies, their stalks wrapped in newspaper.

'A cup of coffee, and then it's home,' Dolores said as they walked back to the car.

'I'm surprised you're allowing us to have breakfast,' Marianne said as they ordered two cappuccinos in a street cafe.

'I've been here before and know the importance of putting the best foot forward. We won't get a second chance. The small things count a great deal towards the overall experience. We know all the pieces you've designed are stunning and the models are fine young women. What we need to make sure of is that Kilteelagh is looking its best. The collection must not be let down in any way.'

'I guess.'

When they got back to Kilteelagh, Jack was already in the drawing room polishing the runway. 'I wanted to make sure I gave the final polish early, so it has time to settle; we can't have anyone slipping. I'll get the chairs in place once they arrive around lunchtime,' he said.

Dolores made her way to the kitchen and began looking for vases.

'I will have to go home and get some of my own, I forgot there wouldn't be enough here,' she said.

'I will run you there, you won't be able to carry them alone,'

Jack said, and they both left as Marianne entered her design studio.

The sketches were lined up against the wall, all framed and ready to hang in the hall. Each dress had been pressed the day before and they were hanging on a rail, with the name of the model pinned to the hanger. A hair and make-up station had been set up near the fireplace with the first model up at lunchtime. Marianne stood in the centre of the room listening to the silence. This was the special moment when it was still before the frenetic activity behind the scenes of a show.

'Is there something wrong, sweetheart?' said Dolores, catching sight of her as she came into the room carrying a big jug of roses.

'Oh, you're back. Could you get Jack to hang the sketches? I need to go upstairs.'

Dolores opened the door for her, touching Marianne lightly on the elbow as she passed by.

'Don't worry, we'll get on with everything here. You go and rest.'

Marianne saw Katherine and Bridie drive up the road and she quickened her pace on the stairs.

She didn't go to her room but to Collie's chair on the landing. Sinking into the velvet seat, she sat watching the avenue. How had Collie done it all these years, waiting for Lucas to come round the rhododendron grove? There must have been the pain of faded anticipation intermingled with sparks of hope, followed by a desperately lonely desolation as time marched on. Collie had no doubt filled her days by devoting herself to her family and particularly her grandchildren, but still there must have been a chasm of loneliness. The rhododendron was not in bloom yet. She preferred when in late April the rhododendron flowers began to fade and fall, creating a red carpet on the avenue. How many times had Collie seen the rhododendron flowers fade and fall thickly, covering the avenue until eventually they disintegrated and turned to brown? That her love never faded was testament to its strength and Collie's belief that Lucas would come back to Kilteelagh and claim his rightful place by her side. Sadness crept through Marianne for her grandmother and anger at Lucas for letting her go and never seeking her out.

She smiled when the sharp sound of Dolores bossing Jack interrupted her thoughts.

'Check all those pictures are straight before you finish, and not one speck of dust must be on that runway, Jack. Parking must go smoothly, particularly for the second event. They are the VIP guests. We want them arriving to the house already enchanted by the spectacle of Kilteelagh, not frustrated by dim-witted parking attendants. Have you told the lads helping out, they must wear white shirts and the dickie bows I gave them?'

Marianne heard Jack sigh deeply and she knew from the way he answered that he was doing his level best not to quarrel with Dolores.

Next, she heard Fiknete burst into the hall shouting, 'There are sheep around the gazebo! Are they supposed to be there?'

Marianne burst out laughing when she heard Dolores screech at the top of her voice. Jack seized the moment, saying he had better get it sorted.

'We can't have the fancy fashion types falling over a flock of sheep and stepping in shit,' he called out as he raced down the steps.

'For God's sake, man, go sort it out immediately,' Dolores shrieked, and Marianne giggled so much she had to stuff her hand in her mouth, lest her friends could somehow hear her.

THIRTY-SEVEN

Marianne took her time getting ready. Fiknete had shown her how to tie her hair in a chignon at the back of her head and she liked the look of sophistication it gave her. She was wearing a simple navy silk dress Fiknete had only finished the night before. It had long gathered sleeves and the skirt was full and flowing, which Marianne knew would billow out as she walked down the runway. A stab of anxiety shot through her to think she had to complete the runway walk not once but twice, and she wondered whether they were mad to run two shows in the one day.

Dolores said the first show, for the community, where they wouldn't bother with speeches, would be a good dress rehearsal for the real thing.

Marianne, as she slipped on her dress, had already decided to say a few words at the community showing though, with a special mention for Collie. She took out the Tiffany necklace her grandmother had once gifted her and put it on. It was the perfect simple adornment to complement the silk dress. She also slipped on the ring Lucas had given Collie.

Fiknete had promised to do her make-up, after she had

finished with the models. Marianne was ready in her head for the event. All she needed was for her designs to wow the buyers and the press.

If they got the orders, the local team were all set up, ready for the cutting and tacking, leaving the sewing and finishing, for the moment, to the Kilteelagh House team. It was a cottage industry, everybody working in their own homes and all managed by Dolores. It was a perfect set-up for any designer, eventually allowing Marianne to concentrate on the design and fabric and leave all the administrative and business details to Dolores. Before she went downstairs, she quietly asked Collie to give her the strength to get through the next hours.

Both Dolores and Fiknete had changed into the black silk dresses which Fiknete also had found time to make.

'You look stunning. How are the nerves?' Fiknete asked.

'I can hardly breathe, but don't tell Dolores,' Marianne whispered, and Fiknete gave her a reassuring squeeze on the shoulder.

'All the models, bar one, are here.'

'What do you mean? How are we missing a model?'

Dolores rushed into the hall, her cheeks red and her phone to her ear.

'What are we going to do? Ciara Hayes has come down with a bad cold and her mother says she will never make it down the catwalk.'

'Which dress? Can we get someone else to double up or something, you know, to start and finish the show?' asked Marianne.

'Great idea, but it's not the way I planned it, and it's the design for the finale – the blue silk number to go down the aisle with Collie's dress.'

'Surely *somebody* can double up.'

'I've already asked, and they're nervous. It's not going to fly,' Dolores said, her voice high-pitched.

'We need to come up with a plan,' Fiknete said sternly as she ushered Marianne and Dolores to sit at the kitchen table. 'Come on, we have to figure a way out of it. That's all,' she said a little more kindly.

Dolores made to get up, but Marianne pushed her back into the seat. 'Fiknete is right, we have to get around it. It's not a complete disaster.'

Rachel walked into the kitchen and opened the fridge. 'Can I get my make-up done too, Fiknete?' she asked as she opened a carton of orange juice.

Fiknete elbowed Dolores, who immediately jumped up and stood beside Rachel. 'Darling, would you save the whole fashion show for us, and we will forever be in your debt.'

'Yes, free make-up lessons for a month,' Fiknete said.

'And a one-night homework pass from me,' Marianne said.

Fiknete and Dolores stared at her severely.

'OK, a weekend pass,' Marianne said.

'What's going on, what do you want?' Rachel asked suspiciously.

'She's a perfect size,' Fiknete said.

'And she is Collie's granddaughter – the two granddaughters on the runway together,' Dolores said.

'Hold on, I'm not going on any runway,' Rachel said.

'Why is Rachel getting a chance to wear a new dress down the runway and not me?' Katie said as she burst in the door.

Marianne gritted her teeth and tried to stay calm. She turned away and held the mugs which had been left in the sink under the tap to wash them. Katie pulled at her arm. Rachel made for the door, but Dolores stopped her. When Marianne turned around, everybody stared at her.

'Rachel, I need you to wear the blue silk dress. We're in a bind, and it's our only way out of it. You are a beautiful young woman and Collie would be so proud of you for stepping up to the mark like this. Katie, I will need you to go out and find a vase of roses and take all the petals off and put them in a basket, or a bowl or something that looks nice, because for the two shows, you will walk down the runway ahead of us throwing a few petals each time. I will wear Collie's dress. We should be proud to do this for Kilteelagh.'

Katie jumped up and down with excitement.

'Can I wear my red sparkly dress?'

'Of course.'

Rachel didn't say anything for a few minutes.

'Do I have to?' she asked.

'I understand you're nervous, but I really need you to do this,' Marianne answered, and Dolores gave her a thumbs up.

Katherine and her family arrived early for the dress rehearsal, taking up seats at the front near the bay window, so they could best see every twirl on the runway. Bridie, when she arrived with her granddaughter, took up the seats opposite and also put reserved signs on three more seats for their friends.

When Marianne walked into the room, they clapped, making her blush.

'It is going to be a fine show, Marianne. I hope you're pleased with yourself,' Bridie said.

'Let's wait until afterwards. Is everybody from the town coming?'

'And some, I've had a lot of enquiries so I've arranged for Steve to set up a screen on the front concourse so those who couldn't book a seat don't have to miss the show. I hope you don't mind,' Katherine said.

'It will have to be taken down before the second show.'

'Steve is going to look after that, don't worry.'

Bridie laughed. 'It's a full house and front garden too, and everybody paying five euros a head. Thanks to your generosity, there should be enough to help the needy, and not just in our town either.'

'I didn't realise we were going ahead with that suggestion.'

Bridie looked a little embarrassed. 'I've shot off my mouth again. Dolores said we could request a donation for a local charity. You don't mind, do you?'

'No, it would have been nice to know though.'

'I have a speech ready, can I run it by you?' Dolores asked as she walked into the room to pick up a vase of flowers to take to the hall.

'Not now, Dolores. I'm sure it's fine. You should go with the first telling, which is always the best. I know I will cry, and I can't afford to have red eyes before the show,' Marianne said, and Dolores wondered why she was so on edge. Dolores, who had several pages in her hand, folded them back into her patch pocket.

'Time for a quick rehearsal. Everybody gather,' Dolores called out to round up the models. Bridie turned on the lights and music. Dolores, making sure everybody was in line, stood behind the dais under the painting in the drawing room.

'I'm not going to go through the full introduction, we're making sure the sequence is right,' she said before she called out the first dress: 'Perfect for a summer day in the country or the city, dress up this silk number or let it stand on its own.'

Marianne's stomach heaved; she couldn't watch the rehearsal. Quickly asking Fiknete to take her place for the last design, she escaped upstairs to her room, where she stood inside the bay window. The frost had thawed, and the garden looked tired, as if it had spent the night fighting off the cold. In the distance, she could hardly make out the sea where it blurred into the sky on the horizon. When she heard the delighted squeals and clapping of Katherine and Bridie, she knew the rehearsal was over.

Dolores knocked gently on the door before pushing it open.

'Marianne, it's going to be spectacular.'

'I don't know what I would have done without you, Dolores.'

'Got another Dolores to help, Bridie would have been the first in the queue.'

Marianne thought she detected a certain resentment in her friend's voice.

'Yeah, but she wouldn't have your style or little black book.'

They laughed together and Marianne felt better.

THIRTY-EIGHT

Kilteelagh had never looked so good. The gates were swept back, and the avenue lit up with solar lights. The gazebo twinkled down by the lake. Even the weather was kind and the guests remarked on the moonlight on the lake. Every design was greeted with applause and the seasoned buyers and press appeared to be impressed. When the first model stepped onto the catwalk, tears bubbled up inside Marianne. It had been such a hard slog to get to the point where guests took to their seats on either side of the runway and began to clap the first dress displayed to the world. Dolores and Fiknete gripped her hands as if they were taking off in an aeroplane and she was the nervous passenger who needed reassuring.

When it came to Marianne's turn on the catwalk with Rachel and Katie, she felt sick.

Katie grabbed her hand and squeezed it tight. 'Don't worry, Mum, we can do this,' she whispered.

Rachel threw her arms around Marianne as well. 'Come on, Mum, let's show them what we can do,' she said.

Marianne at that moment felt complete. She was exactly where she wanted to be, beside Katie and Rachel at Kilteelagh

House. Katie stepped out first, scattering the rose petals as Rachel and Marianne walked hand in hand down the runway.

If only Collie could have seen the reaction to her ball gown, the reverence for the beautifully handcrafted vintage piece. Dolores announced it, telling a brief story of how Collie had made it over several weeks at her kitchen table. 'No wonder she inspired her granddaughter, Marianne Johnson, to become the designer we see here today,' she said.

Katie walked ahead, carefully letting the rose petals flutter around her. At the end as the three stood facing the fireplace, they bowed to the portrait of Collie Keane and the audience, including the American press, pushed back their chairs and stood up to applaud.

Marianne, holding tightly onto Rachel and Katie, allowed herself to savour the moment. The rhythm of clapping filled the room and from the far corner came a long, low whistle.

She had shown off the Kilteelagh Design dresses and the crowd had sighed with satisfaction as summer strutted down the ramp; the soft wafting of the silk and chiffon calling up individual memories of warm, carefree, summery days.

Afterwards, as their guests sipped Prosecco, Marianne and Dolores made sure to have long conversations with the Irish and American buyers present. Hours passed by in a blur for Marianne. She smiled her way through it, and her head thumped. Many more glasses of Prosecco were handed out, and many guests hung around in small groups long after the show was finished.

When the last of the buyers had left and the local newspaper photographer had snapped all his shots, Marianne sat in the drawing room enjoying the quiet after the frenetic activity. She heard Dolores and Fiknete tidying up; she felt guilty she wasn't helping. When there was a knock on the drawing room door, she jumped. Bridie stepped nervously into the room.

'I came to say my goodbyes, and to thank you for all you

have done for us, bringing the women of Balgaddy together. I have a feeling there will be sewing past midnight most nights as the order book is filling up.'

Marianne smiled and made to say something, but Bridie put a hand up to stop her.

'Look, I want to say you are a right fit for Kilteelagh, and while I would love to buy the place and the land if you ever want rid, it's fantastic to see the place so alive, and you have done that. Well done, girl.'

Bridie backed out of the room without giving Marianne a chance to reply, and she later heard her chat to Katherine as they both headed down the avenue to their cars. Dolores came in, buttoning up her coat. 'Fiknete is giving me a lift home. Everybody had a ball, and the order book is already full.'

Marianne got up and pulled Dolores into a hug. When Fiknete walked into the room, she joined in. 'Great day for hugs,' she said, squeezing extra tight.

'Thank you both. Thank you for making my dream come true,' Marianne whispered.

'You're welcome. Let's try to do it every year,' Dolores said, and they all smiled.

Marianne turned back to Kilteelagh House. When she saw the letter propped against the vase on the hall table, Marianne knew it was from Collie. Dolores must have put it there before they left.

Walking to the kitchen, she sat at the table before pulling the letter from the envelope.

Kilteelagh House
Balgaddy
Co. Wicklow

My dearest Marianne,

You must be quite tired of getting my letters, so please note I am nearing the end of both the letters and this life. I am very tired these days, and it takes such an effort to write. It is time for me to retreat and leave Kilteelagh to you, to do as you see fit.

I think I have conveyed to you about my life here and how important Kilteelagh House is to me. I only ask one more thing of you, and that is to scatter my ashes at Kilteelagh, but remember: only when Lucas can join me. That day may never come, but it remains my fervent hope that in death we can, even if only in a symbolic way, be united. I keep asking because I hope by doing so, it will make it come true. I am sure you love Kilteelagh at this stage, but I want you to make your own decision whether to go or stay. I know Rachel and Katie love you to bits and you them. Bring them up in New York or Kilteelagh, all that I ask is that you love them.

You must step out in life now and make your own way. My letters to you, I hope, have brought some comfort and an understanding of life at Kilteelagh. I think you know I regret not following Lucas when I became free, but I was tied to Kilteelagh. As I approach the last turning in the road, I realise Kilteelagh will always be here, and we must make our own way and find our own happiness. I arrive at this decision too late, and there is no comfort to know my life could have been so different. However, I can say I have loved my life at Kilteelagh. If you are going to sell, please make sure it is not for development. This house deserves to have a family to love it.

I hope you stay, and I don't say this to influence you, but maybe you can combine it all, the happiness and fulfilment, where Kilteelagh is part of your life.

Be happy, Marianne. Don't walk away from happiness, but towards it. Stay true to yourself and everything else will fall into place.

All my love,

Collie xx

Marianne stood on the top step of Kilteelagh House and pulled the wool shawl around her shoulders, holding it tight. She was still wearing Collie's dress.

It was almost morning, and Kilteelagh House was ablaze with light and somewhere, somebody had forgotten to turn off the low-level mood music which flowed through the downstairs rooms. Marianne was too happy to feel the tiredness which came from staying up all night. Orders had already been made by the American buyers, and two department store buyers from Dublin had asked for further private viewings. The ladies of Balgaddy had scrambled to buy the dresses and were disappointed when Marianne could not run off a few copies for them or sell the catwalk samples. They were only placated when the local newspaper photographer took their photographs and their names for the next edition of the paper.

She noticed the gazebo lights which Jack had strung up at the last minute were still twinkling. Everything about Kilteelagh, at this moment in time, felt just right.

Katie summed it up well as Marianne tucked her up in bed sometime after midnight, when she sleepily said it had been the best time ever at Kilteelagh House.

Before turning back into the house, Marianne stood for a moment and surveyed the Kilteelagh land. The frost of the night before twinkled in the light thrown out from the house. A single camellia rose which had never unfurled,was still on the bush nearest the drawing room window. Frost sparkled on the bud, the beauty of the ice masking the harm it was causing the flower. The sun was slowly emerging, sending tentacles of streaking dawn gold across the sky as the birds began to stir. Soon the sheep who had huddled in the far corner of the front field would begin to spread out and the cows would wander nearer the house.

Stepping into the hall, Marianne stopped to breathe in the aroma of the lilies in the high vase on the mahogany table. Making her way to the drawing room, she peeped in as if she were a visitor to the house instead of the owner. The room was resplendent with huge church candles still lighting either side of Collie's portrait; bouquets of flowers were dotted around the room and at the end of Jack's runway.

Walking over to the fireplace, Marianne reached up and blew out the candles.

THIRTY-NINE

March

Two weeks later, Marianne stood on the stone steps and waved as Jack drove down the avenue. It was too early for a Sunday morning, but Jack had called round to invite her to lunch later. She asked why he couldn't have phoned or texted.

'I've been hiding away studying and this morning I wanted to see you, talk to you face to face. If I go home and get to grips with some more study, do you think we could spend the after-noon together? Bring Katie along, because I have Sarah today anyway. We could chat to them about us.'

'Yes, sure thing.'

'Right, so,' he said, brushing her cheeks with his lips, before he hopped in his car. He beeped as he drove down the avenue. Marianne saw his car pull suddenly to the side and push in near the rhododendron as another car rounded the bend. She watched Jack roll down the window and speak to the driver, then continue on his way.

Marianne tightened the belt of her dressing gown as the other car came closer to the house. It swept around to park at the bottom of the steps. An elderly woman wearing a dark suit got out. She waved, before reaching into the front passenger seat to pull out a fur stole, which she arranged on her shoulders as if she were cold.

'Forgive the intrusion, but I was looking for Collie Keane.'

'I'm sorry to have to tell you this, but my grandmother died last year.'

The woman looked taken aback as she climbed up the steps. 'I'm so sorry to hear that.'

'Did you know my grandmother?' Marianne asked.

'In a manner of speaking, yes, though we never met.'

'Would you like to come in?'

'That is very kind of you, if you are sure you don't mind. I assure you I don't make a habit of calling on people so early, but my flight into the country was at dawn and I hired a car and came straight here.'

'Do you know Kilteelagh then?'

The lady appeared to hesitate as she stepped slowly into the hall.

'Your home is beautiful. In my mind I had imagined something different.'

'Excuse me?'

The woman smiled as she looked around the hall. She pointed to the drawing room. 'May I?'

Marianne wasn't sure how to reply, but her visitor quickened her pace to reach the drawing room door.

'I promise I am not mad or an intruder,' she said as she turned the brass knob on the door.

Marianne followed her as she tentatively stepped into the room as if she were afraid of what she might meet. She noted the woman's shoulders rippled and shook as she crossed to the fireplace and stood in front of Collie's painting. Marianne sensed she should keep her distance, that for her the viewing of the painting was an intensely private moment. Placing her hands on the mantelpiece, the stranger leaned in to study the canvas closer.

After a few moments she spoke, her voice low and trembling.

'Is this Collie?'

Marianne moved in front of the fireplace. She saw the tears on the woman's face.

'Yes, but who are you? Why are you so interested in this painting and in Kilteelagh?'

Swiping away the tears, the woman smiled at Marianne.

'I appear to have mislaid my manners, and I apologise. My husband is the artist, I so wanted to see this work.'

'Lucas?'

'You know of him?'

'My grandmother, after she died, told me about him in a series of letters.'

Throwing off her stole, the woman pointed at the couch.

'Do you mind if I sit?'

'Please do.'

'You know their story?' Marianne moved from one foot to the other. The woman clicked her tongue. 'My name is Irina; I was Lucas's wife. But I'm not here to cause any trouble, believe me.'

She gestured to Marianne to sit beside her.

Marianne sat at the far end of the couch on the edge of the seat, her hands around her knees as if she was waiting to be ticked off.

The woman giggled. 'Dear girl, I'm not going to bite. We have no argument between us. In fact, I don't have an argument with anybody at Kilteelagh.'

'Why have you come here?'

'I came in search of Collie Keane, the woman who shared my husband's heart.' She stopped, shaking her head fiercely to correct herself. 'We both know Collie had my husband's whole heart all these years. I know he loved me, just not like that.'

'You knew about them?'

'Not until Lucas was dying and he told me.' Irina stopped to wipe a tear from her cheek. 'I shouldn't cry; we had a good marriage. I loved him so much, and he was a wonderful husband and father. I always knew that Lucas was different after that trip to Ireland. I could never quite put my finger on it, but there was a sadness and a remoteness about him, Neither I, nor our family could ever completely wipe it away.' She stopped to cough delicately into a handkerchief she had taken out of her skirt pocket. 'Lucas was a good husband and the best father, but a man who pined for something or someone he could never have. I backed him as he gave up the day job he hated and followed his passion for painting.'

Marianne shifted uncomfortably in her seat.

Irina reached over and took her hand.

'Lucas, when he died, had quite a reputation; I suspect your painting is worth a lot of money now. His reputation in the last years has soared in European circles.'

'Do you want it? Is that it?'

Irina guffawed out loud. 'I have more than enough of my husband's paintings, and why would I want this one?'

'Isn't that why you are here?'

Irina sat back and folded her arms.

'Tell me: is that Collie in one of those urns?' She pointed to the urn nearest the painting. When it was delivered by the crematorium, Marianne had placed Collie's there as a temporary measure, but it had stayed on the mantelpiece beside Aisling's urn. Now the truth was that even Marianne had almost forgotten it contained Collie's ashes.

'Yes, it is. We like to have her near us.'

Irina rummaged in her handbag and took out a plastic bag with a box inside.

'Meet Lucas,' she said, and Marianne couldn't help giggling.

'You may laugh; I was afraid your customs officials would think it was drugs and confiscate him, but we old ladies get away with murder, even these days,' Irina chuckled. She placed the box beside the urn. 'It is where he would want to be,' she said quietly.

Marianne pretended not to show any surprise and said she would make some coffee.

'Come with me to the kitchen,' she instructed Irina, who followed meekly behind her.

'Are you afraid I will run off with the painting?'

Marianne grinned. 'I'm not sure you would get it off the chimney breast, it's quite heavy.'

Irina pulled a packet of coffee out of her bag.

'Would you be insulted if I offered some of my own? I travel the world, and I bring my own coffee everywhere.'

'I'm beginning to wonder what else is in that bag.'

'I left on the spur of the moment – I didn't even tell my family. So, I took Lucas and my coffee.'

'Why the hurry?'

'I finally worked it all out. Before he died, Lucas told me he had loved Collie after meeting her over just a few days in Ireland. He said he never saw her again but had painted her and sent the framed work to her. He was very weak and when he named the place, I couldn't quite catch it. He asked me to take his ashes there. I promised I would, and I meant it, but I had no idea where it was in Ireland. After Lucas died, I had his ashes with me all the time, but it gnawed at me that I couldn't fulfil his dying wish.'

'It must have been devastating for you.'

Irina got up and took the pot of coffee from the machine.

'May I pour?'

Marianne nodded, placing the two mugs on the table.

Irina spoke as she poured. 'What was devastating was to

lose my husband, when we had planned so many things, so much travel together. He passed away in early March last year. To hear he had loved another woman was a surprise and rather intriguing. I no longer felt jealousy – I had the man I loved for all those years. There was no point immersing myself in a quagmire of resentment and bitterness and ruining my last years as well as my happy memories.'

'I think you and Collie, if you had met, would have got on.'

Irina threw her head back and laughed.

'I doubt it. Two women who love the same man could never get on.'

'But how did you find Kilteelagh?'

'Our son was in Ireland on business, and he had picked up a newspaper magazine. I was flicking through it when I saw the picture of your sitting room and the painting over the fireplace. I knew my Lucas's work straight away. I read about your success with Kilteelagh Design and I booked the next flight to Dublin.'

'Collie died on March fourth last year.'

Irina stared at Marianne. 'Just after two in the afternoon?'

'Yes, I believe so, though I wasn't here.'

'Well then, maybe it has worked out after all.'

'Worked out? What do you mean?'

'Lucas passed away just after two on the fourth of March. I was holding his hand.' Suddenly, Irina got up and walked down the hall to the drawing room. 'Life has a funny way of throwing things at you, doesn't it?'

'Are you OK? Can I get you anything?' Marianne asked, following quickly behind.

Irina shrugged and stood in front of the painting.

'How can you look at the painting, knowing what you know?' Marianne asked.

Irina rubbed her eyes with her fists. 'I can't deny what happened; if I was reading about this, I would say how beautiful. I hope she loved him as much as he loved her. I know he loved her to his dying breath. Imagine, on his death bed, he was reaching for her and here she was, probably reaching for him. I can't resent that type of love, only mourn that I never had it myself.' Marianne took Irina's hand and held it. 'I have had over a year to come to terms with it, dear. I loved him with all my heart, and he loved her with all of his. I know he loved me too, if in a different way, but I want to respect his wishes. Love is a funny old thing,' she said, gently pulling away her hand. 'I so adore the dresses you design. I guess you don't want an old woman like me wearing them, but I think they're so beautiful. I could imagine in my younger days walking along by your lake wearing one of those floaty creations.' Irina stopped. 'I guess Collie wore dresses like that.'

'Not when I ever knew her, but she did sew and make her own clothes.'

'I am milking you for information about Collie and I promised myself I wouldn't do that, because with that type of information, the small incidentals can hurt the most.'

Marianne heard Katie move about upstairs.

'It's my younger daughter; although the children don't know anything of Collie's past.'

Irina stood up. 'And they won't know of it from me. I should go, but first, could I ask a favour?'

'Yes.'

'Is there any way you would consider allowing me to scatter my husband's ashes here at Kilteelagh? It is here he will be most at peace. I realise it is a most unusual request, but—'

Marianne put her hand on Irina's arm. 'Only if you let me scatter Collie's ashes at the same time.'

'Could we do that?'

'Yes, down by the lake.'

Irina beamed with delight but then frowned.

'Collie wanted this too. She has been waiting for him,' Marianne said quietly.

Tears streamed down Irina's face. 'Don't worry, I am happy for them and proud that I have managed to do this. I am staying in Balgaddy until tomorrow evening, so when could we do it?'

'Would you mind if we do it when I have the house to myself while the children are at school tomorrow?'

'Of course.'

'Maybe at eleven, the lake is beautiful in the late morning.' Marianne got Irina's stole and walked with her to the front door. 'Lucas was lucky to have you to carry out his wishes.'

'I loved him, and I still do. Love doesn't conquer everything. I am not a hopeless romantic, but a deep, enduring love can surmount most obstacles.'

Marianne stayed on the top step and watched Irina drive off along the avenue as Katie came down the stairs.

'Who was that?'

'Jehovah's Witness, but the lady was very nice, and we had a cup of tea.'

'Grandma always banged the door in their faces after she gave out that they had some cheek coming around to her back door.'

'Well, Collie could be very impatient,' Marianne said as they made their way to the kitchen to make breakfast.

FORTY

After Marianne dropped Katie at school the next day, she got ready for Irina's arrival. Fiknete and Dolores were due, but she had asked them to take the morning off as she was not opening the design studio until the early afternoon. Dolores knew better than to ask her why, but Fiknete, who did not like her routine to be put out, cross-examined her, wanting to know why she could not work on her own in the studio.

'Fiknete, please just accept I need some time on my own at Kilteelagh. Normal service will be resumed at two o'clock. You should be glad to have a morning off.'

'Not so good, when I have to spend the rest of the day catching up. I have to have an order out by tomorrow and there is so much to do.'

'This is not something I can change, so we will have to work around it,' Marianne said, her voice firm, so that Fiknete did not argue further.

Marianne went into the design studio to calm down after the call, and it was there she saw the ball gown. As she stepped into it now, up in her bedroom, she was afraid that the gesture was too over the top and Irina might not like it. But Collie would, she thought, and that sustained her and made her braver. Scooping up her long hair, she tied it in a chignon at the back of her head and wore the Tiffany necklace Collie had bought her for her eighteenth. As she closed the jewellery box, she noticed the velvet ring box. Snapping it open, she took out the Tiffany ring. Slipping it on, she smiled at the diamonds glinting in the morning sunshine. This was the occasion to wear the ring, she thought.

When she saw Irina's car come up the driveway, she took one last look in the long wardrobe mirror. Taking Collie's bolero jacket, she swept down the stairs as she imagined Collie had when Lucas got her to sit for the portrait. When she pulled back the front door, Irina was already out of the car.

'Oh my, don't you look beautiful,' Irina said as she stepped back and took in the length of Marianne. 'Your grandmother and Lucas would be so proud to see you in this magnificent dress.'

'I was afraid you might think it was too extravagant for such an occasion.'

'Nonsense, the dress has so much meaning for Lucas and Collie, it is perfect.' Irina ran her hand along the satin skirt. 'Your grandmother was very talented to be able to make such a beautiful garment.'

'She's the reason I became a dress designer.'

'In another world and in another time, I would like to have met your grandmother,' Irina said. She picked up Marianne's hand to look at the ring.

'So beautiful, you wear it well,' she said.

They stood in front of Kilteelagh, the young woman in the ball gown and the smartly dressed older woman, neither entirely sure what to do next. The kitten played under the hem of the ball gown and Marianne gently nudged him out of the way.

'Collie loved the lake. That would be a good place to scatter the ashes,' she said.

'Lead the way,' Irina said, after returning to her car, reaching into the back seat and lifting out a basket.

'I brought champagne and glasses and some roses we can throw in the water. Just like the movies.'

Marianne gathered up the long skirt of the dress and they made their way down the path to the lake.

They walked on in silence, each absorbed in her own thoughts.

At the gazebo, Marianne stopped.

'How do you want to do this?' she asked.

'Do I look as if I have ever done this before?' Irina smiled.

Marianne let her dress fall in a rustle of satin folds as she took the urn out of the plastic bag she was carrying.

'Let's have a glass of Prosecco to give us courage,' Irina said, opening the bottle. It popped and she poured the Prosecco quickly, letting it froth up the glasses.

'To Collie and Lucas, wherever they may be. Let's hope they find each other,' she said.

'To Collie and Lucas,' Marianne murmured as they clinked glasses and downed the sparkling wine.

'This must be the lake in Ireland where he skimmed stones. He always said it was the best place to skim and the only water where he achieved ten bounces,' Irina said, a tear plopping down her cheek.

The two women walked to the water's edge, where they stood side by side. The ducks swam to them, creating a racket as they pecked the water in expectation.

'Shall we do it together?' Marianne asked.

'Yes, please,' Irina said softly.

Each poured out the fine dust into the air. The light breeze whipped it away; the dust of Collie and Lucas dancing together across the water, forming a grey cloud which glided high and low, until resting where the water sparkled in the sunshine. The mingling of the two lives had, for a moment, resembled a murmuration over the lake until each speck fell down, surfing the lake top as the dust was brought to shore onto Kilteelagh lands.

'A job well done,' Irina said as she let her rose flop into the water.

Marianne flicked her bloom further out.

'What will you do now?' she asked.

'Go home, keep his secret. There is nothing else to do. And you?'

'Go home too, to Kilteelagh House. Take off the ball gown; keep Collie's secret. Be the best mom I can be to Rachel and Katie.'

They walked back across the grass side by side, and up the avenue to Kilteelagh House.

Marianne stood on the stone steps and waved off Irina as she drove down the avenue, past the rhododendron, which was resplendent in colourful bloom, and the daffodils, which were swaying gently in the breeze.

FORTY-ONE

Marianne was in the kitchen when she heard a light tapping on the front door.

Thinking Irina had forgotten something and still wearing Collie's ball gown, she wandered up the hall and pulled back the door wide.

'Ms Johnson, do you remember me? I'm your solicitor, Sean Eager,' the man said, smiling as he took in the luxurious ball gown.

'I do, but is there something wrong?'

'No, at least I hope not. I'm here to find out if you intend to stay on at Kilteelagh. May I come in?'

'Of course, but why do you ask?'

A stocky man with glasses, he stepped into the hall and continued into the drawing room, placing his briefcase on the velvet couch.

'Your grandmother was not only a client, but also a good friend. She asked me, when your year was up, to personally come to Kilteelagh to find out if you had made up your mind to stay.'

'I didn't think it was necessary to tell you.'

Sean slipped off his glasses and polished them with a white handkerchief he took from his trouser pocket.

'There was no legal obligation to inform me; I am here as Collie's friend.'

There was an awkward silence between them which the solicitor rushed to fill.

'You've done a fine job with the house; it looks like a beautiful family home again.'

'Thank you. Kilteelagh *is* our family home. I would never consider selling it. And Rachel and Katie – we are a family.'

'Your answer gladdens my heart, though I had hoped and expected it,' he said as he snapped open his briefcase. 'Collie never doubted you, but I guess she put the get-out clause in the will in case the city had changed you and you found Kilteelagh too much.'

He took out a white envelope from on top of the stack of documents he had in his briefcase.

'I personally handed you a letter at the start of your Kilteelagh journey, and now I hand you a final one. I do not know the contents, but I do know that Collie wanted you to have this, but only if you were staying on at Kilteelagh. I spoke to her a few hours before she died, and she checked with me again that I knew what to do with this envelope. She said I was to place it in your hands and walk from Kilteelagh House to leave you to read it, and that is what I am going to do now.'

Marianne accepted the envelope then waited as he shut his briefcase and made to walk from the room, stopping briefly to look at the portrait of Collie over the fireplace. He bowed low in front of the painting like you would to a judge in the superior courts.

Letter in hand, she listened as the solicitor made his way down the hall and out the front door. He crunched across the gravel, and she heard him open his car door, the engine starting up soon afterwards. It ticked over for a short while and she imagined Sean was looking at Kilteelagh and remembering his friend, who always waved her guests off from the front of the house.

Turning the envelope over in her hands, Marianne sat on the velvet couch directly in front of Collie's portrait as she eased the gummed flap open.

Kilteelagh House
Balgaddy
Co. Wicklow

My dearest Marianne,

You know I was always one that liked the dramatic moment. Sean is a good friend, and I knew I could trust him with both the content and instructions around this and the other letters.

In my heart I never doubted that you would love Kilteelagh as much as your mother did and as much as I did. Kilteelagh has been so important in our lives.

The time has come now for me to address why I chose you to take over Kilteelagh. To do that I must also confront one of the biggest regrets of my life. It is time to make it right.

Your mother Chloe was the most beautiful daughter anyone could wish for, and when she died my heart was smashed into pieces. There was so much left unsaid.

Katherine and Aisling had Mike's dark hair and his practical streak. But Chloe was always such a quiet child, one of life's observers; but then, so was her father. She had his sense of humour too and his blonde hair.

Because Chloe was my child with Lucas. Yes, Lucas is your grandfather. My regret is that I never told her the truth. The time never seemed right, and then it was gone. I must admit I was anxious and afraid that if I unburdened to her, our special bond might have been permanently damaged.

All my life I have come across as a strong woman, but in truth that has been a front. Like everybody else, I have been afraid to step out, afraid of what others might think.

I should have gone to Lucas after Mike died. I should have given Chloe a chance to know her father. I should have given you a chance to know your grandfather. Too many regrets.

The truth is that Chloe sustained me all my life. Every time I saw her, I saw Lucas, and that brought comfort and pain in equal measures. I was wrong not to tell her, I know that now.

I think my hiding of this secret affected Katherine badly. She knew there was something special about Chloe, no matter how much I tried to hide it. As she grew older, that developed into a deep resentment of me, even though I knew she loved me with all her heart.

Katherine was right to be resentful. I loved Aisling, my firstborn, and Chloe, because she was my child with Lucas. Katherine was stuck in the middle and, though I tried, she grew up feeling somehow outside of the family and yet unable to leave Kilteelagh and forge her own path. My love for Katherine was never enough; she felt the secret that was there. Even now, I can't bear to tell her.

I am not sure if I am right in this, but this is what I have decided.

So, there you have it, Marianne. No doubt I have shocked you and I am sure I have disappointed you. In my defence, I would ask you to consider this: Mike never once raised the matter with me; he loved me too much for that. He loved Chloe too much; he must have known in his heart she was not his, but he loved her as if she were. She, in turn, of all my daughters, clung onto a good memory of him, always talking about his kindness and gentleness. And I was the coward who was too afraid of undermining that, and my own standing with her, to tell her the truth.

By the time you read this, I will be well gone. What you do with the information is now your decision. Know this: Kilteelagh was where your grandparents were happiest and all I wish for you is the same happiness in life. My hope is that Kilteelagh has become as precious to you as it always was to me.

Live a long and happy life, Marianne; live it your way.

All my love,

Collie xx

Marianne, the letter in her hand, trudged up the stairs to take off Collie's ball gown. Stopping at the landing window, she looked down the avenue. The daffodils, a ruffle of lemon down both sides, were swaying gently in the wind; the rhododendron stood sentry at the bend. From here she could see across the fields to the sea. She moved on to her bedroom and carefully unzipped Collie's gown and stepped out of it. Folding up the letter, she pushed it in her jeans pocket, before making her way downstairs and across the grass to the lake.

She didn't need to keep this letter; she needed to keep the secret. Taking the letter from her pocket, she stood and read the words one last time before tearing it apart over and over until it was in small shreds. Tumbling the paper strips into the lake, she stood and watched as the water, speckled still in places with the dust of Collie and Lucas, weighed down and sank each scrap to the bottom of Kilteelagh Lake.

The lake water gently lapped on the shore; the ducks gathered and somewhere overhead a red kite called out. Turning to look back at the house, Marianne smiled.

Kilteelagh House stood tall and proud. This was home.

A LETTER FROM ANN

Dear reader,

I want to say a huge thank you for choosing to read *The Irish House*. If you did enjoy it, and want to keep up to date with all my latest releases, just sign up at the following link. Your email address will never be shared and you can unsubscribe at any time.

https://www.bookouture.com/ann-oloughlin

My writing space overlooks the garden. Day after day, I observe the subtle changes as spring turns to summer, drifting into autumn and winter.

In spring, my favourite flowers are the yellow daffodils and red tulips; in summer the poppies and cornflowers demand attention, competing with the roses and the cottage garden blooms.

It was as I looked out on my garden that the character of Collie Keane came to me. Collie was a strong woman sustained by the land and her home, Kilteelagh House.

When she dies she leaves her beloved old mansion in Wicklow, Ireland, to her American granddaughter, Marianne, who must also be the keeper of Collie's great secret as well as finding her own peace at Kilteelagh.

Along the way she learns that women, when they support and hold each other up, can reach for the stars.

Welcome to Kilteelagh House.

My wish is that you enjoy this story as much as I enjoyed writing it.

I hope you loved *The Irish House*, and if you did, I would be very grateful if you could write a review. I'd love to hear what you think, and it makes such a difference helping new readers to discover one of my books for the first time.

I love hearing from my readers – you can get in touch on my Facebook page, through Twitter, or Goodreads.

Thanks,

Ann

facebook.com/annoloughlinbooks

twitter.com/annoloughlinbooks

instagram.com/annoloughlinbooks

ACKNOWLEDGEMENTS

Writing is a solitary business, but after the last words have been put on the page, getting a novel to publication becomes a team effort.

There are so many to thank, but top of the list is the home team.

To my wonderful husband John and my two children Roshan and Zia, thank you with all my heart for your love, unstinting support, patience and the numerous cups of tea to help get the novel over the finish line. I couldn't do it without you.

Thank you too to my superb agent, Jenny Brown of Jenny Brown Associates, who has been my champion for so many years.

To my terrific editor Isobel Akenhead, thank you for your passion for my writing, and your sound advice.

I am incredibly lucky to have the backing of the dynamic Bookouture team to help bring my writing to readers all over the world.

Finally, to the readers of my books, I say thanks a million. To the new readers who happen on this novel, I hope you enjoy your time at Kilteelagh House.

Ann

Made in the USA
Las Vegas, NV
18 May 2023